All My Days are Trances

[Shattered Dreamers Book 2]

By

Gary M. Jaron

(Based on the dream journals of, and interviews with, Lamont Corazon and Basha Edelman) [1]

---

[1] [Note: As for the names of the participants and places they have been changed to protect myself from any legal repercussions that might incur due to the publication of this record. As for the names of deities mentioned herein, hopefully, they will not take offense. At least they're membered. As it has been said, 'What is remembered, lives.' Any resemblances to actual locales, persons, living or dead, is purely coincidental.]

Cover artwork created in Photoshop by inverting the original colors of "Bat Out Of Hell", Monotype w/pastel © 1999 Barbara McLain. (http://www.barbaramclainart.com/)

Cover Design: Marianne Nowicki;
www.PremadeEbookCoverShop.com

Interior by Gary M. Jaron

GMJ Books
Berkeley, California

Gary M. Jaron can be reached at grayravensf@gmail.com
www.garyjaron.com

ISBN 9781795294188

This book uses Palatino Linotype font. This selection was based on the font used in my hardback edition of Ray Bradbury's *Dandelion Wine*. Palatino is the name of an old-style serif typeface designed by Hermann Zapf, initially released in 1949 by the Stempel foundry and later by other companies, most notably the Mergenthaler Linotype Company.

"The myth is the public dreams and the dream is the private myth."
Joseph Campbell, *The Power of Myth with Bill Moyers*, pg. 40, Doubleday, 1988.

...

And all my days are trances,
And all my nightly dreams
Are where thy dark eyes glances,
And where thy footstep gleams-
In what ethereal dances,
By what eternal streams.

To One in Paradise
Edgar Allan Poe, [1834]

Take this kiss upon the brow!
And, in parting from you now, thus much let me avow-
You are not wrong, who deem, that my days have been a dream.
Yet if hope has flown away, In a night, or in a day,
In a vision, or in none, Is it therefore the less gone?
All that we see or seem is but a dream within a dream.
...
I stand amid the roar of a surf-tormented shore,
And I hold within my hand grains of the golden sand-
How few, yet how they creep through my fingers to the deep,
While I weep - while I weep!
O God! Can I not grasp them with a tighter clasp?
O God! Can I not save one from the pitiless wave?
Is all that we see or seem but a dream within a dream?

A Dream within a Dream
Edgar Allan Poe, [1827, revised 1849]

TABLE OF CONTENTS

FROM THE EDITOR

As I began to present this next section of their journals, I felt the need to clarify things in my head just so I have it straight, so forgive me as I indulge in a bit of backtracking here.

Lamont Corazon is this child prodigy, born on January 6, 1964. Perhaps the most fantastic thing about him is his ability to recall memorable passages in books verbatim, even to the extent where the passage is located in the text he had read. He is highly inquisitive and reads complex, abstract material that would challenge many adults. Two of his heroes are Sherlock Holmes and Don Quixote, which given his history, have a noticeable influence on his actions.

Let me describe him to you. His overall appearance would enable him to easily blend in on the streets of his ancestral Toledo, Spain. His five feet six inches slender body is now firm and strong, forged through Tezcatlipoca's efforts. This transformation started when Tezcatlipoca took possession of him and put him through a fitness regime to strengthen and tone his physique in anticipation of her hopes to take over Lamont's body. That takeover of Lamont was ultimately foiled. He has raven black hair and bright, mischievous blue eyes. Lamont always felt that his hands and feet were taken from some spare parts meant for someone taller and bigger than his own frame.

His parents were Hector and Helen. Hector was ashamed of his Hispanic heritage and upbringing to the extent that he left the Catholic Church. He joined the fundamentalist church of his wife while they were dating. Which explains why he conveyed none of that rich heritage to Lamont.

Basha (Susan) Edelman was another child prodigy, born December 31, 1961, with a similar ability to recall verbatim text that she had read. She has the overall Italian look of her heritage; with a twist, she has remarkable red hair. When commenting on her own voluptuous form, Basha remarked that she agrees with the statement made by Sophia Loren when Loren was describing her own bountiful hourglass form that it was all due to pasta. Basha's intense long wavy red hair falls beyond her shoulder blades. She has intense, emerald eyes flecked with gold.

She is also Five feet six inches in her stocking feet. She always appears taller than Lamont due to constantly wearing her favorite three-inch heeled red leather cowgirl boots. Basha explained that she started to wear these signature boots when faced with boys and adults who did not take her seriously due to her femininity and size. She couldn't do anything about being attractively well-rounded, but she could add to her height. Thus, with her taller stature, she placed herself on more equal footing with those she was confronting and dealing with.

Her father is Herschel, a Hassidic Rabbi assigned to run a yeshiva in Berkeley with his wife, Miriam. As their only child, Susan was taught Hebrew by Herschel, which she had a natural talent for. She was able to learn Hebrew and mastered it enough to study both the Talmud and the Rabbinic Kabbalistic books as she was growing up. As she got older, Herschel realized that he had made a mistake in allowing her to study those texts and tried to pull her away from that involvement. Herschel and Miriam's marriage was approaching a crisis when Susan was 11 and said she wanted a Bat Mitzvah. Herschel would not hear of that. And the problem festered. Eventually, when Basha was 13, Miriam moved out, seeing that she wanted a different sort of life for Susan. They came to live in San Francisco, ultimately getting a divorce. Miriam became involved with the feminist magic bookstore, the Gift of the Goddess in the Haight, and the prior owner who wished to retire sold it to her. So, she and Susan, who had taken on the name of Basha, lived above it.

Basha and Lamont were destined to find each other as if they were bookends to a shared soul.

Miriam, Basha, and Lamont were vivid lucid dreamers all their lives. Miriam and Basha both had, at an early age, encountered the alternative dimension that they call Dreamland.

Perhaps I should explain what Dreamland is and how things work there? To begin, Dreamland was first described by Howard Philip Lovecraft in his short stories and novella written from 1919 through 1929. His description of Dreamworld responded to his biases and views and thus filled solely with males. It was a sexually innocent, almost childlike fantasy world, though not a world without lurking dangers. Randolph Carter, a dreamer, made famous by Lovecraft, had lost his natural ability to enter Dreamland when he was thirty.

Lovecraft wrote concerning Carter the following passage[2] to explain that loss:

'He had read much of things as they are, and talked with too many people. Well-meaning philosophers had taught him to look into the logical relations of things, and analyze the processes which shaped his thoughts and fancies. Wonder had gone away, and he had forgotten that all life is only a set of pictures in the brain, among which there is no difference betwixt those born of real things and those born of inward dreamings, and no cause to value the one above the other.

---

[2] H. P. Lovecraft, The Silver Key, It was first published in the January 1929 issue of Weird Tales.

...Wise men told him his simple fancies were inane and childish...They had chained him down to things that are and had then explained the workings of those things till mystery had gone out of the world.'

Lovecraft's world was oddly and noticeably devoid of children or young adults despite his explanation concerning the need to believe in wonder to sustain one's existence in this realm.

However, Dreamland was not the creation of Lovecraft. It existed before he mentioned it, and it still exists today. The Dreamland has always been crafted by visitors who dream and those who call that land their home. Thus, the Dreamland that Lamont and Basha explore and live in is much different than the one that Lovecraft described. How Dreamland worked was never really explained by Lovecraft, but from Lamont and Basha's account of their ongoing visitation, we have discovered many things about its workings. Let me briefly summarize some of the pertinent points now.

When you first come to Dreamland, the lucky ones get themselves apprenticed to be taught how Dreamland works; lacking that assistance, they have to figure it out on their own. The first Dreaming skill is being able to transform your appearance to match your intentions. After that skill is mastered, you begin to discover what talents you have. They vary from only being able to control your appearance to be able to create and shape the stuff of Dreamland itself. Basha, for example, has mastered her special gift; in doing so, she personifies the element of fire. She reminds me of the Human Torch, a comic book character created by Jack Kirby and Stan Lee.[3] Whereas Lamont's abilities developed over time. He was a late bloomer who came to have shamanic-like powers.

Lamont only stumbled upon this world through the plotting and machinations of the immensely ancient being, known as one of the Outer Gods. They made herself/himself known to Lamont as Tezcatlipoca, Smoking Mirror. Tezcatlipoca was seeking revenge on Cortez for destroying the Aztec empire. So, after many long years of attempting and plotting, he chose Lamont, whose ancestor was an officer in the troops led by Cortez.

There was a less powerful entity that had taken on the name of Lilith, who involved herself with Basha and Lamont. This entity was one who Basha had only known as the Queen of the Night, and it was at her temple in Dreamland where Basha was initiated. Lilith had caught wind of the schemes of Tezcatlipoca, so from the beginning, she was watching over Lamont, trying as best she could to aid and guide him.

[3] The Fantastic Four #1 (Nov. 1961)

Tezcatlipoca wanted to seduce Lamont into compliance and thus appeared to Lamont as a seductive female. Tezcat, as Lamont called her, wished to escape from wherever she was trapped. She desired to travel through the Gate of Dreams into the Waking World to once more rule and be worshiped as she believed was her due. To do this, Tezcat used two other teenage lovers as bait. Tezcat caused Lana to bring Jon to the top of Strawberry Hill in Golden Gate Park on September 3rd of, 1979. There Tezcat opened the Gate of Dreams that brought Jon physically into Dreamland. Tezcat needed Lamont to be there on Strawberry Hill one year later. On that day, Tezcat's plan was to alter or take control of the magick spell that Basha would cast, thus enabling Tezcat to escape from her prison of death in Dreamland.

Lamont met Basha, who was not only a magickal adept in Dream Magick but was also knowledgeable of Kabbalah. Together throughout 1979, they worked to find a magickal means to foil Tezcat's plan. To that end, Lamont and Basha enlisted her magickal coven, the self-proclaimed 'Wicked Witches of Atlantis', made up of Basha, Boots, Zeh'Brah, Oolong, Selene, and Lenore.

How one appears in Dreamland is a matter of intention. Each Dreamer crafts their persona, consciously or unconsciously. How their Dream body and Dream self look is eventually a matter of choice and skill. With the power and magick of Dreaming, one can take on any appearance. To the extent that your age is also an illusion. You can be 8 or 80 in the Waking World; however, in Dreamland, your apparent age is your choice. Once you understand that, you will appreciate how Basha's coven members chose and crafted their Dream suits. So, I will describe their Dreamland personas and costumes.

Let me start with Boots, Basha's oldest friend in this realm. Boots is always seen wearing her signature thigh-high high-heeled python leather boots with matching long leather gloves. She is a tall, slender 20-something with a prominent full chest and tight derriere, both suggestively covered in python leather in a bikini top and short shorts. She has bright sky blue eyes, thick red lips, and a full mane of auburn hair falling below her shoulders. Overall, she appears as the quintessential not-someone-you-would-take-to meet-your-mother and, more likely, someone you would expect to see in Playboy magazine centerfold.

Zeh'Brah reminds one of a provocative humanoid zebra; her only clothing item is black calf-high boots, while the rest of her pale Caucasian bare body is strategically covered in thick black zebra-like bands. Of course, she has a sable mane of hair.

Oolong is the stereotypical seductive Asian dragon-lady clothed in the tattooed image of a Chinese dragon that overtly covers her body; the dragon wraps from the chest down, between her legs, and up her back. Her only conventional clothing is black high-heeled sandals and smoky black thigh-high stockings.

Selene is a large bountiful hourglass-shaped African American woman. Her dark black skin is the black night sky emblazoned with a starry bright spiral Milky Way galaxy to cover her front and backside. Her black hair is short and styled like an Egyptian queen. Her only conventional clothing item is the leather sandals with their straps wrapping up her legs.

Lastly is Lenore. She is a Southern California beach babe. With bleached blonde hair and azure blue eyes. She is clothed in a tattooed Octopus wrapping and covering her body. Her only conventional clothing item is white leather go-go boots and scalloped shells that adhere to her breasts.

These ladies take the moniker of Wicked Women to the stratosphere and beyond, tantalizing and provocative.

Then there is another coven of Dream Land witches recruited to help Lamont and Basha. The individual members of this coven were never really introduced to our heroes, so I don't have any description to offer you. However, this coven was led by Sarah and Rebecca. Let me describe these two lesbian lovers and Lamont's mentors in Dreamland. Sarah is a five-foot-tall slender woman with shoulder-length fine brown hair. She first appeared to Lamont in an ankle-length burgundy dress with a cinched waist. There is a hint of lace at the sleeves and neck. A pink ribbon secures a cameo brooch tied around her throat. She is the image of a very proper Victorian woman in every way. She prefers long dresses and lace, always elegant and refined. Both she and Rebecca are uncommon in that they appear as they are in real-time. No youthful projections. Rebecca is a stocky and tall amazon of a woman of around six feet in height in her bare feet with short brown hair.

With a kind and commanding yet pretty face with lush brown playful eyes. She usually dresses in sensible, practical, and context-appropriate attire, with only a hint of playful.

Also, there was Peter Robinson, a slender African American youth from San Francisco who was also a Dreamer. When Lamont first met him in Dreamland, he projected a rock-hard exterior vaguely reminiscent of *The Thing* in the Marvel Comic *Fantastic Four*[4]. That hard outer shell contains the

[4] He was created by Jack Kirby and Stan Lee with his first appearance in The Fantastic Four #1 (Nov. 1961)

proverbial heart of gold and kindness. Peter became a friend and aid to Lamont as they tracked down Jon in Dreamland.

Lamont and Peter discovered that Jon was taken and trapped by an associate of Tezcat, Kaliya, the mayor of the city of Thrall. Kaliya is one of the ancient beings created by the Outer Gods to serve them. These beings were known as the Nephilim. Lamont and Peter got trapped by the mayor for many days as they kept dreaming and finding themselves back in Thrall. Lamont was tortured by Kaliya and Tezcat these many nights until Lamont had an epiphany, which brought him into his Dream power. With this newfound power, Lamont escaped from Kaliya's clutches taking Peter and Jon with him.

Finally, on Sept 1, 1980, Basha, Lamont, Lana, and Peter went to Strawberry Hill's top. Basha, Lamont, and Peter went into a trance state and arrived at the other end of the gate site in Dreamland, leaving Lana in the Waking World. Lana was to be the anchor and beacon to enable Jon to latch onto her and, therefore, to come back across when the Gate of Dreams was once again opened.

Things did not go as planned. Once the Gate was opened between the two realms, the veil between all the worlds was thin enough for some entities to come across from some unknown dimension and attack them all. In the ensuing battle, many people were killed (or were taken?) Neither Basha nor Lamont at that time knew which. They only knew that Peter and three young women from Basha's coven and two from Sarah and Rebecca's coven were gone.

Lamont did manage to bring Jon across to the Waking World. Lamont did stop Tezcat from coming across as well. But, at the time, it seemed that he did so by sacrificing his own life.

To be honest with you, I could not take it seriously when I got to the end of what I printed as book one in recounting these events from the dream journals.

First off, I knew Lamont did not die. I met him and Basha. When I finally tracked them down and met the two of them in 1999 and began the series of interviews that enabled me to first publish this manuscript in 2002, I was convinced of their sincerity. They did, in fact, believe what they told me was real. They were not trying to perpetrate an elaborate con or hoax. Though it pushes what we accept as real to the very stretching point and beyond.

I had hastily produced that first version of this book. It was very raw and created at a time before the ubiquity of the internet; hence it contained an abundance of footnotes in that first version of the book.

We remained in contact and became friends. It seemed like kismet that these two child prodigies would meet and fall in love. I wanted to update the book and, more importantly, include their personal story, first date, etc. I finally convinced them to let me do this, giving me the impetus to create that new version of the book *Through the Gate of Dreams* I published in 2019.

It is a fact that we all dream, even if some of us never can recall those dreams. It is also a fact that lucid dreaming is a real skill that a person who perseveres can acquire. Indeed, we can communally share a dream experience, like sharing and all participating in a mutual guided trance work. So, all that these books describe are theoretically possible.

Dreamland is real, though you, the reader, may not wish to believe that.

If you like, you can treat this as a work of fiction. Since I am writing this as if it were fiction, I have taken it upon myself to create book titles, chapter headings, etc. I will even use different fonts to convey and reveal the nature of those beings who appear in this text. I now know who and what they are, even if Lamont and Basha at the time did not know. All of this adds to the illusion that it is all fiction. I do have the literal benefit of 2020 hindsight.

If you wish to hold onto your sanity and sleep soundly and comfortably, you should treat this book as fiction. In the end, some things are better left alone.

Gary M. Jaron,
The editor, July 5, 2020

PART TWO

TO BOLDLY GO INTO THAT GOOD (K)NIGHT

You only live twice; once when you are born, and once when you look death in the face. Ian Fleming *(After Baasho, Japanese poet, 1643-1694)*[5]

Labor Day, Monday, SEPTEMBER 1, 1980

DREAMLAND

BASHA[6]

The adrenaline high is gone and in its place is relief and exhaustion. I am lying on my back, looking up at the white shade of pale moon in the azure sky. The moon shines clear and bright with half its face in darkness on the cusp. Just like I feel. Half in this world and still half of me is trapped in dark Dreams of their aftermath. My body is stiff and sore from the strain of all that intense focusing on that spell. Now that it is over, I am beginning to feel the loss, regret, and guilt. It hits me like a blow to the stomach—it was all my fault.

The black monolith, that ebony shaft of marble, returned to its prior girth and length, though its surface glistens from the blood smears of all those summoned by Tezcatlipoca's call. I should not be surprised that it came through, the act of going in and out of the openings between the worlds unharmed, still solid and erect. Beyond this clearing lies the dense old oak and ash trees in this once hidden and unknown part of the Enchanted Woods. I can still smell the lingering foul stench of brimstone and sulfur. I hear the cawing of crows checking out the scene all around me now that those foul things from beyond are gone.

Jon is gone, back where he came from. We did it. Oh dear Goddess, but at what cost? As I walk around and check up on everyone, I do not see Lamont. Damn it! Where are you? I spot Boots, we hug, and then it dawns on me that Lenore, Oolong, and Selene are missing. Tears run down my cheeks, and Boots and I hold each other as we silently weep. Fleeting images of those things from beyond engulfing my friends and how many others?

---

[5] Ian Fleming, You Only Live Twice, 1964, Gildrose Production Inc., opening pages.

[6] Just to keep us all on the same page, I am weaving Basha and Lamont's two dream journals together. In this manner, I will mark the passage of time, where the events are taking place, such as in San Francisco in the Waking World, or in what city or location in Dream Land. I will also mark each section with who is the first-person narrator of that section. That person will be the "I" who is speaking and describing the events as they occur from their perspective.

Are they gone? Dead? Dream dead, that seems to be the case. Bloody Hell! Where the hell is Lamont? He would not leave without telling me. Something is not right…

I go over to Sarah and Rebecca; at least they are all right. No sign of Lamont's friend Peter. Damn! Sarah and Rebecca tell me they cannot account for some of their coven members at the moment; most seem all right, apart from bruising and being shaken up.

People start departing from the scene, some in a flash of light, like a light bulb going off, others just fading like a fleeting memory. All were returning to the safety of normality. The felines, led by Zuki, Zip'pora, and Isis First Riser, are being attended to. They check them out and account for all of their folk[7]. Many of them were harmed in the fighting against the rats—some dead. I offer my condolences. As for the giant rat things, those Zoogs, that our feline warriors fought, I am not surprised that I do not hear the chittering of those massive rat things lurking in the forest underbrush. They presumably are licking their wounds and possibly consuming their dead that they dragged with them as they hastily fled, routed in the battle.

Zuki says the battle took a toll, but at least they did not have to deal with those other things. Those things focused on us humans. Boots says she is heading out; we will talk later, she says as she fades from view.

Where is Lamont? Did he go across with Jon? I cannot recall clearly the events. Damn it! Where are you? It is not like Lamont to leave without saying something. I have a bad feeling about this.

I best wake up and ask him why he is not here in Dreamland. I cannot believe he left me here by myself! I am so pissed!

*[8]

GOLDEN GATE PARK, SAN FRANCISCO

The air is crisp and clear, not a cloud in the azure blue sky. I smell pine leaves and hear the delicate chirping of small birds and the distant sound of the waterfall…ahhhh, normality. There is no place like home. But wait…is this real or a dream?

Suddenly I am floating like a boat on a stormy lake. Every inch of me is complaining. Then, images form and fade quickly against the reddish black of my eyelids. I try to reach out to Lamont, but I am slipping into an exhausted sleep. No! I need to wake uppppp…

---

[7] I need to mention that all cats in the Waking World co-exist in Dreamland. Hence the reason that they seem to sleep so much in the Waking World, in their sleep they are in Dreamland. They can of course talk.

[8] This will designate a passage of time and or space from the prior segment.

I hear a scream...Noooo! It is Lenore...wait...she is not alone. I hear Oolong and Selene...Their voices are like a cold blade thrusting into my heart. Then suddenly, they are gone. The silence afterward is like the twisting of the blade. This was not supposed to happen. It was all just a ritual. We have done rituals like this many times before. Oh, Goddess, I am the one responsible for them being here. For everyone being here. I misled them. I let them down. It was all such a great game before. But I led them into something else.

It all starts to replay before my eyes. One by one, I listen and watch as they disappear, screaming in flames of horrible green terror.

Then something new. I see a cold shadow cast by some winged form that flies across the sun. It comes closer, and I realize it is a huge bat that is the color of cold ashes. It is coming right at me! It shrinks in size as it comes closer and its frigid fangs pierce my breast. Funeral blackness seeps into me and smothers me. The sky burns blood red. I reach out to the sun to grasp it to keep me from drowning in the pain and darkness. I burst into flames, searing that bat off me; blood drips from the wound where it bit into my breast. I feel so weak, and I lose control. I plunge towards the dark green ocean water beneath me. Then, all there is is the surging roar of the ocean tide pounding on the beach where I lay.

I float in the sun's soothing warmth, lying on this wet sandy beach. My scarlet leather catsuit has been torn to shreds. I lay there aching and exhausted. The memories of my friends who are gone sift through my fingers like sand as the images fade from me. I try to grasp them tightly, but the memories slip between my fingers and fade. I weep as I try to keep them safe and prevent them from disappearing. But I fail.

Gone! They are gone, and they cry out it is my fault! I let loose the horror that took them away! I opened the gate and in it came. I should have done more. Could I have done more? It all went so horribly wrong. I need to find them. I pray that they only disappeared from Dreamland and nothing else. Dear Goddess, let that be all!

Please, they must be safe somewhere? I must find them, but how? I only know their Dreamland identities. Who are they in the Waking World?

The Waking World...I must leave this nightmare and wake up! Return to the world of the waking and return to Lamont! Lamont and I are going to be busy little bees! Wake up, Basha! Wake up!

*

I open my eyes and look around. I'm in a place that is sane and familiar. Atop Strawberry Hill in Golden Gate Park. This time I know I am awake. There lying next to me is silly sleeping, Lamont. Lana and Jon are already up and about.

Lana: "Basha, you and Lamont did it!" The words erupt.

Basha: "Hello, Lana. Hi Jon," replying weakly and exhaustedly.

Jon smiles back. I do not think he knows who I am or even how much of all that had happened to him he can recall. Hmmm…there is something about Jon that is bothering me, but I cannot put my fingers on it.

Jon: "Basha, you look worried. Is everything okay?"

Basha: "I am not sure. My mind is trying to tell me something. Something I am not paying attention to. Hmmm. Jon, what are you wearing?"

Jon: "Huh? A white tee shirt and blue Levi's jeans. What's the big deal? Lana is something wrong with your friend. I don't understand the question."

Basha: "I think that those clothes were made in Dreamland."

Jon: "Yeah? How can you tell?"

Basha: "Something about them does not seem right. I may have leaped to a false conclusion. Could you stand up and let us check them out for a manufacturer's label?"

He does so, and we find none on the outside, and after some prompting, we look inside and find none.

Basha: "Just as I thought."

"Jon: "So, what's the big deal with what I'm wearing?"

Basha: "The deal is that hypothetically you should be wearing either what you wore when you first stepped into Dreamland, or you should be wearing nothing. Either way, those Dream clothes should not exist. Not on this side of reality. They should not exist here. Yet there you are, wearing them. How in the name of the Goddess is this possible? I do not like this one bit. Lamont! Wake up, lazy head! We have a very interesting impossibility here for you to mutter over."

I shake him, but he does not respond. His eyes are closed, and I brush his tussled raven black hair back off his forehead. He does not respond to my touch. Something is not right—black horror nibbles at my gut and the corners of my mind. I try to ignore their gibbering. He is so still. Way too still.

Basha: "Damn it, Lamont! This is no time for jokes!"

His eyes are not opening. Those long lashes on his eyelids do not flutter. My hands shake as I touch his throat and his wrist.

Lana: "Basha, what's going on?"

As I touch Lamont, I notice that he does not feel right. I am scared. Very scared.

Lana: "Basha?" she speaks my name with desperation and a need for reassurance.

I touch Lamont's face, and it is cold. I do not feel a pulse. I know what this means, but I refuse to believe it. My breath stopped as I put my head on his chest, trying to hear the sound of his breathing or his heart beating. Yet, I don't see him move. I don't feel him move. I don't hear his heart! I...I...tears start to well up and flood out. I don't want to give voice to what I fear and what I know.

Lana: "Basha, what is wrong with Lamont?" She pleads.

Basha: "He's..." the words are like bile in my throat. "He's...dead." I sob, and tears flow hot and fast down my cheeks. "Dear Mother. He's dead." I pound on his chest, trying to start his heart to beat. I begin doing mouth-to-mouth resuscitation like I have seen done on TV shows. But nothing is happening. Nothing! "Bloody damn Hell!" I keep pounding on him. I shudder as I silently sob. Lana tries to hold me. The world has been ripped away, and I am left with desperation and fear. I hear someone keening.

It is me.

Jon: "Lana, Basha, the black kid is breathing. But he is not waking up. Not at all. He is totally out of it. We need to get help. We need the cops. We are all in big ass trouble."

Lana: "Basha, Jon's right. We've got to get the police. We can't keep this from them. How do we explain all this?"

Basha: "We tell them the truth," I state with flat blackness.

Jon: "The truth Basha? Are you nuts? We tell them I've been missing for a year? You tell them that I was in a world of dreams? You tell them I just got back because you did this magic spell? If we tell them all that, we'll be locked up."

Basha: "Not that part of the truth. What we tell them is we do not know what happened." I explain slowly and painfully. "We tell the police that we all came up here together to hang out. Then we dozed off. When we woke up, Peter, that is his Waking World name, by the way, was not awake. As for Lamont..." I cannot bring myself to say it.

Lana: "We found him like he is now," Lana says in despair. "We found he had no pulse. That is when we went and got help. You're right, Basha; that's the only thing we can tell them. It is true. We don't know what happened, right? Everything went okay in Dreamland, right? Lamont and Peter were okay when you last saw them, right?"

What do I tell her? What do I really know about what happened back there?

Lana: "Basha, you haven't answered me. Did everything go as

planned in Dreamland?"

*

GATE SITE IN DREAMLAND
BACK WHEN THE GATE WAS FIRST OPENED[9]

September 1, 1980

LAMONT

Okay, Mr. Superhero, I must do what we came here to do and get Jon to Lana.

Jon is huddled around the base of the Monolith. I gently lift him up in my arms, as I frantically beat my tired bat wings, to carry us up. Uh Oh. I've just had a horrible idea. Now that the spell has served Tezcat's purpose, does she no longer need it, and will She close the Gate? Who controls the magick? Can she close it? I fly alongside the Monolith's surface, racing toward the Gateway. I struggle against the convulsive and turbulent currents of the winds as I force my way through the purple edges of the Opening.

Once beyond those edges, only two things provide reference points for my sanity and my journey. The first is the sound of Lana's voice, which keeps me focused on the direction of travel. The second is the pulsating black surface that I'm flying above. The two keep me from wandering off into the oblivion that surrounds me. All around me are fluid-like flowing coils of colors that no mortal eye should see. I hear and feel resonating in my bones a powerful pulsating rhythm. It's like waves of liquid sound pounding on the shores of my ears. I feel an urge, an ecstatic call for union. To surrender my lonely singularity and submerge myself into the soothing void impinging on my frail mortal mind.

I fly close to the center of the storm along the shaft of the monolith. Above me, the currents ripped out into Dreamland; below me, the storm is a spewing force that rushes toward the Waking World. The somewhat calm area within which Jon and I travel is a narrow tunnel that exists between the natural forces that have gone mad. This small zone of quiescence seems to be getting smaller. Which I fear means Basha and the Coven members are nearing the end of their fortitude.

Lana's voice is getting louder and so I take heart. I must be on the verge of entering the Waking World. Then I see the Gate, and beyond it, I see Lana. She has anchored herself against the stone altar/fireplace. Her eyes closed in concentration. The storm wind whips out at her. She chants softly to herself. For the first time, I feel Jon stir as he lifts his head in the direction

---

9 Jaron, *Through the Gate of Dreams*, Kindle Direct Publishing, 2019, p366-371.

of Lana's voice.

Jon: "Lana." Jon speaks the word as if he was struck by a revelation. "Lana." He says it again like a prayer of hope. "Lana!" He struggles to reach out to her.

As I fly closer to this Gate's entrance, I feel some barrier pushing me away from it. I cannot fathom how or why the way through is barred to me. There is a tremendous inpouring and outpouring happening all around me, and yet I cannot pass. I concentrate and try to force my way through this unseen wall. It refuses to yield. Time is running out; I must get Jon past this last obstacle. But how? Can I burn my way through that which I do not see? An idea illuminates my mind and begins to dispel my fear. Maybe my fire can paint what is unseen and make it visible? I focus my thoughts and spray the area ahead of us with gray flames.

Lamont: "Damn! No effect."

Lana: "Lamont! Is that you? I feel your presence but I can't see you. Do you have Jon? Bring him to me!"

Lamont: "I can't Lana. I'm trapped on this side of the Gate! I don't know how to get through!"

Lana: "You must get through! I can't bear to lose Jon again when he's so close! I refuse to accept this!"

Damnation! How can I get through that which I can't see? What is the nature of the thing that bars my way? This is no time for Philosophical dilemmas! Bloody Hell! I try to calm my thoughts and focus my jumbled mind on finding a way through this barrier. Wait. What will happen if I bring my Dream body into the Waking World? Is this possible? Is it dangerous? Is that what Tezcat meant when She said I could not follow Her? That the consequences are too great for me to follow Her into the Waking World? Consequences as, in my death? Was this what Basha meant by a rule that I must obey? Can, or should, anything of Dreamland go beyond into the Waking World?

Suddenly, the mysterious force that was keeping me out is weakening! How did this happen? Who cares! The Gate is getting slightly fainter and perceptibly smaller. Basha and the coven are tiring. There is not much time left. I'm afraid. I hesitate.

I don't know what will happen when I go through the gate.

But I do know what will happen if I don't.

Jon and Lana will never be reunited. I must finish this. Jon must be brought over to Lana. Should I just let go of Jon and let him alone pass beyond? Then I can accomplish my mission, not enter the Waking World and perhaps avoid those ominous consequences that Tezcat spoke of?

No. It won't work. If I let go of Jon he will fall through the opening and fall to the ground. The impact will surely kill him. I must bring him safely to the ground.

Bloody Hell!

I lunge forward into the heart of the storm center that is the Gate opening at this end of reality. I penetrate that cleft, carrying Jon and myself through, into the Waking World. As we emerge from the shimmering Gate, Jon's Dream garments start to fade. I swoop down to Lana and land next to her. Jon steps onto the firm earth of the Waking World naked as on the day he was first born. I see him wrap his arms around Lana as she opens her eyes and arms to him. They stand clinging together, supporting each other. All around us are hurricane winds shooting out of the Gate and an equal force sucking the air around us back in. But then Jon's Dream garments reappear. This is bizarre. How can that be possible?

I suddenly feel very dizzy and weak. My doom is upon me! I'm being drained of all my energy. I shut my eyes and focus inward, grounding myself. I see myself, my body lying on the blanket below me. I see but can't feel my own body. What does this mean? It means you idiot that you're going to die!

Tezcatlipoca: Corazon![10] This is not possible? How can you be here? Do you not know how foolish this act is! We did not consider that anyone was capable of such folly.

Lamont: "Damn you Tezcat! Stop calling me a fool! I'm no fool I'm a hero! I feel your presence, Tezcat. But I can't see you. I know you're here. Where are you Tezcat?"

Tezcatlipoca: Here. We dwell within your flesh! But who would have thought? Never in the long annals of time would we have considered this. You have somehow done what should not be done. You cannot be here as you are to the place of your flesh. No!

Lamont: "I feel like I'm being pulled apart. I'm dying; is that it, Tezcat?"

She does not respond with Her usual laughter. Instead, I hear Her cry out in pain! What is going on here?

Tezcatlipoca: We cannot remain within your flesh. Your very presence here is driving us out! Damn you, Corazon! Damn your stupidity! You will pay for this! That is not a threat but a certainty! Remember my words. There is no escaping the consequences of your heroic folly!

---

[10] The entity that is speaking here is known to Lamont and Basha as Tezcatlipoca, Smoking Mirror. Who, according to what Tezcat told them, is in actuality the personification of cosmic power born out of the Big Bang. It seems that these ancient beings had been called by H. P. Lovecraft as the Outer Gods.

I can feel Tezcat being ripped out of me. The pain is intense. I... I wake up. I blacked out. I'm alone. Tezcat is gone. I feel alone. She has left me. What does this mean? I feel so weak like I can barely breathe. Wait. There's an incredible ghostly little fairy light, a mere spark, lifting up from my Waking World body. I watch it leave my body and then drift aimlessly off. What is happening? What does this mean? I feel stretched out. As if I lack substance. I feel an eerie emptiness, a sensation of dreadful coldness, and tremendous loss. I fear that something irreversible has taken place.

*

RETURNING TO THE PRESENT
SAN FRANCISCO, GOLDEN GATE PARK

September 1, 1980

BASHA

Basha: "Yes, Lana, the spell was a success. We did run into some trouble, and Peter did get hurt. That may explain why he has not woken up. But nothing happened to Lamont as far as I know. He should be fine. I do not understand."

Jon: "Look, you two ladies can sort that out amongst yourselves," Jon says. "I'll go find the cops. You stay here with them."

Basha: "Jon, you are right. You should both go and get help. I will stay here. But remember, just tell the cops that Lamont is not waking up. Do not tell them about the no pulse or the not breathing. Got it?"

Lana: "Are you sure? You'll be okay?"

Then everything goes weird. The world goes way too still. Birds and insects stop in mid-flight. Lana and Jon stand before me, unspeaking and silent.

Basha: "What the…?"

Tezcatlipoca: Hear us, Bright Eagle. We were very angry with Lamont, our Dear Heart. We wanted to kill him and you. We were burning with revenge. However, we realized that we had not been challenged by the likes of you two mortals since the time when Randolph Carter dreamed across the realm of deepest sleep. However, Carter was just annoying and not clever like our Dear Heart. Carter did what he did for his own satisfaction. Nothing noble. He was stubborn, and, as you Bright Eagle would say, Carter had Chutzpah. Carter never realized what he sought was a mere illusion from his childhood.

We then laughed at ourselves. Our Corazon had been willing to sacrifice so much for so little. That insignificant fool, Jon Dale. We were proud of our Corazon. We finally realized we would need you two. You could be of great service once we get past our blinding anger. We must serve you two in this hour of your darkest time and need. However, the time for acting is now. We must not delay. It is dire for our Corazon and may be too late. We heard you call to us, and here we are. We will help. We have brought you to stand before our mat of the eagle and the Jaguar. Listen to us. Hear our voice and focus only on that. Hear our voice and obey us. It is all going to be for the best. Trust us.

Basha: "Tezcat! I..."

*

Tezcatlipoca: Now, wake up Bright Eagle, and know that you had chosen wisely, O' keeper of our chosen one's heart, O' bright and shining one. You have protected our Lamont Corazon. With your gift. We now wish you to notice that we have left you something important. We have placed a stone from this site in your keeping. You will need it. Understand that the stone will need to return to the soil of its birth to maintain its special properties. Now we shall depart. However, know that we shall speak again. You will find a way.

There is a blinding flash; deep laughter fills the air, and uncertainty claws at me. What just happened? Bloody Hell! I need time to think, study, and ponder! I need to figure out what just happened. I am certain I heard Tezcatlipoca. Chosen? What did I choose? What did he mean? What did he do? I can't recall. It is all slipping away like so much sand. Everything is going dark...

*

I awake and realize I am not in the Waking World or Dreamland. I am in my private dreamscape. I look around; there are dark woods, and it is the dead of autumn when all the leaves have fallen off the branches; they lay as dried husks of blood reds and pale orange scattered all around, almost completely covering up any sight of old paths amongst this thick foreboding wood. It is a dark night, the star-filled sky, and the woodland landscape seems to be endless.

I see a hooded knight with an ill-kempt white straggly beard, clad in an ill-fitting armor covered by a battle-stained white robe watching me. That robe is too large for him.

Did it once fit him better in his prime? Perhaps he has kept it out of pride in his station and his obtained status. Now it just hangs on his body. He is hunched over and grasping a tall polished wooden staff for support. The top of his staff glows with a feeble light.

Basha: "Where am I?"

He does not answer. I follow him, not knowing what else to do. We take an overgrown path that leads down to an ocean beach. I cast my eyes to the waters as he steps into them. He then turns to me as he steps further into the waters. It soaks into his robe that billows around his torso like frozen smoke. He says like a prayer these words, "Please remember me." The sound of his voice pierces my heart, and I embrace his plaintive cry as if it came from a lost lover. "Please remember me," he begs.

My eyes have been cast to the sea as he begins to fade. I feel my soul reaching out to join with him as he disappears into the endless night, leaving me with only his plaintive plea as it is carried toward me with the soft rush of the incoming tide as the only thing left in my feeble grasp. "Please remember me."

I swear to him that I will not ever forget him.

Then it all goes silky ebony.

*

I am still in my dreamscape. I am running, running in dark misty woods. Darkness is on the edge all around me; surrounding me are shadows. I notice my skin covered by a white wispy linen nightgown, and I catch the scent of sweet perfume from my wrists. There is a full moon that hangs over this mist-filled dream of woods. It flutters behind me like shimmering wafting steam. I am holding a single lit candlestick; it and the full moon is my sources of light as I walk confused and dazed in these woods. I look down at my bare feet. It is funny how here in this dream they never touch the earth. I can not tell whether it is spring or fall as I run through these woods—the trees grow and shed their leaves in a flux of seasonal transformations. The scene recalls memories of gothic romance novels. Before long, I approach a crossroads. There stand three bloodstained and torn cloaked figures, and they are pointing at me. Accusing me. They are silent, yet it is as if I hear them shriek out in pain and denounce me as the source of their pain. I feel like I failed them. Then they fade, dissolving into mist.

I hear glass breaking and see a gray bat staring at me and then darting into the darkness. I need to follow it, so I do still with bare feet that continue not to touch the ground in this dream. These dreams just go on even when I close my eyes, these strange dreams in the mist

Up ahead is a house. I float closer to it and see that this side of the house has floor-to-ceiling glass panels. The bat slips through the window. Something compels me to enter, but I can find no doorway. The glass dissolves and feels like cool water though I can somehow still feel its sharp edges. I carefully push the cool, wet glass aside as I step into the house without getting a single cut. Inside the house, it is empty and still. Yet I feel that someone is here; as I continue to follow that bat, both trying to hide in the shadows. I wander through still, cold, and empty rooms.

I keep floating through rooms filled with unused furniture draped in white sheets that shimmer with the moonlight and by candlelight.

Ornate chandeliers and candle holders are everywhere unlit. They seem to be waiting patiently for someone to come and give them light. I hear it first—a fluttering of soft dark wings. I will try to find it. I follow the sounds as I catch a fleeting glimpse of the bat in the shadows ahead of me.

I climb a circular staircase to the next floor in my search. There seems to be someone at the far end of the dark shadowy corridor, a cloaked figure in the shadows. Suddenly he bursts out into laughter, dark and ominous. I see eyes gleaming in the dark. There is a gust of wind, and the figure melts into that small gray bat and hovers. Cold wind and the sound of rain, then thunder and a flash of lightning. Cold...so cold. Cold as the grave under winter's snow. I start to shiver. My candle is blown out, and I am left in the icy darkness. The shadows engulf me and whisper into my soul.

*

I am back again in Golden Gate Park. I feel Lamont's presence as I lay upon him. I cannot tell if he is breathing or his heart is beating. He seems so horribly stiff and silent. A sense of urgency takes me. And a compulsion. I recall his parents. Why? I must not let them lose hope, even if I have little of it myself. I must do something. Perhaps if I can convince them, I can also convince myself of it in that act of reassurance. A plan forms—I think I can do this. I focus on Lamont's mother. I feel Lamont's warmth seeping into me the more I fix upon his mother. I did it! I have entered into her dreams.

Basha: "Trust me. All will be well, no matter what you are told. I trust that all will be well. Lamont will be well. I swear it. I promise it."

Then, finally, everything is back to normal ordinary time and space, with the comforting sound of chirping birds. Lana and Jon ask me if they should go and get the police. I realize that Tezcatlipoca had put me back into the river of ticking time.

Basha: "Of course. What else could go wrong? Now go, you two, go! Remember; tell them only that we just could not wake Lamont up. And do not worry; everything is going to be okay."

Lana: "What are you saying, Basha? Has something changed with Lamont?"

Basha: "Just go! I think it will all be alright. Just leave me alone with Lamont. Now, go!"

Jon: "Okay, we'll go get the cops."

I watch them head down the trails and try to make sense of what happened. Lamont...silly, cute, foolish, bright, brainy, talkative, trusting, naïve, but oh so good. A young man who sometimes sounds like a wise elder. He saw someone hurting and just assumed he should do something about it. Damn it, Lamont! You bewitched me! I am supposed to be the witch—but you wielded magic more powerful.

When I met you, you were just this young kid who clearly had a crush on me. You seemed so young, too young to be taken seriously. But over time, the longer we interacted and I got to know you, you were not a kid anymore to me. You were this paradox of naiveté and maturity. Your spell of good nature touched me. Your love was infectious. It was like being bewitched. It was a magic spell that I willingly gave myself over to. I could not help myself. Damn it, I love you. You...you cannot be gone! We only just kissed...we promised to wait...I would give anything to make this right.

I have a strange feeling about all this. What would Lamont say? He would quote Doyle, '*When you eliminated the impossible, whatever remains, no matter how improbable, must be the truth.*[11]' Well, what I am thinking is highly impossible, but I do not believe so improbable. Okay, Tezcatlipoca, we have unfinished business. Tezcatlipoca! I need you. Be here now!"

Everything is normal. He does not appear.

Basha: "Damn it! How do I contact Tezcatlipoca? Bloody Hell. Wait, blood. That is the key, is it not Tezcat? You always ask for blood. But I have no knife. I should have brought one." Then, I spot something black and shiny lying on Lamont's chest. I pick it up. It is a piece of obsidian about the size of my fist.

Basha: "How in Heaven's high name did this get here? Wait. Now I remember Tezcatlipoca came to me and then left. Is he playing games with me? At this time? Damn him! Hmmm...no, he said something about offering to help. Okay, let me see if that was for real. That is why he created this; I will bet. He wants me to do something. Okay, here goes. I squeeze it tightly.

Lamont: "Ow!" I can feel its sharp edges cut into my palm and watch as a bit of my blood soaks into the stone. "I thought so. You transformed ordinary stones into this piece of obsidian, which I believe is proof that the magick of the Dreamland variety somehow is an effect caused by the opening of the Gate of Dreams. Well, Tezcatlipoca, here is your blood. I offer it freely. Come to me, O' Smoking Mirror! Come to me O' Tezcatlipoca! I, Basha, keeper of Lamont's heart, need you! "

I hear, but not with my ears, soft, sibilant laughter.

---

11 William S. Baring-Gould, *The Annotated Sherlock Holmes*, Clarkson N. Potter, Inc., 1967, *Sign of the Four*, Vol I, Chap. 1, p. 613 &Chap. 6, pg. 638. "The Adventure of the Beryl Coronet" v. II, pg. 299; "The Adventure of the Bruce-Parrington Plans" v. II, pg. 446; and in "The Adventure of the Blanched Soldier" v. II, pg. 720.

Tezcatlipoca: Well done, Bright Eagle. You learn well. Are you ready for what must be done next?

Basha: "What are you talking about? What must I do? Explain yourself? How can I help Lamont?"

Tezcatlipoca: He is in the sleeping dream of death; your blood brought him this far from out of death's clutches. Now, more must be offered to bring him out fully from its grip. Know that death can die, but there is a price to pay. Are you willing to pay that price?

"What must I do?"

He will be dead soon without someone giving him life. You must be willing to provide him with some of your life so that he will return to the waking state of life. Are you willing to part with a piece of your very soul?

Yikes! What have you gotten us into, Lamont? What in the name of the Goddess does Tezcatlipoca mean? But Lamont must live. "Yes. Yes, O' Tezcatlipoca, I will give of my very soul to bring Lamont back to me."

Brave Bright Eagle. Wise and faithful you are. We only require a small offering of your life. A year of your life will be traded to bring Lamont, our Corazon, back to us both.

"A year? Explain!"

The days of your life are not entirely determined, but at some point in the future, when that path becomes fixed, what you will do this day will be noted. Your life's blood and breath will be shortened by this offering. You will die one year sooner than your allotted time. How and when this will be, we do not know. You will die sooner than you would have been if not for this bargain you had made. That is what you are about to do with this act. Do you heed my words?

"I do. One year of my life so that he may live again. Okay. We have a deal."

Know that there are no guarantees. Dear Heart will rise, but he will not be entirely as he once was. Death does not like to give back what it has taken. But he will be able to walk amongst the living once again. Are you still willing?

"Yes."

Now we shall call in one other to aid us both. We call to join us O' Queen of the Night, O' Lilith, she who is attuned to the Tree of Life. We call you! Be With us! We need you! As you watched over our Lamont Corazon, come to his aid in his hour of need!

Moonlight filters into this space, and I feel a silvery presence.

Lilith: "I have heard your call. You of the dark night and the dark wind, O' Tezcatlipoca. And to you, Basha Edelman, I offer greetings as well. What brings such an unlikely pair to call upon me?"

Wow. After all those years of doing rituals and calling to Gods and Goddesses, I realize that I never really thought I would ever interact with them. I am not sure I ever really believed they were real. Now, besides talking to someone who claims to be a god, I am actually getting to speak with someone who Tezcatlipoca says is a Goddess. She must be the one whose temple I studied at in Dreamland. I did not realize that she would call herself Lilith. Interesting choice of name. I will have to ask about that some other time.

Be not coy, O' Lilith, you who partook of the Tree. You know why we are all gathered here outside the River of Time. It is Lamont that brings us all together. You and we can aid him and aid Basha, this Bright Eagle. You must know what we desire, do you not?

"Basha, do you truly understand what Tezcatlipoca wishes to do? Basha, we would have guided and helped Lamont. Helped him on his journey as he passed through the veil. We would have allowed him to come to you. However, only when he awoke to this the final end of all mortal journeys."

You would have simply brought Lamont back as a ghost, a voice on the wind, in the shadows, and the shade. We offer him more.

"You deceived Basha once; will you not do it again? Can she, or I, trust such as you? Will you, O' Dark Trickster, tell all the truth and keep to your word? Can we trust that you are not holding something back?"

Basha: "Deceived me? What is she saying, Tezcat? Explain!"

Yes. When we first talked at the gate site, I caused you to forget what we had done. We possessed you briefly out of your desire, love, and grief for Lamont. We took advantage of those unconscious feelings to take from you an offering of your life's blood, a small part of your soul, to cast a spell of undying and stasis unto Lamont. To keep him from falling deeper into the final clutches of death. We needed you to trust that we would genuinely aid you and Lamont. We feared that you would not listen to us. We had to act quickly, then, or all would be lost. Our time to weave that enchantment was fleeting, and we could not let the time slip out of our grasp by chatter and argument. It was then or never.

"So, you took from me without my full knowledge."

Yes, only to save our Lamont.

"Why should I trust you? You are evil. You did your best to possess and harm Lamont."

We don't think of ourselves as evil. We are givers of a gift of the night and the wind. We ask for what we need and give our gifts in return.

"And all those slaves and captured prisoners that your priests sacrificed to you by cutting out their hearts? That was not evil?"

What those who have done in our name, directly or indirectly, many would call evil. This is not for us to decide. Such things are of your concern but not of ours. Evil and Good are human words. They are things that little godlings such as you, O' Queen Lilith, have to contend with. Beings such as you are made of human desires and needs and thus bound up with human limits.

Such things are without meaning to beings such as us. We are not of the mud born and made. We are children of the stars. Ancient ones we are. We danced and walked amongst the first stars. We require and ask for offerings of blood given freely. We have our own needs, desires, and dreams. We are above the petty limits of the human mind. Even the lesser star-traveling beings are above your level O' Lilith. They roam free amongst the stars while you are trapped on this ball of mud and water.

You are correct; possess Lamont we tried. We wished to be free of the cage in which we had been cast, hence the opening of the Gate of Dreams. But no true and final harm was ever planned for Lamont.

"If I recalled, you would have killed me, is that not true?"

Well, that was true. You stood in our way. We were angry. We had spent all that time trapped in a prison of death. We deserved our freedom! We would not let anyone stop us from being free!

However, you proved your worth, O' Bright Eagle. You challenged us, and you were right. We stood down. You both were so clever. Hence, we did not take your life. In the end, you tricked us. You defeated us, you and our Dear Heart. We deserved it. We were foolish. We acted hastily without care and thought. You and Lamont are now both precious as jade and as sweet as chocolate to us. You foiled our plans, and few have done such a thing. You had earned our respect.

"So, now I have your word that you wish us no harm or ill. You wish to bring Lamont back to me?"

This is what we have been saying, O' Bright Eagle. To restore our Dear Heart's soul to his corporeal vessel as fully as he once was, we cannot, but to allow that vessel to walk amongst the living and taste life once more, this we can. Hence, we need the action of Queen Lilith in consort with our efforts, and yours as well, to make this magick work.

"You must make this clear to Basha, O' Tezcatlipoca; you need to speak the truth to her. You cannot bestow upon Lamont true life, Tezcatlipoca. Admit that."

You speak correctly, but we can remove from him, for now, the true death and thus aid him to awaken to the living.

"But not as he was. He will walk between life and death. You will make Lamont into a creature that is undead."

True. But more alive than dead. This gift we can bestow.

"How do you know this is even possible?"

I know that something like this has been done before.

"What? By who? When?"

That is no concern of yours, Lilith, young human-made godling.

"Yes. I know my place. I believe there is a high price for such acts."

Yes. So, we have told Basha, the Bright Eagle and keeper of both our hearts. We have not deceived her in this.

"You were right. I could only offer Lamont a voice. Help him to be a presence. This is all that can be accomplished in the flow of the natural order. I would have helped him speak beyond the veil separating life from death. To bring Lamont back from the dead is to violate the laws of Heaven and Earth as laid down by the Infinite Divine herself. What Tezcatlipoca proposes is to make Lamont an unnatural being. Is this what you wish for him and for you, Basha? This could jeopardize yours and his very soul. I want you to be very clear and certain about this path you are about to take."

"I want him to return to me, not as a mere shadow, not as merely a voice alone. I wish to hold him in my arms and him to hold me. I do not care what it takes. I need this. I cannot live without him. Tezcatlipoca says he can do this. Is what he says true, O' Lilith?"

"It is as he says. However, Basha, heed my words. What Tezcatlipoca is about to do imperils Lamont's soul. I did know that this has been done before; I have watched them walk the Earth. I did not know how such things were made and by who. Now, I perceive who can do such things. You of the higher Gods—the ancient ones who were made of the stuff of stars. You, I gather, now must have this knowledge and power. This I now know. I did know that some of those creatures who feed off the living have come to rue that day. Let me make this clear to you, Basha; Tezcatlipoca wishes to make Lamont a creature that can only live by feeding off the life of others. Is this truly, what you want for Lamont?"

"What? I do not understand. What are you saying?"

"Tezcatlipoca's solution to bring Lamont back from the dead is to make him a drinker of blood, a vampire. He will forever be defiled. Lamont's soul will be stained forever. Is that what you truly want for your beloved?"

Oh, dear Goddess! No! This cannot be. Think Basha, think! I carefully recall all that Tezcatlipoca said, and there it is. The hints were clear. Lilith is right; what Tezcatlipoca was telling me is that he will make Lamont into one of the undead. "Tezcatlipoca, is what Lilith is saying true? You are offering to transform Lamont into a drinker of blood?"

Yes, Bright Eagle. This is so. This is the only way. You must choose for Lamont. Shall he have a life as an undead nosferatu or death? All that Lilith can offer is to allow Lamont to talk with you as an unsubstantial ghost.

"Lamont may rue this day. Do you understand that, Basha?"

"Tezcatlipoca, how long do we have to do this deed? Can we wait till Lamont awakens as a shade, which is what Lilith can do on her own?"

If we do not act now, it cannot ever be done. Precious time is slipping away.

"Does Tezcatlipoca speak true, O' Lilith?"

"He does Basha."

"Then I cannot wait to act. I have to do this on my own." Dear Goddess. Ghost or undead creature? A mere voice or someone I can hold and touch?

Decide Bright Eagle, choose. The time to act is slipping away like grains of sand in an hourglass. You must now decide!

I want him back as best I can get him. I never believed in this whole damned soul stuff. Superstitious nonsense. Nor did I ever go along with the entire ritual impurity stuff. The Rabbis were just freaked out by blood; that was their problem, but never mine. They fabricate all these rules about ritual Kashrut killing of animals to drain out every last drop of blood. They were disgusted by menstruation. Again, they were repulsed because of their imagined taint of blood. It was just an excuse to control women and dominate them. I have disregarded the rabbis about witches, so why not this as well? Think of it; Lamont can live! Yeah, but only by drinking blood. Okay, I have to admit that the thought is more than just gross. Damn it! Their religious guilt has been pounded into me. The guilt trips of the fathers have corrupted the children—tainted me with their bias and superstitions. What do I do?

Decide Bright Eagle, please. Decide. Tell us what we must do for our Dear Heart.

"Bloody Hell! I want what I want! And this is my only certainty! Damn it! I do not care what this may mean later. I will deal with tomorrow's troubles when tomorrow comes. I want Lamont to live. I want to be able to hold him in my arms. Damn it! Do it, Tezcatlipoca!"

You speak wisely, O' Bright Eagle. We shall allow Basha to give the gift of her life force, you O' Queen Lilith, shall aid in bringing Lamont's souls back into his vessel at one and the same time; thus, the deed will be done.

"I know what I need to do, Tezcatlipoca. As Lamont said, he could always find Basha, even in the darkness. I will simply facilitate his coming here."

Then let us begin.

"Yes."

Basha, hold our stone and place your hands onto Lamont, and we will begin.

"Wait…I remember now; you said something earlier to me about this stone…that it had to return to the soil of its birth or something like that."

Yes. This is true.

"Hmmm…so you are saying that like the storybook vampires, they have to spend time in the soil, so it is some kind of sleep cycle thing?"

Yes.

"I better gather some soil up from here then, since this is the soil of his new life…hmm…where can I put it? My backpack, so I will have it when we leave this place."

I get up, go to my backpack, dig up a good amount of that dirt, and fill the bottom of my backpack. Then I walk over to where Lamont lies, hold the stone in one hand and place my other on his heart. I pray that I am doing right by him. I breathe deep and concentrate. I feel bathed in the moonlight as I ignite into flames. My blood is seeping out of my hands and goes into Lamont.

Then there is searing hot pain. I am being wrenched and burned by the fire. Lamont glows with silver moonlight, and I sense this is Lilith's contribution.

Lamont screams in pain. His body is lit by silver flames and my red blood, which he reacts to as if molten lava was being painfully poured from me into him. We both respond to the burning pain. Oh, dear Goddess! What have I done to him? Was this a mistake? It is too late to ask that now. I can only go forward.

I am the fire that is pouring into Lamont. His body is being consumed. If I break contact, the horrible pain will stop, but my life force will no longer flow into him. The life force that I have offered to give will not replenish Lamont. The world is a blur of thick smoke and the smell of burning flesh. I can barely stand. I can barely breathe. I have to focus and ride the pain till this is done.

"Lamont!" I scream as I hold onto his body and drown in a pool of fiery pain, blood, and moonlight.

(BASHA AND) THE NEWLY RISING CREATURE WHO WILL BE KNOWN AS THE **NIGHT**

DREAMLAND, ABOVE THE CITY OF ATLANTIS

Night: I feel as if I have been in the dark and cold for a long, long time.

Basha: (Why do I feel this way? Those thoughts and feelings are not my own. And why do I feel that this thing is connected to Lamont?)

But with the ticking of time, there is the accompanying beating rhythm within. With each new beat, I feel the cold fingers of Sheol slip further away. I hear pounding in my ears and in my very being. The beating of my heart matches the beating of my leathery black wings. Together they beat to the same rhythm in the night sky.

I am alone. I am hungry. I burn with a consuming hunger. It is as if the night has coalesced into me, and I have been born. I am the unseen but ever-present. I am the night itself that watches over everyone.

(Fear grips my heart in its icy claws. Get a grip Basha and just wake up! I have been controlling my dreams since I was a little girl. I should be able to stop this nightmare. I struggle…but I cannot…)

Ice-cold serpents slither in my empty stomach. Who am I? Where am I? I feel a burning need and hunger.

To live, I must feed! Below me, I see food walking upright on two legs all around. I can smell a strong coppery and sweet smell coming from them mixed with the scent of sweat. My yearning drives me, compelling me to attack them.

(I feel that this thing is trying to pull himself up out of some deep dark pit as it claws its way through Lamont and me. I cannot make sense of these feelings and images. All I know is that they scare me, and I cannot ignore them.)

I approach a young couple walking hand in hand…they smell so sweet…I need to feed, and they are food.

Basha: "No!!!"

Night: Who dares question my needs!

Basha: (Holy Crow. It heard me!) "You must not do this. They are innocent!"

I do not care. I must feed on blood! I have no choice.

Basha: "You can choose to feed on those that prey on others if you must feed."

Why do I feel this need to heed your words? Who are you?

Basha: "Maybe that is why I am here. Heed me. Find some others. Do not attack the innocent."

I can hear a voice within me crying out that what you say is correct. Your words and that inner voice compel me as much as my needs. I can sense innocents from evil. I am the one who knows what evil lurks within. I will find that evil and feed on them. Will that satisfy you?

Basha: "Yes."

Alright. Not here, not yet, not now. I am mad with hunger! But I will wait and search for my prey.

Then I come to the fog-bound water's edge, where it kisses the marbled wharf softly. The scent of fish, living, and days old dead is palpable in the air and seems to cover everything inches deep. It seems a familiar place. I hear and smell fear here. I sense cruelty and pain, and it calls to me, singing sweetly to come and feed.

There. I hear a cry. A child's cry in the night. She is drenched in anxiety and sweat. The sound of cruel laughter. The sound of a hand striking innocent flesh. A man drags along a child who cries helplessly as they travel down the streets amongst the labyrinthine alabaster walls of this city. Hopelessness drips off her, carried by her tears.

The man's lust matches my lust. Now I can feed. I come out of the darkness. I am the dark. "Let the child go," I hear my voice say.

Unknown man: "Look, man, this is none of your business. Who do you think you are to tell me what I can do? I bought this one. Leave us be for your own good."

I laugh. "I know what evil lurks in the hearts of men[12]," I say as I envelop him in my shadow.

He feels fear. He feels terror. I lunge with bared teeth into his flesh and rip savagely into him. Delicious blood spurts out, and I feed. The taste of copper and salt and the sweetness like honey from his terror fills my mouth. I smother him, and not even his screams fill the air. I hear and feel his fear. It is in his blood. I love it! I hear little feet running, fleeing, and seeking shelter. I swallow down his hot salty, gushing fear.

Basha: (Oh dear Goddess. Such horror. I want to vomit from the stench of blood and urine. This is awful...)

My need has been slaked for a moment. Back into the shadows and the night, I return. I float over the city. The night revelers are wandering the streets, enjoying the darkness that gives them the stage for passion and pleasure. My hunger drives me on. I sense food walking the streets all around me, but I feel two voices, one within and one without arguing and insisting I must not. Alright! Leave me alone! I will find just the right food to take. So, I continue my hunt. I travel over great distances to another shore. Desire, hunger, and need carry me toward the city of Dylath-Leen.

---

[12] Here the Night is tapping into Lamont's memory of the Shadow radio broadcasts and published stories. Lamont is an Old Time Radio fan and collector of republished Shadow stories in paperback editions. The Shadow was the creation of Walter B. Gibson, under the pen name of Maxwell Grant. The first Shadow magazine was April 1 1931 published by Street & Smith.

Damp and darker. The creaking of ships moored at docks. The pungent, dank smell of the sea is even stronger here. Perhaps here I will find what I yearn for. I search on. I am reaching out to find fear and pain. I smell it...large quantities...young. I melt into the shadows and find myself in a massive room of comfort, debauchery, and excitement, all carried on the wafting scent of sweat. There is also the scent of roast meat, fermented butterscotch, honey, and yeast. The room is filled with adults lording over a cadre of adolescents and teenagers. All collared and drugged, being used as toys and playthings for the others who are predators with their guards and procurers. The air stinks of wine, drugs, sweat, fear, pain, and sex. They think they are in control and can perpetuate and dominate.

I laugh at them, and my laughter sends a chill through the room. Everyone stops in their tracks. "This debauchery has come to an end. I am the night who comes to reap sorrow and pain. A time of reckoning is upon you!" I call out from the shadows. "I know what evil lurks in your hearts! The weed of your evil bears only bitter fruit! As you sow evil, so shall you reap evil!"

Voices raise in challenge. A ripple of guilt and fear permeates the room. Muscle men search in the dark shadows for me. The laughter of my hunting and the knowledge that I can joyously feed fills the air. Out of the shadows, I strike.

I tear quickly into throats and limbs to drink of their coppery honey-sweet pain. I rend and slash to slack my need.

Basha: (Oh dear Goddess…the carnage…)

I take their life force from their blood. In return, I, with my touch, transmit the pain and fear of their victims as my parting gift to them. One by one, I pounce and feed, chasing them down. No escape for anyone of them!

Basha: (Oh dear Goddess…this is a massacre…I feel sick at the sight and the smells…)

Their weapons and arms find me not. They feebly strike at me but connect with mist, fog, and shadow. I am a whirlwind of darkness reaping revenge, feeding on them, and sending them, who preyed on the weak and the helpless, back to the Waking World in pain and fear as I drink of their life's essence. Now the room stinks of sweat and fresh piss, the heady bouquet of terror. On and on, I strike and feed—terror and my laughter echo through the room in my wake.

Finally, the room is empty save for the victims of their evil. They are left in safety to find comfort with each other till they slowly fade back to the Waking World, free of fear and pain.

I melt back into the night. My hunger is satiated for the moment.

*

BASHA

Uggg…my gut wrenches, and I heave up. My bile smells and reminds me of the stench that I could taste. What the Hell was that? Why did that horrible dream come so vividly to me? It must have been a dream…what else can it be? Yet, I felt that I was that…thing? Why? How? Then I notice that I am holding on to this obsidian stone. It feels important. I just feel I have to keep it…

I toss it into my backpack. I feel this strong connection to Lamont. What does that mean? Please, Goddess, let him be alright!

Then, I hear the sounds of approaching people. It must be Lana and Jon bringing the cops and help. I wave to them and motion for them to come to me...but I feel weak, and I slip…

*

I am awake. I am in a bed, not my own. I hear the soft hum of equipment and the scent of antiseptic, and I sense I am not alone. I try to sit up, speak, and look around. I manage to softly moan.

Miriam: "She's awake."

I know that voice. It is my mom. I look around me. I am in a hospital room. Why? How?

Miriam: "Daughter, are you well?" she says as she helps me sit up in this bed.

Basha: "I…I think so. Feel weak. How...?"

"The police found you with Lamont. From what they told me, you had fainted. They noticed that you had cut yourself on an odd stone. It was the one that you were holding. You were dazed and confused. You kept drifting awake and then fainting again. The paramedics took you with them. They brought you here with them. And here is San Francisco General Hospital. Lamont and Peter are also here. What I overheard about your friend Peter is terrible news. Besides being in some kind of coma, they said his blood work shows that Peter is very, very ill; he has been that way for a long time. The doctors are not sure what is wrong with Peter something is odd about the results from his blood tests."

Basha: "That doesn't make sense? How could that be?"

Miriam: "The doctors don't understand it. All I know is that they are worried about Peter."

Basha: "What about Lamont? Is he alright?"

Miriam: "Yes, Lamont is fine, he just seems to be asleep as well, but they can't wake him."

Basha: "But he is alive? Right?"

Miriam: "Yes. His condition is odd to them. Sort of exhaustion and something else, they don't like that he won't wake up."

"But he is alive?"

"Well, yes. His vital signs are very weak, though they don't understand it."

"Good. Then it will all be okay. Mom, when I woke up from Dreamland, I found him without a pulse, but I must have been mistaken. I think he almost died. Lilith, the one whose Temple we care for in Dreamland, appeared to me, and she did something to restore him. But I think that changed him somehow." I do not want to tell her about Tezcatlipoca's involvement. Not now. Not yet. Maybe never. "Anyway, I am certain he will be okay, but different. I am not sure."

"You're not making sense, daughter. You're worrying me."

"Sorry. I do not have a clear head at the moment either. I feel very drained as well. I think they took some of me to aid in the healing of Lamont. That has me weak. Tired. I…feel sleepy again."

"But you are alright? And who is this *they*?"

"I will explain…later…I just know that this worked…I am tired...I…need rest…I..."

Wednesday, September 3, 1980

SAN FRANCISCO GENERAL HOSPITAL

BASHA

I wake again, not knowing what time or day it is.

Helen Corazon: "My dearest Basha, are you awake?"

I recognize the voice as Mrs. Corazon's. "What day is it?" I feel so confused.

Helen Corazon: "Today is September the third. It is still morning. You gave your mother quite a fright when you fainted. How do you feel?"

Basha: "Weak. Tired."

Helen Corazon: "I was told that you were lying next to my son when you were found."

Basha: "It is not my fault that he is here. Let me explain…"

Helen Corazon: "I know. I wasn't implying that you did anything wrong. I know that you would never harm my Lamont. I was upset when the police came to the house, and they told me that you and my son were taken to the hospital. He had told me about you and some friends going to Golden Gate Park for a picnic. But we grew concerned when he was gone for so long. My husband and I rushed to the hospital. The doctors told us that you were all in some strange sleep from which you could not wake. That night I was so worried that I had a hard time sleeping. I admit I was angry at the two of you at first."

Basha: "I am sorry about all this. Let me explain..."

Helen Corazon: "It's all right. I understand enough. You see, you told me everything was going to be all right. It was amazing! You came to me in my dreams. You explained that you prayed long and hard for him to help heal him. They said that they found you lying over Lamont in tears. This is how I know that you truly care for my son. I think you two are soul mates. Is that right, my dear?"

Ahhh...what do I say? "Yes, honestly, I do think we share a bond. So, I guess Lamont and I are soul mates.

"You two were meant for each other. I knew that when you came to me in my dreams. You told me not to worry. You told me you would not let any harm come to my son. You must have said special prayers for him, right? Those prayers were answered by our Lord. Your people, the Hebrews are a very old race, am I right? Your people have been to many places and have learned old things and old ways. You have studied such things in your books, am I right?"

"Yes," I guess that is one way of putting all this.

"Those studies enabled you to come to me in my dream so that you could tell me that my son will be all right. You told me not to worry, no matter what I heard. Am I right?"

"Yes."

"The doctors here are concerned for you. But I knew from what you told me that you and my son were okay. I think you used old Hebrew magic to talk to me in my dream and help my son. The doctors don't understand these things--the power of old prayers taught in old books. They are puzzled about him. They said he is now very weak and in a deep odd sleep. This makes them concerned for him. But, we know the truth. God answered our prayers. Especially your ancient prayers that you learned. It is because of you that we were granted a miracle. You helped God bring about that miracle, which the doctors don't understand. But we do."

Basha: "Yes, I am sure you are correct, God did answer our prayers, and I did use some ancient learning to come to you in your dream."

Helen Corazon: "I thought so. I have prayed for you to recover and be well. Your mother wanted to stay, but she had work to do, running that shop. I told her I would stay and be here. I said I would stay with you and Lamont. I watched over you two. Now things are better. You must be hungry, yes?"

"I think I am."

"I will go get the nurse and the doctor to check on you. Your love for my son is strong and true. Basha, You will always be in my prayers."

"Ahh…thank you."

Mrs. Corazon goes to get the nurses; I lie back feeling like a great weight was taken off me. It worked! Tezcat and Lilith did whatever magick they did, and Lamont will be okay. He just needs to wake up, I guess. The doctors quiz me about why I was slumped over Lamont when they found me. I just made something up about being concerned for my boyfriend. After checking my vital signs, they called me an overwrought and overly sensitive girlfriend.

They could not find anything wrong with me despite my being excessively tired. The nurses give me a clean bill of health. They tell me to call them if I have any further fainting spells. They offer me breakfast. They bring it quickly, and I devour it. When they take the tray away, I ask if I can get up and walk around. They say yes.

Helen Corazon: "I will look after her. Now, Basha, do you really want something else to eat?"

Basha: "Yes! I have suddenly got your son's appetite!"

Helen Corazon: "I don't understand where he puts it all," she says, laughing.

Basha: "Let's get you to the cafeteria."

As we walk, we talk. She has many questions. I try to come up with a reasonable explanation of the bargains I made without telling her that I actually spoke with Gods. As I eat, I tell my tale. I'm sure that the truth would not go over well. Ancient Jews who learned the secrets of old Egypt and Babylon sound much more believable to her. I tell her I have learned how to enter a dream of someone I can emotionally connect with. She must not tell anyone what I did. I had been sworn to secrecy and told never to use that knowledge. I explained that I broke those oaths of secrecy. I needed to make sure she had hope, just like I did. That I just felt that our prayers would be answered. She is grateful that I did.

I ask about my motorcycle, and Mrs. Corazon tells me that Mr. Corazon brought it to the store. She tells me that my friends Lana and Jon had been in and out trying to see me the other day, but I had been bedridden. When we get back to my room, I tell her I want to rest. While I rest, she will call and tell my mom that I have been up.

I need to get to Dreamland and speak with Lilith if I can.

*

I appear at the Goddess of the Night's temple's courtyard. I make a hasty greeting to the Keeper of the Flames and go directly to the audience room. It is odd to have met and spoken to beings claiming to be Gods. The hall is quiet, dark, and empty. The chamber has a hint of smoke and sweet spices. Clean marble and alabaster, brightly painted walls depicting the moon over many Mediterranean landscapes. I have been here for rituals and ceremonies many times but never thought I would speak with the Goddess directly. Only with some high priestess speaking in the name of. It was clear that this chamber's art and architecture had the look and feel of what I saw in Minoan temple pictures. The high priestess wore those layered bell-shaped dresses with the open bodice revealing her bare breasts.

Basha: "O' Queen of the Night, I, Basha, call to you, asking if you will grant me an audience," my voice is soaked up by the quiet emptiness of the hall.

I light the braziers next to the altar. I wait. Finally, moonlight filters into the room, and with it, a voice.

Lilith: "You may address me as Lilith, O' Basha Edelman, one of my dutiful daughters. Well trained you are in our arts. I have been watching Lamont Corazon since he arrived in this realm."

"Are you related to the Lilith of the legends of my people?"

"I am the same. Though I never had very good relations with your Rabbis."

"That is what I understand. I notice that you do not act in the manner that they slanderously attribute to you. Their own misogynist bias created that version of you, and thus they failed to understand you. That is their loss and their problem. It is one that I think that Freud would enjoy pondering. As for me, I am honored to speak with you."

"I helped a little to assist Lamont once I realized that he had gotten involved with that Higher God, Smoking Mirror. I was concerned about Lamont's well-being and his soul. In the end, I was wise to be concerned. I was compelled to participate, against my better judgment."

"I am grateful that you helped him as you did. Through all of this, I am reminded of how Lamont was complaining for much of his time in Dreamland that he had no dream skills. But I think he actually did have a very singular skill. I learned amongst my childhood lessons in Dreamland that one who dies in Dreamland cannot return to it since their Dream body had been destroyed and thus ceased to exist. But somehow, Lamont had seemingly died many times and yet kept on returning. I think that was his unique and most amazing Dream power. One that I did not believe possible."

"Yes, that is his most remarkable talent. One that I do not fathom."

"It is a mystery to you as well?

"I have my suspicions. The only explanation for this impossible ability is that I speculate that it was Lord Tezcatlipoca's doing. He must have imbued Lamont with such resilience for his own mysterious purpose. He needed Lamont then, and his actions demonstrate that he needs him still, as well as he needs you. The two of you are his chosen ones."

"Great. Chosen for what? Do you have any ideas?"

"No, I do not. I cannot fathom why. The cliché is right; Tezcatlipoca does indeed work in mysterious ways."

"All very disturbing." But there is nothing I can do about it. I will have to be wary. "Anyway, I am grateful to you, and no matter his motivation, I am grateful for Tezcatlipoca. But you said you were concerned for Lamont; why? Also, why did you say you were compelled?"

"You need to understand when Smoking Mirror asks something; it is actually a command. *I had no real choice. I would never have done such a thing. Nor would I ever have thought it in the realm of possibility. It violates the laws of the natural universe. It was unwise and dangerous. I wish I had nothing to do with it. It reeks of dark forces. Tainted forces. However, Smoking Mirror commanded it to be so."*

"How could Smoking Mirror command you? Who is she? I know from books that usually, Smoking Mirror is referred to as masculine, but Tezcatlipoca appears to Lamont in female form. You two talked about there being many different types of Gods and Goddesses. Is this true, and are all Goddesses created equal?"

"Firstly, yes. Tezcatlipoca can command someone such as me. Not all goddesses are created equal. For instance, I am one of the many gods that humanity has created through their dreams, hopes, and fears. Humanity has created hundreds, if not thousands, like us. Some even of us think they are more

than they are. The god of your people claims the foolish title of 'The One True God', trying to pretend and forget the history of its own making. That god, the one who is called simply 'The Name' by some, and others as Lord Adonai, or by the mystics as Ayn Sof, is simply one of the many human-created ones. Like the other two gods of the so-called 'monotheistic faiths, it is merely like me, a human-created deity. "

"Wait, the three monotheistic religions claim there is just one God and that they simply call it by different names. Are you saying that is not the case?"

"Of course, I am. Those three just pretend to be the only one. Those monotheistic gods are actually three different but very popular gods. They just try to convince everyone to think that there is only one. They would have more competition if all the people on the Indian sub-continent ever got around to believing in only one deity. Still, they are too committed to their polytheistic roots. Anyway, there are a lot of us gods of humanity. I'm just one of the oldest. I managed to pull myself up by my own sandal strings when I mastered the power of the Sefiroth and ascended to potential divine status. To be truly divine requires worshipers."

O' Queen Lilith, I am puzzled. Is not the Sefiroth the emanation of Ayn Sof? It is not a personal deity but a force of the cosmos. Did it not create everything?"

"Well, that is a question of semantics. The word as you use it could point to the actual and true so-called 'Creator of the universe'. I must say that there is creation, and there is formation. The entity that claims the title of The Crafter-of-All is the supreme deity of the pantheon of the Outer Gods. It is a vast entity, but it still is a finite being with a personality like all the gods of whatever rank and title. It is not an impersonal force as your Kabbalistic mystics think of it."

"Is there no ultimate non-personal force that created everything?"

"That is a philosophical question I cannot fully fathom. All I do know is that I have talked with many gods and goddesses. I have never spoken with or heard the voice of such a Being. All that I have met and talked with, these are all beings with personalities. I do not understand this obsession with abstract things that mystics, rabbis, and philosophers write and talk about. I can neither confirm nor deny the existence of some abstract supreme force such as Ayn Sof or the Dao or Brahman. I can only say I have never encountered such a thing. Not

even in Gan Eden. As I mentioned, I do know that the one who claims the title of the Crafter and Shaper of the universe, that being is the supreme entity of the Outer Gods. One of its names is Azathoth. Whether there is a nameless force behind it, I cannot say. Thus, the title Ayn Sof points to Azathoth this seems to be pragmatically the same, as far as I have experienced."

"That is something that is hard to comprehend. I believe that the true creator of the cosmos is the force known as Ayn Sof. As you said, all the beings you encountered are vast but finite creatures, even one's such as you and that Azathoth you talk of."

"Yes, I agree. I know that those deities are merely finite creatures with immense power but still finite. You, humans, have such strange ideas that I don't understand. Just know that all human ideas concerning the divine are just that, a human concept. It is not anything but that."

"Okay. Please continue to explain things as you have encountered them, O' Queen Lilith."

"As I said. I have learned the truth as far as I can about creation and all the deities. I know and acknowledge the truth. All of us gods of humanity are small children to beings such as the one that has taken the name of Tezcatlipoca. That one is a force of the universe. Those like her are as old as the universe itself. We do not really know. Well, most of us gods of humanity recognize the sovereignty of the ancient ones known as The Outer Gods. All except the 'Big Three'.

As I just said. Those three monotheistic gods have immense hubris and vast egos concerning their self-importance and place in this infinite cosmos. They had forgotten or pretended to ignore the ancient knowledge. It angers me how they demean and dismiss the others like myself. Pretending to be the Only True Divinity. Yet also pretending that the other two claimants for the title of 'The Monotheistic God 'do not exist. I'm sorry, I'm repeating myself. Don't mind me; it just irks me even after all these long eons.

Anyway, as for our status and position here on Earth, amongst humankind, all of the gods, whether we are talking of the Earthbound and human-created ones such as myself or the star spawned ones – our ultimate status here all comes down to a popularity contest, to tell you the truth."

"What do you mean by that?"

"Well, all gods need worshippers; otherwise, we cease to exist. For us human-made godlings, that is literally true. The star spawned, and the Outer

Gods do not need humanity, but they crave and need worship. That is the stuff of life for any deity. We are vampires of a sort in that we feed off our worshipers' energy. Though, those who know how can sustain and tap into the power of the cosmos itself. That force you know in the form of the Sefiroth aka The Tree of Life and Knowledge. I acquired such abilities when I mastered the Tree's power and learned true magick. Thus, our rank amongst each other depends on how many worshippers we can claim."

"So, we give power to the Gods?"

"Yes. By your worship. To continue the list of gods and godlings, besides the deities that humanity had created, such as myself, besides the ancient Outer Gods, such as Tezcatlipoca, there are also beings who had come to your planet a long time ago. Humanity treated them also as gods. They are star-born and star-traveling beings. We human-made gods are less powerful than some of those star-traveling beings. We are at the bottom of the totem pole of deities that humanity has known. Since we dwell solely on this sphere, the others can swim amongst the stars."

"Wow. That is a lot to take in. As Lamont would say, I appreciate the cosmic civics lesson. However, I am not sure how this impacts us, especially Lamont?"

"Correct, as you say, all of that is not important. Our discussion drew me into topics of history and philosophy and not to the matter at hand. What is important is this, for Lamont, know that he may walk and talk but that he will never be normal again. He is a thing other than merely human. He is undead."

"Okay, now explain what this all means. Lamont is undead. Do you mean that he has become a vampire as described in all those horror novels and movies?"

"Yes, to an extent. Though not exactly like the storybooks. He will not live forever, even if in Dreamland, he seems unkillable. He will not ever get ill, though he will grow old and, like all things, wither in his allotted time. Since you gave your life so that he may live, you are forever connected to that thing that has risen out of him."

"You said that Lamont became a vampire through your magick spell that you and Tezcatlipoca wove. What do you mean by a thing rising out of him? Explain?"

"Lamont lives because a vampire was created out of a portion of his soul. He and this vampire entity are joined, two minds in one vessel. You are bound to

this thing as well."

"I had a dream in which I saw and felt this thing clawing into life and going out to hunt for blood. That was not a dream but this vampire creature that I connected to?"

"Yes. So long as Lamont and it feeds, Lamont will seem mostly normal. He will require psychic energy conveyed through the blood to retain his existence. His body will function like any living person with that stolen life force. But he will need to feed on life from others throughout the days of his allotted life. The Vampire will always be a part of him. I tried to warn you, but as I said already, I had no choice. Lamont could become as monstrous as that vampire thing if Lamont is not careful. The two of them have the power of life and death now that he is a living dead. This vampiric life is something that is not right. It is a terrible power. No human should have this. You must watch over him. Don't let it take him over."

"I will make sure Lamont does not become a monster. Although, I do not think he has that in him."

"One never can be sure of that."

"Do you think Tezcatlipoca turned Lamont into something like this so that Lamont could become a monster?"

"Actually, no. I do not think that is what Tezcatlipoca had in mind for Lamont. I think Tezcatlipoca truly does seem to care about you two. You are his favorite pet, perhaps even more. But for how long, I wonder? He wanted Lamont alive for a reason, his reasons. So, he allowed your wish. It is what you wanted, and more importantly, it is what Tezcatlipoca wanted. So, I had to do my part. I am sorry. I may be able to offer some further council in the future, though my powers to intervene are limited."

"I had to do what we did. I needed him back. We appreciate what you have done, and will do, on our behalf. I thank you, O' Lilith."

With that, the moonlight fades, and the room feels empty indeed. Lamont is possessed by a vampire. Dear Goddess, I did not consider fully what I was doing to you, Lamont. Will you forgive me?

My Waking World ears hear a familiar voice, speaking very weakly and faintly, a voice that brings joy to my heart. I need to wake up!

*

Lamont: "What time is it? Did I miss breakfast and lunch?" In a weak yet clear voice, Lamont asks as the diffuse sunlight seeps onto him from the shut window blinds.

Basha: "Lamont!" I call out as I struggle to get out of this hospital bed.

Helen Corazon: "My son, you're awake. And you're hungry. Of course, you are," she says with happy relief.

Lamont: "Mom, could you go get me some food?"

Helen Corazon: "Yes, I will go and leave you two alone. But only for just a little time. I was young once, and I remember what it was like."

As she leaves the room, I do my best to gather my dignity in this hospital gown and get to Lamont's bedside.

Basha: "No peeking, Lamont!"

Lamont: "I wouldn't dream of it."

Basha: "Ha! Of course, you would; you cannot fool me."

It is so good to see his bright blue eyes again. His face is ashen, and he feels feverish. His raven black hair is a mess, a bad case of bed-head hair. I run my fingers through his hair to fix it somewhat. He just smiles weakly up at me with a happy grin. We both laugh; it is good to hear his laughter.

Basha: "Now, pay attention. One: you were dead. Two: Tezcat made you not dead. Three: Tezcat and the Goddess Lilith brought you back to this form of life you now have. I am reasonably certain that you are fine."

Lamont: "What?"

Basha: "You are alive...sort of...you are kind of different now. But fine as well as can be expected since Tezcat had used me to bring you back from death's door."

Lamont: "You do realize that you're not explaining this very well?"

Basha: "Yes, I know that. But there is more."

Lamont: "Okay, will table me and my condition for now; what else?"

Basha: "Four: Peter, well, he is very sick. I am sorry to say that he is mysteriously ill. Not sure of the details."

Lamont: "What! Was it something to do with what happened to him at the dream site? He was attacked by those...things. Oh God, no..."

Basha: "As far as I know, he had some illness from a long time ago that never got treated. He is ill from something other than the attack. Though I guess he is not in any pain, he is in some kind of REM sleep and will not wake up from it. Five: Lana and Jon are fine, I think. Six: I think we can Dream like we can in Dreamland here in the Waking World."

Lamont: "What?"

Basha: "At least I think this is true, for we who were at both sides of the gate when it opened have been affected. For us, the gate between the two realms is still open to some extent or something like that. I am not quite sure. This is the kind of puzzle that you love to untangle. Other than all that, I just recounted, everything is normal."

Lamont: "What? Dead? Tezcat? What? Is the gate still open? Hell! I hear mom coming back; we need to meet in Dreamland, say at Zuki's place; I need more details than you could give me in that quick recap. But later, I need to eat first. Okay?"

Basha: "Absolutely." I quickly kiss Lamont. "So glad you are back."

When Mrs. Corazon returns with the nurse, she mentions that Lamont is still running a mild fever. They noticed it started once it was daylight. Hmmm. Vampires and sunlight don't mix. I wonder if that is the problem. Good thing the blinds are tightly closed. He is only getting indirect light. Sunlight could be disastrous to him if they open those blinds. But, I am anxious to test out the effects of the open gate. I have an odd idea that I need to check. I ask if I can get dressed. The nurse says yes. She says that if I feel fine by the end of the day, I could go home. I gather my things from where they got stashed and go to the bathroom to get dressed—time to test a hypothesis. When you eliminate the impossible, etcetera, I imagine a small flame appearing in the palm of my hand. Nothing happens. Why not?

But wait. What if it all has something to do with the stone from the gate site? Maybe that is the connecting link. I go back and get it out of my backpack. Hmmm...it is buried in that dirt at the bottom of the pack. Tezcatlipoca said something important about that dirt. What was that? Anyway...I need to focus on the task at hand. I take the stone and head to the bathroom. Now holding it in one hand, I try to create a small flame in the palm of the other. It works. Oh, great Goddess, it works! This is crazy!

This is definitely a Holmesian impossible-improbable that I just have to accept. The fact that it worked means that a direct connection to the gate site is the key. Presumably, if I was there, I could do this. Holding something from that place enables me to maintain a connection to there. Reasonable hypothesis. Now, can I make this stone more portable and less conspicuous?

I have an idea. I could make this stone more portable if I made it into a piece of jewelry, like a ring. Hmmm...Let me get my earrings and see if I could fashion a ring out of them.

First, get dressed. Well, let me put that Dreaming to use. I take my socks and my panties, soak them in hot water and then use Dreaming to dry them off. Crazy. Weird and crazy. Not perfectly clean, but good enough. I dress and then go back out to get my earrings that should be with the rest of my things.

Lamont: "Basha! What are you doing?" As he is about to take a bite of food.

Basha: "Maybe you should hold off on eating so soon..." too late.

Lamont: "Why," he says with a mouthful of food that he swallows.

Basha: "I have an idea. Hold that thought." I grab them, step back into the bathroom, and shut the door. I hold the obsidian stone in my hand with the gold and silver sun-moon earrings that Lamont bought me. I imagine two rings, one a gold ring and the other a silver ring, each blended with some of the obsidian stone. I close my hands around it all and focus.

I can feel the heat and power surging in my hands. If I was not already used to playing with fire, I might have been in trouble. It takes a bit of time and concentrated effort. I am sure they are wondering what is going on. Oh well, focus, Basha, focus.

Finally, I feel that it is done. I open my hands. The earrings are all gone. Instead, I have in my hands two rings. I see that a small chunk has been taken out of the obsidian stone from this process. It worked. This is so weird! This is fantastic! But it is now beginning to make some sense.

This is what Tezcatlipoca was talking about in his oblique way. He has done something to make us have this power. He used our gate spell to connect the two realms, and he has made that connection manifest through this obsidian and the soil from the site. So, as long as I am in contact with the obsidian, even with a connection to this small amount of the stone in the rings, I can do Dream magick. Wow! I have magick here in the Waking World. This will change everything! Maybe I can do something to protect him from the sunlight?

Then there are the others. We need to help Peter and the others. Somehow. We have to make this right. I do not think we were given this ability for a lark. We were given it for a purpose. One final test to confirm my hypothesis. I slip the gold ring on my finger, put the stone down on the sink, and then try to make a flame. It works. I was right. Now one last test. I try to conjure up a pencil. I picture it in my mind and focus on it. I feel the energy sputter and just not do anything. I focus harder. I focus all my will and desire that I can muster.

My head starts to hurt. I stop and look at my hand. Nothing. Then there are some limits to our newfound powers, just like in Dreamland. What powers we have are connected to the stone; that is a fact. I wonder if our magick abilities are limited to conjuring our Dream attire? Does what I did to forge the rings a one-off special exemption? Makes sense that it is. Since it is related to what Tezcatlipoca did to us and for us. More experimentation needs to be done to ascertain our true limits. But no time for that now. I take off the ring and head out to Lamont. Maybe the rings can help him.

Lamont: "Hello, beautiful." Says around a mouth full of food.

Basha: Damn, seeing that, I have a bad feeling about all that food he has been eating. I hope I am wrong, but I do not think so. "I had hoped that your mother taught you not to talk with your mouth full?"

Helen Corazon: "I tried my best to raise him right, but you know how boys are."

Basha: "Yes, I do. Boys are not very trainable."

Helen Corazon: "So true."

Basha: "Lamont, I have been keeping those rings you bought for us safe, and now that you are awake, let me put it on your left hand."

He spots the two rings in my open hand and looks at me, puzzled but knows something is going on. He does what I ask and holds out his right hand to me.

Basha: "The other Left hand, Lamont."

Lamont: "Oh."

He holds out his actual left hand, and I am about to slip the silver and obsidian ring on his third finger. Then, I decide to slip it on his middle finger instead at the last moment. He might get the wrong or right idea if I put it on his third finger as I was about to. That's the engagement-slash-wedding ring finger. So, for now, it is not going there. My unconscious may have no trouble announcing a commitment to each other and making it public, but I am consciously scared of that idea. I do not want to admit it all to myself, not just yet. Let's just keep it on the death-will-not-part-us-but-we-are-just-extremely-good-intimate-close-friends level. I hold it tight, causing it to conform to his finger to fit better; it glows as I do this. I was making sure to conceal what I had just done from Mrs. Corazon's sight.

Basha: "There. Now you will not misplace it. How about…"

Lamont: "No!" says in a loud whisper and uncharacteristically complaintive, "I...I was supposed to get the gold one…please."

I can see a tear trickling down and that he is trying to hide a grimace of pain.

Lamont: "Please take it off and give me the gold one."

Basha: "Sorry, Lamont. Sure." What is going on? "I apologize that I forgot what we discussed," I say as quickly as I can take the silver ring off his finger. As I do, I notice that his skin is burnt! An idea from books and movies springs to mind—silver and supernatural creatures do not mix! Holy Crow! His vampiric nature cannot touch silver.

Helen Corazon: "Is something wrong, dear?" Spoken in a concerned and puzzled tone.

Basha: "It is nothing, Mrs. Corazon. I just forgot that I promised Lamont the gold ring," I say as I slip it on him.

Helen: "But why? That seems odd."

Lamont: "I wanted the gold ring to remind me of Basha, she's dazzling like sunlight, and the gold reminds me of that. That way, I can keep her with me always."

Helen: "That's sweet."

I then slip the gold ring on his finger. I notice a brightness of health appears across his pale countenance as I do. He looks more relaxed. I touch his forehead, to my surprise, and he no longer feels feverish. His very pale skin is cool to the touch. So, I am about to put the silver ring onto my third finger, but then with conscious thought, I put the silver and obsidian ring on the middle finger of my left hand. I touch the ring to make it fit snuggly. I give him a quick kiss on the cheek.

Basha: "I forgot to tell you I really appreciate the matching set of rings you bought us."

Yes, the fever seems to be all gone. Could the ring be protecting him from the harmful effects of sunlight?

Lamont: "Oh. Yeah, you're welcome. I'm glad you like them." He blushes. He looks at the rings and me.

Lamont: "They are cool rings. Tell me again what kind of stone is mixed into the rings; I forgot."

Basha: "They are obsidian, silly. You are so forgetful sometimes."

Lamont: "Yup. That's me, forgetful Lamont. These are really cool. I'm so glad I bought them."

Helen Corazon: "Matching rings. You two are officially going steady now, I see. "You are good for each other."

Lamont blushes again.

Basha: "I told him he did not have to get them, but he is the sentimental type. We are young, but we are very invested in each other."

Helen: "Well, I'm happy you are in my son's life, Basha."

Basha: "I am too."

Lamont: "Uhhhh…"

Basha: "Lamont, what is wrong?" I ask, noticing the grimace on his face.

Lamont: "My stomach...it hurts. Bad. I need to get up...get to the Bathroom...I'm going to be sick…"

Helen: "Lamont! What's happening?"

I quickly help him out of bed and put my arm around him.

Lamont: "I...feel...sick…bathroom...quick..."

We get into the bathroom, I shut the door, and Lamont lunges for the toilet. He vomits up what he just ate, obviously in pain and distress. I get some paper towels to help clean him up.

Basha: "Lamont," I whisper so only he can hear. "I believe that this must be a side effect of you coming back from the dead. I do not think you can eat solid food for a while. I think you should be able to handle liquids."

Lamont: "Why?" He whispers back.

Basha: "It makes sense from what Tezcat and Lilith were saying. And it explains your reaction to silver. Brace yourself. To bring you back, I had to agree to Tezcat's bargain. It was my only option. You are alive, but not alive. No longer a normal human being. The word Lilith used was, I am afraid to say it aloud, but she called you a *vampire*."

Lamont: "Oh God…oh God…it's true...oh God," Lamont whimpers as he stares into the bathroom mirror. "I'm like something that walked out of Bram Stoker's novel. See!" He shakily points at the mirror.

Basha: "What is wrong…" Then I gasp as I look in the mirror. Lamont has no reflection. "How is this possible?"

Lamont: "I don't know…but it is. The mirror does not show my reflection; that is the proof."

Basha: "I am afraid so, Lamont. Dear Goddess, I am sorry. But it all happened so fast. I panicked. I did not want to lose you. I…I…"

Lamont: "This is all crazy. Am I not human? Am I a monster?"

Basha: "No. I do not think so." Oh, Goddess, I hope not. "Lilith would have stopped me if I were turning you into some kind of monster." At least, I think she would. "But, I think you are condemned to a liquid diet, and you need to avoid silver as we just discovered with the ring. Let me see your hand."

We look, and it still shows a burn mark; it has not healed.

Basha: "Is it painful?"

Lamont: "Not much now; it just doesn't look so good. But the gold ring hides it from sight. I'm definitely avoiding silver from now on."

Basha: "Oh, Lamont, I think direct sunlight is harmful, but wearing the ring somehow protects you from that. What have I done to you? I am so sorry."

LAMONT

Basha looks so terrified and guilty. I need to reassure her. I'm just happy to be alive—sort of alive anyway. "But, hey, it's okay," I hug Basha tight. Her comforting sexy, spicy hot scent of cinnamon is strong. "I'm here with you. I want that. Anyway, I can. I didn't want to be dead. So, you did the right thing. We'll figure this out." I sure hope to high heaven I'm going to be okay. She allowed them to turn me into a vampire! I guess being a vampire is better than being a zombie. Bloody damn Hell! Nothing will ever be normal ever again. But I can't think about that now. Mom is here. Have to act all normal. I have to put on a good face even if I can't see it anymore.

Helen Corazon: "Son? Are you okay? Should I get the nurse?"

BASHA

Lamont: "I'm okay now," Lamont says in a normal tone of voice. "I'm coming out in a moment. Quick, what's with the rings?"

Basha: "They enable us to do Dream magick. They connect to the open gate between the worlds, and I believe they will block the harmful effects of direct sunlight."

Lamont: "Really? You've tried this?"

Basha: "Yes, the magick part of it. It is how I made them. But Tezcatlipoca said something about having to return to the soil of their birth. I am not sure about that."

Lamont: "Hmmm...do you have some of that soil?"

Basha: "Yes. In my backpack, I have soil from the gate site."

Lamont: "You made out rings from the obsidian stone that Tezcat made for us. That must be what he means. We need to keep that in the soil to keep it and the rings magickally charged."

Basha: "That seems to make sense."

Lamont: "You realize that you almost had me put them on like engagement rings! You do realize that."

Basha: "Yes, Lamont, I did do that. However, I will swear under oath that it was acting under the influence of temporary insanity."

Lamont: "Ha! "

He quickly kisses me. Now I blush.

Lamont: "Waking up from the dead isn't all bad. We're an *item*. Wow! Too much to try and deal with now. We just need to pretend everything is normal in front of Mom."

Basha: "Yeah. Right."

I open the door, and Lamont heads back to bed.

Lamont: "I'm okay, Mom. I just don't seem to handle solid food yet. Maybe I could get some soup, or juice, or both?"

Helen Corazon: "Are you sure? Should I go get someone?"

Lamont: "Let's buzz them to see if I could go to the cafeteria. Also, I preferred if I could get dressed. I don't like the idea that I just flashed my mom and my girlfriend."

The nurse returns and Lamont asks if he could get up and walk to the cafeteria with us. She responds with maybe and goes to get the doctor. They check his vitals and see that his temperature and blood pressure are now back to normal. Sort of, both are below the normal range; it is not dangerously so. They want to keep him under observation for a bit longer as for getting dressed, nope. However, she does permit him to go to the cafeteria if he feels up to it. They say they will give him a walker. He gets up and walks around the room to show that he is okay. They compromise on a cane just to be on the safe side.

Lamont: "Okay, let's get me something I can eat. And try not to make too much fun of me in this silly hospital gown."

Basha: "I would never dream of it."

Lamont: "Oh yes, you would. Just keep it to yourself, okay?"

Basha: "I think the cane suits you. It gives you an air of distinction and elegance." I say with delightful sarcasm.

Helen Corazon: "You do know that you two bicker like you've been married for years?"

We both just look at her and each other with embarrassment and then giggle at the astute observation of our mutual compatibility.

Lamont: "No. We don't!"

Basha: "That is preposterous!" I say, trying to deny everything with a grin on my face.

Helen Corazon: "I'm just calling it like a see it. Now, will you two just stand around and snipe at each other all day? Or are we going to get something to eat?" She says, laughing with delight.

Lamont: "Hey, I don't need the cane if you two young ladies would just grab an elbow."

We all smile, Mrs. Corazon tucks her arm into Lamont's left elbow and me into his right, and off we go laughing and sniping at each other like children at a playground. Whew. It feels so good just to be alive, happy, and ignore all life's problems for a while.

When we get there, Lamont asks for three bowls of chicken soup, just the broth, a container of apple juice, cranberry juice, and orange juice.
Lamont steers us to a table just out of the direct sunlight streaming in from the windows. He places his tray on the table and then looks at me with a grin, then with a shrug, approaches the window. Oh, Goddess…what if? He hesitantly reaches his hand out to the direct stream of sunlight. This is crazy and so dangerous! Why is he always so impulsive and reckless like this? If he reacts, someone, like his mom at the very least, could notice. I am about to say something or grab him, but it is too late. The sunlight covers his hand, and he just stands there.

Nothing happens.

Helen Corazon: "Lamont, come to the table. Your soup will get cold."

Lamont: "Sure, mom. I just wanted to look outside on this beautiful day."

Nothing happened. Whew. My hypothesis was correct. So long as he wears the ring, sunlight does not harm this vampire. Weird, but wonderful! Lamont sits beside me, squeezes my hand, and grins.

Lamont: "Hey, Basha, care to share a milkshake. It is a liquid. I hope that my tummy can take it. But if not..."

Basha: "No problem. You are right. Best to be cautious."

He happily discovers he can hold down some of the milkshake. To be safe, for once, he only consumes a quarter of it. Mrs. Corazon and I split the rest. We are both antsy to get to sleep and dream. But we engage in idle chatter, and when we get back to the room, Mrs. Corazon takes out a deck of playing cards from her purse. She says that she plays Solitaire with them to pass the time. We agree to play some rounds of three-handed rummy to occupy time while waiting for my mom to come and pick me up now that she was told I am up and about and could be discharged.

*

Mom shows up, and I give Lamont a quick kiss on the cheek and get hugged by Mrs. Corazon. Mom barrages me with whispered questions as we leave the hospital; she is anxious to learn what happened to us back at the gate site. I give her a bit of an explanation. I want to leave out Tezcatlipoca, but as I explain the spell that we cast to open the Gate of Dreams, she pulls more and more of the facts out of me. Truth be told, I want to tell her; I need someone to understand what is happening to us, and so the truth is told. She goes from shock to anger, back to shock, and finally to reluctant acceptance. What is done is done, and nothing can be done to undo this mess we made. She is not happy with all that I tell her but grateful that we are as alright as can be expected given these extraordinary circumstances.

When we finally get home, she goes back to the store and lets me go to my room. My first order of business is that I need to find somewhere to put this dirt and the precious magick stone! I see a plastic file box that I was keeping some papers in. I will just have to buy another one for the papers later. I again place the obsidian stone within that enchanted soil from the Gate site. Damn, stuff is hard to get out of the bottom of the backpack! I think I got it all, but what a mess it made!

Looking at this...dirt, it just seems so ordinary. It does not feel anything special. It is just this brownish-gray stuff. And yet, Tezcatlipoca made such a big deal of it. There must be more to it. Well, maybe it will make sense later on. Right now, I am excited to try out my Dream magick powers again. I strip off my clothes, wearing only my birthday suit and the obsidian and silver ring.

Here goes something…I focus on flaming on, and wow! To my amazement, I become like a fire elemental and float up a few inches off the wooden floors of my room. I can do this in the Waking World!!! I wonder if I will ever get used to this? I hope not! I carefully extinguish the flames and fall back down to the floor. Next on my agenda, I need to do a Lamont and go off in search of some books on vampires. It is just like being in Dreamland. I can conjure up my Dream suit in any manner I so desire. What shall I wear?

I focus on what I wish to wear, and viola! All of the conjured outer garments cover my bare skin. This is so cool! I have a functioning Dream suit in the Waking World! I feel so giddy as I grab my now empty backpack, my iconic black leather double-breasted motorcycle jacket, and go downstairs to get on my bike and go off in search of a good bookstore. I head over to the bookstore on Irving and begin to peruse the shelves searching for my research material. I find *Interview with the Vampire* by Anne Rice. Then keep on hunting. Once I am confident that I have depleted this store of books on vampires, I then search for another bookstore to see what I can find. It is getting late when I gather them all up, a good selection of novels and even an encyclopedia on vampires and vampire lore.

When I leave the store, I see the sun is about to end its day. As I ride back home, I feel the sun begin its blood-red dying as it sinks below the horizon. Something is going on. My finger that has the ring is starting to tingle; then, my whole body is soon tingling. What the? I pull in behind the store as the sun dies entirely beneath the horizon for another life and death cycle. For a moment, I feel the cool air and how nice it feels against my skin, and I notice the feel of the leather on my bottom and my—Holy Crow! My Dream suit…is fading. Hell! This cannot be happening! I focus, and it dimly reappears.

How can this be? I quickly, in a panic, look all around the alley to make sure no one sees me like this. Thank the Goddess; I am all alone. I muster up every ounce of self-control and focus on maintaining my control over myself. In a panic of embarrassment, I hastily get the bike inside the store and do my best to quickly run upstairs before mom finds me back here like this. It keeps on fading in and out…almost leaving me completely exposed. Bloody Hell! Focus!

I run to my room and shut the door, and I feel my heart pounding as I lean against the door and try to get my brain to work. I am now completely naked, and I cannot get it to reappear. What is going on here? "Think, Basha.

There has to be an explanation. Dreaming magick worked in the Waking World till it did not. How? Why? It stopped with the setting of the sun! Why? It is all happening in the exact opposite way of vampire lore. Vampires wake up into their power with the coming of the night! Why did my Dream magick vanish with the dawning of the night? Is it gone for good? Hmm…the rest of the obsidian stone has been in the soil from the Gate site all day...I wonder if that makes any difference? One way to test this is to pull out the box with the Gate site Soil. I do so and hold the obsidian stone in my nervous hand. Okay, Basha, think clearly now. I try to make some fire appear while holding the stone. Hey! It works!

I keep my hand on fire, releasing the stone and letting it fall onto a pillow. I don't want it to break. The flames go out as soon as I do this. What is going on here? The stone maintained its connection to Dreamland and thus to Dream magick power. What does that mean, think! Well, it has been in the soil all day long. Ahh! My ring that has been on my finger lost its power with the setting sun! But the rest of the stone nestled in the soil maintained that connection. So, it has kept its charge even with the passage of time as marked by the sun. What to do with this bit of insight?

Ahhh…I pick up the obsidian and hold it in both hands. I focus and try to conjure my desires. I feel the fire and the heat as I forge something new. I open my hands up, and there are two new obsidian rings. I put the stone back beneath the soil and then slip off my silver ring and bury it in the soil. Then I put on one of my new rings.

Okay, here goes…I burst into flames! It works! These new rings have the charge from the obsidian that has been in contact with the Gate Site. Therefore, the rings have a charging cycle. They have to be in the soil when the sun is up or down. The silver ring was out of the ground during the day and thus lost its powers with the setting of the sun. The new ring was made from the stone that had spent the whole day in the soil, and now it still has its charge. Presumably, it will maintain that charge till the rising of the sun when it needs to return to the soil. Lamont and I need to switch between the two rings to keep using Dream magick here in the Waking World.

Now I need to turn these new rings into replicas of the first pair that I made. I go to my jewelry box and find some hoop earrings, one a set of gold and the other a set of silver. I hold the new pure obsidian rings and the gold and silver hoop earrings in my two hands. I imagine the gold and the silver wrapping around the obsidian, and with that thought, I concentrate and complete the forging of these new sets of rings.

Okay, now I need to make Lamont a box of soil to keep his rings in and get him this new one.

I find a small plastic container for Lamont and fill it with some of the dirt from the Gate Site. I need to eat dinner. All this magick has me starving! I conjure up some clothes and go to the kitchen with *The Interview with a Vampire.* I make a hasty meal and devour the food and the book like it was an overdue homework assignment.

Whoa. This is hot stuff. It gives a girl something to think about, and I seriously feel like Mae West drifting again[13]. Vampires need to feed, and they are consumed and driven by their hunger. According to Rice, they can become monsters if they do not control themselves. Lamont needs to stay in control. I need to ensure he often feeds so he will not lose his humanity with his blood lust. But, there is this very erotic component to all this bloodsucking. I realize how bad this all is, but that Mae West part of myself wants to test this out with Lamont tonight at Zuki's when I fall asleep. I have a lot to tell him! But, wait, I really need to get him his ring and the box with the soil. I think visiting hours have not ended yet, so I better get a move on. I conjure up my red cowboy boots, red jeans, and a golden turtleneck sweater, then stuff his box into my purse, grab my black leather motorcycle jacket and gallop down the stairs to my cycle.

*

When I bound into his room, I can see how excited he is to see me by that happy, silly grin on his face.

Lamont: "Basha! I didn't expect you back tonight!"

Basha: "Well, I have something important to tell you," and I do as I hand him the plastic box with his new ring nestled in the Gate site soil. I explain carefully everything I figured out, but not without going through a jillion questions as he constantly bombarded me and interrupted my telling him what I found out.

When I am finally done, I slip the new obsidian and gold ring on his finger, put the one he was wearing inside the soil, shut the box, and hand it to him.

Lamont: "Ha ha ha! You really mean that you were out in public all naked?"

Basha: "If you say another word Lamont, I'll deck you! Besides, I was not naked in public, just when I got to my room and the sun was completely set. Now, I came here out of concern for your safety—not to be laughed at!"

Lamont: "Okay. Okay. But, come on…it is kind of funny."

---

13 *"I used to be Snow White, but I drifted."*, Life magazine, April 18, 1969, Interview with Mae West, Source: https://en.wikiquote.org/wiki/Mae_West

Basha: "Errr…yes…in an embarrassing and almost humiliating way! Never say another word about this! Or I swear…"

Lamont: "My lips are sealed. I promise!!! So, I see why we need to switch out the rings with the sun's rising and setting. I have a question, will these rings work for anyone?"

Basha: "Good question, Lamont. Hmmm…Let us think this through. They work for us because…"

"Well, I'm now a vampire…"

"Yes, but I am not."

"We both have been in Dreamland?"

"Hmmm...I think more than that. The rings need the soil to work…"

"Therefore, it is the place that is the connection."

"Not merely the place but the when. We were involved in a spell at that place to open the Gate of Dreams. That is the key."

"That makes sense. This means that I, you, and Peter are the only ones with this connection to that place and that event. The rings would only work for us alone?"

"That is my hypothesis."

"But this means that someone else could have had Dreaming magick abilities in the Waking World."

"Who?"

"Tezcatlipoca? That must have been Her plan all along. She would have gone through the gate and had Dream Magick powers here in the Waking World."

"Right."

"If someone had done a similar spell, they could be here from Dreamland and have this ability as well."

"True. But doing that spell requires a huge amount of magick. Look at all that Tezcat had to do to almost pull that off."

"True. Hopefully, no one has ever done this."

"Hopefully.":

"On that note, it is getting late; I got to go. See you in your dreams."

*

I appear first at Zuki's; she asks me to make us tea. I relax and clear my head as I prepare and drink the tea in silence. She laps up her tea in her saucer, and I sip slowly. Then, as she sits on my lap and grooms herself so daintily, I regale her with all that has happened to us since we last meet at the battle of the gate site. Finally, Lamont puts in his appearance. I assume it is harder for him to drift off to sleep in the hospital without seeming too suspicious. Zuki offers to give us some privacy, we thank her, and then, once she bounds off, we embrace and kiss.

I untangle myself from Lamont's clutches.

Lamont: "Basha! You can't imagine what it feels like. I have such an incredible need, Basha. It's frightening. I need to eat, but I can't just drink juice. That didn't really help. I need something more. If I don't eat something soon, I feel I could die. What am I going to do?"

I take a deep breath and try to calm myself as I take in what Lilith called Lamont, undead, like the Rice and Stoker books. He needs something. Oh, Goddess, I know what he needs. I then offer Lamont my wrist.

Basha: "Go ahead, Lamont. Bite me. Let us see if blood really will feed that hunger in you." I try my best to hold my arm steady. I bite my lip and pretend it will only be like he is giving me a hickey.

He hesitantly takes my arm and brings it to his lips. A strange and slightly horrific look comes over his face as his skin takes on that unnatural whiteness. His eyes widen and turn icy blue, and his skin coloring takes on this incredible lighter shade of pale as his lips pull back, and his two front canine teeth begin to elongate to frighteningly sharp points. Then he lunges at my wrist.

Oh, Goddess! What have I done! There is a sharp burning pain as he pierces my flesh. Damn, it hurts! A thin river of crimson trickles down my arm as Lamont sucks on my wrist. My blood gushes around his mouth as he struggles to drink it down. Frantically he tries to swallow my blood and thus force life back into him. All goes red hot, and I am gone. Help meeeeeee...

I am lost in a world of overwhelming emotions, pain, and something deeply primal. My body shudders with waves of erotic pleasure. Time fades as I am lost in the sensations. I feel myself being drawn into Lamont…joining with him in all these erotic emotions and feelings. I am getting more and more aroused. I feel weak…and I am getting fainter…hard to focus…then a voice of my conscience rings in my ears. That urgent voice rises in me and cries out in fear and guilt.

Basha: "Stop!" I hear myself say. "Lamont, stop…you can kill me…" The pleasure is immense, and I can barely continue to stand up. This has to stop…it has got to stop! I burst into flames to try and get myself away from him. "Stop!" I cry out hoarsely. I struggle to stand up and keep from fainting.

For a time, we are locked in fiery pain and passion. Finally, the pain of his burning flesh causes him to release me. I fall and look up at him; both of us are still possessed by our desires.

Everything goes black.

*

Lamont: "Basha, what happened to you? You were unconscious. You wouldn't wake up. I thought I killed you...but you had a pulse. I kept trying to wake you. I was so afraid..." I hear Lamont weakly say. "I'm...so...sorry...I couldn't help myself. I..."

Basha: "It is okay, Lamont. It is okay. I am exhausted. What happened?"

Lamont: "You were out for a long time. I don't know how long. You're okay now?"

Basha: "Yes, I just feel drained. However, Rice was right."

Lamont: "Huh."

Basha: "Lamont, that was hot but easily could become way too good. We promised your mom to be good."

"What? I'm sorry...I didn't mean to..."

"Rice, the author of a book on vampires, was very right. That—what we just did— is dangerous, very hot, and very addictive. I want to do that again. Sometime later. But, we have got to be careful." I get up and take him in my arms. "And for me, that was so good. You are definitely my favorite vampire."

"You realize what I did? I drank your blood, and I enjoyed doing it! I am a bloody damn vampire!" Lamont physically slumps down and steps away from me. *"I'm really a God damned vampire!"* Tears begin to pour down his face.

I rush over to him and hold him as he cries. "It is okay, Lamont. Breathe. Do not panic. You are still you. Even Rice said that there is such a thing as *good* vampires, vampires with a conscience. If ever there was going to be one in real life, it would be you."

Lamont: "You're sure? Please tell me it will all be okay. I won't turn into some kind of monster."

Basha: "I am sure. Oh...I am very, very weak. Hmm, I just had a thought."

"What? Is there something wrong with you?" Lamont asks, all in a panic.

"I am okay. Hey, Lamont, did your burn from the ring ever heal?"

He looks at his hand under the gold and obsidian ring, and it is perfectly smooth.

"It healed when I drank from you. It never healed until then. It was so cool watching it heal! It seems that the burns from silver only heal by taking in blood."

"I just was thinking. You just sucked my blood in Dreamland. What did that do to me in the Waking World? Also, do you feel…satisfied? Is the hunger gone?"

Lamont: "Yes, it is."

Basha: "So, being a vampire in Dreamland probably takes in whatever life force you need to sustain yourself. The question is, what does it do to me in the waking world? Be right back."

*

I wake up in my bed and look at my wrist and the bedding. Bloody Hell! Clearly visible on my wrist are his vicious bite marks with dried blood. And my sheets are marred with large crimson stains from where my arm lay. Dear Goddess! I will need to see if I can get the bloodstains out. I might be able to clean the sheets, but the mattress might be stained permanently. Life with Lamont just got very messy. Hell! I'm going to need to hide these marks. I hope they heal quickly. I close my eyes and refocus.

*

I reappear in Dreamland. "Okay, here you drank my blood which contained my life force. Lamont, my body, shows your bite marks and dried blood on me and my sheets in the Waking World. It was your first feeding, and it was messing and unskilled. So, whether you feed here or there, you bite into my Waking World body and leave signs of that mess behind. That will make things difficult, and we will have to do something to conceal that. Ahh…the excited high is fading...and now I…"

*

I find myself in Lamont's arms. I feel weak and tired and like I just woke up.

Basha: "What happened?"

Lamont: "You fainted. Again. You were out for about an hour. I was in a panic. Are you okay? You're not going to turn into a monster like me?"

"Still feel woozy, but better now. Lamont, when you are feeding, it drained me. I am also famished; giving you sustenance means I require sustenance afterward."

"Bloody Hell."

"I did recover. I still feel woozy, but I should be fine after more rest. It would be best if you learned to get my blood in a more controlled and less messy manner. I will need to wear long sleeves or a scarf to hide those bite marks. Where is Miss Manners'[14] guide to vampires when you need it? But we did find out that you cannot avoid the blood-drinking by feeding in Dreamland. Either in the Waking World or here, blood is needed to sustain your life. Though you may be able to consume any liquid, it may not yield much in the way of sustenance. I believe you will be stuck on a permanent liquid diet. Milkshakes may be as solid a portion of food as you can handle. Do you understand?"

Lamont: Yeah," saying with deep guilt. "But how did this happen?"

Basha: "Hmmm...I have a hypothesis. To understand what happened to you, we must consider the differences between normal dreaming, lucid dreaming, and entering into Dreamland."

"Well, to begin with, our mind-body unity can be mapped out as having three layers. A Consciousness, unconsciousness, and a sub-conscious."

"Correct. Our subconscious is connected directly to our body and our life force."

Lamont: "When we normally dream, our consciousness goes to sleep and enters our unconsciousness. When we lucid dream, our consciousness wakes up while in our unconsciousness."

Basha: "I agree. When we enter Dreamland, it is when our awake consciousness finds the doorway to that realm in our unconscious mind and then goes through it. In doing so, we are still connected to our subconsciousness and our body. When we enter Dreamland, our unconscious creates a *tzaleem*, like a vessel that holds our life essence, consciousness, and unconsciousness. Tzaleem literally means in Hebrew shadow; that is the Hebrew word the Rabbis used to refer to our astral body, which we know as our Dream body.

When we leave Dreamland, our consciousness goes to sleep, and our unconscious, which is our tzaleem, dissolves when we return to our body in the Waking World. Now I think that what you did at the Gate site was to take your conscious and unconscious that was encased in your tzaleem and travel through to the Waking World. Meanwhile, Tezcat had taken his consciousness with his unconscious and awoke in your body."

Lamont: "Which meant that my Waking body that was still connected to my tzaleem sensed that somehow?"

Basha: "Yes! This was something no one had ever done before. Your subconscious and life force were being pulled to join with your conscious and unconscious mind housed in your tzaleem. It did so. However, that caused

[14] Miss Manners is the pen name for Judith Martin (nee Perlman) an American columnist, author, and etiquette authority. The Miss Manners advice column began in 1978.

your body to no longer have a life force, and it began to die. This dying body repelled Tezcat's conscious mind. He had to return through the Gate or simply wake up, wherever his physical body was. Otherwise, he would dissipate and cease to be."

"That was how I killed myself and defeated Tezcat simultaneously."

"He called it foolish and a sacrifice. That eventually impressed him, and he decided to help you. That help, with the aid of Queen Lilith, used my life force to kick-start your body into creating its own life force and a new subconscious. However, that process had to turn you from dying to the undead."

"That makes sense to me. I have to consume blood, which is how to carry the life force into me. Now, what about me feeding on you? Will that turn you into…a vampire?"

"I do not think so. It took a great deal of magick from Tezcat and the Queen of the Night Lilith to change you. I would think it would take a lot more than just feeding on me to turn me."

"You will try and find this out for certain?"

"Yes. I promise."

Lamont: "Now, this whole dying and coming back as a vampire is annoying- no more Italian food! No popcorn! My life sucks!" He jokes to cover his fears, tries to say that last bit with a straight face, and fails.

We both start laughing hysterically in relief.

Lamont: "We do have one crisis," he says this with a bit of hysteria in his voice. He is clearly still in a panic but trying to humor himself out of it.

Basha: "What is that?"

"I think I need a new set of Dream clothes."

"Ha! You are joking. Tell me you are joking."

"Actually, no. I think my whole Batman outfit doesn't feel right anymore."

"Why not. He is a BAT guy, and vampires are bat-like?"

"I'm just not feeling it. I think I need to go for more like my namesake, Lamont Cranston.

"You want to be the character's alter ego? The Shadow?"

"Yes. Cranston was one of the identities of the Shadow in the books. On the radio program, he was the only other identity."

"So make yourself a new outfit."

"I can't. I can't make new stuff up. When I made your clothes, I had to see and touch the real thing or a picture of what I wanted to create those things. So, I need to find pictures or something in the Waking World that I can copy."

"Okay, tomorrow we will go shopping for your new outfit."

"You are kind of goofy; you do realize that?"

"Yup. Whew. I feel fine again. Fit as a fiddle. Now, here is something we can try at home. Wake up and try to change into something. Like alter your appearance or become an animal. Then report back on what happened. I will do the same. I have a hypothesis I want to be tested."

"Okay. See you shortly."

*

I awaken again in my bedroom. I get out of bed wearing a white cotton tank top and panties. Okay. What should I try? How about shapeshifting? That sounds like an adventure. Hmmm. Tezcat kept calling me a little eagle. Why not become a California golden eagle?

I glow, and then a weird feeling overtakes me. When it stops, I look at myself, and I have done it! I am this big raptor with dark brown and gold plumage on my feathered form. I stretch out my wings, and oh wow, they are about five or six feet long! On the floor, I spot my top and panties. So, that is what Lamont was wondering. My body can act like a Dream body, but I cannot seem to change other objects here in the Waking World.

I look down at my left claw and spot the silver and obsidian ring. That remained with me, which makes some sense. It is what enables me to use this body as a Dream body. I reimagine myself as my usual self and see that I am naked. Which is probably what Lamont was thinking would happen. Of course. This is so fantastic! Our Dream powers enable us to change ourselves, but we cannot make something new out of nothing. If I can become an eagle, I can fly like an eagle in the Waking World! Oh, great Goddess. I rush to my window and open it up wide.

I turn back into the golden eagle. It feels so strange and so...real. If I want to use my Dream body's ability in this Waking World to change, I will have to start off naked and just Dream of myself covered by clothing. Which has never been a problem in Dreamland, so I guess it will not be one here. I am always naked underneath my clothes in the Waking World, so it is visually still the same to someone looking at me, whether they are Dream clothes or Waking World clothes. However, I need to keep my eyes focused on the time. I cannot let myself be caught with the sun's changing and find myself powerless and end up naked!

As for now, this is so bloody amazing. I hop over to the window ledge and get my body through the opening. Then I spread my wings, and I take flight! I soar and dive through the sky above. I take to the night, and I fly! I *can* fly! Doing this in Dreamland is commonplace, but it is all so extraordinary and incredible here in the Waking World.

After a few minutes, I head back to my house, get myself into my window, and become my naked human form. I get back into bed and dream myself back to Dreamland.

*

Lamont was impatiently waiting for me at Zuki's, and I report back to him. Yes, I can change shape. Yes, when I do it, all Waking World clothes fall off. The ring stays on my left claw.

Lamont: "I've never done this before. I always had problems changing my Dream bodysuit and my Dream body. But now maybe I can."

Basha: "Try it, Lamont. Try imagining yourself as a bird."

Lamont closes his eyes and then glows all blue, and in a cloud of smoke, he starts to take on a new form. He does it. He is a raven. I change into a California Golden Eagle, and we take flight. We soar and dive in the Dreamland sky. Lamont and I sing out our birdcalls. We call out with primal joy, filling the night air with our songs of play and hunt—as we fly!

Thursday, September 4, 1980

SAN FRANCISCO

BASHA

Eventually, we both feel that the sun is nearing its time of awakening. We can see the waning crescent of the moon in the sky. Here in Dreamland, the rising and setting sun is not significant. But we both feel that we need to wake up. The power of Dreaming will soon wane and then end. We need to get home now before we lose our chance. We go our separate ways and return to our homes in the Waking World just in time as the Dream Magick fades.

*

I wake up back in bed. It is not yet morning which is when I can get to Lamont. I am naked, sweaty, ecstatic, and worn out—time enough to drift off to sleep happily.

*

It is dark. Yet I know where I am. I am there. I am back atop Strawberry Hill in Golden Gate Park, where it all happened. The gate site. I am alone. I feel scared. Why? Something is not correct. Something is wrong. I know it.

LAMONT

Where am I? I smell dampness, earthiness, and decay. I can't stop shivering. My teeth are chattering. I try to open my eyes to see, but it is all pitch black. I can't tell if my eyes are open or not. I try to get up but feel all confined. Then I feel this odd burning sensation like sitting on a stovetop, and someone just turned on the burners. I cry out for help.

BASHA

Then I hear something. Or should I say-- someone. A muffled cry in the night. Where is it coming from? I...know that sound, that voice...Oh, dear Goddess! Lamont!

LAMONT

The heat is getting more intense...it is going from discomfort to pain. I keep calling out, but no one answers. Can anyone hear me? I reach out, and when I touch the walls of my chamber, they are red hot. I try to move and realize that I'm in a small container. It and I smell awful. Putrid and the smell of something being cooked.

The pain is becoming intense, and I can't seem to maneuver in this tight space to prevent me from touching the heated surfaces. I begin to panic. I frantically feel around as best I can in this confined space; all the while, everything that I touch and touches me is burning hot. Oh, God...no! I realize I'm trapped in a rectangular-shaped box. Then panic wells up as I realize what this all means. I'm in a coffin. I'm buried in my own coffin! I'm also being burned as if I am being burned alive. I start to scream even louder.

BASHA

The sound of Lamont screaming is coming from right below me. Under the very ground I am standing on. I frantically dig into the moist earth.

"Lamont! I am coming to get you! Hold on!"

Frantically I dig and dig and dig. The smell of moist soil is thick. Finally, I come to something solid. Big and solid. Oh, Goddess! It is a coffin! Lamont is in this coffin; I just know it!

LAMONT

I keep crying out in pain, panic, and hysteria. I have to get out of here! Despite the intense heat radiating from all the walls, I push and pound to no avail. I can't get out...I can only continue to be burned, and I scream and scream and scream...

BASHA

I pound on the coffin and try to break into it. My hands hurt and bleed, but I manage to rip it open. The smell is horrible!

I see Lamont, his face full of terror. I rip more of the lid apart to get him out. As I do, I see him begin to decay right before my eyes. The smell is overwhelming as his body putrefies, and then...oh Goddess...as I reach out to him…he is just a skeleton. My hands touch bare bones, and then they turn to dust. "NOOOOOO!!!!"

LAMONT

I wake up. It was only a dream. The scent of panic and fear is carried on my sweat. My body is damp as I shake in bed. Oh dear God, help me. I was so afraid. It was horrible. I was sure I was in that coffin. It felt so real. It was only a dream. It was only a dream. As I curl up in a ball, I keep saying that, still shaking. Eventually...I feel myself finally drifting back to sleep.

BASHA

I can feel my scream echoing in the night, yet no sound comes out of my mouth. I shudder, and my heart races, but I realize I am awake in my bed. It was horrible. All my fears flood through my body and mind. But I know that Lamont is not dead. He is alive. Well…sort of. He is undead. He is a vampire, and I agreed to help make him into a vampire. Oh, Goddess, forgive me. Oh, Lamont, forgive me. Tears run down my cheeks. I cannot tell Lamont about this. He has enough to deal with. It was only a bad dream, a nightmare. It's over now. I cry myself back to sleep...

*

THE NIGHT (AND BASHA)

Night: I coalesce into a huge dark bat and take flight.

Basha: (The vampire creature has arisen again! That creature of darkness is a thing of the night.)

Hunger is all I know. Ravenous for revenge. To feed on injustice, I seek my prey in the darkness.

I feed on cruelty.

I feed on fear.

I know what evil dwells in their hearts.

I will Drink deep of those who thought they could prey on others. They will learn as their last lesson in Dreamland that their time here has come to an end.

On and on, I hunt and feed.

I am this giant bat seeking out my prey. I drink from my victims till the glimmering light of dawn compels me to dissolve back into dark dreams as I dissipate in the morning light.

BASHA

I tried to control it, to lessen the savagery when it feeds on those people. But I can barely blunt its desires. I am so exhausted by the effort of trying to have an effect on this creature.

LAMONT

I wake up feeling full and disoriented. Something is wrong…what happened last night? I can't remember. I dreamed, but I can't remember my dreams. How is this possible? A feeling of dread creeps over me. Nightmarish images flitter in the corners of my mind that I cannot grasp and then dissolve into mist. Why?

BASHA

I wake up in the morning, see the bloodstains again, and shudder. I am sickened by feeling what that vampire did to those people. Then a powerful realization takes over in my stomach. Holy Crow, I am so weak with hunger. I try not to dwell on that creature and focus on the memories of last night when I was with Lamont. I was an eagle and him a raven. Whew, flying takes a lot out of a girl. I take off my obsidian ring and switch it out for my silver one.

I conjure a red silk kimono-like robe with a fully charged ring, tie it around my body, and head to the kitchen to rustle up breakfast. I get out mushrooms and eggs. I start sautéing the mushrooms in pinot griot wine and butter to make my breakfast as I gulp down very un-lady-like my coffee.

Poor Lamont, he will be starving and only fluids to drink! Oh, Goddess, I hope he has enough self-control not to go all vampire and take a bite out of one of the nurses. My mom is already dressed and making coffee.

Miriam: "You're a hungry, sleepy head this morning, daughter? How come? Have you spent too much time with Lamont in Dreamland? But, wait…what *were* you two doing there to make you so hungry?" Mom eyes me with suspicion and a bit of concern. Oh Hell! Did she spot the bite mark on my wrist? I look down and see that they are gone. I wonder how long it took for them to heal?

Basha: "Ahhhh...we were flying! All night long, I was flying like an eagle! It was incredible!"

"Flying. Ahh…to be young again," she says, giving me a motherly kiss on the cheek.

"I'm off to work."

Once she leaves, I snap my fingers and make the kimono robe disappear for wicked fun, just because I can since it's only a Dream garment. I finish eating just all naked. I realize that I can conjure anything with these rings. This is going to be fun.

After eating and quickly cleaning up, then showering, and the rest, I stand in front of a full-length mirror still unclad and look at myself while I run a brush through my long thick red tresses. I notice some unwanted hair forming on my legs and under my arms. I look at my hands, and a thought occurred to me. I ignite the palms of my hands and recall something about permanent hair removal and lasers.

A laser is just concentrated light and heat…I concentrate and intensify the fire. I can create fire, but it does not burn my skin…hmm. I run the palm against my underarm and watch in the mirror as the little bit of hair flitters away, leaving warm glowing skin. This could work.

I repeat and do the other arm. Then I decide to remove all of that unwanted hair on my body. I run my hands slowly over my skin, leaving smooth bare skin in my wake. I can feel the intensity of the process without any discomfort from the flame and heat. I notice the light strands of hair all disappearing. This beats a razor any day. No burns. Eventually, I am done. All of me is just soft, smooth, glistening olive skin without a trace of any hair anywhere except my mane of hair on my head. If it were not permanent on the first go-round, I would think it would be so with a few treatments. I admire my handiwork in the mirror. I am both vain and naughty. Okay, Basha, with that done, what does the fashionably dressed Dreamer wear this season? I giggle to myself. Why not red! I say as I snap my fingers. I conjure a pair of tight red jeans to cover my hips and legs. I can feel the tight toughness of denim on my body.

Dream magick—you got to love it. For some, it is the most remarkable and their only usage of magick in all of Dreamland.

The first Dream magick one masters is controlling one's Dream suit. It is remarkable stuff. It is the essence of Dreamland attached to your body. It takes on the feel, texture, and appearance of whatever you will it. In its pure form, it feels either oddly like you are not wearing anything at all or like a second skin of permeable super strong nylon. The Dream suit keeps out the ambient temperature and protects you from the outside environment. No feeling cold or too warm, nor any sensations of the terrain you may be waking on if you choose. It covers you from head to toe.

It can even seal you off from the pressures of the deepest waters and contain you in a safe zone of breathable oxygen—if you know how to truly tap into your power. It takes skill and effort to make it feel to you and to someone else who touches it, like some material of your choosing, such as silk, denim or leather, or even metal armor plating. Wearing this Dream suit will enable me to ignite into flames via Dream magick at a moment's notice.

I reach down for my cinnamon oil; I apply a dab to my wrists, behind my ears, and then between the valley of my breasts. I notice my polished red nails. Hmm…I am due soon for a manicure, and a glance at my toes confirms it. And a pedicure as well. I am overdue. The Dreamland superhero gig gets in the way of the important stuff that needs maintaining.

Oh well, such is my lot. Next, add a cream-colored long sleeve cotton blouse with the top buttons undone. I snap my fingers, and they all appear. Oops…I forgot a bra. One of those push-up bras that Lamont is so fascinated with. I snap my fingers again to bring them into existence. Now, that feels interesting. Noticing how my breasts now feel after having a bra form around them for them to rest in. Hmmm…Oh yes, Lamont's sun and moon earrings! I then apply scarlet red lipstick and gloss. Then my red high-heeled cowgirl boots.

I snap my fingers, and there is the icing on the cake as my red leather jacket appears! One last thing…just in case. With a finger snap, a wide crimson leather choker is now around my neck. Last but not least is my leather motorcycle jacket.

Okay, admit it, Basha, wearing only Dream garb here in the Waking World feels naughty! And I really like it! I stand there both feeling clothed and yet feeling naked underneath my clothes simultaneously. Yes. I am always naked under my clothes, but now being dressed like this, I feel more naked than I ever do in Dreamland. But the powers are limited to conjuring up clothing and anything else that I would wear on my body as adornments. I can also wholly morph my body into animal form. But I am guessing I still cannot make any new objects.

Hmmm…I pick up a used pencil and try to restore it to its original length and form before I had used it up. Focus. Concentrate. Oh, I begin to feel a pain in my head. Nope. Nothing happens. I cannot alter other objects. I, at least, do not have that ability. I think some other Dreamers can do something like this. As I said, there are limits. Whatever I could do in Dreamland, I can do here in the Waking World with the help of the open gate and the ring I wear. All in all, I do not think that having Dream powers in the Waking World will ever seem normal. I sure hope not.

But, I like the comforting thought that I have things to do, everyday things, and obligations. I guess that is why rabbis mystically inclined were told to wait till they were mature married men before doing and studying. That way, they would have ordinary obligations and connections to keep them grounded. I need the ordinary stuff to escape Dreamland's worries and pressures.

I bound down the stairs, take my bike out of its place in the back of the store, and am off to Ambrose Bierce High school with a roar. I need to get the word out to everyone who knows Lamont that he is okay. When I arrive at school, everyone is looking at me strangely. Why? For a moment, I panic at the thought that the Dream garb did not work, and I appear naked to everyone. But that is not it. They are not giving me that sort of look.

Ahhh! I am not in black. I am not mourning! They do not know that Lamont is alive and well. Lana, who graduated like me last year, must have contacted some friends at the school and told them about Lamont. I have to quickly end this. Whom do I tell? Of course, I head to the library and ask for the head librarian. She immediately knows who I am and starts offering condolences. I interrupt and explain that he is okay.

Basha: "The reports of his demise have been greatly exaggerated. He came out of it just yesterday and should be back in classes tomorrow." I explain with complete honesty that the doctors do not know what happened to him. "But they admit he is okay now. They are keeping him for one more day for observation." As I leave them, I realize that they know me as 'the one who is Lamont's girlfriend'. Kind of odd to be known because of my relations with someone else. I was just this rumored-to-exist person.

I wander by Lamont's locker and see a large pile of pennies. It takes me a minute to figure out why. 'A penny for your thought.' There are all sorts of Post-Its and notes put on his locker from people I do not recognize. Obviously, Lamont made an impact on people. Of course, he did. He was, is, so generous with his time. He probably always is helping people out with assignments and just being kind. He is a *mensch*. I wonder if he even knows how much he touched people's lives. It will be a pleasant surprise when he sees all this tomorrow. After getting his assignments and books, I realize I need to take off and head over to SF State to get to my classes. I missed the first day, so I need to catch up.

*

Wow. I forgot how much fun and intense it is to begin a new semester. This is going to be great. Lots of work, but great. I will need to burn the midnight oil to keep up with my studies. But hey, that is fine with me. I would much rather focus on schoolwork! Right now, school is just what the doctor ordered. Thinking of homework and doing it is my fantasy and a pleasant escape, whereas Dreamland is just way too horribly real with all that guilt hanging over me. And speaking of the burdens of Dreamland, I get home and call up Lana to check in with her.

Lana: "Basha! I got calls from some of my friends at school saying that Lamont is okay. Is that true?"

Basha: "Yes. It is."

"That is fantastic! How?"

"It essentially came down to divine intervention and magick. Crazy story. I have a question: Jon's clothes that he wore when he went through the gate, did they vanish at any time?"

"Yes. We were lucky that he wasn't wearing them at the time. They disappeared about a day after he got back. Is that significant?"

"Kind of."

"Is Lamont in the hospital? Will he be getting out soon?"

"Yes, currently in SF General. He should be able to leave the hospital today. We want to stop by and talk to you tonight. Would that be possible?"

"Sure. I'll give you our address just tell us when. That is so great about Lamont. Thank God!"

After exchanging the information and a few more pleasantries, "Okay, I got to run. We will talk later, right?"

"Right. Bye."

I get on my bike and ride over to San Francisco General, where Lamont is, and I discover that I was right and he can leave today. I get to his room, and his mom is chatting away with him.

Lamont: "Hey, Basha!" Lamont calls out as I just barely come to the door. He can sense my presence, and I can sense him before we even see each other.

Basha: "Hey, Lamont! You are dressed in street clothes. Does this mean what I think it does?" I keep a sense of decorum and do not run into his arms. But face it, Basha. You want to. I also spot the leather jacket I gave him last year. His parents must have brought it over, knowing he would need a coat now that he is going home.

Lamont: "Yup! They did a huge battery of tests and took blood like *they* were vampires! I kept on coming back mostly normal. Low blood pressure, a bit lower body temperature, but nothing that set off any alarm bells. They see I can walk around and stuff. So, they reluctantly give me a clean bill of health. We can stop focusing on me and start focusing on others, like Peter, for instance," he points to him, looking like he is just in a deep sleep. "They don't know what to make of him."

Basha: "Correct. Mrs. Corazon, would it be okay to take Lamont home on my motorcycle? I promise to be careful."

Helen Corazon: "Yes, Basha, you can. I know my son is safe with you. You have more than proven that."

Lamont: "Great! So, we'll see you at the house. Dad should be here shortly to get you, right?"

Helen Corazon: "Yes, shortly. I will be okay. Do you want to stay for dinner, Basha, if that is okay with your mother?"

Basha: "Thank you. That would be nice. My mom works at the store, so we do not often eat together. What time do you want us to show up for dinner?"

Mrs. Corazon tells us the time as Lamont picks up his coat, and we take our leave and walk off holding hands. Once we are down the hall, Lamont directs us to go into the stairwell. Once the doors to the stairs shut, we embrace.

Lamont: "Ohhh…I love your cinnamon scent..."

Then he kisses me. With the rush of relief of all our worries seeming now past us, it all feeds our passion. Eventually, we stop kissing, but we are still wrapped in each other's arms.

Basha: "Hey, Lamont. How are you holding up?"

Lamont: "Ahh, actually, I'm ravenous. I had to fake eating and hide that I couldn't eat solid food. Then I flushed all the food down the toilet so no one saw that I couldn't eat it. It was tricky, but I found out I have a new skill. Just like the Shadow on the radio, I have the ability to cloud people's minds. Which seems to be a vampire ability. I can impose my will onto someone else – sort of like hypnotizing them into seeing or doing something, like a stage hypnotist who gets someone to strut around and cluck like a chicken. I didn't like it, but I used it to make my mom think I was eating when I really wasn't. I had to do that. It is so wrong. I violated my mom and the nurse. But they would go bonkers with fear and lock me up if they found out I was this Vampire-thing. I had to do it." Lamont says, on the verge of hysterics.

Basha: "It is okay, Lamont. You were right. You had to do it. You had no choice. You must keep this all a secret from everyone."

Lamont: "I also used it to find out what is wrong with Peter. He has swollen lymph glands, some odd purplish sores on his body, and night sweats. They are not sure what that all means. Since they can't talk to him. They are monitoring him. The doctors do not think it is related to the coma thing. They think it is related to some older untreated illness."

Basha: "They are doing everything they can for him, yes?"

Lamont: "Yes. But nothing seems to be working. It's terrible. As for me, I'm going crazy with hunger. I need to feed. I almost can't think straight. All I can think about is feeding on you. I need to do that. I need to feed. I'm a growing vampire boy. Please, Basha. I need this." Lamont says, feeling very embarrassed and guilty.

Basha: "Yeah. Well, we are going to have to figure this thing out. You need to feed now?" My heart starts to pound.

Lamont: "Ahh…yes. Oh God, yes!"

Basha: "Okay. I think you should go for the neck from now on. It is easier to cover up the marks. See, my latest fashion statement should work just fine." I start to take off my choker.

"No. Not here. I think there will be less of a mess if we do it in Dreamland. I'm hoping that will work."

"You need not worry, Lamont; I do not believe Dream clothes will show bloodstains."

"Oh. You've taken to wearing a Dream suit in the Waking World."

"Yes. Much more convenient. Do you still want to go to sleep here and now? Close our eyes and drift off?"

"Yes!"

"Meet at Zuki's or…"

"No. Just close your eyes. I have a weird feeling about this. "

"Okay," I close my eyes and begin to drift off…but this time, it feels a bit odder than usual...

WELL OF DREAMS

Suddenly Lamont and I are somewhere…a place of power. A temple? Whose? I do not recognize it. It feels like somewhere between ordinary dreams and Dreamland. How did we get here? Is this Lamont's doing? He said something was going to be different. Did he find this place? The air in this immense cavern feels warm and moist. I realize that this is caused by steam rising off the inky black water in this large marble-encased pool that is in the center of this chamber. Black Columns, or pillars, of polished marble, I always get the two confused, in rows and rows fading into the shadows all around us. Power and energy emanating from that well's water.

Then I am seriously distracted. I feel the pain of Lamont's teeth penetrate the skin of my neck...This time, there is no frantic savagery this time…just pain and the flowing blood...I feel him sucking and feeding on me. I am losing myself in him.

Then…Oh, Goddess! Such a powerful rush of sensations. It is all so passionate as I feel him…take me...but ohhhhh…! My body is on the verge...no, we promised...it feels so good. But...no. Have to stop him...I hear myself scream out. I burst into flames to ward him off me.

Basha: "Lamont, stop!"

SAN FRANCISCO

Basha: "Ohhhh, Lamont..." I am back in his arms, collapsed on the floor in the Hospital. I instinctively look at my clothes. No torrent of bloodstains on my Dream suit. I touch my neck and feel the unmistakable marks of his teeth there. "Oh, Goddess, I hope I didn't scream out loud." I feel all flushed. Mmmmm…" Lamont…dearest…" I reach up to kiss him softly. "I am liking this vampire thing way too much. It is all erotic. Very intense. However, we promised your mom, so we have to stop this sooner rather than later. We almost did something very bad. You do not seem as hot and bothered as I feel. Did you not react the same way?"

Lamont: "One: you were asleep, out of it again for a good while. I knew that you had a pulse. I knew it in my blood that you were alive. But you were so weak. I drained a great deal of you. You were out for about an hour. You're okay, right?"

Basha: "You avoided my question, and to answer yours, I am alright."

Lamont: "Two: no, I can't tell you if you screamed or not. But I guess not, since no one came bursting in to check up on us. Three: as for how it felt for me, it feels like a joining. All kind of mystical. Me becoming you, getting lost in the joining or communion of souls or something. It is hard to describe. Floating and blissful…"

Lamont leans in, and eventually, we stop kissing.

Basha: "Lamont, you need to pay attention."

Lamont: "To what?"

"To knowing when to stop."

"Why?"

"Because you could drain me."

"Oh. I can't tell when we've gone too far."

"Great. As usual, proper sexual conduct is all up to us girls. Cosmically typical! I am okay. I am very weak but recovering. I am hungry and drained. What you describe sounds nice. Cerebral, sweet, sunlight, and gentleness. Very Lamont. As I have been saying, for me, it is all physical and emotional union—bodily sensations. Very, very hot and erotic sensations. Oh my. I hope you like doing this. Because I sure do. But the problem is I like it way too much." I kiss him again to show him how much I do like this. "Now, I think we should get going and stop making out in the stairwell. I wonder how long the bite marks will take to heal? Anyway, shall we head over to your house now?"

When we get there, Lamont's parents are there, and dinner. Mrs. Corazon made a thick, hearty soup that is simmering and filling the kitchen with its moist, tasty fragrance.

LAMONT

When we get inside, my dad motions for me to follow him. I do, and we step down the hall and out of earshot.

Hector Corazon: "This Basha girl seems to be very taken with you. I was surprised that such an older girl would be interested in you and such a good-looking girl. But then again, you have always charmed your teachers and those librarians. So, I guess it makes sense."

I'm very embarrassed by this but manage to reply lamely in the affirmative.

Hector Corazon: "And you two seem serious about each other, is that true, son?"

Lamont: "We are, Dad."

Hector Corazon: "That's a good son. I'm hoping you will do the right thing by her."

Lamont: "Of course." That feeling is beginning to grow…like something waking up in the pit of my stomach…

Hector Corazon: "I knew my son would understand. I raised you right. So, you two probably talk about all kinds of books and such. Well, when you do, don't forget about The Good Book. I know I taught you well, and she needs to be led into the True Light. You will be doing her a good turn. She seems to dote on you, and I'm sure she'll be a good obedient wife someday."

I'm kind of stunned into silence as I try to grasp the implications of what he is saying. That sickening feeling is becoming more painful. I can't believe this.

Hector Corazon: "I know your mother will like a big church wedding. Once this Basha is shown the Light, I bet she'll learn our ways even better than you, being such a learned girl. I know that you won't disappoint us. She has a lot to learn, so you should start to teach her the Good News of our Lord soon."

I don't know what to say. I feel trapped. I can't let him do this to me. I need to tell him this is not going to happen…

Hector Corazon: "To be honest, son, I wasn't sure about you. But you seem to have charmed a good one. I can't say I understand how."

Lamont: "But…she's Jewish, Dad…"

Hector Corazon: "I know, son. But you must show her the error of her ways. Her people had a chance to embrace our Lord; you must help her and guide her."

Lamont: "I don't think so…I…" There. I did it. My stomach pain is not going to go away on its own.

LAMONT, **NIGHT** (& BASHA)

I can feel him getting upset. Who dares to do this to him?

Hector Corazon: "What? Her immortal soul is at stake. You must bring her to the light…"

Lamont: "I don't think she wants this…" I have to stop this. I need to set my dad right about this.

Hector Corazon: "They don't know what they want. Men like us must tell them what is right."

Lamont: "No." There. I've taken a stance against him.

Hector Corazon: "What did you say, son?"

Lamont: "I…said no. This is not…"

Hector Corazon: "Son, I thought meeting this Basha was a sign that you left behind your foolishness."

I see my dad's face turn into anger, a look that I know all too well.

Hector Corazon: "I don't want to make a scene…"

I must not let any harm come to him.

Lamont: "Dad, she doesn't want this and isn't interested in converting."

Hector Corazon: "Son, you need to understand. You have to be strong with girls; they appreciate that. Your mother understands this."

I must come to his rescue. This man is upsetting him, and he feels he is a threat. Something needs to be done. Something I can do.

BASHA & **THE NIGHT**

I can feel shadows cold and drenched in anger crawling down the hall. Holy Crow! No! Vampire, Listen to me! Take us both out of time! Now!

I hear and obey. It is done!

What are you doing?

I have done nothing—yet. I was about to act. This man is a threat to Lamont. I must intervene to protect him…

I see the dust motes stuck in the air as I jump out of the wooden dining room chair, knocking it over, ignite and blast down the hall to where the heart of the dark shadows lie, where Lamont and his Dad stepped away to talk. I can see the Vampire, all blazing ice blue eyes holding Lamont's father off the ground.

Basha: "Night! Do not harm him."

"Why not? Lamont feels like he is threatening him. I can feel Lamont's fear and anger. I also sense that this is not the first time this man has threatened Lamont. It must be stopped. I can and must stop it."

"No! What you say may be true, but he is Lamont's father. You must not harm him."

"He is his sire? I didn't realize that. Ahh...yes, I am searching Lamont's memories...I should have known this. What should I do, mistress of Lamont's heart?"

"You must let Lamont work this out between them."

"Lamont is so angry. Does he not need my help?

"No, this is not your place to intervene between Lamont and his father. It is his fight. He must deal with whatever this is. You must allow this and just have faith in Lamont. Do you understand?"

I understand. I will not interfere; it is not my place to get between him and his sire."

The Vampire lets go of Lamont's father and draws back into the shadowy darkness that had filled the room. The vampire's anger recedes and turns to resignation; his presence dissipates and returns to Lamont's unconscious mind. I leave them and return to pick up my chair and sit back down.

"Okay, bring us back to the normal flow of time."

LAMONT

Hector Corazon: "My son, you are being foolish. You don't understand women like I do. They need to be told what they want."

Lamont: "No, I, Dad. I don't think so. Especially not Basha."

Hector Corazon: "You have much to learn. Now, consider what I have said and don't disappoint me like you used to. I'm happy for you. Now that you heard me, I'm sure you will come around and do the right thing. It's good that we had this talk." Dad puts his arms around my shoulders. "We better get back to the women-folk now. Just know we're proud of you and don't expect you two to rush to the altar anytime soon. We figure you should wait till you at least graduate from High School and find a good job."

Bloody Hell! I can't believe this.

Hector Corazon: "We're so glad you won't be disappointing us," My dad continues. "I know you won't disappoint me. Your mother and I are so looking forward to a nice church wedding."

He didn't listen to what I said. But, this is not the time to argue with him. Not that I think that would do any good. Bloody Hell! I just return to Basha and try not to let her know how angry am I. Not now. I had hoped things would have changed. I should have known better.

BASHA

I could just barely hear their continuing whispered conversation. It feels so intense. No wonder the vampire reacted the way he did. Finally, they return to us. I wonder how it all went. Lamont looks strange when he and his father come back into the room. I wonder what it was all about. Well, Lamont will tell me when he is ready. I offer to help serve to distract me from worrying, but both Mr. and Mrs. Corazon will hear nothing of that. They insist on Lamont and me sitting while they tend to us.

I discover that Mrs. Lamont told her husband that I provided a blood transfusion for Lamont at a critical moment. She did not say to him about anything related to praying or me appearing in her dreams.

What she told him is even closer to the truth. So, she said I now have been given honored status for my contribution to Lamont's recovery.

We are all served big bowls full of this soup chocked full of good stuff. But I know Lamont cannot eat it. What is he going to do?

LAMONT

I stand up and get all shrouded in darkness. The tasty smell of boiled chicken, onions, olive oil, and laurel is a wafting scent. I look at them with icy blue eyes and use my powers. I force my will onto them as I command them.

Lamont: "Mom, Dad, you will see me eating your soup and loving it. You will not notice anything out of the ordinary. Do you understand?"

Helen and Hector Corazon: "Yes."

Lamont: "Basha, I need to hypnotize them, so they don't discover the truth. That's what I just did. I don't feel right about this, but I didn't know what else to do."

Basha: "Yes, you are right."

Lamont: "I do not have any other ideas to see that they do not have a meltdown about your condition. Normally I would agree that lying to them is not great, but the alternative, in this case, would freak them out. Your Dad would go crazy with horror and anger. I think it is for the best, Lamont. You have no choice."

I pour my bowl back into the crock-pot and just ladle out a big bowl of broth and return to my seat. Its aroma is warm, thick, and yummy. "At least the broth will be really tasty, and I can eat that."

BASHA

Then the dark Lamont disappears, he is back to normal, and we eat. The soup is excellent, quite filling, and I hope nourishing and satisfactory for Lamont in some manner. One thing is for sure, on this liquid diet, his kidneys will be working overtime and be really healthy. When we finish eating, I again ask if I could help with the dishes, and once more, my offer is politely refused.

While they are doing that, I excuse myself to go to the bathroom. I want to see if Lamont's bite marks on my neck are still there or have they have healed up. In the privacy of the bathroom, I discover that the bite marks under the choker that I had conjured up actually healed, and now my neck shows no effects where Lamont bit me.

I figure it took about an hour after I woke up to disappear. I think it takes two hours to heal from when I got bit. When I rejoin everyone, Lamont asks if we could go out for a ride and be back later. They said yes. I am obviously trusted with their son's care now.

Lamont puts on a denim vest for extra warmth under the leather bomber jacket I bought him, and then we head out the door.

Lamont: "I'd like to go to that clothing shop where you got me this leather coat. I'm looking for some new items for my new Dream suit."

Basha: "Are you saying that you still cannot conjure up a new Dream suit even with the ring?"

Lamont: "I tried, and I still can't."

Basha: "Ahh, just like me, whatever limitations on your Dream abilities in Dreamland, you have them here in the Waking World."

Lamont: "Correct. But I seem to have other abilities, as you might have noticed, like going to that place of power that I call the Well of Dreams. Anyway, I can only make something from a picture if it shows all angles of the outfit. Hence my being able to make the Batman-like suit. I've been looking at comics for years. I need to copy something in the Waking World to do something new. Which is how and why I was able to make your birthday-slash-New Year's outfit."

Basha: "Okay, I get that, but what are we looking for?"

Lamont: "I want to take on a version of the Shadow's[15] outfit."

"Well, so what does that look like?"

"Well, on the old radio programs I listen to with my parents, they never described his outfit. However, I own this hardback book, a collection of some Shadow stores from the old Shadow magazines; there were pictures and descriptions of him. According to what I read, Walter Gibson, the character's creator, described the Shadow as wearing a dark suit with a black cloak with a red lining and a black slouch hat, plus a red scarf."

"So, since you have a dark suit at home, all you need to get is the cape, the hat, and a scarf? Other than the cape, the rest should be easy."

"Hmmm...I guess. But something feels like I'm looking for something else. Not sure. Just going on instinct here. I guess I'll know it when I see it."

"Okay. Your wish is my command. Hop on the back of my trusty steed, and we will be off."

We get to the store on the Haight, park the bike on the sidewalk, and direct Lamont to where the guy's clothing is located.

"Cape, hats, and scarfs, right?"

"As I said, I'm not really sure. I just got a feeling that it will be here. Sort of like when I search for a new book. I just got that intuitive feeling that the universe will provide it if I pay attention. I'll know it when I see it."

So, I let Lamont wander through the store as I watch, content to have him back.

"Wow. This is cool!" He says, holding up a long wool charcoal coat.

He scrutinizes it as if he were a tailor going to have to replicate it, which I think is what he intends. It is a British World War II bluish-gray double-breasted coat with wide lapels and collar and four stripes on the epaulets that designate it as a captain's coat. It has two large pouch pockets on the outside and two inside pockets. The brass buttons let us place it as a Royal Air Force officer's coat.

Lamont: "It was owned by J. Harkness."

Basha: "How did you deduce that, Sherlock?"

---

[15] Walter Gibson, under the pen name of Maxwell Grant, created the character The Shadow for Street and Smith magazine publishers. The first story produced was 'The Living Shadow', published April 1, 1931. The Shadow's true identity in the Radio Program version was Lamont Cranston; while in the magazine stores starting in issue 3, 'The Shadow Laughs', October 1, 1931, The Shadow assumes the identity of Lamont Cranston since the real Cranston was traveling outside of the United States. It was only on August 1, 1937, in issue 131, 'The Shadow Unmasks', that the real identity of The Shadow was revealed to the readers as Kent Allard a World War I American aviator serving in the French Air Force.

Lamont: "By the laundry mark. How this coat made its way to San Francisco would be an interesting story."

When Lamont puts it on, I can see that he would look rather dashing in it if it ever fit properly. I recall that dream I had about seeing the old knight in his ill-fitting outfit for a fleeting moment when I first thought Lamont had died. I wonder why? Oh well. If Lamont did get this coat, it would be practical. Since it is just like an old western duster with a split back, which allowed cowboys to be covered from the weather while on a horse. That will work the same way when he rides on my motorcycle's back.

Lamont: "This feels so cool, you can pull up the collar, and it stays up on its own. Hmm…this definitely feels right. This is why I came here, to find this.

When he tries it on, it is way too big for him, and he looks like some frail old guy wearing his coat tying to look again like he did back when he was in his prime and was proudly attired in his officer's coat. Once Lamont finishes and carefully inspects every inch of it, he says he will buy it.

Basha: "But Lamont, it does not fit."

"I just think I need to have it to help me make a Dream version of it. As I think it over, I don't think I need the scarf; a red tie would do. But let's look for a hat. An old military wide-brim slouch hat."

We locate a scarlet red silk tie that he puts on. Then he finds an old Australian hat and puts it on. It does not fit off course, nor is it the color Lamont wants.

"How do I look? You have to be my mirror since I can't look at one anymore. Be honest?"

Basha: "If it all fit, you would look good. Very dapper and dashing hero-like."

Lamont: "Great. All of this will do. It is enough for me to get a fix on it. I don't need to buy all of it. Just the coat."

"Okay, Lamont. Pay for the coat, and we can leave."

He takes off his leather coat when we return to my bike.

Lamont: "I have a feeling about this, so sit back and watch the master tailor at work." He says, closing his eyes. He swings the coat and slips his arms into it, draping his form as he lifts the collar. I see that his obsidian ring begins to glow, and gray smoke engulfs him as he puts up the collar. The vest disappears, the crimson tie appears, and the coat turns black. To my complete surprise, the coat shrinks and starts to fit him. The lining turns blood red to match the tie. The black slouch hat appears on his head. His face is completely shrouded in blood red and darkness, with only his eyes glowing icy blue against his white marble skin. The RAF unbuttoned officer coat billows out behind him like a cape in a breeze. He starts to laugh softly and weirdly, deep and resonating.

Lamont: 'This is what I will wear as my incarnation of the Shadow! Since I have become a thing of darkness, I think I should call myself the Night.'

Basha: "Hey! You altered a Waking World object! How did you do that?"

"I don't know. I just assumed I just could, and I did it."

"You seemed to have acquired a new Dream magick ability. Perhaps it helps that it was just your attire, like conjuring up a Dream suit. If that is the case, did you change its physical shape, or is it an illusion that it now has that appearance?"

"That might be a difference that doesn't make a difference, as William James would say[16]."

"I am not sure of that. But it is an interesting thought. At least you might be able to change the shape of an object that you will then wear. The results are the same in this case. As for how you look, you always were a bit of Don Quixote, tilting at windmills and helping damsels in distress. So now, you are an elegant and modern version of a mysterious knight errant, very suave and sophisticated, all very mysterious and heroic." As for me, to keep things straight, I will call Lamont in his superhero persona the Knight, while the vampire, which is a shadow of his soul, I will refer to that as the Night, just to give that thing a distinctive separate name.

Lamont: 'One more trick to show off.'

Now, this is odd. Lamont's voice has suddenly gone whispery soft, yet very clear and close. He would have to be speaking directly into my ear for me to hear him with his voice that low. Yet he is standing across from me.

Lamont: "Can you tell the difference in how I sounded a moment ago and now?"

Now he is no longer whispering; it is his usual clear voice I hear.

Lamont: 'Just think the answer to the question but don't say it out loud.'

There he goes again, all soft and quiet. But wait. It is not an external voice I hear. I hear him inside my head! His voice is clear, just like my own thoughts.

Basha: "Why should I just think the answer? What are you getting at?"

Lamont: "Humor me."

---

[16] Lamont is referring to William James's concepts of pragmatism as explained in his 1907 book *Pragmatism: A New Name for Some Old Ways of Thinking*.

Hmmm, I think to myself. 'Lamont seemed to be simply whispering and then speaking louder. Or was he? That does not seem like such a big deal, so what is he getting at?' Then, Lamont answers with what I realize is his voice in my head! I hear him inside my mind just like I hear my own thoughts!

Lamont: 'I was channeling my inner vampire powers,' Lamont's voice is a soft intimate whisper in my mind. 'I felt like I could do this as a new act of Dreaming now that I have taken on the persona of the Night. I was right. I have a mix of the Shadow radio character's abilities and the vampire's abilities. I can speak telepathically with you, my Margo Lane[17]. You are hearing me in your mind, not through your ears. I can transmit my thoughts to you, and you can direct them back to me. My new self has intimately connected to and joined you, so who knows what our range is.'

Basha: 'So, turning into a vampire has given you the abilities associated with The Shadow from the radio and book forms, interesting.'

'That or just my Dream power that we can access via the rings. It might be another Jamesian pragmatic difference without a difference. Either way, I can do the vampire body change thing and turn into mists and shadows—dissolving into darkness. I should be able to be bat as well as a raven.'

Basha: "That is very cool. But can you read my mind?"

Lamont: "I don't think so. I could only hear your thoughts when you were thinking about me."

"Still both creepy but might be useful. You can make your mom and Dad do things and read people's thoughts. Can you make me do things?"

"I wouldn't do that, not to you, Basha."

"But you have powers, Lamont. You could do things to others and me. This is terrible. It is like a violation of their bodies. This is not good."

"I know. What am I to do?"

"Well, how do your comic book heroes deal with these ethical dilemmas?"

"Well, to begin with, this reminds me of what Peter Parker, aka Spiderman said. '*With great powers comes great responsibilities.*[18]'"

---

[17] Margo Lane was a friend and companion to the Shadow. Her first appearance was in 1937 in The Shadow radio drama. Her first appearance in a print story was in 'The Thunder King', in the June 15, 1941, issue # 224 of The Shadow Magazine.

[18] The phrase is attributed to Peter Parker's Uncle Ben. However, in Amazing Fantasy #15 (August 1962, written by Stan Lee). Where it first appears, it is not spoken by any character. In fact, Ben has only two lines in the entire comic. The original version of the phrase appears in a narrative caption of the comic's last panel, rather than as spoken dialogue. It reads, "...with great power there must also come -- great responsibility!"

"Exactly! You need to have a code of conduct, rules of ethics to determine how and when to use your powers."

"That's it. I just have to be careful and only use these powers to help people, not for my own needs. But, what I'm doing to my parents that's not to help them; it is clearly just to help me."

Basha: "True. But as Rabbi Hillel said, '*If you are not for yourself, who will be?*[19]' You need to care for yourself so that you can care for others. It is okay, Lamont. You need to do that to live. If you did not, they would be frightened into doing something that could get you killed. Hmm. I got it! Let me give you a simple example of some ethical guidelines. You have read Isaac Asimov's stories?"

Lamont: "Of course; what are you getting at?"

"Consider Asimov's third law of Robotics: *A robot must protect its own existence as long as such protection does not conflict with the First or Second Laws*[20]. Therefore, it is ethical for you to hypnotize your parents. You have to do that to protect your own existence."

Lamont: "Okay. I might need a tee shirt with Lee's quote on one side and Asimov's three laws on the other. Or maybe a poster and hang it on the ceiling over my bed or plaster it on my dresser mirror or something. Anyway, I can now change my Dream suit to wear this coat, tie, and hat as my Night form. And since we will do this body-transforming thing, we can't be wearing Waking World clothes. They will fall off. You recall what happened to our clothes when you changed into the eagle in the Waking World?"

Basha: "Oh yeah. Everything I was wearing fell to the floor. Too bad you were not there to see me. You might have seen me naked when I changed into an eagle last night."

Lamont: "Would you believe I'm too much of a gentleman to let myself see your naked flesh?"

"Ha! Good try, Lamont. You may be able to hypnotize lesser mortals into believing what you want, but you will not cloud my mind, buster! I will break your arm if I find out you did that!" I say part joking and part serious. I grin and lean in and give him a quick kiss. "I will not tell anyone what you did or did, not see. That is for sure."

---

[19] This appears in the *Pirke Avot* (*The Sayings of Our Fathers*) 1:14.

[20] The rules were introduced in Isaac Asimov's 1942 short story "Runaround" (included in the 1950 collection *I, Robot*), although they had been foreshadowed in a few earlier stories. The Three Laws, quoted as being from the "Handbook of Robotics, 56th Edition, 2058 A.D. The other two laws are First Law – A robot may not injure a human being or, through inaction, allow a human being to come to harm. Second Law – A robot must obey the orders given it by human beings except where such orders would conflict with the First Law.

"Okay. The last thing on tonight's agenda is to find out how much Dreaming power Jon might have since he came through the Gate of Dreams, as we did."

Basha: "Good question. Hop on the bike and let us head over there. Lana is staying with Jon. You'll be happy to hear that Lana told me that Jon got his old job back, and she also got her first job. She moved in with him, and she gave me their address. They live in a one-bedroom apartment in the Richmond district at the corner of California and Ninth, a few blocks below the Presidio. Do you want the scenic route?"

Lamont: "Sure."

I take us down the Haight towards Stanyon, where John F. Kennedy drive leads us into Golden Gate Park; eventually driving past the large glass greenhouse that is the Conservatory of Flowers that is off in the distance sitting up on a hill. It is a majestic wood and glass structure built originally in 1879. A Victorian masterpiece of 12,000 square feet of beauty married to utility. It proudly survived the 1906 earthquake showing that, while it may look like a delicate fairy princess, it regally stood firm and tall, revealing that it was like a Queen mother bound tight in an ornately decorated corset beneath a gown of glistening glass.

It has been closed down for renovations since 1978. It will be wonderful to be inside it once more when it is finished, whenever that may be. We exit the park at 8th Avenue and head up towards California Street. This area is known as the Richmond district's Lake Street section. I know this area well since it is just a block from my favorite used bookstore Green Apple Books, on Clement Street. This two-story store is as close to the archetype of a used bookstore as you would find. Crammed into every corner are bookshelves bursting with books for sale. It is a maze and tight warren of bookcases, all roughly organized by overarching topics to each area. A delightful place to get lost in books for hours on end. Almost always coming away with some new, unexpected find. A very dangerous and addictive store.

The surrounding area is populated by many Russians who came to the area fleeing the Russian revolution and civil war. I was told that the Holy Virgin Cathedral on Geary Street between 26th and 27th Street is the largest one of its kind of the Russian Orthodox Church outside of Russian soil. It is a huge and impressive white building with five gold leaf onion domes on the structure, proudly displaying crosses on each. The front has six arched segments with giant painted icons, three on each side of the central doorway arch with the gold leaf Russian Orthodox Cross over the door. It seems incongruent and out of place in its location as it towers over the residential buildings that nestle around it as if for protection or guidance.

Another prominent immigrant population is the many Chinese, whose arrival was facilitated by lifting the Chinese Exclusion Act in 1965. Those Chinese immigrants began to replace the ethnic Jewish and Irish-Americans who had dominated the district before World War II. Chinese of birth or descent now make up nearly half of the residents in the Richmond district. One of my mom's favorite Chinese restaurants, Ton Kiang, is not too far from here between 22nd and 23rd street and Geary Boulevard. I wonder if Lamont likes Chinese food? Oh, Bloody Hell! I forgot, he cannot eat anything now. Will I ever get used to that?

My musings end as we take a left on 8th and turn onto California Street, where they live. I park the bike on the street in front of their four-story apartment complex. The bottom of this simple building is five-garage door entrances, and the three floors above are the apartments.

The only interesting architectural feature is each apartment's three-sided bay windows and the red round clay tiles on the roof. The color of the building is indeterminate due to the wind and fog that pours into this area almost every day. The structures butt up tightly against one another, with that smaller apartment house proudly showing off its recent white and red paint job it received.

We dismount and ring the bell, Lana buzzes us in, and we head up to their apartment.

LAMONT

As we step into their apartment, I feel a sudden warmth under my feet. What is going on here? I look down and see their apartment has nice polished wooden floors, which to my Dream covered feet feel like a stovetop was just turned on. Bloody Hell! How is this possible? Why is this happening? I do my best to ignore the mild discomfort as I look for a place to sit down, get off my feet, and figure this all out.

Lamont: "Can we sit on the couch?" I ask in haste. Basha notices my ill ease and looks at me. I smile to keep up appearances as I try to understand what's happening.

Jon: "Sure, take the couch. Is everything okay, Lamont?"

Lamont: "Oh, sure. Everything's fine. Just perfect."

Everyone is looking at me like I just grew a third eye. I ignore them and just make a beeline towards it. I sit down, keeping my feet off the floor, hidden under their large wooden coffee table. I am nervous, and when my feet brush up against the table, I can feel that same warm reaction from contact with its surface. Bloody Hell! Why is this happening? Does it have something to do with their house?

Jon: "I'm glad to hear everything is okay," Jon says, clearly puzzled but trying to not pry.

Basha joins me on the couch. 'You really are okay?'

Lamont: 'Oh, sure. Everything is just peachy.'

I ignore her concern and pretend to be distracted by a careful survey of the room. I can see that it shows clear evidence of Lana's encroachment into Jon's territory. I spot a recently added small bookcase crammed with books on dreams, dream symbolism, lucid dreaming, Charles Fort, hauntings in America in general, and some specifically concerning California, books on Atlantis, Mu, and Lemuria, Astrology, Tarot and Starhawk's *Spiral Dance,* some Agatha Christie novels, Armistead Maupin's *Tales of the City,* and some old hardback *Yermah the Dorado* by Frona Eunice Wait. The overall room has a tidy messiness showing that Lana had cleaned it up around the disarray Jon had left when he was unintendedly taken off to Dreamland. We ask both of them about how they are doing Dream wise.

Lana: "Well, we both aren't dreaming at all."

Jon: "We don't remember our dreams now, including the normal kind. I just don't think we want to anymore. It's all been too much stress and bad memories."

Basha: "That makes sense. I am sorry how it all worked out."

Lamont: "Well, you two had a bad time, so it's understandable. Hey, just give us a holler if you need anything, right?"

Jon: "We are so glad you are alive and well, Lamont. We were both worried."

Lamont: "Yeah. I'm all better now. Right as rain."

We chat about this and that, and the conversation ball is dropped slowly. We politely begin to make our exit. We all stand up, and then, as soon as my feet come in contact with the floor, I notice the sensation of warmth underneath radiating from it. I try to ignore it as we all hug, then leave. The carpeted hallway and stairs feel cool and comforting to my feet as we leave. Thank heavens all that weird stuff stopped happening. What was causing all that trouble back there?

Basha: "You still seem preoccupied, Lamont, everything okay?"

Lamont "Sure."

Basha: "Well then, I guess we are the only two active Dreamers who were at the gate site on both ends, excluding Peter, since he is not exactly active at the moment."

Lamont: "Presumably, he has the same powers?"

Basha: "However, we have these rings. It takes both things and influences to give someone the ability to Dream in the Waking World."

Lamont: "Which means it is just the two of us."

Basha: "Correct. Time to get you home."

Soon we are back at my parent's house. I appreciate my parent's wall-to-wall carpeting under my feet; it feels pleasant and soothing.

Lamont: "Maybe I'll sneak out and come by your place later?"

Basha: "Sure. After we get caught up with our homework, night Lamont."

We kiss but not too long; I don't want my parents to notice.

Lamont: "More later? Right?"

Basha: "Yes. Love you."

*

BASHA

After all that reading for my assignments, my brain is fried. I need to relax. I cuddle up under the covers with a good book waiting for Lamont to show up. I replay my cassette recording of John William's soundtrack to John Badham's version of the movie *Dracula.* I was told that this version starring Frank Langella was very romantic, and I have a hold on it at the video store, Le Video, on 9th Ave. I am almost finished reading Fred Saberhagen's novel *The Dracula Tapes*. I am especially interested in reading next, Les Daniel's two novels, especially his second novel, *The Silver Skull,* and his take on Tezcatlipoca. I wonder if Lamont has read this one? I never was that into vampire stories, but now I have a vested interest in doing as much research as I can on the topic.

My stack of research has only a few of the thirty novels by Marilyn Ross in her *Dark Shadow's* Barnabas Collins series; of the more recent vampire novels, besides Anne Rice, I have two by Les Daniels, three by Saberhagen, and two by Chelsea Quinn Yarbro.

'I'm leaving now.' I hear Lamont whisper in my mind.

A bit later, I hear a familiar rapping at my chamber window and spot a raven with bright blue eyes. Obviously, it is Lamont. I get out from under the covers, wearing a Dream suit consisting of a red flannel shirt, a proper red cotton panty, and thick red knee-high socks. I was not going to be caught naked. I open the window, and Lamont flies in.

He quickly goes from raven to shrouded in shadows naked human form and just as quickly conjures up clothes so I do not get an indecent peek. He now has a pair of Converse Chuck Taylors All-Star black and white high tops, black 501 Levi jeans, and a white cotton shirt with a blood-red tie. His wind-mussed hair is the same color as his raven feathers.

He is all bright-eyed and happy to see me but suddenly...

Lamont: "Hey!" Lamont exclaims, trying to keep quiet to not wake my mom.

Lamont: "It's happening again."

Basha: "What do you mean, again?"

Lamont: "My feet. The longer I standstill on the floor I notice heat radiating up into me. What the Hell? Basha, it burns!" Lamont says as he loses his balance and teeters over, catching himself from falling by holding onto my wooden bookcase. "Bloody Hell! That really hurts!"

He takes his hand away from the bookcase, loses his balance, falls to the floor, and then yelps

Lamont: "Gangway...coming through!" He says as he rights himself and hurriedly gets over to me on the bed.

Basha: "What is going on, Lamont?"

Lamont: "Hell if I know, but look at me," he shows me his hand where he touched the bookcase and reveals his bare feet. Both show signs he suffered from severe sunburn.

Basha: "Why?" I ask. "How?"

Lamont: "Hey, it's like when I touched the silver."

Basha: "Holy Goddess! Did this happen before?"

Lamont then tells me about what was happening at Lana and Jon's apartment. I ponder all of this. Hmm. A light bulb goes off.

Lamont: "Well, Watson, when you eliminate the impossible[21]..."

Basha: "Yes...so I'll play the Watson. Tell me what is happening to me?"

"It means that you are reacting to touching wood!"

"Bloody Hell! You're right! That is the common factor in all of this pain. I can't touch wood!"

"And it means that the ordinary impermeability of a Dream Suit is affected by your vampiric transformation. Thus, counteracting the normal ability of the Dream suit to protect you from contact with the environment."

Lamont: "I know that vampires can be killed by wooden stakes, but I don't recall not being able to touch wood."

Basha: "Neither do I. That is not normal."

---

[21] *'How often I have said to you that when you have eliminated the impossible, whatever remains,* however improbable, *must be the truth?' (Sign of the Four,* Sir Arthur Conan Doyle, The Annotated Sherlock Holmes, edited by William S. Baring-Gould, Clarkson N. Potter, Inc., 1967, p. 638), Sherlock Holmes has spoken this maxim five times, twice in The Sign of the Four, then in 'The Adventures of the Beryl Coronet', 'The Adventure of the Bruce-Parrington Plan', and lastly 'The Adventure of the Blanched Soldier'.

"Then again, I'm not your average vampire. I'm a custom-made job by Lilith and Tezcat."

"True. So different rules seem to apply?"

"I guess. All I know is that when I touched your wooden floor, I reacted just like Lana and Jon's place! It hurts. Same thing when I touched the wooden bookcase. It's just like touching silver! Both can burn me. Now that will make things complicated!"

"Well, at least you do not have any problem being in the sunlight, thanks to the Dream Magick of our rings."

"That is a blessing. Not being able to eat pizza, pasta, and popcorn, and I can't touch any wood, which is just about everywhere—this is really crummy."

Basha: "Just 'crummy'?"

Lamont: "Hey-I'm alive, and I got you, so I'm looking on the bright side! Those burns I received from contact with the wood didn't heal."

"That could be like I've read in the literature. Burns from sunlight or, for traditional vampires, touching holy objects all do not heal like any other wound."

Lamont: "You mean I'm permanently scarred?"

Basha: "No, I did not mean that. I just meant that wounds like that require the vampire to take in some blood in the literature, and only with that act will the vampire be healed."

Lamont: "I would be willing to put that hypothesis to the test. Especially since you're looking good, as usual, and still smelling wonderful', Lamont whispers in my mind and then moves in for a kiss.

Basha: I can feel his sharp fangs touching my throat. I get the message. But I pretend not to take his apparent hints. So…'You are semi-formal compared to my casual bedtime attire.' I reply in my mind.

He answers with some more smooches and little nips with his fangs. Drawing a little bit of my blood. I fade out for moments, and then I hear his voice in my mind as I return to the here and now.

Lamont: 'Did you hear me when I left my place?'

Basha: 'I did. We seem to have a long-distance connection with this telepathy thing.'

'I wonder what the range is. Hmmm…Hey, I see you're reading up on vampires. Good. Somebody needs to, and I just can't bring myself to launch into that reading list. Though if you think I need to…'

Basha: 'I will mark pages that I think will be important for you to read.'

Lamont: 'One burning question, before I feed on you, and I do need to...but, before that, how infectious is this vampirism? I vaguely recall that the vampire's bite victims turn into one themselves soon afterward. Isn't that what happened in Stoker's Dracula? It's like the spreading of some infectious disease by contact. I pray that isn't true!'

Basha: 'I have not become a vampire even with all your feeding on me recently, Lamont. I do not believe that it works that way. Even starting with Stoker's original novel, when you read it carefully, it states that to have someone cross over and become a vampire, that person needs to drink a vampire's blood. That's what Dracula did with Mina Harker[22]. Anne Rice takes up this idea in her novel *Interview with the Vampire.*

Lamont: 'But I recall from Stoker's Dracula Lucy seemed to become a vampire just from Dracula biting her!'

Basha: 'Calm down, Lamont. I think I have an alternative explanation for what happened to Lucy. I believe that it was due to Dracula completely draining Lucy Westenra. She died by that act, which was why she rose from the dead as a vampire[23]. Therefore, my assertion stands, mere feeding will not turn someone into a vampire.'

"But I'm not your average vampire!"

"True. You were not made a vampire in the ordinary way of either books or the movies."

"So maybe all those books you're reading don't apply to me?"

"Possibly. However, if your special creation is truly the deciding factor, it would follow from that fact that turning another into a vampire will not happen easily. Thus, you regularly feeding on me should have nothing to do with me catching the vampire virus or whatever you have. So as I said before, relax. It seems only movies have people turn into vampires from a simple act of feeding. I think we are safe. You're feeding on me all by itself only makes me doze off and very hungry. I am sure that the books are right and mere feeding will not do it.' (Reasonably sure. At the very least, hopefully sure.)

Lamont: 'Whew! You're telling me the truth?"

Basha: 'Yes. I promise I am not lying. I would never lie to you. I swear. We will be okay, Lamont. Trust me.'

---

[22] Bram Stoker's *Dracula,* 1897, as recounted in chapter 21.

[23] Perhaps Basha is correct. Or it could be that Lucy drank some of Dracula's blood as well, in a scene not shown. One could reach that conclusion from a reading of the text. Leslie S. Klinger editor of *The New Annotated Dracula,* W. W. Norton & Company, 2008, pg. 397 note 40 presents this very idea.

'Okay. I do. What you've explained is a great relief. Thinking about how I've constantly been feeding on you was causing me much apprehension.'

'Also, just so we are clear- since feeding on someone is a highly intimate and erotic act, you are only doing that with me. Got it, buster! If I catch your fangs on anyone else, I will rip them out of your mouth.'

'Yes, ma'am! I promise to be a good little monogamous vampire. And as for feeding...'

WELL OF DREAMS

I find myself in Lamont's embrace and back at that 'well of power' temple site. The water is varying shades of swirling blackness, and the place is humid from the steam rising off its surface.

Suddenly I feel his fangs carefully and deliberately piercing my flesh and pulling me into Lamont…I can feel my blood flow out as he begins feeding, and though he is a lot calmer and relaxed...the feeding is soft and slow…it is highly erotic as we comingle. Ahhh...

SAN FRANCISCO

Eventually, I realize I am only Basha once more. I am still feeling drained. It felt great—very intense, spilling over into the erotic. And I think he stopped a bit sooner this time. Whew. I touch my neck and feel the place where his teeth entered to feed on me. Chokers will be a permanent part of my outfit from now on. Once again, I am reassured that my Dream suit does not stain from any of the bloodlettings. The only evidence of his feeding in the Waking World is the bite marks and my blood-stained pillowcases.

Basha: 'You seem to have more control over your needs, Lamont. How long was I out this time?'

Lamont: 'For only about half-hour or so. During that time, I got to watch my skin heal up. This proves that taking blood is the only way to heal from the burns from wood and silver.'

Basha: 'As for that,' I grab one of my Blackwing Palomino pencils off my desk. 'The pencil is coated with a thin layer of paint. Will that protect you from burning?' I hold out the pencil to Lamont.

LAMONT

Lamont: 'Don't know.' I don't think so, since the floors here and at Jon and Lana's place were probably coated with some kind of varnish. 'But here goes…' I tentatively touch the pencil with the tip of my finger. 'Ahh…good news, no reaction.'

Basha: 'So that means it is direct contact with exposed wood that does it.'

I grip the pencil tighter and hold onto it for some minutes, waiting to see if there is any reaction.

Lamont: 'Ah...one moment, Houston, we seem to have a problem..."

Basha: 'What are you talking about, Lamont?'

Lamont: 'Hey!' I let go of the pencil. 'It seems the longer I hold that it begins to hurt.'

Basha: 'That means even a coating of paint or polish...'

Lamont: 'Or some layer over the wood only protects me for some moments. Given enough time, it begins to hurt. Even though I'm wearing these Waking World cotton socks, I can still feel the warmth from the wood. So, things are just a temporary layer of protection. Sustained contact won't indefinitely protect me even with an intervening layer between it and the wood. So, wood and silver are deadly to me like Superman is to Kryptonite.'

Basha: 'Explain, please?'

Lamont: 'Oh, come on, Basha, are you telling me you don't know about Superman?'

'I seem to have missed that topic in my American literature class.'

'I hadn't realized that you were so culturally uneducated. Superman, the DC comic book superhero[24], is vulnerable to Kryptonite- the stuff left over when his home world exploded. But for him, lead containers will keep the radiation from harming him. We have yet to find my equivalent to lead.'

'Why the interest in lead?'

'Ahh...the problem with dealing with an illiterate.'

'Hey! Who are you calling illiterate? I started to read Torah when I was six years old!'

'Well, you never read the literature of the American Comic book; thus, you can be considered a cultural 'illiterate.' If you had, you would know that lead shields Superman from the deadly effects of kryptonite."

'Okay, we will have to work on finding out if anything shields you from wood or silver. Now we know that you are vulnerable to silver as well as wood. It must relate somehow to the legendary motif that a wooden stake can kill a vampire. In your case, it is just any wood in any form that can harm you.'

Basha: 'That seems a logical deduction. '

[24] The character was created by writer Jerry Siegel and artist Joe Shuster, and first appeared in the comic book *Action Comics* #1 (cover-dated June 1938 and published April 18, 1938).

Lamont: 'And my Dream clothes do not protect me. Only Waking World materials did offer some form of protection.'

Basha: 'What about in Dreamland?'

Lamont: 'Hmmm…hypothetically real wood and real silver–mined and grown in Dreamland, could act as it does here and give me the third degree. I hypothesize that I would need non-Dream magick-created material to shield me from the effects even there. At least that is my tentative hypothesis and a caution I will have to take there.'

'That sounds reasonably cautious of you. So, it is all good. Now, I have a question. Where and what is this place you keep taking us to for our make-out sessions?'

'I don't really know. Something within me called out to me and guided me to that place. Sort of like how I came to make my way to Dreamland in the first place. Anyway, I was drawn to it. It feels like it is not either Dreamland or the Waking World though this place has elements of both. I'm not making sense, I know. It is connected somehow to dreams, ordinary dreams. It is a place of power that called to me. The name Well of Dreams came to me as if it was introducing itself to me. It does seem to be connected to everyone who is dreaming. I can hear the whispers floating on the steam coming off the waters. Can you hear it as well?'

Basha: 'Not really, but I feel the energy of the place. When I can pay attention to my surroundings. You keep me occupied with other things when you take me there. So I do not focus on much else other than you. Now that you are stable, we need to consider what happened to everyone else during the battle at the gate site. We only know where Peter is because he came with you to Golden Gate Park. We do not know where the others are.'

Lamont: 'Hopefully, they are in a similar condition to Peter, just in that deep coma form of REM sleep.'

Basha: 'Hopefully. But we need to locate them. I only know the Wicked Witches by their dream names. We have to find them to help them.'

'Let's check in on Peter tomorrow after school and see what we can figure out.'

'Sounds like a plan, Lamont. Oh, and I can give you a ride to school on my bike if you would like.'

'That sounds great. I was wondering if I get a little nibble? I'm still feeling puckish; I was cautious about the amount I took previously. It cared for my needs, but I'm a growing boy.'

'According to the literature, the newly turned has a greater need to feed regularly. It should subside, and the need to feed lessened. So, yes, you can get a bite. I need to check in with Boots, so Lamont, let us make this a quickie, and then I will head off to Dreamland proper?'

We kiss deeply and passionately, and Lamont starts to nibble on my lips, then ow! He draws blood, and he begins to feed again. Ahhhh…slight pain becomes…mmm...communion is bliss. Ohhhh!

*

TEMPLE OF THE NIGHT, WHERE QUEEN LILITH RESIDES
CITY OF ATLANTIS

Whoa. That boy puts a whole new spin on the term 'necking'. I think Mae West would approve. I find myself alone, feeling warm and yummy, though I can barely stand on my own two feet. I wonder how long I was out? How much and how often does he need to feed? Though I like it, I am unsure if I can keep up with this feeding schedule. I hope it will settle into just once a day or less. Anyway, I need to compose myself. I realize that I am outside Queen Lilith's temple. I hope to locate Boots from there.

I approach the open courtyard. The air is wonderfully crisp and full of the scent of burning leaves. The trees in the courtyard are a mix of yellow, gold, pale to intense orange, and bright red. They crunch under my boots as I walk in. A well-built twenty-something Native American with dark, intense green eyes and shoulder-length chestnut brown hair is Tending the sacred fire. He is bare-chested and clad in leather armbands, skintight buckskin pants, and moccasins. He looks good, and he knows it. He is checking me out, and I can tell he finds my red and gold form-fitting outfit meeting with his approval.

Native American Lad: "Hail and welcome to the Queen's temple!" He says with a wolfish grin. "Are you hopefully here on 'pressing' business? This humble servant would be honored to attend to your needs."

I am sure that he has helped many a gal or guy with their pressing needs. But not this gal. She is happily spoken for. 'I have come on urgent business, and besides, I have pledged myself to another. You can help me, though."

Native American Lad: "Any boon I may grant is yours to request."

Basha: "Do you know if the lady named Boots is anywhere on the grounds this night?"

"I know of her. She is here now. You can find her in the chambers dedicated to the Egyptian God Thoth."

"Thank you."

I teasingly sashay past the young man, and I can feel his gaze locked onto my swinging hips as I enter the halls and head toward Thoth's chambers. I pass and greet a lounging group of wild felines, a lioness, a panther, and a tiger, all with a few cubs dozing. Due to my ruminative mood, I ramble through the temple grounds, passing its many halls and chambers. I recall my early years of Dreaming when I first came here and grew up here. When I was a novice at the temple, this place was my school, my playground, and a place of solitude. My mind back then was filled with wonder and joy.

My only worries back then were simply mastering lessons in the arcane arts of the Craft and the kabbalah and whether that cute boy in my Dreamland class actually liked me or not. A wistful sigh ends my reverie as I find myself at my destination.

I find Boots seated before an altar dedicated to Thoth. The statue shows the ibis-headed Thoth in ceremonial attire measuring the heart of a deceased against the feather of truth in the Hall of Judgement of the Dead. Boots is clad in a tight-fitting black leather dress, with long black gloves and her signature thigh-high black boots. For her, this is being modest. Oh, my Goddess! I just realized she does not know about Lamont. She does not know that Lamont is not dead, well, mostly not dead.

Basha: "Boots! Bad news travels fast, but unfortunately, good news takes a bit longer."

Boots: "What are you talking about, Basha? What good news?"

Basha: "Lamont is not dead! He is alive. Though he was on the knife's edge the last few days before he came back to us." Not sure yet, if I should convey all those little details to Boots about Lamont's condition, such as the fact that he is now a vampire. Perhaps later.

Boots: "That's great news! Have you seen him?"

"Yes, I have. I have been with him since they took him from the gate site in the Waking World. It has kept me occupied and worried ever since. This is the first night I could make it over. I am sorry for not sending word or something."

Boots: "I'm so relieved to hear that. Despite the dark attire he cast himself in, he is still bright and playfully cute. I don't think he can really pull off the dark and brooding look. You telling me he's alive is the best news I've heard concerning that miserable event you got us roped into. Since this is the first time you've been in Dreamland since then, you haven't tried to find Zeh'Brah either?"

Basha: "No. I have not."

"Well, we've talked. She and I had come to an agreement. She asked me to convey a message for her. Oh Basha, why in the name of our Mother didn't you warn us!"

"I thought I tried. I really thought I did."

"I don't recall being told about any blobs from Hell attacking us!"

Basha: "I do not think they were from…"

Boots: "I don't give a Holy Mother's damn where they're from! Did you know about them, yes or no?"

"Not really. I knew it could be dangerous, but I never really knew what form the dangers might take. Nor did I think we would be attacked. I honestly did not know what would happen when we opened the gate."

"You just brought an escort of cats, Lamont, that black kid, that dyke all decked out for a fight just on the off chance that something would amble by for an unfriendly visit?"

"I was just erring on the side of caution." (Come on, Basha, don't lie to her. Tell her the truth. You know you did fear something terrible would happen, and you just tried to ignore those feelings. If you had been more honest with them, maybe none of this would have happened. Tell her! But I can't. I'm too ashamed.)

"You erred all right! You erred big time! You should have told us more. You shouldn't have kept us in the dark. And we should have asked more questions! Damn it! We had a right to know what we had signed up for! We just blithely volunteered for all this as if it were some kind of lark."

Basha: "You are right. I should have spelled things out better and more fully. I should have thought this through. I didn't. I failed everybody. I am so terribly sorry."

Boots: "We were simply a coven, having some fun, not some sort of magick military squad!"

"I made a big mistake. I am sorry. I should have handled things differently. I let myself get swept up in the whole fantastic situation. I promise it will never happen again."

Boots: "That honey is for damn sure! I'm sure I won't be able to forget that night. It felt like my heart was ripped out when those blobs attacked Selene."

Basha: "I did not mean for this to happen. Everything just went…wrong. Selene, Lenore, Oolong, that gay kid, Peter, and all those cats. I feel so guilty. Like it all was my fault."

"What are you going to do about Selene and the others?"

"I do not know. But, if what happened to Peter happened to the rest, then there is hope. His body is there in the Waking World in deep REM sleep."

"I can live with hope. Okay. I can forgive you, to an extent. You didn't really understand what you were doing. Now you got to fix this. You and Lamont are the clever people. If there is a way, you two can figure something out. You will do that, won't you?"

"Yes. I swear we will do everything to fix this for everyone."

"Okay. We thought so. Good. If you find them leave word for me at the temple."

Basha: "Boots, do you know their Waking World names and where they live? Anything about their lives over there?"

Boots: "No. I only know their dream names."

"Yeah, same here. That is our first problem."

"Yes, it is. Okay. I'm exhausted from all of this arguing and worrying about everyone. I'm done in. But I don't know about you, but I could use a long hug."

We hold onto each other and let all the anger, guilt, tension, and anxiety leak out of us with our shed tears. Then suddenly, Boots pulls back.

Boots: "Now, here is the deal. Zeh'Brah's not coming back. Not ever."

Basha: "What?"

"Well, definitely not as she once was. If she comes back to Dreamland, it won't be as Zeh'Brah, so you won't be able to find her. Same with me. New name, new look, new identity."

Basha: "What?"

Boots: "We don't want any part of that kind of magick spell casting. So, you won't see or hear from us again. We're done. I will tell you this. I desperately needed to escape my situation in the Waking World and stumbled onto this place. To confess, I was a runaway who was lured into becoming a damned streetwalker. That's as much of who I am as you need to know. So, just leave a word here when you find them, and you can tell us they're okay. Okay, it was a fun lark for all those years we had together. I really looked forward to sleeping and escaping here for all those years. This was the best thing in my life. Up till…well… Damn it! You might as well have killed me. You did kill us. At least Zeh'Brah and Boots are dead forever. We will be back in a way that you'll never find us—ever! We won't let you take this place from us again! "

Tears of shame and guilt leak out as she fades from view. Because of what I did, I lost two of my oldest friends! I feel cold, alone, and even guiltier than before I got here, if that is possible. She is right. I did kill their beautiful dreams.

*

LAMONT

After feeding on Basha, I let go of her connection and feel her fading off to Dreamland. I transform into a small gray bat and fly home. Once I get back into my room, I become my human self. Good thing the floors here in this place are all carpeted. I get in bed and drift off to the Well of Dreams. I want to understand this place better. The air is moist, and there is a hint of the metallic scent of blood and chocolate. I think I'm connected to this place and drawn to it due to Tezcat's involvement in bringing me back to this life. It's a place outside the Waking World and Dreamland's usual time and space. I somehow feel the presence of Tezcat when I'm here. She is tied up with this place and its power.

I feel and hear voices, mere murmurs. The sounds and feelings of people, thousands if not millions of people. But I can't make out what is being said. I feel confident I'm here for a reason. Somehow, I feel that I can connect to those voices. But how do I connect to them? Perhaps I need to step into the water? I reach down and touch the water; it is hot, scalding hot! In the moment of contact, there is searing pain but a fleeting image and voice.

Gwen: "Help me. please…"

Who is this? She needs my help. Hell! I've got to touch the waters to see if I can connect to her.

Arrgh! The pain is intense…focus on her voice...I can feel her pain…her need. Focus on that call... that plea…I feel it like a stream flowing from the source to its confluence downstream.

*

I am floating...in dark waters...warmth...wet...slowly things begin to coalesce. I can hear her voice and her whimpering. The feeling is tangible. She is alone and both helpless and feeling hopeless. Finally, I am a shadow in the corner of her dream. She is in a dark, dank, damp cell. The scent of stale sweat, urine, feces, and mildew is thick. It looks familiar. But is it just that all dungeon cells have the same interior decorator? Or is it because I've been here for way too long? My olfactory memory confirms that this is a cell in the depths of the mayor's abode in the city of Thrall.

The dreamer is a young girl named Gwen, perhaps ten or so. I am in her dream and her mind. She knows she was taken to serve in the city of Thrall. Then I look upstream to its source and see her far away, sleeping in her bedroom in Seattle, Washington.

I whisper in her mind, "Help is on the way. Take heart. Your voice has been heard."

*

I pull my hand out of the water. Damn! It hurts! I wonder if this is what third-degree burns feel like? It looks like a mess and feels both numb and painful simultaneously. If how fast the bite marks heal is representative of vampire healing rates, I should heal soon-ish.

I need to go to Thrall. She is probably not the only one there, I'm sure.

*

I become a bat and make my way to the city of Thrall. Eventually, I see the tall inward, leaning alabaster stonewalls of the city below me. The walls enclosing the metropolis have a hundred gates and two hundred turrets. Overshadowing the prominent walls are white clusters of towers with golden spires that pierce the gloomy gray clouds floating above Thrall. Under some of the city's gates, the deep jade green water flows from the river Styx. Jutting out into the wide river are wharves constructed of marble where ornate galleons, made of cedar and calamander wood, dock and unload their wares of spices, livestock, dusty and musty fabrics, and fresh wood.

I pass the metropolis's main gate with its red-robed and hooded city sentries. I approach the Mayor's citadel. The colossal building has over its center a multicolored mosaic dome. I melt into human form with my long black coat, blood-red tie, and black slouch hat. I noticed once again the garish gigantic breast-shaped ruby doors covered with bizarre, aberrant, arabesque designs. As a mist, I pass through them.

I am now in darkness, but that does not matter to one such as me. I am the darkness that walks. The room has a blue-gray tint and the lingering miasma of dank hashish, lavender, sandalwood, and stale burgundy wine scents, as I peer around the palatial deserted halls heading for the stairs that will take me to the cells below.

I notice that all my senses have been heightened, which is good. However, the smell is more pungent, an all too familiar stench of human suffering in these dim, dank cells. I hold out my ringed hand to feel my way to the young girl I seek. She is just a small, slender youngster with once glistening silver hair tied in a ponytail, all sweaty with purple oiled skin and dark brown eyes with strength and dignity in their depths. It is such a shame that she got trapped in this horrible place. I should help her first, and then the others. The cell door is never locked, so I swing it open and step in. I kneel next to her and reached out to touch her shoulder. I remove the glamor of darkness that surrounds my face.

Lamont: "Gwen, I have come to help you. Awake," I whisper.

Gwen: "Hello. You came. I was afraid I made you up. Are you a knight errant like Lancelot in the stories?"

"Yes. I'm the Night, and I have come like a knight from Camelot to rescue those in need."

Gwen: "Can you really get me home?"

Lamont: "Yes, and I believe I can make sure you'll never come back here. Furthermore, you'll be able to go back to anywhere else in this land of Dreams if you want to. To do that, I need to look a bit scary, Okay?"

Gwen: "I'm not sure if I want to come back. It has been bad for so long since I got brought here. But, it is nice to know I could. It's okay if you look scary. Please just do it now. I want to go home."

As I speak, I can feel my face darken, gathering up my Dream magick powers. "Listen to me and do as I say. You will wake up and no longer feel compelled to return to Thrall ever again. You are free. Never return here. Now wake up!"

I watch as Gwen vanishes. It worked! I have some new abilities between Dream Magick and having turned into a vampire. I can get into people's minds. Through the Well of Dreams, I have power over others' dreams and their Dreaming. I can enter their dreams and even locate them in the Waking World. This means that I can help all these people here. All these Dreamers were ensnared by the seductive allure of Kaliya. I can help them escape from their enslavement and break the Dream spell that keeps them returning to their slavery under Kaliya's enchantment. I'm not just a vampire monster; I'm more than that; I'm a righter of wrongs.

Well, Gwen isn't the only one here. One down, and as I look around at all the filled cells, there are many more to go. They all need to be freed.

Lamont: "I can help you if you want that. To you wish to be free of this place?"

I see expressions of shock and disbelief on many of their faces.

Lamont: "Yes, I am really here to help you. Just like I did for Gwen. I set her free. If you want, I can do this for you as well."

"Really?" I hear one of them say.

Lamont: "Yes, really. I have come to help you. All you need to do is tell me you want this. I will help you like I did, Gwen."

There is just silence, wide-eyed silence. Then the quiet is shattered by a single sob and the sound of tears falling onto the floor.

"please..."

"please..."

"yes...please..."

"help me..."

I start going to them, beginning with the youngest. There are so many teary eyes as I walk in to help them.

Lamont: "I will help you wake up and be free from the compulsion of having to return here."

Through their tears, they thank me as I work my Dream magick on them to help release them. I am a bit overwhelmed as well. I feel like a real knight of the Round Table as I help them. Perhaps this is my real destiny! To help people. I have been granted a new life to give others a second chance. I focus on my task of using my powers to release them from their compulsion to return. With each success, one by one, they disappear.

As I assist in their rescue, I hear a guard approaching leading two more enthralled Dreamers. I can't stop to break the connection with this teenager with who I am working. Luckily, I finish before they enter the cellblock. I fade into the dark corners of the cell and just wait. Perhaps the guard won't do anything. The guard shoves a college kid all skinny, naked, and dazed with short blonde hair and owl eyeglasses into one cell and then another dazed naked late teenage boy with purple hair and purple skin into another empty cell.

Seeing them reminds me of how helpless I was when I was trapped in Thrall. Stripped naked and made to serve. It was so humiliating. And to think I let it happen. I actually enjoyed it or seemed to when it was happening! I will free all of them, I swear it! I won't let this happen any longer to them!

I watch silently from the shadows as the guard glances around to check up on all the occupants.

I hope he doesn't notice that Gwen and the others are gone.

He then just turns and heads back up the stairs.

I can't tell whether he noticed anything or not. I just return to my task of waking up all the victims of Thrall.

After waking up another four, I hear a substantial creature approach. From the heavy reptilian musky smell and ponderous sound, I can tell that the being is the mayor, Kaliya, in his Lovecraftian form. As if I needed further confirmation, I could hear his familiar voice. Then something strange happens. A new feeling, a slight humming in my bones. As if we resonate the same. How is this possible? How can it be that we are similar? I don't understand?

Kaliya: "What is this? How is this possible? You smell like a Nephilim. But I know all of our kind, and you are not one of us. Perhaps it is simply that you're recently made? Yet, why would one of our kind act as you and care for these lowly creatures? Who in their foolish poor judgment sired you? Tell me so that I can inform your sire when I eliminate this mistake."

THE NIGHT (& BASHA)

What is this creature called Kaliya saying? He smells and feels something like me. I know this. I know it in my blood. Like me, he feels like one who can feed off the living. He calls himself a Nephilim.

(Holy Great Mother! Lamont is some sort of Nephilim? Does that mean all Nephilim are vampires?)

Yet—there is something different about him. I don't think we are precisely the same. It does mean that there are other blood drinkers and life feeders despite our differences that I know in my blood. We share something. Shall I reveal who and what I am to this one? Do I let him know that I am different? No. I think not. I do not trust this one. I shall bide my time and let Lamont do what he will with this one. Lamont speaks rightly; I know the evil that dwells in that one's heart.

(How and why does the Night think and know he is different? What does all this mean?)

LAMONT

Kaliya: "Creature! You came here to this place traveling under the open sky bathed in the sun's light. That means you are a Day Walker! We are not the same after all!"

THE NIGHT (AND BASHA)

As I suspected. I am different. He now knows this as well.

(Day Walker? That must mean Nephilim are more like the traditional literary vampires fleeing from daylight!)

LAMONT

Lamont: "I am called The Night, and I know the evil that dwells within you! I am here to put an end to that." He doesn't recognize me as Lamont. Good. But he thinks I'm a Nephilim? What is he saying? What does that mean? I can't be like him. That can't be possible! Either way, I don't have time for this. Put it aside, Lamont, and focus on the task at hand, Lamont. You came to do a rescue.

Kaliya: "You cannot be some newly made one of us, not with the ability to Day Walk. What are you? How did you come to be?"

Lamont: "I am mystery and majesty. I am the Night who walks even in the light of day."

Kaliya: "Well, whatever you are, know that I have spent millennia gathering my powers. So, you shadowy strange new creature, beware! You should not have meddled in my affairs; you will be dispatched back to dust if you do!

Lamont: "You will find that death's arms cannot contain me. Whereas you are mortal, so beware." I ignore his approach. I simply walk to another cell and try to calm everyone that remains, telling them that I will do my best to rescue them all.

Kaliya: "Idle boosts. None have such abilities. This I know for a certainty. All creatures can only postpone death's embrace. I warn you, leave my guests alone! I won't hesitate to kill those who meddle in my affairs."

Kaliya likes to appear as a walking nightmare, a hybrid of space alien and humanoid. If his two snakeheads stood still and erect on their long necks, they would reach twenty feet. The two snake forms become one as they reach the torso. Around the joined meeting of the two independently moving snake necks forming into one neck is a necklace of chopped-off hands and human hearts. Fanged mouths are at his elbows, and those hands end in two large crab-like pincers. Around his waist is a skirt of hanging serpents strung together. He stands on two reptilian-clawed feet like some Hollywood idea of a dinosaur. His single voice comes out of both the snake's heads simultaneously.

Lamont: "You are the monster! I am the dragon slayer, so beware! Now leave me. I would rather free your prisoners than waste my time fighting with you. So, go away!" I continue to concentrate on placing my hands over the eyes of a terrified young dreamer. I whisper to my new charge, "Focus only on my voice. Hear only me. You will wake up in bed once more. You will no longer feel compelled to return to Thrall. You are free from this nightmare. Listen to my voice. Listen to only me…" I repeat over and over, trying to get him to obey me and awake.

Kaliya: "Foolish youth, feel my wraith!"

I feel Kaliya's pincers cut into my arms as I try to pull myself away. I can't be insubstantial while also needing to connect with the child. I try to get the child to focus on my physical presence and hypnotic commands. Damn it! I push the pain away…fight to focus…need to help this child…repeat my commands to enable him to wake up.

Kaliya: "You are damned Knight of darkness! I will haul you up and beat you as if you were some disobedient child! You're taking my playthings away! A futile gesture. There are so many who desire what I offer!"

I can barely focus between the prior burns and this cutting into my arms. But then the child vanishes. Thank God.

All the human prisoners cower in terror at the sight of the monstrous Kaliya. Their screams and whimpers add to the confusion. I don't think I can do much more to help them.

Lamont: "I am the Night who embodies primordial fear! Once you realize the extent of my powers, it is you who should tremble. You cannot harm me." I turn myself into darkness itself and fade. I no longer have a form or substance.

Kaliya: "Your words do not scare me. I'm not some tiny monkey cowering when the sun goes down. Your little parlor trick will not stop me from teaching you a lesson."

I lunge at Kaliya and wrap my arms around him as my fangs extend, and I bite into one of his snake necks. I wonder if I can drain the life force out of him, as I now am a vampire. His blood is sweet like honey though it burns in my mouth as I feed on him. I can feel his essence and strength flowing into me as I drink his blood. My fingernails lengthen and sharpen as I rip and slice his neck. He bellows with pain, and blood pours down hot and thick from the gouges I cut into him. He tries to break my attack on him by swinging the serpent neck I am attacking. I hold onto him tightly with my fangs and my hands. He tries to knock me unconscious by repeatedly smashing me into the wall.

I can feel his life force draining and him weakening. However, he is like a well too deep, and I realize I cannot drain him dry. He is so very ancient, and that adds to his power. I don't think I can match him even now.

Kaliya: "Knight! You are annoying. I will smash you to a pulp long before you have swallowed your fill."

He switches tactics, and his other snaked head begins to chomp onto my back, its teeth penetrating my coat and piercing my flesh. I can't take much more of this. He is right. I have to retreat and leave these dreamers. Bloody damn Hell!

*

I return to the peculiar sweet, moist mixture of metallic scent and chocolate and realize I am in the Well of Dreams. My body is bleeding, and I can barely stand the pain...the loss of my precious blood...ohhhh...I can feel my body trying to absorb the life force of Kaliya and trying to heal. I just think I won't be able to...not yet...I sink into a pool of darkness and let it take me in its embrace...

*

THE NIGHT (AND BASHA)

That was a most engrossing encounter Lamont had. This means that beings such as I am are not unique. There are others. He calls himself a Nephilim. He said that they were as evil as he? We both feed off of others, yet we are different. He seems like the traditional nosferatu, whereas I am

the living night! For now, I will not dwell on such things. Now is the time to hunt. In the form of a giant bat, I traverse the skies of Dreamland, seeking to feed. Hunting time has begun once again. I cry out with mad laughter and primal joy as all who hear me tremble in fear.

(I continue to try to reign in this monster as it attacks. And it is a struggle to contain its savage hunger, the righteous anger, and the desire for revenge it feels as it strikes these evil people. But it is like trying to tame a Tyrannosaurus Rex, and it is still not happening. I am exhausted and sick with the struggle.)

Finally, coinciding with the new day's coming, I feel satiated. My hunt once again comes to an end.

Friday, September 5, 1980

SAN FRANCISCO

LAMONT

I wake up with clinging wisps of nightmares rising off me like the morning dew. I can't recall clearly any of it. How? Why? Also, I feel both full of sustenance and aching. I need help. I need Basha. But first, I need to swap out my evening pure obsidian magick Dream ring for my gold version, the daytime one I get out of its container where it was charging in the Gate-site soil. Then it is off to her place!

BASHA

I fitfully rise out of Dreamland into lucid dreaming as I remember Lamont meeting with Kaliya and me wrestling with the Night. I must not let him know that I know about this, not now, since there is nothing he can do about it, so why add to his burden? Then, I hear my alarm going off as I ponder all this. Next, as the clarion bids me rise to greater levels of consciousness, I sense a familiar presence in the room. I open my eyes and see Lamont asleep on the chair at my desk. He's with the store cat, Gizmo, curled up on his lap. What in Heaven's name? What is he doing here at this hour? When did he get in? Why did I not notice? He is here, so I better find out why. I mentally call him.

Basha: 'Lamont, what in heaven's name are you doing here? Cannot a person have some privacy?' I say angrily to cover up what I know.

He does not respond. What is wrong with him? I conjure a rose-colored camisole and cotton panties and then get out of bed to check on him.

Basha: 'Lamont, are you alright?' At my touch, he opens his eyes.

Lamont: 'I'm sorry. I needed your help.'

Basha: 'Well, I am flattered. Okay. We cannot have you getting overwhelmed with needs. '

Lamont: 'I had a rough night. I ache everywhere. Though I don't think I'm bleeding.'

'What do you mean bleeding? Lamont, what happened to you?' I say as I wrap my arms around him as he lays his head in my lap.

Lamont: 'I was dancing with Kaliya, the Nephilim Mayor of Thrall, last night. He plays rough. Ohhhh.'

Basha: 'What in the name of the Goddess were you doing there?'

'Playing Lancelot for a ten-year-old Guinevere. I was doing the knightly thing and rescuing the princess from the dragon. She and a lot of other young dreamers were enthralled in Thrall. But damn it! He showed up before I could get them all out of there! That's when I got a bit of a thrashing. I'm glad we're talking telepathically. I wouldn't want to freak out your mom with my presence in your room. She does head off to work soon, right?'

'She does. I generally just say good morning before she commutes down the stairs to the store. So, you rescued people from Thrall. That is good. But why did you decide to do that last night?'

'When I went into the well's waters, I heard little Gwen calling me. She was a kid in Seattle. I can trace a dreamer to where they live in the Waking World! A really cool trick! So that is why I rushed out to Thrall. Then I limped back after Kaliya smashed me up and stopped me from helping everyone. I collapsed asleep back in bed. When I woke up, I was mainly healed up this morning. I then flew over as a raven. Doing knightly rescue things as the Night tires a guy out. I wonder how Bruce and Lamont manage this kind of lifestyle? It seems easier in the comics. More people back there need rescuing, and this time I would like to do this with some backup.'

'Are you referring to me as backup? You are finally learning Lamont. If you are fending off foes, especially one who seems as formidable as Kaliya, then I strongly recommend we do this as a team. You barely were able to get out of his clutches the first time you encountered him. Besides the fact that he held you enthralled for over a month.[25]'

'I agree. But I did drag myself out of there on my own when I awoke to my Dream powers. I couldn't defeat Kaliya then, and I didn't do so last night, so I could use your help to rescue those held captive by him.'

'How many more are in that place?'

'Hard to say. And we may not have the element of surprise this time.'

Basha:: 'So, this will be difficult and dangerous?'

---

[25] As recounted in *Through the Gate of Dreams*. Those events when Lamont was enthralled by Kaliya covered the dates from May 1, 1980 –June 9, 1980, pp 278-319.

Lamont: 'Yes. But they need help. This won't be easy. I'm hoping that perhaps the two of us will make the difference.'

'Great. Just great. I did not realize that we have become knight errants. But you are correct. We cannot leave them enthralled and trapped in that awful enslavement. I am not sure there is anyone else to call. Okay, we will do this come the evening. Meanwhile, you should rest on my bed while I get showered.

Lamont: 'Sounds like a plan to me.'

Basha: 'Oh, and I have something for you. Here catch.'

I toss him a pair of my red knee-high socks, all nicely balled up. He catches it easily.

Lamont: 'Socks! I can wear them so I can avoid the wooden floors! Excellent idea. But they're red; don't you have some black ones?'

Basha: 'Just be grateful they were not girly pink. If you want something different, you will have to buy a pair yourself.'

He struggles to get them on, and I realize that he really hurts from that beating he received. I go off to him, help get the socks on him, and then help him to my bed; he winces as he moves. He settles in, curls up, and drifts off to sleep. I conjure up a red silk robe and head out of the room. I step out of the room and get a kiss on the cheek from mom as we go our separate ways, she to the store downstairs, and I to the bathroom. There are advantages to Dream clothes, as I click my fingers and make my robe disappear. This certainly does away with the tedium of doing laundry.

After my shower, I get an idea. I heat my skin. I see and feel the steam rising off it as I dry. Now that was a neat trick! I run a brush through my wavy red hair and notice it's getting longer; I bet it falls below my shoulder blades. I poke my head out and call Lamont to see if he is awake.

Lamont: "You are a cruel taskmaster, Basha! I had such a nice dream; your scent is all over the bedding. Don't ask me to tell you; we might both get embarrassed."

Basha: "I promise I will not ask about those kinds of dreams if you do not ask about mine. Now, do you need to feed?"

"I would never turn down such a tasty offer."

"Okay, you can get a quick bite, but only if you make yourself useful before and make me some toast and eggs. All our smooching makes me hungry! So, start making breakfast and a cup of tea this morning with a bit of honey. I will be out in a moment."

I hear Lamont get out of bed and make kitchen noises. I apply my cinnamon oil to my skin, then materialize a pale pink satin push-up bra, some fire truck red jeans, a red leather belt with the sun buckle, then red cowgirl boots over my feet, and finally a tan cotton blouse. Last but not least, a blood-red choker. Lastly, I create a version of those gold and silver sun-moon earrings and a version of the gold mezuzah my Dad bought for me. I check out the length and polish on my fingernails.

I notice they could use trimming and touch-up. With a snap of the fingers, I adjust the look of red nail polish on them until I get them properly taken care of. I again realize that I need to find time to schedule a pedicure and manicure. I put on cherry red lipstick and am ready to make an appearance.

LAMONT

Lamont: "Wooden cabinets are everywhere! I had to use kitchen towels to protect myself. I think I'm going to need to keep gloves here. However, enough about me; you look gorgeous as always," I say while stirring the scrambled eggs in the pan, smelling the sharpness of the red onions and the slight sweetness of the white wine in which I sautéed those onions. I hope she likes this. The fabric protects me, sort of. But I can still feel the heat under my feet from the wooden floor. I may need thicker protection. Perhaps leather? Something to think about and plan for next time. Oh well. "Tea is on the table; I choose Twinning's Lady Grey," the subtle scents of lemon and orange mixed with the bergamot appealed to me.

I liked how the faint sweetness of the honey rose out of the warm liquid as I stirred it in.

Lamont: "I'm having the same. Toast should be popping up at any moment. I will butter them and add some jam.' I chose a jam sweetened with the fruity flavors of apricot and green grapes.

BASHA

I sit down and get served. I definitely could get used to this. Lamont sits across from me at the wooden kitchen table., hands in his lap. Presumably, the chair's thick cushion protects him, but I notice that his feet are floating almost imperceptibly above the floor.

Basha: "Now, as soon as I eat, we can do some vampire necking. But just a bit. We need to get going, and I cannot have you lay me out for an hour!" I say between bites, "Now, we have to locate the others."

Lamont: "I agree."

"Well, I only know their Dream names, so this will be difficult. We conjectured that they are all in a coma similar to Peter's in some hospital in the western half of the US, right?"

"Though the time zones are only separated by an hour, I think that our Dreamland is at the very least built off of everyone in the Pacific, and the Mountain Time zone creates and inhabits our Dreamland. I'm guessing that the major influences are Los Angeles, San Francisco, Seattle, and Las Vegas."

"What about Taos and Sedona? I would think there would also be influential Dreamers from those two cities."

Lamont: "Yeah, you're probably right. The important point is that ours is just one of many versions of Dreamland with some overlap as the evening hours goes by."

Basha: "So, all we need to do is get access to hospital records to find people admitted on the same night as Peter and you. As you were alluding, they might be in our time zone, though technically, they could be anywhere in the U.S. Yikes. How in Heaven's name are we going to do that? Hire an army of private detectives?"

Lamont: "The place I take us to, I call it the Well of Dreams. I heard the voices of people as they were sleeping and dreaming. It seems to be a conduit to dreamers everywhere."

Basha: "Is that true? Can you really tap into someone's dreams from there?"

"I did with Gwen, the young dreamer from Seattle who I helped escape the nightmare prison of Kaliya. I know we were able to do dream magick for me to project that image into Lana's mind. Queen Lilith said I had that ability, and she was right. So, it seems from the Well of Dreams, I can. I need to go back there and explore this further."

"Well, we need to clean these dishes and get you to school. That is first on our agenda. Then after school, we need to check on Peter to see how he is doing and what we can learn about where he is. Your ability to read minds or get into dreams will be tested."

"Sounds like a plan. So, are we riding to school on your bike or flying?"

Basha: "I would love to fly. Parking is always a hassle. However, you have schoolbooks to carry."

Lamont: "Yikes! I forgot my homework and books! I was so focused on getting here that I left it all behind! Damn!"

"Silly Lamont. I am sure they will forgive you one day since you almost died."

"True. I wonder how long I could get away with this excuse? Do you think a few months?"

"Lamont! You are terrible! Now, hop to it, man and help with these dishes; otherwise, you will be late."

*

After a short bit of vampire feeding and me waking back up, we head out. We pull up to the Ambrose Bierce High School parking lot on my red Honda CB400 Hawk. Lamont enjoys how cool he looks with his Charcoal RAF coat flapping in the wind behind him. We conjured up our favorite attire; we both like to indulge our desires to show off. Lamont's wearing Chuck Taylor sneakers, black 501s, a white cotton button-down shirt, and a black cotton vest underneath the leather bomber jacket I gave him. I added a red leather version of my usual black double-breasted motorcycle jacket and a hooded sweatshirt to the outfit I had on earlier. It is a brisk high of 50 degrees with a cloudless pale blue sky and perfect fall coat-wearing weather. We do not need to wear coats to keep warm – any Dream Suit, even if it is just a veneer of color over one's skin, can keep out the cold, but it is best not to be conspicuous in our attire.

Though we do seem to be noticed. I realize that it is like we were the Home Coming king and queen or something for all the attention we are getting. Lamont's basking in all of it; I am trying to deal with it. He enjoys everyone knowing that I am his girlfriend.

An acquaintance of Lamont's approaches us and notices the rings. "Hey, you two, the matching rings are cool. You two are officially an item now?"

Lamont: "Yup!" he happily pipes in.

Basha: "Lamont got them for us, and I did not think about what it implied when he slipped it on my finger," I confess with embarrassment.

I wander the halls with Lamont for a bit. Everyone we meet is so happy that Lamont is alive and we are an item. Lamont is bursting with pride, and I feel so awkward. Why? I guess I was not ready to take out a billboard and announce it. But, if I am honest with myself, I have to admit we are good for each other, he is head over heels in love with me, and I am in love with him. We are literally in a death-do-us-part kind of thing; except for us, even death cannot part us. Damn, my life has gotten crazy since Lamont walked into it. A quick kiss, tell him I will pick him up at the day's end, then I leave him and rush out the door to get to my classes. I go down 19th street to Holloway Ave, pull into the campus, and locate where my first class is held.

*

When I head back to pick up Lamont at the end of the day, a group of four of the school Jocks seems to be following Lamont as he heads over to me in the parking lot. One of them I recognize is some guy who had approached me to go on a date with him. I had declined. He was in a state of shock. I am sure I hurt his male ego. They block our way and surround us as we walk toward my bike. A crowd begins to gather like people who cannot help but watch a train wreck.

Jock No. 1" "Hey Basha, what are you hanging out with the young kid? Now that you decided to leave behind the girls, you should try a real man." The football jock that I recognized, blonde and muscle-bound, said with a swagger.

Basha: "Look, boys," I say, eyeing them all, "I am not interested. So, bugger off. We are leaving."

Jock No. 2: "We just think you need to know what a real man is like."

Jock No. 3: "Tell the child to take a hike."

Lamont: "The lady said she is not interested, so take the hint, leave her and us alone."

Jock No. 1: "Or what little one? Are you going to throw a fit or something?"

They all laugh at the joke.

Lamont: "I really hate bullies."

Basha: "You do not want to mess with us."

Jock No. 1: "Let's get rid of the kid and grab her."

Jock No. 2: "Yeah."

One lunges at me, and I quickly grab his arm, pull him in, and use his momentum to toss him to the ground. Those self-defense classes I took all those years from the JCC paid off.

Out of the corner of my eye, I spot Lamont, and something is going on. As they approach him, it is as if he is the center of the growing darkness that envelopes them. Suddenly it is not him but someone else. I am reminded of an image from my nightmares.

A figure of darkness towers over them, with his black double-breasted RAF coat, upturned collar, crimson tie, and black slouch hat. His face is enshrouding in darkness and blood red. Deep hushed ominous laughter

whispers all around us. A chill of horror shudders through me. I realize that this is Lamont becoming the one I call the Night! Oh, my Goddess—that thing is making itself present in the Waking World!

The Night: **"I know the evil in your hearts. You cannot hide from me. Feel the pain and fear you wish to inflict on others."**

His eyes glow icy blue, his skin takes on that marble deathly white, and I can see his incisors elongate into fangs. He has a wild, almost primal animal look on his face as his black fire forms around his hands; he looks like he will either lunge and attack them or hurl something at them.

Holy Robert Louis Stevenson[26]! My sweet kind Lamont has been consumed by this angry and vengeful Night that stands before me. I fear he will do something terrible to them if I let him. I have seen that thing rip people to shreds! The boys just stand there in shock and fear, not knowing what is happening.

Basha: "Night! NO!"

The beast that is now Lamont turns to face me in surprise and anger that I got in the way of his attack. I create a flaming barrier to protect those boys.

He looks at me with such out-of-control anger baring his fangs at me.

"Stand aside! I know the evil that lurks here!"

He shoots shadowy black daggers at me in his rage! I have to act quickly to burn them away with my flames.

Basha: "You cannot do this, Night! Stop! Please, Night, leave and become my dear heart once more. Come back to me."

"No! This evil must be put down!"

I blast this monster with my flames. It roars in anger. It turns and, at first, seems ready to pounce on me. I continue my own flaming attack.

"Why are you stopping me? I must end their evil reign!'

Basha: "No! I will not let you. They are just children. Wicked though they may be, they are only children. They are just bullies. Stop this, Night! Do not harm them!"

"There is malicious evil in their hearts. It will only fester and grow if you let it. They must be stopped before real harm is done by them. You must not protect them. If you do, I will have to take you down as well as them!"

Basha: "I will not let you rip them apart! You must stand down! I will not permit this!"

"They are bullies; if nothing is done, they will just grow up to be worse. I must stop them. Let me pass!"

I send forth another blast of flames at him. It chokes back its chilling mad laughter when that happens. I can see the fiery anger in his icy blue eyes fading as his skin tone returns to normal, the black flames and his fangs recede.

Lamont is acting like he just woke up from a dream. He looks at those boys, and they are all in a daze. They huddle on the ground shaking with dread. Lamont gently reaches out and touches each of them quickly. It is as if he punched them because their reaction to his touch is to buckle over and

---

[26] The author of *The Strange Case of Dr. Jekyll and Mr. Hyde*, 1886.

begin to whimper. Lamont leans into each of them, and for a moment, he is lost in darkness as he whispers in their ear with that ominous voice, "Let this be a lesson. Your bullying days are over. I will be watching and always remember, the Night knows."

Then Lamont faces the crowd in his Knight persona and waves his hand to point at all the onlookers. In that instant, they are all enveloped in dark shadows. "Forget me," his deep, ominous voice commands and then turns to laughter.

Lamont's laugh is scary but not tinged with the madness that the nightmare beast projects.

Everyone just stares at us, puzzled. Then the darkness fades, and simple Lamont is back at my side. The hat is gone, his RAF coat is back to charcoal gray, and the collar is back down. The only evidence of what happened is the four jocks huddled on the ground, eyes closed and whimpering.

Basha: 'Lamont,' do you know what just happened? Will that mass hypnosis work?'

Lamont: 'Yes, it will.'

Basha: 'Lamont, take us out of the River of Time. We need to talk!'

Lamont: 'Okay. Done, we are outside of the flow of time. Hey, you don't need to be so upset. I just hypnotize them, that's all.'

Basha: 'That is all! You became a thing. A monster! You were about to slaughter those kids.'

Lamont: 'What are you talking about? I just leaned in and made them feel a little bit of the pain they caused others, that's all."

Basha: 'Hell no! You became a bloodthirsty monster back there! It was all I could do to stop you!'

Lamont: 'I don't know what you're talking about, Basha? Are you going nuts? Nothing like that happened.'

Basha: 'I had to blast you with my fire to get you to stop.'

Lamont: 'What? Now, what are you talking about? I would have remembered if you attacked me. And why would you do that? What is wrong with you? Are you sick or something?'

Basha: 'Lamont, you became the thing you feared for a moment. The vampire monster possessed you. It was terrible. You might have done something horrible if I was not here to stop you.'

Lamont: 'Nothing like that happened. All I did was make them feel the pain they caused in others. That wasn't acting like any monster. What is wrong with you? I couldn't do something like that. Please tell me you're just teasing me.'

Either Lamont blacked out the whole incident of turning into Mr. Hyde/Night-thing, or he is lying. I am not sure which. But we are not getting anywhere on this. Just going in circles.

Basha: 'Okay, Lamont, I guess it is all good. Yes, I just made it up to mess with you. Sorry about that.' I need to watch him. He has the potential to go all Hyde/Night monster if he gets angry.

Lamont: 'Basha, what I did to them, make them feel the pain. It was instinctive. Those bullies made me so angry. I just lost it. I'm sorry.'

Basha: 'This is all so new to both of us. Presumably, it will get better as time goes on. I do not think using your powers is how to handle that situation. These dream powers are not some kind of all-purpose fix-it tool like a Swiss Army knife for you to pull out when the going gets tough. I think you need to learn how to take care of yourself more normally.'

Lamont: 'Hmm…you mean like flight or fight like the average Joe? But, I am not an average Joe, not anymore.'

'No, not average, but still human, and you need to be reminded of that humanity. So, I am thinking, yes, you need to find a way to deal with your anger and your need to feed. You must not let blood lust have an opportunity to take over your normal decency.'

'I guess I need to take up boxing lessons or something. You want me to deal with this anger in an ordinary way.'

'Some form of self-defense, martial arts training, yes. Or do the meek and mild Clark Kent thing and just take the bruises.'

'Hmmm…I just don't like bullies.'

'I can see that. But that is no reason to let yourself go all dark on them.'

'It is just that I've been that afraid young kid growing up, and now, I don't want to run away anymore; it just doesn't feel right. I want to stand up to that kind of behavior. But I get it. I have to be careful. So, no big bad, but taking care of it as Lamont. Something else to add to my burgeoning to-do list.'

Basha: 'You are certain they will all forget what happened?'

Lamont: 'Yes. As they say on the old-time radio program, I, like the Shadow, have the power to cloud men's minds. But, what you said about Clark Kent, you're right. We do need secret identities. When I become The Night, I take on a different form, and you were right to address me by that name and not call me Lamont.'

When he becomes that vampire monster, he does become a vengeful demon of the night.

Lamont: 'Hey, Basha, that goes for you as well; you need a new name when you go all flaming superhero. Actually, we need this here in Waking World and Dreamland.'

Basha: 'You are kidding, right?'

Lamont: 'Not really. We need to keep our powers hidden and a secret, and if we go off and challenge Kaliya and his cronies, we can't be doing that as Lamont and Basha; we need to do that as someone else. I as the Night and you costumed and masked and taking on some other name.'

'We took on Tezcatlipoca without any of that; what makes this situation any different?'

Lamont: 'Yes, Tezcat knew who we were, and as for all those volunteers from the covens who helped in the Gate spell, they were all bound by the seal of the coven, so they kept our identities a secret. Now we are up against strangers who will oppose what we do. They will try to stop us and may want to harm us when we succeed.'

Basha: 'I guess you are right. We will be upsetting the wrong kind of people. People who I never thought were actually here in Dreamland. It all felt so safe growing up here. But you showed me the underside of this place. We cannot have them trace us back to who we are. Okay. I could disguise myself by making a fire elemental appearance so that my body is solid flames. That way, my face will be hidden, and besides, I will truly end up with flaming red hair. Will that do?'

Lamont: 'Yes, sounds perfect. You will need a name to disguise your true identity. I'm the Night, and since you light up my life and your all fire and light, how about The Dawn Fire?'

Basha: 'No 'the' and not Dawn Fire either, too corny for me. How about just Dawn? Will that work?'

Lamont: 'Works for me. Now, shall we go see Peter?' Lamont asks, pointing to my bike.

Basha: 'Yeah. Sounds like a plan. Take us back into the normal flow of time, and then let us blow this pop stand.'

*

When we get to SF General and into Peter's room. We see that he seems to still be in deep REM sleep. We ask the nurse about his condition, but she replies that only the family could have access to that information.

That is when Lamont's icy blue eyes start to glow the light then seems to reflect off his marble skin, and the darkness seems to form all around us.

Lamont: "We are family," the Knight commands the nurses and the Doctor at the station. "Mark that in the record. Now please keep us informed of Peter's condition. Also, we will be coming by to spend time just sitting with Peter. Do not be concerned with us, no matter how long we remain there. You may monitor us for any signs of severe trouble. Otherwise, just let us be."

Lamont is way too quickly using those Night vampire powers of his. I will have to watch him like a hawk and be his conscience. Though I can see how useful that can be and thus such a continuing temptation.

We are told they do not understand his condition, but it has not changed. It still is similar to a coma, and yet he is clearly in REM sleep and cannot be made to awaken or react to anything. I find out that his blood tests are odd. They say he has some kind of skin cancer, Kaposi's sarcoma. But that is usually found in someone older with Mediterranean or Jewish background. It does not make sense that a black kid in San Francisco has this disease. Besides, typically this form is a skin cancer that is not supposed to pose any real danger, yet the doctors seem very concerned with his condition. They think somehow he got it through a gay sexual act. I sure hope he will be okay.

Basha: "Lamont, this cancer thing that the doctors say Peter has. It must have come from all that unnatural sex that he indulged in. His wicked ways finally caught up with him, I guess."

Lamont: "Basha, that is a terrible thing to say."

"Come on. It is true. What Peter has is not normal and what he does is not normal either."

"Hey, sex is perfectly normal."

"Not that kind of sex. What he does is not natural and disgusting."

"Basha, your homophobia is showing."

"What are you talking about? Do you think guys having sex with other guys is normal?"

"It can be."

"Is that what you want to do?"

"Ahh...no. But just because I don't want to do it doesn't make it unnatural. It's just not in my nature."

"Well, the Torah calls it..."

"Yes, I know what the Torah says about homosexuality. But hey, I'm not like your average Yeshiva boy. I'm a blood drinker. That has to be as far away from kosher behavior as you can get. I'm sure no rabbi has written up the proper rules for offering your blood to a vampire."

"Okay, you got me there, Lamont. Blood is treyf. What we are doing is not sanctioned by any rabbinic authority. Your point is well taken. But I cannot stop, and you would not want me to. We are stuck in this mess. I am sorry, but I had to have you back. I...just could not go on without you."

"Well, I'm grateful that you did. But we have to admit that what we are doing is…to use your phrase—unnatural. So, let's just drop this whole commenting activity that the rabbis would not consider kosher, okay? However, he got it; the bottom line is that he is my friend and seems to be dying. Show some empathy for a fellow human being here. Okay?"

"Well, yeah, it is terrible that he is dying. I do not wish that on him or anyone. You are right, and I am sorry, very sorry. My biased upbringing just leaked out. Sometimes I cannot help it."

"Let's just focus on trying to help him, okay?"

"Yes."

We go into the room and to his bedside, saying hello but otherwise ignoring the other patient in the room.

We both reach out to touch Peter. I feel nothing unusual.

Basha: "Well, Lamont, can you sense anything?"

I watch Lamont as he keeps his hand on Peter's forehead and as he stands entranced and silent. I wait. Then Lamont becomes the Knight, and the room seeps into darkness. The air around Peter begins to shimmer. Slowly he and his bed seem to be encased in a glowing, milky white gelatinous mass. The mass appears connected to and pouring out of Peter's forehead.

Basha: "What in Eve's holy womb is this all about?"

Lamont: "The thing from the other side," The Knight's ominous voice speaks. "His body is here, but his mind and soul are not. They have been taken through some sort of gate to another realm. We must get him and all the others back."

Then the darkness subsides, and Lamont is back. He opens his bright blue eyes.

Basha: "This is sort of good news. How can we get him to awaken and return to his body here in the Waking World? Do we need magick?"

Lamont: "No. When I touched him, I think I felt a gate of some sort. I think we can just step into that mass, and that is the gate to wherever he, and hopefully everyone else is."

Basha: "Okay, then we should just go through and see where down the rabbit hole this takes us?"

Lamont: "Hmmm…yes and no. I think this will take a while. We need to come back as early as possible and do this. That gives us the maximum amount of Dream Time to accomplish this. Hopefully, one day will be enough to locate them and bring them back. So, tomorrow we should come here first thing in the morning."

Basha: "That sounds like a plan. We should inform my mom what we are about to do so she knows what is going on, and we need to give her a cover story if it takes more than one day."

"Agreed. There is nothing more we can do and learn here so we can depart. I want to check in with Sarah and Rebecca before tackling Kaliya."

"I want to check in with Zuki and Queen Lilith. We do this all tonight and then meet at my place around nine-thirty to report back and begin our rescue?"

"Yes."

"Well then, let us head back home. I need to eat dinner, and you probably have homework?"

Lamont: "I guess. Let's not talk about it now. I would rather get all my nourishment from my sweet cinnamon and red-haired love of my life." He says as he reaches out to take me in his embrace.

Basha: "Not now. Let us go back to my place, smooch, and then you better get home and get cracking on your homework. Have you caught up yet?"

Lamont: "Almost. Okay. I will control myself till we get to your place."

*

LAMONT

After helping to clean up dinner, I head down the hall to my room. I then do as much schoolwork as I can handle tonight and feel that I deserve a good night's sleep. I dissolve my Dream bathrobe and underwear, slip under the covers, turn off the light, and drift off to sleep and Dream.

I soar above Atlantis in the crisp azure sky on raven's wings. From the air, this part of the city looking down on the crowded buildings resembles piles of autumn leaves. I locate the outer rim of the eastern district, where the streets are flanked by maple trees dressed in their autumn royal splendor.

They are so lovely but now so deadly to me. I need to remember that and not land on a branch even in my raven form. No matter its form or shape, I will now be vulnerable to wood.

I catch the fragrant scent of burning leaves. As I descend, I transform into my human shape, wearing a white button-down shirt, scarlet tie, black 501's, Chuck Taylor high tops, and charcoal RAF coat, which fails to impress a couple of visiting cats grooming themselves. I step up to the front door and knock. Sarah responds to my knock.

Sarah: "Whoever it is, I'm in the back; if you wish to talk, come around to the back."

I walk around the house to come upon Sarah tending her vegetable garden. I notice the pungent scent from the tomato plants and the refreshing scent of mint from turquoise leaves. The tomatoes range from lavender to deep purple, with an abundance of tiny pearl tomatoes as well. She has orange zucchinis, scarlet peas, zebra-striped carrots, iridescent pumpkins, and squash. I also notice the shadow I cast; it is not what I expect. The shadow on the ground shows I'm wearing the wide-brimmed slouched hat, my collar is up, and my coat is floating around me as if blown by a wind, although there is no wind. Hmm. The shadow I cast is more like my Night form than my ordinary form, which is how I am currently garbed. Interesting side effect. My shadow is my inner Night revealing itself.

Lamont: "Good afternoon, Sarah." I see her kneeled over on a mat, attending to her colorful garden, in a long teal frocked Victorian dress, hemmed with white lace at her neck, sleeves, and along the bottom, wearing sensible tan leather flat-heeled laced-up boots.

Sarah: "Like the new coat. Very dapper. It's about time you showed up. You're overdue. I expected to hear from you sooner."

Lamont: "Sorry about that; I was indisposed and couldn't make house calls for some time."

"Still flippant after everything that happened. Will you ever change? Oh well. I've wanted to ask you..."

"Could I just ask a quick question of my own first, totally irrelevant, I suspect, to the topic you're dying to launch into?"

"Oh, alright. What burning question do you have?"

"Your vegetables are beautiful, and I bet they taste incredible. They are not what you would find in the Waking World, but why have you invested your time and energy to dream them? I don't understand."

"We all come here to do what we cannot do in the Waking World. I don't have access to the land in the Waking World where I live. I loved gardening. When I was a child spending time with my grandmother, we did gardening together. So, here I get to relive one of my fondest childhood memories. This is literally getting to live out a long-sought-after dream of mine."

Lamont: "Makes sense. I totally get it. Thanks for explaining that to me. One more question? Please?"

Sarah: "Oh, all right, ask away."

"How did you and Rebecca meet? You are so clearly in love. You were the first loving couple I've ever had the honor to meet, other than my parents. And now that me and Basha..." I leave that unsaid, and I can see by her smile that she knows. "So, I was wondering. How did you meet, and how did you know she was the one? Did you meet in the Waking World?"

She sets down her gardening tool and looks in my direction with a wistful gaze, staring off beyond me to another time and place as she slowly begins to answer my question.

Sarah: "We did not meet over there. She lives in Alaska, and I'm in Arizona. We met here. Hmm, it's been almost thirty years. Now, how did I know? Hmmm. I could see it in her eyes. In the way, her hand felt in mine. She made no demands. She had no needs. She just wished to be truly with me. The first whoever did. So, we fled into each other. Fled away from children, grandchildren, husband, and parents. All who wanted a piece of us. All with their endless wanting. She just wanted to share and be. She was the love I had dreamed of all my life. I was just lucky enough to find her. Does that answer your questions? Humph, "she says as she takes up the tool to go back to attending to her garden. "I wonder if this is what confession feels like?"

Lamont: "Did you know it from the moment you saw her?"

She looks at me with a smile as bright and clear as sunlight dappling on dewdrops after a summer rain. "Yes," she says in a reverential whisper as if making an offering.

"Thank you. I really appreciate this. Now, what were you going to say before I interrupted and sidetracked you?"

"Well..." She says like a schoolteacher telling me that I need to stay after class. "Did you have any idea what you were doing when you gathered us all together to open that gate?"

"Sort of."

"That's the exact answer I expected from you. You didn't know what you were getting yourself, and all of us, into? You simply thought it would all work itself out? Or that you'd figure it out as you went along. Typical," she says sharply as she snips an offending weed vigorously. "Did you consider what risks might be involved?"

Lamont: "I had some idea. I just didn't think it would endanger anyone other than myself."

Sarah: "It would have been appreciated if you had elaborated on them before you called for volunteers."

Lamont: "Didn't Basha fill you in when she spoke to you?"

"No. She made vague references to dangers. All the while rhapsodizing on heroic virtues and bravely facing adversity. Adversity is one thing, but what happened there is more like a nightmare."

"Aren't you getting a little hysterical about all this?"

"Really? Don't you call four people who vanished and missing at the very least, possibly dead, a good reason for worry? If not, a good reason for outright hysterics? Which doesn't even consider the number of cats who died."

Lamont: "You're jumping to conclusions. We don't know what happened to them."

Sarah: "That is precisely my point. We have no clear notion of what happened to them. And it is your fault. You and your foolish heroics. I expected better from Basha. But one can be easily blinded by a pretty face and infatuation. She should have known better. She is an experienced dreamer and a mature woman. Or so I thought. Letting your emotions get the better of your judgment is something I would have expected of you. But not her. I knew that the object of the spell was to open that gateway. I know enough from my study of the Craft that you shouldn't get involved with such things. It borders on the Black Arts. I should have listened to myself. Instead, I let myself get fooled by your silly sweetness and innocence. I was as bewitched as she was," emphasizing that last remark with a shaking of her garden shears.

Lamont: "Maybe I should come with a warning label? Or is there a place to post public notices advising people of the dangers of involving themselves in my affairs?"

Sarah: "I may have to institute such a thing if I could only decide where to post it. Perhaps in multiple locations, the city square in Atlantis, then at the Queen's library. Where else I wonder…"

"What?"

"Ha! You are not the only one who jests. Now, do you have any idea what those translucent things that attacked us were? Or where they came from?"

"I have a hypothesis."

"Wonderful! What is your hypothesis?"

"I think they come from a dimension between the Waking World and Dreamland. What they are, I'm not certain. The opening should not have enabled them to have access to our dimensions. That ancient grimoire did not describe fully what was involved in that spell."

Sarah: "That sounds great. But it doesn't tell me much that I haven't already guessed. I was hoping you had more. But I shouldn't be surprised that you didn't fully check things out first."

Lamont: "I know. I feel responsible. It is up to Basha and me to find our friends and do whatever I can to bring them back."

"Noble thoughts. But that, unfortunately, is the same sort of thinking that got all of us into this disaster. I'm not sure that doing anything is the best response. That is precisely what happened to cause all of this. Maybe you should finally consider that some things weren't meant to be done."

Lamont: "No. I disagree. I can't just witness a tragedy, especially one I helped cause, and do nothing. I must do something."

Sarah: "But where did that get us? Maybe we would have all been better off if you never met Lana. Or, at the very least, you never should have tried to reunite her and her boyfriend."

"How can you say that?"

"Look at what has happened, Lamont! It wasn't like you simply had to hop on a bus and bring Jon back to her. What you had done violated the cosmic order! It was so reckless."

Lamont: "So, you're saying what I did was wrong?"

It was so bloody damn wrong! I got myself killed…dead and brought back from the dead to be this blood-sucking thing I am now. What is Tezcat's plan for me? She brought me back from the dead for what reason? Did I defeat her plans, or did I just get manipulated into serving her final plan for me? God, I want to tell her about what happened, but how can I? I can't bring myself to do that.

I'm so afraid of what she'll think of me now. I really made a mess of all of this. She would shun me and want nothing to do with me. I can't have that. I need friends and support now more than ever. Should I have just walked away from Lana and not done any of this?

Sarah: "Well…It was a noble gesture. But, looking back on the results—what came at us, what we did was wrong. Allowing a Dreamer to go through the Gate of Dreams back into the Waking World was dangerous and terribly wrong. We brought together something that was never meant to be together. You eliminated the separation between the worlds. That is what was wrong."

Lamont: "But Lana was in such anguish it would have been cruel to have not done something." I have to keep telling myself this. That I did it for a good reason. That it was all worth it in the end.

Sarah: "Then you should have found some other way to help them. Taught Lana how to Dream her way into Dreamland. That way, they could be together. Better that than endangering everything else. You could have tried to find out if the writings of that 1920 horror author…oh, what was his name? You know, the one with those unpronounceable names. All that Ka-thul-hoo stuff."

Lamont: "I believe it is pronounced Kuh-THUL-loo, emphasizing the second syllable. The author you're referring to is Howard Philip Lovecraft."

Sarah: "Right. So, the point was, didn't Lovecraft mention that there might be paths between the two realms. Ways of going from Waking World to Dream Land? There are rumors about those paths, which mention them as dangerous places. Still, that wouldn't threaten cosmic order. Given what occurred, one thing is indisputable, neither I, you, or Basha had thought this through. Or had been thinking clearly."

Lamont: "I think all of us, especially myself, were just caught up in the moment, in the process. When we found the spell to open the Gates between the worlds, we got caught up in the technical aspects of how to do it. Maslow supposedly referred to the same type of trap when he evaluated the work of strict behaviorism. Maslow said, '*If the only tool you have is a hammer, you tend to treat everything as if it were a nail.*[27]' We were so trapped by the fixation."

Sarah: "Lamont, you're rambling. Presumably out of guilt. But you're not the only guilty one. I agreed to help you both in this mad scheme of yours. I should have done better as well and tried to stop you. But I didn't. We were all fixated. Because of that, we all failed to consider whether this was the best solution. I've read of demons and deities coming through such gates. But I don't recall any instance of a human going through them. Maybe, humans were not meant to pass through such gates."

Lamont: "That logic is faulty. It's a variation of 'if humans were meant to fly, why weren't we born with wings'. We weren't born with wings, but we were born with a mind that could conceive of a way to fly without them. We had the ability to open gates so we could use them. We tried to take precautions, but they weren't enough. We couldn't prevent others from using the gate while we were using it."

Sarah: "Ahh, but it is not the natural means for us to fly. Perhaps we really were not meant to travel through such gates in this case. As for the other point, look at the consequences of unnatural flight of airplanes. Air and noise pollution, using fuel in the manufacture results in pollution."

Lamont: "That doesn't mean we were not meant to fly. All that goes to show is that we need to take care in how we act."

Sarah: "Yes, there are unintended consequences."

"And if perhaps we were wiser, we could anticipate. As it is, we just need to mitigate the harm once we are aware of it."

"What if there are no ways to completely mitigate the harm. What if the very tools we use to fix the harm lead to more unintended harm? Perhaps that is the Goddess's way of telling us not to tamper in things beyond our ken."

---

[27] Robert E. Ornstein, The Psychology of Consciousness, pg. 23, Pelican Book, (1972).

Lamont: "Right. So it's best to go back to the Stone Age, to those good old days of dirt and disease, since our technological tools create harmful side effects."

Sarah: "Now, who is exaggerating things out of proportion?"

"Am I? I am only taking your idea to their logical conclusion."

"But that logic is just artificial-a product of debate and discussion. To be fair and realistic, the extremes of any technology or none are not the only real-world choice. Like everything else, this isn't a matter of either-or, black or white. We aren't faced with only two choices."

"I know. I know. I call it the Aristotelian dichotomy of either or. It is a false one when applied to the real world. There is a continuum of choices, with two extreme positions at either end. Those extremes are either not possible in the real world or inappropriate. So, what were the extreme choices in Lana and Jon's situation?"

Sarah: "Perhaps they were between doing nothing and doing what you did by opening the gate."

Lamont: "You are implying that our choice of using the gate spell was extreme and thus, according to my analysis, inappropriate. Is that it?"

"Perhaps. The results of that choice seem to point in that direction."

"Perhaps you're right. However, we made that choice, fixation, coercion, or tool trapped whatever reason was; it is what we did. Now it is up to us to accept responsibility for our actions and deal with the consequences. We need to find a way to help those who disappeared. Those who were taken by those blobs that came through the gate. We need to set right what we had a hand in doing wrong."

"There you go again, meddling with things. Maybe you should leave things alone."

"How could I? These are people who were harmed. We're not talking about a pile of stones knocked over."

"Yes, but the damage was done by taking action. Perhaps now is the time to consider what is called 'non-action'. All our troubles may have been caused by your taking action in the first place. By upsetting the cosmic order. By upsetting the Tao."

Lamont: "What do you mean by the term non-action? And what is the Tao?"

Sarah: "Hold that thought. Let me go inside and get a book." She returns with a handmade book bound with cording.

Lamont: "Now, you'll tell me that Lao Tzu himself gave you that copy?"

"Don't be silly, Lamont. Not every famous person came here. This is merely an English translation. Though there is a legend that Lao Tzu himself hand wrote and left it in the Queen's Temple library thousands of years ago. Though like all good legends, they exist without confirmation. I don't know anyone who's ever seen it. Now shush. Let me explain. The Tao is Lao Tzu's term for the infinite Divine. For the principle of cosmos. The cosmic flow and the natural way. The main text of Taoism is the *Tao Te Ching,* written by Lao Tzu. Non-action in Chinese is wu-wei. Consider this from the *Tao Te Ching,"* She leafs through the text to find the page she wants and then reads aloud, "Listen to this. '*He who takes action fails. He who grasps things loses them. For this reason the sage takes no action and therefore does not fail. He grasps nothing and therefore he does not lose anything. People in their handling of affairs often fail when they are about to succeed.*[28]' You are meddling with the Tao. The sage sometimes does not take any action. Other times the sage does not take direct action. Action that is aggressive and goes against the flow. The sage takes non-action. An action that goes with the flow and rhythm of the cosmos' way. Direct action will fail. But non-action will not disrupt or destroy what is acted upon."

Lamont: "This wu-wei is not taking action and not taking aggressive action?"

Sarah: "Yes. Aggressive action is yang action. Whereas non-aggressive action is yin action. Yang tends to be the way of the stone. It involves lots of bashing and smashing. While yin is the way of water. Flowing over, under, around, or slowly wearing away the rock over time. Your opening of the gate was yang action."

"So, Wu Wei is both yin and correct?"

"Wu Wei is realizing the subtle and the slow. As in '*Ruling a big country is like cooking a small fish.*[29]' Too much forceful action, too much stirring, turns the small fish into a mess. The proper application of action is what is needed. '*A good general achieves his purpose and stops. But dares not seek to dominate the world. He achieves his purpose but only as an unavoidable step. He achieves his purpose but does not aim to dominate.*[30] Lao Tzu knew that there were times when action was needed. Lao Tzu was admonishing against aggressive, violent, coercive yang force. Cook the fish to feed the people. But do so in a way that does not destroy the fish in the process. Lao Tzu instructed taking action carefully. To act by following the way of nature, the Tao. '*Cautious, like crossing a frozen stream in the winter. Being at a loss, like one fearing danger on*

---

[28] *Tao Te Ching,* translated by Wing-Tsit Chan, Bobbs-Merrill Co. Inc., 1963, Chapter 64, p. 214.

[29] Supra, Chapter 60 p. 207.

[30] Supra Chapter 30, p 152

all sides. Reserved like one visiting, supple and pliant, like ice about to melt.[31]' This does not describe how you do things. When were you careful, Lamont?"

Lamont: "Well…I admit I am a bit too hasty at times." How about stupid and reckless? Like some addictive Don Quixote who can't leave well enough alone? "Okay…I get your point. I need to learn to be less foolhardy. Perhaps I need to learn from this Lao Tzu guy. Maybe it will help. I have some studying to do. There is nothing better than that. Which translation were you quoting?"

Sarah: "Wing-Tsit Chan's."

Lamont: "And did he make that copy of the translation you hold?"

Sarah: "No, it was made by some other Dreamer. Not every person who was important and wise makes their way to Dreamland."

Lamont: "Well, I'll go and study the *Tao Te Ching*. I'll try and discover a way to help without doing harm. I'm sorry for the mess I created," more than I can ever tell her. "But I'm grateful for you and your coven's help. I believe two of your coven went missing during the gate ritual, correct?"

"Yes."

"Do you by any chance know their Waking World names and locations?"

"I just know their first names, which were Annabel and Laura. That's all I have.

"Oh well. I should get going. I feel it is getting late. Thanks for your advice and the book!"

"Before you go, would you like some fresh sweet peas?"

"Sure, could you put them in a small bag?" At least I can give them to Basha to eat.

"Okay."

She gathers some up, goes inside, and puts them into a bag for me. I'm curious, so I take the smallest pod and open it up. It bleeds red fluid. Inside is a small cluster of red beads rather than the usual solid little peas. I cut into one pea with my fingernail, and it bursts into a smear of red liquid. I lick up the nectar, and it has a hint of strawberries mixed in with the natural sweetness of sweet peas.

I carry the bag in my raven's claw and leave it at Zuki's for Basha. I return to the Waking World, open the window, change into a raven, and fly toward Basha's place.

*

BASHA

[31] Supra Chapter 15, p 126

I hear a tapping at my window and see a raven hovering as he keeps tapping away. Presumably, that is Lamont. I get a floor rug so Lamont can land on that when he drops in. I slide open the window and step back, allowing Lamont to fly in, and he spots the rug and then transforms into his human shape, decked out in his black RAF coat, red tie, and slouched hat.

I guess I should change out of this pale red tank top and black cotton leggings into something more super-heroic. Should we really be doing this? Yet, who else can do this? We have gotten this power and as Lamont said when he quoted Stan Lee, with great power comes great responsibility. I guess this is why we were given this power. This is our part of Tikkun Olam. Our way to make things right for others. We have to do this. So accept it, Basha, and just gird those loins. So, with a snap, I don my superhero outfit. I am now clothed in my tight red catsuit with the golden belt, sunburst belt buckle, and red cowgirl boots.

Lamont: 'Hello, love,' Lamont says as he takes on his human form. 'I brought some fresh peas from Sarah's garden for you and left them at Zuki's. They are delicious and very cool!'

Basha: 'I will give them a try, but later. Now that I have agreed that we need to do this, we need to help those who are helpless. You are right about that. So, let us get this show on the road. Lamont, since I have never been to Thrall, you will need to lead the way. Where is the closest location that I might know?' I say as I project my thoughts toward him.

'Hmmm…I know. Have you ever been to the Enchanted Woods where the hummingbirds perform?'

'Yes. It is breathtaking. Something that does live up to its legendary hype.'

'Perfect. We can meet there and travel to Thrall.' Then in a burst of black smoky darkness, he is gone.

Basha: 'Lamont! Will you ever learn to be less impetuous?' I close my eyes and let myself fall onto my bed as I go into Dream sleep.

*

I see Lamont, all Shadow-like, waiting for me in the center of the clearing.

Basha: "Now, Knight, what is the plan before you fly off the handle again?"

Lamont: "We fly into the city and head over to the huge domed building that is Kaliya's lair. Down below are the cells where he keeps everyone imprisoned. If we are alone, I will do my hypnotic thing to get everyone un-enthralled while you stand guard. If Kaliya shows up, you can see if you have better luck keeping him occupied than I did. I will need all the time I can get to wake everyone up. I don't think I can just do it all at once. I think I need to give everyone individual attention."

Basha: "What if I cannot, as you say, keep him occupied?"

Lamont: "Then get my attention, and I'll join in. If we defeat him together, I can wake the remaining ones at my leisure."

Basha: "Describe what he looks like again to me in his human and non-human form."

Lamont does so, and I ask him to map out the floor plan of the place in the dirt. So, I know ahead of time where we will be going. I tell him we must only disable any guards we encounter, and if we meet any servants, we will need to ascertain if they are enthralled or not. If they are not, then they can leave under their own power. Lamont will also have to clear their minds if they are compelled to be there. Having gone over everything I can think of more than once, we are as ready as we ever will be.

Basha: "Perhaps we should fly there as eagle and raven to keep the element of surprise?" I suggest.

Lamont: "Good thinking. Let's do this."

We transform and take flight with raven-Lamont leading the way. My heart is beating fast as I am nervous about all this. Doing this superhero fighting when defending myself against Tezcat is one thing, but I am not used to deliberately going in like this. The last time I did something anywhere like this was going in to do the gate spell to get Jon out of Dreamland. I watch the Enchanted Woods, a thick green canopy pass by as we wing our way toward the city of Thrall, leaving the isle of Atlantis that contains the Six Kingdoms.

On the other side of the mainland, at the mouth of the Ourkranos River, where it meets the Southern Sea, we can see gleaming in the morning sun reflecting off the alabaster of Thrall's port city; beyond that is the mighty port city of Hlanith. Both port cities are below and nestled next to the perfumed rainforest jungle of Kled. It is a shame that this ancient city of Thrall, once known as Thran, was taken over and ruled by Kaliya.

The city of Thrall is an impressive sight. There are supposed to be a hundred gates topped with two hundred turrets in the walls surrounding this ancient city. This place had been crafted a thousand years ago when the first mayor and settlers came there. I have heard the story of this place but never before came to see it. The story goes that down through the years, the inhabitants undertook this Dreaming building project. They began to train their Dreaming skills to craft all these distinctive gates, each uniquely crafted by the city's living inhabitants, who became the new builders in those neighborhoods.

It took hundreds of Dreamers to combine their efforts to learn how to shape the stuff of Dreaming to fabricate the towers and turrets. The merchant inhabitants of the city, those non-Dreamers, also got into it. They used the Dream magick from all the Dreamers who passed visited the city. That Dream magick was stored in the merchant's gems as payment for some item. That allows non-Dreamers access to Dream magick, and thus they, the non-dreamer, those who live here in Dreamland, can make use of Dream magick.

With all that stored up Dream magick to be utilized, over the centuries, the inhabitants of the different sectors of the city competed with the others to craft and recraft those gates and the turret walls.

It takes exceptional Dream talent to accomplish this. To craft physical stuff or manipulate physical property to make and shape it. I cannot do it even with the power from the rings. It just is not where my talents lie. I am always impressed by those who can. Any craftsperson is a real artist.

Once they were all alabaster white with gilded gold turrets, over the centuries, differing materials and architectural and cultural time frames were brought to bear on the city's environment. They matched the time and culture of the natives who were brought into Dreamland from the Waking World. The city's overall structure was done so well that those who came after them kept it up as their inheritance to preserve. That's what happens—time brings changes even as the traditions frame the scope and context of the situation.

Standing at each gate are two robed red sentries. That tradition was the invention of the millennium's old first mayor and ruler of the city. We bypass all of this in our bird form as we head toward the domed center where the mayor, Kaliya, holds court. Now, with Kaliya – he christened the city in his decadent and corrupt vision – Thran became Thrall, and the central palace was his epicentral web of sin and decadence to lure and lure and hold onto his power overall. We hover in front of the strangely open circular doors of the palace and transform into our human form. Lamont in his Shadow-like outfit of the RAF coat and the hat, while I ignite so my Dream suit is all flame. Even my face is cloaked in fire, and my flowing locks of hair are flames.

Lamont: "Well, I must say, you look really hot!"

Basha: "Are we being literal or figurative, Knight?"

"Clearly both. You know how to light my fire, Dawn."

"Enough with the bad puns. Stop staring and start focusing on what we came there to do. Hey, the main door is ajar. What do you think this open door means, Knight?"

"Not sure. Let me go first; I can see in the dark and hide in the shadows."

I watch as Lamont fades from view and a mass of shadowy darkness floats inside.

Lamont: "Hey Dawn, come on in and bring some light; this place is as dark as the proverbial tomb. You're going to need it."

I create a small fireball and let it float in front of me as I make my way inside. The entranceway would have been entirely dark. It is silent, and I quickly gather, empty. I increase the size of my fireball to create enough illumination to let me see the whole huge room. It is filled with old worn-out couches, cushions, tables, and settees, all scattered about. Shadows cower beyond the area of illumination created by my light.

Basha: "It appears that Kaliya and his entourage have abandoned the palace. Let's head down to the holding cells and see if they took everyone. Let me do a quick recon of the place. Be right back."

I let myself become as insubstantial as pure flame, so I float. I travel through the place like a slow-moving comet. I pass by room after virtually empty room, a few old cabinets, storage bins, dressers, and desks; otherwise, the whole place is open and almost entirely bereft of contents. The building has been meticulously cleared out of anything valuable. Some old tapestries and worn, frayed, or stained rugs and pillows. Not even breadcrumbs were left behind in the kitchen and pantry. I did find a few hungry and disappointed mice and rats.

After checking a few more areas and finding them all dark and emptied of all but old and worn items, I head back to Lamont.

What were they doing with those beat-up and overly used items they left? It does not match the voluptuous and lavish display Lamont had described. Then it slowly dawns on me. Those old fabrics and items were well-used relics of the past. They were templates. They were used as templates, or canvases, for a dreamer to craft more luxurious versions onto and out of them. These items were dreamed of to replicate more of them. It is easier to adjust a physical item than to create it out of nothing. It is not something I can do, but many craft dreamers specialize in just this kind of skill.

These craft Dreamers can turn plain cotton to cashmere or silk, plain brown into various tapestries of vibrant colors. Or simply take an old canvas, dream it into something bright and new, replicate it into many of them, or enlarge it to fill a wall. They left behind the old and worn and took what was new and fresh.

Basha: "As we thought, they left and did the proverbial stripping of the place upon leaving—taking everything that was not nailed down."

Lamont: "Okay, then let's head down into the cells and see if they took them when they left this place."

Lamont leads me down into the dungeon area, and we find the cells still filled with only about a dozen enthralled prisoners.

Not as many as I thought would be here from Lamont's account of his last visit. Most of the cells are empty except for this group. They are all dreamers of varying ages, sexes, and races, and all of them wearing what should be suggestive and sexually provocative lingerie-like outfits. The really odd thing is that they are so ordinary-looking. There is no attempt to be glamourous. They are like a group you would find in the Waking World waiting for the bus to come by and take them somewhere, except for the weird fact that they are almost naked.

They are not embarrassed at being seen this way, but clearly, Lamont and I are. We avoid as best we can to stare at them, but I feel compelled to like they are all daring me to say something is wrong with this. They are so passive and immodestly costumed that I cannot help but feel that they have been staged and waiting for us to show up. The only thing in common is that they were all once innocents, at least I assume so. Presumably, they got caught up in the web of enticement that the mayor and his minions wove around them.

Basha: "Bastard," I mutter. "Okay, we are here to help you, rescue you, and get you home. So, it is all going to be alright. Just follow us upstairs, and we will get you all out of here."

Lamont shows me that the cell doors that hold these Dreamers as prisoners are not locked. With facile acts, we help them out of their cells. They just passively obey our request to leave their cells. I assume it is because they have been so psychologically beaten down. We gather everyone together; they seem dazed and compliant.

I feel terrible at seeing what happened to them. What an awful mess they have gotten themselves into. I imagine this is what complete addicts look like when they have hit the very bottom. They hide their faces; I assume they are so ashamed of themselves, which is why they cannot look us in the eyes. I cannot tell if they recognize us as other slavers or can see us as the rescuers that we are. I try to explain to them that we are here to help free them, but they do not seem to understand what I am saying. They cannot seem to take in the idea of anyone coming to rescue and help them. Then one of them, a young Asian High School girl, starts to giggle. I assume out of embarrassment and shock at our turning up.

Aki, Asian teen: "You just don't get it," she giggles. She is an Asian teenager with jet hair tied up in two ponytails with bright jade ribbons, wearing a matching bright pink satin bra and panties with bright pink pumps.

Overworked housewife: "No, they don't," a plump 50-something Caucasian lady, looking the part of an overworked housewife with short gray hair wearing a scarlet and black accented merry widow corset, red nylons, red platform high heels, a big grin, and her delicate diamond wedding ring, pipes in. "Just like the master told us."

College student: "The master said they would be clueless," says an over-weight scruffy blonde-haired college-age guy clad in nothing but a bright pink teddy and pink backless heels.

Elderly Black woman: "We all asked to be left behind, so you could find us," A large black elderly woman explains, wearing a white satin corset with white stockings and black stiletto heeled pumps.

Bald guy: "We don't want to be rescued, you, foolish children," a tall, slender balding guy wearing a black velvet bustier, matching thong emphasizing his beer belly, who stands comfortably on his black stiletto pumps. "We like serving the Master."

Elderly Black woman: "All our lives are dull and boring. We're trapped in that ordinary rat race back in the Waking World."

Aki, Asian teen: "Here, we get to live and enjoy something exciting and naughty."

Basha: "I do not understand? None of this makes any sense." I cannot believe what they are saying. "Are you saying you want to be slaves to that monster, the mayor of this city?"

Lamont: "You're all still under the spell of Kaliya. You need help to wake up. Trust us, we can help you."

Bald guy: "No, you kids are the ones who are deluded. The best thing that ever happened to us is when we found our way here."

College student: "When the Master was leaving. We asked to stay behind. To show you the truth. All who come to Thrall want to be here. Here we finally found some escape from the monotonous dullness of our Waking life."

Lamont: "That's a lie! I didn't want to be here! I was taken against my will. And so did Jon, the guy who I was searching for."

Elderly Black woman: "Honey, you and Jon were the exception to the rule. You were the only ones who came here not by choice."

Lamont: "That's a lie! I was here just the other night, and I helped rescue a group of young children brought here against their will! They told me that. They all were desperate for someone to come and help them escape from that evil Kaliya!"

Bald guy: "They were the ones who lied to you. What they told you is just not true."

Lamont: "Enough of this!" Lamont yells as his eyes turn icy blue and take on his vampire form.

THE NIGHT (& BASHA)

"I can find the truth that lurks in all your hearts!" Time stops as I reach out and place my hands on the black woman and the bald guy. What? This can't be!

Basha: (What cannot be, Night?)

What I am seeing. I can see them and this place through their minds; it is so utterly different.

Basha: (Can you show me?)

Yes, I think so. Just touch me, and I think I will be able to share their dreamscape with you.

Basha: (I step closer and touch Night's forehead. His skin is icy cold! Then the room shimmers all with navy-tinged darkness. I look around the room when that stops, speechless at the changes. What was once a dank and dismal collection of prison cells is no longer. Each cell is now more like door-less bed chambers decked out with inviting soft and colorful beds, clean porcelain bathtubs, shower stalls, a sink, and a toilet. The rooms are small but rather comfy looking. I do not understand what I am seeing? Is this really the same place?)

We are seeing this same chamber as they experience it in their Dreaming.

(But that cannot be. This place is a dungeon filled with prison cells.)

Lamont tells me that is how we experience it. But I can now share in their Dreaming. To them, this place is no prison. They were telling the truth. At least for them, they were not prisoners in some cell but had these rooms as we now can see them. Everyone who comes to Dreamland has their own unique experience of this realm.

(Are they being deceived by Kaliya? Is this all an illusion he created when he enthralled them and trapped them here?)

I can't tell. All I can say is that they have a different perspective on this place than Lamont, and you have of it.

(But when Lamont and Jon were here, they were both tortured. That is what he told me. Then there is Gwen, who he met yesterday. She said she was a prisoner as well. Which was true of all the other children Lamont rescued. What is going on? Who is delusional?)

I cannot say if they are under any enchantment. I have revealed what is in their minds and enabled you by touching me to see this as well.

(Okay, Night. Take us back to ordinary time, and let Lamont come back as well. We need to figure out what to do next.)

As you wish.

BASHA

I take my hand off of Night, and after the shimmering light show ends, everything is back to what we call normal. We are once again standing in a prison area beneath Kaliya's abandoned palace.

Basha: "Well, Lamont, what now?"

Lamont: "So, you're saying that you don't need rescuing?"

Elderly Black woman: "You're the ones who will need rescuing. If you persist in interfering with the Master's wishes.

College guy: "We've said our piece. Let's depart!"

Basha: "Wait! Please do not go..."

Aki, Asian teen: "Why should we?"

Basha: "We just want to understand what is going on."

Elderly Black woman: "Well, we are leaving!"

Then she blinks from view, as all the rest, except for the Asian teen.

Aki, Asian teen: "You two really just came to help us?"

Basha: "Yes. That is why we came. I am Dawn, and my partner there is Knight. What is your name?"

Aki: "I'm Aki. Was a friend of yours here? Maybe I can get word to her."

Lamont: "Not really. We just came here because we thought people were being kept against their will."

Basha: "Aki, how and why did you come here?"

Aki: "Well, to be perfectly honest, I came here out of boredom and to find some interesting friends."

Basha: "I do not understand? Can you explain?"

Aki: "Sure. Say, would you like some tea? We can sit in my room rather than stand out here."

Basha: "Okay, Aki, lead the way."

Aki leads us down the hall and invites us into an open cell which, to our eyes, holds only a chamber pot and straw on the floor. Then as she steps inside, it all begins to glimmer and change. The room has a futon couch with red, gold, and brown autumn striped fabric and a long cherry wood low table in the center with red, gold, and brown cushions. On the table is a bronze tea kettle sitting upon a raised platform, standing in a bronzed circular dish. Surrounding that are four pink glazed teacups. Aki fills the kettle with water from her sink and sets it back on the raised platform. She focuses and holds her hands above the bronze circular dish, and a fire begins to form.

Lamont: 'We are seeing the room as she Dreams it!'

Basha: 'How is that possible, Lamont?'

Lamont: 'Something to do with us having soaked up some of the powers from the Well of Dreams?'

Basha: 'That seems sort of a reasonable hypothesis.'

Aki Asian teen: "I hope you like Jasmine tea?" Aki is now dressed in a white kimono with autumn red maple leaves, a black satin obi, and wooden platform sandals. Her black hair is tightly done up and held in place with polished black wooden sticks capped with copper.

We say we do. Soon the water is boiled, and we watch as she gets tea from an ornately carved maple wood box on the cherry wood table.

We watch enchanted as she gracefully and silently prepares our tea. When it is all done, she sets the cups before each of us, settles down on one pillow, and raises her cup to us.

Aki: "To unexpected meetings."

"To unexpected meetings," we both respond as we sip the fragrant jasmine tea.

Basha: "Now, Aki, why in all of Dreamland did you end up here?"

Aki: "Well, since you are kind enough to be interested in me, I'll tell you. I just wanted something more in my life. My parents care for me, but they have always driven me to achieve, ever since I was little. Never really asking what I want. Just expecting me to be what they want – which is to achieve. Ballet, piano lessons, private tutor, enrolled in private catholic school. So much constant pressure to achieve.

Never have any free time to just be me or find out what I want. My only time for myself was in my dreams. I dreamed all the time of being naughty and free. Then one day, the Kami of this city answered my prayers, and I found my way here."

Basha: "But there is so much to explore and do here. Why did you end up here serving the Mayor of Thrall?"

Aki: "It was fate and my desires that led me to my first bar ever. I got to do something naughty. At first, they wouldn't serve me. But this nice man approached me and bought me my first drink ever! We got to talking. He was so friendly. He told me about where the best party ever is in all of this place. I said I begged him to take me there. I so wanted to be all grown up and naughty for once.

So, he brought me here. This place was so amazing! All these grown-ups doing such naughty things! They all said such nice things about me. When the considerate Mayor asked if I had a place to stay here. I told him I was new and didn't. He offered me a home and a job! I could come back anytime I wanted. So, I did, often! I couldn't wait to finish all my lessons, homework, and chores and was so over being just a good little girl just like my parents wanted. So, I got to come back to this place every night and party with all the grown-ups."

Basha: "How did they treat you?"

Aki: "They were all so very nice to me! They treated me like a big girl! The Master called me his princess. He got me pretty things to wear and taught me how to make dreams come true. It was so much fun!"

Basha: "Was it always fun? Did the Master always treat you well?"

Aki: "Of course. I see you have finished off your tea. Would you like me to pour some more?"

Aki reaches out to take Lamont's cup, and I see a smile on Lamont's face, reminding me of the proverbially a cat about to swallow a canary as Lamont reaches out and grabs her wrist.

Aki: "Hey! That is not nice!" Aki says as she tries to pull away from Lamont.

Basha: "Knight, why are you doing this?"

LAMONT

Lamont: "Dawn, look at Aki's wrist. See the marks!"

I pull back her kimono sleeve and grab her other arm to reveal something.

Aki: "Again! That is not nice!" Aki says as the marks fade from view and then completely disappear!

Aki: "I'm leaving! You just don't understand. I shouldn't have bothered talking to you!"

Then as Aki disappears, the room reverts to an ugly empty cell. Lamont: "These marks are familiar to me! I had the same ones when I was here being strung up and whipped by Kaliya! This is proof that he did mistreat her! You saw those marks, didn't you, Dawn?"

Basha: "I am sorry, Knight, I did not see anything on her wrists."

Lamont: "One moment, I could see them, and then the next, they were gone. Did I imagine them?"

Basha: "I want to say no, but what is real here in this land of projected dreams?"

Lamont: "But..."

"We see what we expect and want to see. Is that not right, Knight?"

"Well...yes. But they were there! They were really there. She just didn't want to admit the truth. That's all. They all just wanted to think they weren't prisoners."

"But how do you know that what you saw is real?"

"That Dawn is the 64-dollar question!"

"You could just have seen what you wanted to see."

"Yeah. And Aki was projecting her own dream experience to us. Here we only see what we wish to see. It is all our subconscious projections."

"So, we never see what is real here?"

"The only thing that is real is what we experience. That is literally true here. Only part of the truth in the Waking World. Hmm. In both places, what can be verified by someone besides one's own experience is the key to revealing what is real or not in both realms."

"So, Knight, did Aki have those marks or not? Were they real? I did not see the marks; how does that relate to this verification effort?"

"Hmm. I don't know. I feel they were enslaved and those chained up like me."

Basha: "You do realize that does not prove anything. You are biased against this place, so you would experience evidence to prove your bias. You saw what you wanted to see."

Lamont: "Are you saying I made that up?"

"Hey, I am only trying to be an objective observer here."

"But you are accusing me of seeing things! "

"Well, that is what this place is all about. We project our desires and wishes–both conscious and unconscious onto this place, and then we experience it according to those expectations."

"So, I guess you are saying I wanted to be captured and tortured? Is that it?"

"No. I was not saying that."

"Then what part of making things up are you accusing me of?"

"I believe you were captured and tortured last year, yes. I am only saying that I did not see her marks, which might be your projection of her."

Lamont: "You don't trust what I tell you?"

Basha: "No. We can never completely trust what we experience here; that is all. What happens is partly our projection onto the world. Experience is a cooperative effort. But, on your side of the ledger, trying to prove what is going on here, you said that Gwen and others wanted to be rescued. Hmmm, but some of them could have been drugged into compliance."

Lamont: "So, I forced them to be free, is that it?"

Basha: "Well…there is a vague possibility for someone them. I do not know. It is hard to know, given the nature of what happens to people here willing brought here or not. So, I am just taking on the role of HaSatan, like in Job, the source of the phrase – devil's advocate. We cannot tell what those people wanted."

"So, you think I made them leave against their will?"

"I do not know. I am sorry I should have kept my mouth shut. I just got carried away."

"Yes, you did."

"The point is, I know you have good intentions, and probably you did indeed help those people."

"Probably?"

"Well, even though we might not like this slave scene, they could be masochists. Thus, you were ruining their fun."

"You mean I forced them to leave and not come back when they didn't want that? Is that what you're accusing me of doing?"

Basha: "We are going in circles. The point is we do not know their true motivations, and neither may they. You had the right intentions. You do know that Kaliya abuses people here, so you acted out of good intentions."

Lamont: "But they asked me to help them."

"That is true. Those you helped wanted it. This means we need to find anyone who truly wants out of this place. The others would need a bit of therapy or something, which is not our line of work."

"But we have to do this no matter what they say."

"If they say they do not want to be freed, are you saying we should force them against their will? That does not seem right. If you did that, you would be like Kaliya, imposing your will on someone else."

"But we have to! That man is a monster, literally a monster. We have to stop him."

"I agree. But we cannot become the same kind of monster Kaliya is. We cannot force our will on anyone. So, if we have to accept that some people do not want to be rescued."

"But that's like saying we should just leave an abused wife to stay married to an abuser. We can't let that happen."

Basha: "I agree that we need to help those in abusive relationships like this, those who realize they are and do not need or want to remain that way. Then and only then can we help them."

Lamont: "Bloody Hell!"

Basha: "Think about it, and you know I am right."

"Yeah, I do. Bollocks! I guess you're right. I don't like it, but you're right. If we can't get them to accept help, we just have to let them stay."

"Yes. But for now, we cannot do anything more tonight. We are done here for now."

Lamont: "Well, I'm grateful I was able to help those others, but I have no idea where Kaliya and company headed off to."

Basha: "I do not think he will cease his activities. "I say with resignation and disgust.

"No. I think Kaliya will just set up shop elsewhere, somewhere in Dreamland. We'll have to track him down one day and perhaps end all this."

"But not today. I, for one, need a bath and a decent sleep."

"Yeah. You do that."

BASHA

I lean into Lamont, give him a quick kiss and try to hug him, but he backs away and begins to fade from view. "Night Knight."

I hope he is not mad at me. But he must know that I am right about this. Once he is gone, I close my eyes, try to think happy thoughts, and disappear.

*

In the fog of dreams, I hear something somewhere in the night. I hear my name called to me, calling me out of bed. I arise and feel myself walk out of my room. I am barefoot and wearing a long white flimsy nightgown. Everything is dark. I think my eyes are closed. I guess I am sleepwalking. It is late. Very late.

I walk quietly through the house. I float down the stairs and pass seamlessly through the door and into the alley. I approach a figure all in darkness who has been calling me…commanding me to come to him. I enter his embrace.

I feel pain. Sharp needles pierce my skin. He has bitten the flesh of my throat. It hurts and burns.

I feel weak…

I would collapse if not for being held so tight. I try to break free. I need to break free!

LAMONT

I'm in a dark alley somewhere. I smell blood, and I feel it in my mouth. I am holding a frantic form in my arms. I am frantically drinking down blood. I need to feed. I have such a burning need and desire. I just feed and feed. I feel this person struggling to break free.

She tries to break free of my dark embrace, and I hold her tight and refuse to let her go.

BASHA

I try to cry out, but I cannot. I struggle to free myself, but he is too strong. Stop! Stop! You are hurting me! Oh, dear Goddess, he is drinking my life's blood! NOOOOO!!!! I am dying! He is killing me……noooooo…

LAMONT

Finally, I realize that she goes limp as I drain her completely. I feel horrible but so much better. The hunger has left me. I'm happy and content. I look down and realize that the woman I was feeding on is, to my horror, dead! Dear God, what have I done!

I start to throw up all the blood that I ate and look down to see whom I had just killed.

Dear God! It's Basha! I...

*

I wake up in my bed drenched in sweat and fear.

Dear God. I was only dreaming.

It was all just a dream.

Just a dream…

I collapse onto my bed, curled up in a fetal position, holding on tight, saying over and over again, it was just a dream…it was just a dream…just a horrible dream...

Eventually, I fall back into cold and darkness as I collapse into the arms of a good night's sleep.

BASHA

I wake up in terror. My heart is pounding, and my body is cold and shivering, drenched in sweat. It was only a dream. A horrible dream. It felt so real…so terribly real...I feel so weak…so exhausted...I collapse back onto the bed, and darkness rises to greet and engulf me in the arms of sleep.

PART THREE

THE POWER OF BELIEFS

'Every human society is an enterprise of world building[32]*.'* Peter Berger

Saturday, September 6, 1980

BASHA

I feel a kiss upon my brow and open my eyes.

What? I shudder momentarily as fleeting darkness comes into my memory. I feel and hear Lamont's presence. I realize I am being attacked by Lamont! He is draining me dry. I need to…wait…it was a dream…I feel myself cringe away from Lamont.

Lamont: "Basha, what's wrong? Are you okay?"

It was just a terrible dream. I cannot tell Lamont this. I need to pretend I am all right. I cannot see Lamont; I sense his presence in the shadows. The waning crescent moon does not provide any light.

Basha: "What in Heaven's High Name are you doing here?"

"I…I couldn't sleep, so I got up, dressed, left a note with my folks that I would be working on a project with you, and flew over here."

"You cannot just show up! What if my mom saw you!"

"I was quiet and careful. I'm sorry…I just felt this need to see you. To see if you were alright."

"Are you turning into a stalker on top of being a vampire?"

"Ahh…sorry…I guess I am being a bit intrusive."

"Just a little. You just startled me. Bad dream."

"Really? Ahh, do you want to talk about it?"

"No big deal, just the usual anxiety stuff," I lie. Hmm, does Lamont look relieved that I did not want to share? "What time is it?"

"It's five-thirty, and I slipped in through your window. I was very quiet so as not to wake up your mom."

"How long have you been here?"

"Oh…about a half-hour. I've been reading Holmes Welch's *The Parting of the Way*. I found it downstairs in the store and quietly brought it to your room. I'm studying up on Taoism."

"But you are sitting in the dark. How can you see to read?"

"Silly lady, us vampires can see perfectly well in the dark. No need for a light. All this studying made me hungry, so I thought kissing you would

[32] Peter Berger, *The Sacred Canopy: Elements of a Sociological Theory of Religion*, Doubleday & Company, Inc. 1967, Anchor Books edition: 1969, p. 3.

be a nice, gentle way to wake you up. It worked for Prince Charming and Sleeping Beauty."

Basha: "Well, hello, Prince. It is nice and all, but sometimes a girl just wants to wake up in her bed by herself and not have visitors watching her sleep."

Lamont: "Ahh…sorry. I invaded your privacy. I'm a knucklehead sometimes."

"Yes, you are. A cute, sweet knucklehead. But a knucklehead, nevertheless. Now give me a moment..." I need to conjure some sort of clothing. I've gotten used to wearing Dream Suits, so I just dissolved what I was wearing and did not bother conjuring up anything when I went to sleep last night. "There…that is done. Hmmm…you need to feed, do you not?"

"Well...yes. I do. I'm sorry about this…but I was a growing boy even before all of this happened. I was like a Hobbit if I could so arrange it."

"Meaning?"

"Six meals a day when they, I, could get it[33]. So, now I'm a growing vampire."

"So, you are asking if we could do some discrete and quiet necking?"

"Yes!"

"I get up, or you come down to me?"

Lamont wraps his arms around me in a flash, we kiss deeply, and I am enveloped in warm shadows…

WELL OF DREAMS

...ohhhh…I feel his teeth sinking into my neck, the subtle pain of the bite mixed with the incredible bliss. He is slow and careful. I feel drawn deep into him as I swim in a warm sea of our love. I hear the song of our hearts as one voice. All around us, floating in the steamy air, are whispers of voices of millions of people. "Lamont, remember we promised...!!!"

*

My heart is pounding in my chest. I'm tired, hungry, and feeling all warm and pleasant. I am held tight in his arms, and his lips are sweet and soft. When I can, I open my eyes and see love, the color of deep blue cerulean, by the light of my bedside lamp that he turned on.

It takes us both a while to speak.

Basha: "I keep thinking I screamed while you bit me in the waking

---

[33] J. R. R. Tolkien, *The Lord of the Rings, Fellowship of the Ring*, Prologue, 50th Anniversary Edition, Houghton Mifflin Company, 2004, p 2.

world. You look very scary when you do that if you are wondering. But if that was the case, mom would be here, I am certain. So, it is good that no one can hear you in the Waking World when you scream there in the Well of Dreams. You fed on me nicely, slow, and for a long time. I got a bit nervous when you did not stop."

Lamont: "I was a good boy and was careful. I just prolonged it but kept us from going into any forbidden territory. We're both still virgins. No orgasms. At least I've never had one." I'm sticking to the we-haven't-had-ordinary-sexual activity as logic for my claim to still being a virgin. "But you seem to know when you're close to one. Why is that?"

Basha: "A good girl never talks about such things. But I promise you that you are my first and only lover."

"Okay. We all have our little secrets. Did I tell you today that I love you?"

"Tell me again. I do not think I will ever tire of hearing you say it."

"Basha...I...love...you!" Lamont says as he punctuates each word with a kiss.

"Now, will you give a girl some privacy and entertain yourself in the kitchen. I need to go make myself presentable. While you are at it, make yourself useful, like prepare coffee for mom and tea for us."

Lamont floats across the room with quiet laughter, his feet imperceptibly not touching the ground. Now, that is a neat trick and extremely useful given his type of vampiric vulnerability to wood. He opens the door carefully, touches the metal doorknob, and exits.

I conjure up a fuzzy white robe and slip into the bathroom. I come out fresh, dry, and fully clothed in peach-colored bra, black jeans, and a silk blood red blouse, but barefoot. I smell tea and coffee.

Miriam: "Well, hello, Lamont."

Mom says as she comes out of her bedroom in a fuzzy pink robe and slippers.

Miriam: "Basha mentioned something about an early start, but I didn't think it would be this early. But I can't complain when a man hands me a freshly brewed cup of coffee."

Lamont: "Do you take cream or sugar?"

Miriam: "Just a bit of milk. I'll pour it. So, you two will use your Dreaming magick to see if you can figure out what happened to Peter, yes?"

Lamont: "That's the plan."

Miriam: "Now, can I fix Basha something? A little nosh for breakfast. You shouldn't try all this magick on an empty stomach."

Basha: 'Do not panic, Lamont. I had to tell mom what happened to you when you returned from the gate site. She saw you while you were in the hospital. She knew that something out of the ordinary happened to you and that somehow, I had helped bring you back. I had to tell her something about the nature of your change.'

Lamont: 'Oh God.' "I guess…that makes sense. I…"

Miriam: "It is okay, Lamont; there isn't much that my daughter and I keep from each other. As for the details on any of those topics, not so much. But overall, yes. Ever since we moved out from Herschel, we needed to make a new life for ourselves during the separation and divorce. So, is it true that you can't eat solid food? That's such a shame."

Lamont: "Yeah, tell me about it. No more lasagna or challah or…don't get me started! I can't swallow and digest any solid food. But, Basha needs to eat to keep up her energy levels. The closest I can come is liquids and the vicariously smelling it when Basha eats. Speaking of fragrant scents, I think I smell a lingering scent in the air. Did you make fresh challah bread yesterday?"

Miriam: "Yes, I did two loaves."

Basha: "My mom's challah makes killer French toast! So, let us help get this breakfast thing going."

*

After cleaning up breakfast, Miriam went off to work, and we changed into birds and flew over to SF General. We land in the parking lot, where no one is around to notice as we change back into human form. Lamont is wearing his RAF coat and black 501 Jeans, black and white high-top Chuck Taylor shoes; I have on my red motorcycle leather jacket, red hip-hugger jeans, red cowgirl boots, and a scarlet cotton tank top. We didn't want to pay for parking my motorcycle all day. We start to go up to Peter's room.

Lamont: "I think we need to do some kind of glamor spell so that all the staff doesn't pay attention to us. Also, when we go through that gate, just in case we need to be in superhero identity mode, we don't want anything or anyone to trace us back to our real selves."

Basha: "I am shocked you are being cautious and thinking ahead, so unlike you, Lamont."

Lamont: "I detect sarcasm."

Basha: "Me? Sarcastic, never," I smile as sweet and innocently as possible. "The glamor spell makes sense. Who knows how long this will take. Do you really think we need to go incognito when entering that gateway, aka superhero names and all?"

Lamont: "Just trying to be safer than sorry. We may be pissing some entities off, and we don't want this to come back at us in either Dreamland or the Waking World."

Basha: "Okay, cautious it is. Once we are through the looking glass, capes and cowls, O' Knight. I will set up the ward and glamor spell once we are in the room."

Lamont: "Makes sense, O' Dawn, that brightens my life. As you wish."

"Lamont, are you pulling a Westley[34] on me?"

"You are literally my life and love."

"You are such a romantic," I give him a quick kiss on his cheek, and then we walk hand in hand through the parking lot to the entrance to the hospital.

We head up to the room where Peter is residing. While Lamont talks to the doctors and nurses about Peter, I ponder the spell work we are about to perform. I have not considered doing magick in the Waking World now that we have the ability to Dream here. This will be different. I am not sure how to do this. Should I do it like I would do my personal ritual work, truly skyclad, and have Lamont wait outside so he will not see me naked? Or should we do it together, like we did the dream spells to contact Lana?

Hmm, we are a team, so, yes, we should do this together. We should just do it as if we were in Dreamland, knowing that it will now manifest with that kind of fireworks and power. I postulate that by tapping into Lamont's abilities, he has the power to make this spell even more potent.

Now, should we be actually skyclad, aka—naked? I hear Mae West's whispering naughtily in my ear, encouraging that idea. But…no. I admit that a part of me would really like that, but he is only 16, and he is probably a bundle of raging hormones, so I should not tempt him. So, all things considered, I do not think this is quite okay. Not yet anyway. But damn it! It is times like these that I wish he was my age, and then no one would be able to look askance out our relationship. But he is not. Bloody Hell! Okay. So, not really skyclad—naked. Sigh. I conjecture being in the equivalent of a bikini bathing suit will be plenty skyclad for his hormones.

Basha: 'Lamont, I think we should do this spell together. As we did for Lana. I suggest we go skyclad…'

Lamont: 'What?' Lamont burst forth in enthusiastic surprise.'

Basha: '…which for me would manifest as a bikini and for you a snug speedo brief.'

Lamont: 'Oh. Okay.'

---

[34] S. Morgenstern, *The Princess Bride*, translated by William Goldman, 1973.

I can hear the disappointment in his thoughts as he was dragged rapidly from naughty to nice.

Lamont: 'Ahh...and you should call me Night, even though no one is around. Just to get into and make it an automatic habit.'

Basha: 'Yes, Sir Knight, your princess will try and remember to stay in character.'

'As for what you're suggesting we wear…hey…' His eyes are sharp, bright, and piercing. Devouring me as surely as his fangs. 'When it comes to magick, you're the boss.'

'Okay then, as the spider said to the fly, enter my parlor.' I say, pointing to the door to Peter's room.

We look around, and it is a good thing that right now, Peter is the only one in this room, which makes it easier for us.

"Follow my lead exactly, my dearest Knight," I say as I conjure an average but tightly fitting vermillion bikini bathing suit to hold my curves.

I feel adequately naked and pleasantly indecent standing in front of Lamont, even though I am factually not. Which is precisely what I wanted to be feeling—exposed.

Lamont's eyes get huge, and he blushes almost as bright red as my suit. I turn around—trying to fain casualness as I walk around the room, focusing and feeling the cardinal directions, knowing full well that Lamont can now see me flaunt the ripe peachiness of my backside. My heart is beating fast, and I imagine my breasts rising and falling if they were not forcibly contained by the taunt tightness of my vermillion Dream bikini top. I smile, hearing his intake of breath, and imagine I feel his heart race due to the effects of my spell-work.

After getting a fix on where north is, I turn to face him. I can feel my heart beating fast, and a wicked smile reveals my thoughts as I realize how strange, daring, and provocative it is to be so unclad like this in this hospital room.

Basha: "Okay, Lamont, your turn to strip down to matching magical attire."

Lamont: "Uh…okay."

I am so wicked! I can feel the embarrassing heat and excitement I have caused in him. He dissolves his attire till he is clad in a tight, taut bit of charcoal gray briefs that he conjures to stand similarly exposed in front of me. My wicked weaving is working too well, and I must deliberately focus on acting nonchalant, professional, and proper. I take one last deliberately deep breath and concentrate on dismissing all that Mae West naughtiness to the recesses of my unconsciousness. However, with the tingling of my skin, the beating of my heart, and the hot breath that accompanies my voice, I know those other thoughts linger still.

Basha: "Lamont, not that I have your full attention. I have a new idea about casting and calling in the directions. And well, I would like to try it out. To orient ourselves, that is south," I point toward a specific area of the room. "We will call in the directions starting there. Do you recall the Rider-Waite-Smith Tarot deck[35]?"

Lamont: "Yes. I have seen deck at your place."

"Can you picture them well enough to assist me in conjuring their images up to appear?

"Of course."

"For this spell crafting variant, we shall begin with the South rather than as traditionally done in the North. Since we will be eliciting and drawing forth emotions and the subconscious and then bringing it to manifestation with the aid of the intellect and conscious processes[36]. Therefore, focus on the Ace of Wands from the Rider-Waite-Smith deck and conjure it to float in the air. Do you have it?"

"Yes."

"Now conjure it in front of us. Help me make it appear and stay in the air."

We do it, and the card forms in the air, appearing to be triple the usual card size. It is working!

Basha: "Now repeat after me…By the Fire that is our desires and inspirations."

I next turn and face the west, "Now, conjure the Ace of Cups."

We do, and it appears.

Basha: "By our feelings and emotions…"

---

[35] In 1909 Arthur E. Waite conceived a new version of the Tarot deck and he enlisted the artist Pamela Coleman Smith to bring it to realization. It was the first deck to transform the Minor Arcana half of the Tarot deck, which is roughly equivalent to the four suited playing cards of Diamonds, Hearts, Clubs, and Spades. Prior to Waite and Smith's deck, the Minor Arcana cards simply represented the suits of Pentacles, Swords, Wands, and Cups with the equivalent of multiple images of those symbols in accordance with the numerical value of the card. Now with Waite and Smith, the cards would tell a symbolic story across all the suits referencing the numerological imagery and symbols of aces, twos, threes, fours, etc. All Minor Aracana suits had four Court cards which in this deck were androgynous Pages, Masculine Knights, Queens, and Kings. The deck was published by William Rider & Sons, hence the reference to 'Rider' in the way to name the deck. This deck was the most successful and influential Tarot Deck ever devised.

[36] This comes out of a conversation I had with Seraphina, in January of 2020 concerning Mark Horn's book, *Tarot and the Gates of Light*. See Appendix 2 for the details of this conversation. Seraphina suggested that I anachronistically attribute this to her mother Basha.

We say it together as one voice. As I anticipated, Lamont follows my lead, recognizing my thoughts and ideas as we are joined, as two minds and hearts work in intertwined harmony.

Basha: "Leaving that image to stay in the air, next we conjure up the Ace of Swords. By our intellect and conscious minds."

We turn to face the north.

"Now conjure up the Ace of Pentacles. And then say, we manifest our intentions and bring it into physicality."

Keeping these floating in the four cardinal directions, we cast our hands and eyes downward and form a glowing pentacle.

Basha and Lamont: "By all that is below…"

Then we glance upward and form another glowing pentacle in the air above us.

Basha and Lamont: "By all that is above. We are between the worlds, and what is between the worlds can transform the world. Blessed be."

Basha: "We now ask Queen Lilith to aid us in our task this day; please hear us, heed us and be here now!"

After a dramatic pause, I continue to explain things.

Basha: "Now concentrate and call to mind the Rider-Waite-Smith card of the nine of Wands, recalling the image of a man leaning on his staff with eight other staffs behind him, and then the seven of Cups, recalling the image of someone standing in front of seven cups floating on clouds and coming out of each cup is a fantasy and illusion of one's wishes. These cards will be the focal images to hold the spell of wards and glamour. Conjure them to appear."

Once we can see those two cards floating in the doorway to this room, I recite the heart of the spell.

Basha: "May we be guarded in our work here and let no harm come to us. May those who enter this room see what they expect to see."

We repeat our charm three times while focusing and filling those images with energy and willpower, igniting those conjured images to blaze with the power of our intention.

I can feel Lamont's power flowing into my mind and heart, whispering sweetly and softly, giving potent power to us and our spell work.

Basha: "There it is done. Now, we can devoke by acknowledging the six directions and bringing each of the Ace's images to fade into our hearts and minds. Then we thank Queen Lilith for her aid and assistance in our spell work."

After a few minutes, all was done; the spell was cast.

We both look at each other, feeling all flushed and excited. Lamont takes my hands in his and kisses them. We just hold hands and lock our gaze, not wanting to resume what must be done next. I smile, then take back my hands, and reluctantly, I reimagine my Dream superhero catsuit onto my body. Then Lamont does the same, and I watch as he is re-attired in his variation of the Shadow's outfit. Lamont gets two chairs and sets them next to Peter, and we sit down.

Lamont: "Ready?"

Basha: "Why is it that we ask if we are ready when we are about to do something rash?"

"Tradition?"

"I guess."

"Now, we know that he is inside a portal to somewhere. Let's see how we can enter it." Lamont says as he reaches out his hand over Peter's body.

Darkness like billowing smoke seems to pour out of him to engulf him, Peter, and me. Now I can see the gelatinous, faintly glowing form that encases Peter. The Knight passes his hand slowly through the outer membrane. It ripples like water as his hand goes towards Peter's chest.

Lamont: 'It is working.'

Then I see a flash of surprise in his icy blue eyes, which becomes fear.

Lamont: 'Dawn! I erred! I'm being...'

Basha: 'Knight!' I mentally shouted back in distress and anger at his rashness.

I watch as his form struggles to free itself, then I see his astral slash Dream body gets sucked into the globular stuff. He seems to be sucked into Peter's skull, the energy field source. Lamont's Dream body is quickly flowing into Peter. In a flash, his Dream body disappears as his physical body falls to the floor.

Basha: "Bloody Hell," I mutter as I wrestle Lamont into a chair. "Damn it, Knight! Why can't you learn to say plan something out with me before you dash off! What else can I do but go where perhaps angels fear to tread." I reach my hand towards the globular mass to follow in Lamont's footsteps.

*

LAMONT

I'm pulled down a narrow tunnel surrounded by flowing coils of fluid that glisten with unearthly incoherent colors. Waves of pulsating rhythmic sound buffeted me. My nose twitches, trying to take in a scent; all I smell is hollowness, emptiness, a substantial lack that is contradictory as my eyes can see only emptiness.

The void in which I travel calls out like relentless and merciless sirens, beckoning me to remain and dissipate my lonely singularity into their vastness. I have been here before. I again struggle to maintain my selfhood; the recent memory of my prior successful struggle gives me hope and strength. I pray that this stay in the void will be over soon.

What? I feel like I ran into a sheet of ice-cold sleet. This incongruent phenomenon passes as quickly as I am pulled ever onwards. Off to my right, there is a luminous spherical creature. It is oddly flattened at its top and bottom, and at what would correspond to this thing's front is an immense faceted eye and a peculiar puckered closed orifice. The eye glows with a pale leprous white coloration. Attached to the singular ocular organ are slender translucent ivory tentacles that provide rapid locomotion to the creature, reminding me of a bizarre octopus-like creature. The distance between us is quickly diminished as it closes in.

I watch as the odious eye glows with increased intensity as a blast of shivering cold soundlessly smashes into me. The cold numbs me and allows the creature to ensnare me with hundreds of tentacles. Once in its grip, a horrible blubbery noise fills my mind. Then the blubbery sound begins to take on the attributes of familiarity.

"...elcome creature. Welcome to my neck of the woods, so to speak."

I sluggishly react to the sudden presence of coherent speech, which to my surprise, sounds like the smooth, solemn tones of a British radio announcer.

"We are called Ny'ghan Grii[37]. By what name may we call you?"

I realize that Ny'ghan Grii can telepathically communicate with me now that contact has been established. "I am called the Night."

"We do not often get visitors here."

"That doesn't surprise me."

"Usually, we have to wait a long time till someone opens up the fabric of space and time."

"What are you waiting for?"

"We wait to feed, of course. We rarely get an opportunity to properly get aquatinted with our food before we consume it. We are so delighted that you have ventured into our home territory. Now, would you be so kind as to

---

[37] The Ny'ghan Grii whose existence was first discussed and analyzed in an article entitled *"The Invaders"* by professor Henry Kuttner in February 1939. This information was summarized by Prof. Scott David Aniolowski on page 36 of his scholarly work: *Ye Booke of Monsters; the Aniolowski Collection*, Volume I, Chaosium Inc., 1994. Prof. Kuttner's writings have been reissued in a collection of his works, *The Book of Iod: 10 tales of the Mythos*, selected and edited by Robert M. Price, book 7 of the *Cthulhu Cycle Books* series published by Chaosium Inc., 1995.

tell us about yourself? By the way, could you please cease this rapid moving? It would be ever so helpful if you could just remain stationary while we converse."

"Remain stationary? Even if I was in control of my movement, I would have no intention to stay here and be eaten!"

"Really? Does this mean you're not interested in having a friendly chat?"

"No!" I yell.

"Pity."

The Ny'ghan Grii once more bathes me in a blast of icy cold light erupts out of its eye. It is as if I had sunk into a vast snowdrift somewhere on the dark side of the Himalayan Mountains. I shiver helplessly as the Ny'ghan Grii's translucent ivory tentacles pierce my eyes and sink deep into the center of my brain. I am overcome by shattering and excruciating pain. Pain spreads through my body like a torrent of acid flowing through my veins.

The Ny'ghan Grii moans and quivers in lecherous delight as it dines. The pain I undergo recalls my willing suffering at the hands of the Mayor of Thrall, and that memory transmutes this pain into raging anger and indignation. The inside of my mouth and the tips of my fingers are wrenched and ripped open. This painful sensation quickly subsides when bloodied fangs and claws emerge. I grab the tentacles that are assaulting me and dig my claws into their sponge-like flesh as I yank them out of my eye sockets. This action traumatizes my visual system beyond the onslaught it had already experienced, and I am plunged into blinding red darkness.

I can feel the Ny'ghan Grii taking this opportunity to retaliate with a blast of light from its single eye. The light splashes against the inside of my eyelids as a mixture of virescence and mauve. I feel a baneful and malignant power impinging on my sense of being. I contend with this new psychic assault. Somehow, the light from the Ny'ghan Grii awakens ancient pathways within the body. Those ancient patterns still reside in my DNA. Locked within those chemicals is the complete history of evolution, and now what was once potential is simmering to become manifest. The light is trying to draw out of my cell's buried patterns. So that what was once fixed could become pliable. I strive to suppress the de-evolutionary forces on the verge of being liberated.

We are locked in this bizarre combat, carried by the force that first sucked me into this anomalous realm between Realities. Up ahead, we see the glistening violet ripple in the fabric of space, the opening from which the force we ride is coming.

"Oh dear," the Ny'ghan Grii exclaims with trepidation.

The power of the force that carries us intensifies and we rush headlong into the now churning violet opening. I am pulled through, but the Ny'ghan Grii is barred from making the transition. It smashes into the violet gateway with a prodigious force that splatters it into an oozing flattened mass.

It is as if I had just stepped out of a pool of steaming hot water after being immersed in its soothing effects for the last hour. Deep relief floods through the cells of my body that have once more returned to quiescence. The results of the Ny'ghan Grii's light have subsided. No longer are my cells caught in a de-evolutionary struggle.

I cough as I look around at my new surroundings. Whether it is night or day in this world, I cannot discern. The sky is filled with ashen gray smoke and soot pouring out of a vast forest of tall brick towers below me, belching vivid ivy green flames. The stink reminds me of burning plastic, and gasoline is profuse. The abundance of the fire tinges everything with its sinister virid light. There is a roaring noise that comes from no discernible direction. It reminds me of being at the ocean's edge and hearing the waves smash relentlessly against a rocky shore. Soon I realize it is the sound of churning machinery. The towers are smokestacks from this vast power plant. The green metal on which I stand is covered with dun-colored lichen.

I hear a faint fluttering sound and see a pair of light gray flying figures. They move with an oddly slow but graceful rhythm. These flying beings are carried on enormous moth-like wings. Their wings have intricate patterns of grays and yet are still beautifully mesmerizing. The beings are light, gray-skinned humanoids, clothed in wispy gossamer bands of fabric that seem to be alive.

The bands float and weave around the humanoids like a coiling serpent. Through the gossamer, I perceive the two beings as hermaphrodites with exaggerated male and female sexual characteristics. The creature's faces have no evidence of anything that could recognizably serve the purpose of ears or mouths. The only feature on their perfectly spherical and smooth-skinned head is a ridge about two inches tall and thick that lies in the center of the creature's face and encircles its head. That ridge has slits in it, which I guess allow for it to take in the atmosphere and thus function as the equivalent of its nostrils. The pair land beside me in dance-like unison.

"Offspring of Human greetings."

The sound is like a chorus of human children singing to a fast beat, echoing in his mind. No one creature seems to be its source.

"To our world, welcome."

"Hello," I say aloud; I suspect that the beings are communicating with me telepathically, and my mind is translating their thoughts into English equivalents. Old habits are hard to break. "I am called The Night, and your name is?"

Again, those alien voices seem slightly quicker than normal speech patterns.

"Offspring of Human, many names have you. We address you we will as Offspring of the Night? Your question we answer, one of the designated leaders of drones of the Offspring of Zygo'Teh are we."

"Night is not my family name or the name of my species. It is my own personal name. Do you have any individual names?"

"Individual? What that is?"

"Individual refers to a single person. That is what I am."

"Single person? What that is?"

"A single person is one person."

"`One' is what?"

"One can mean: singular, alone, separate, and one is the name of the first number. Do you have words for your numbers?

"Yes. Two, four, six, eight, ten, and so on are they."

"Ah. That explains it. Presumably, Nothing on this world exists that is not a pair and has shaped your language and culture."

"What is pair?"

"It is two separate things, which are sometimes a set."

"Separate? Unique? These are what words? Two is. Nothing is not two. Think you all things connected with all others of its kind are not? All you exactly alike seem to be to us, yet many names give yourself for the same thing. Why do this you, when not truly different are you?"

"But I am unique. All humans are unique and individual, though we share some similar traits. We each have individual names because we are all individual, unique, and separate members of our race."

"Nonsense sounds, why use? Offspring of Humans, so many bizarre ideas have you. All you feel and act alike. To the true nature all confused of your own being are you."

"I would love to discuss this further, but I have a more important question. You recognized me as human, and you referred to other humans. Have you seen other humans recently?"

"Recently not. To visit us the came hundred years ago the last human was."

"Oh. So much for easy answers."

"What mean you?"

"I am looking for my friends. I believed that they had come here before me. I foolishly hoped that the first person I met would know of their arrival."

"Perhaps know this is by our hive. Come with us, would you Offspring of Night?"

"Yes, I would."

"Good. Carry you to our hive; we will."

"Carry?"

"Pick you up; we will so that all fly there we may."

"Oh. You don't need to carry me. I have my own wings." I melt down into my bat shape. "You lead, and I will follow."

"Humans such difference, some new characteristics we had met had not demonstrated. Understand now we why Offspring of Night called are you. Not similar to the Offspring of Humans some ways you are not. Even though the same species we sense you like as them."

"I don't mean to be rude, but my name is Night, not` Offspring of Night'."

"How odd. Insist if you. Follow us, Offspring of Night."

The pair lift up slowly in unison and flutter off into the air; I fly with them having to make an effort to fly at their pace. They move to the beat of a different drummer, one who is keeping a much slower rhythm. They descend from the metal structure, which towers over everything. They lead me over hundreds of miles of either a single interconnected power plant or thousands of separate ones; I cannot tell which due to the smog and thick smoke hanging over the whole mass.

As they travel, the sky darkens as night approaches. We travel on this third day all through the night, the next day, and still on. Finally, I see an end to the factories, which I now realize is the outermost ring of two incredibly intertwined immense cities where I am being led.

The two cities are like a cell frozen in time when it is in the asexual reproductive process of mitosis. The sprawling cities are made up of skyscrapers, the smallest of which would equal New York City's Empire State Building in height. The sizes of the cities are beyond my comprehension; they spread out in all directions without an end in sight. Bustling in and out of the skyscrapers are millions of flying offspring of Zygo'Teh; their activity reminds me of a beehive. The Zygo'Teh are not all the same. The vast majority are darker and duller gray Then, numerically, the next most extensive collection is light gray ones, and I spot some silver ones.

All the buildings are made of metal and glass. All are built to give me the impression that the homes' entranceways face outward toward the balconies they all seem to have. The buildings, despite their modern design, seem ancient. They are all marred by the soot, smoke, and all-pervasive smog. My throat and eyes begin to feel raw from coming in contact with the polluted atmosphere. It is as if I were trapped in an enclosed basement with a hundred chain smokers. My two native guides are not bothered by their machinery's havoc on the air.

"Arrived we have to the tower marked number 22466288, our hive had assigned to us."

They point to a building whose address, I assume, is marked by the glowing band surrounding the building, which is placed in its middle, and by a substantially circular plate on the building's flat roof. My guides fly onto one of the balconies and step through the open doorway into the building. I follow and take on my Night form.

Inside there is a degree of familiarity. I could be standing in an apartment building in the Waking World were it not for the fact that the rooms have no visible furnishings and no means of illumination. Good thing I don't need any light to see. The room is cast in shades of blue and gray. This is what I imagine a picture would be like on an old black and white TV. I wonder why the rooms are completely bare. Though the walls and even the ceilings are peculiar. They are all textured in a seemingly random manner. Also, they are not uniformly flat. They jut out oddly with bumps and indentations. The walls have been partially covered, seemingly random, with raised markings, reminding me of braille. The room I would call a living room if it were my apartment. I find a tablet with more of that braille-like markings on it. If I touch the edges, the patterns change. Is this a data storage device?

When they had entered the building, the gossamer entities that float around the offspring of Zygo'Teh land and adhere to their flesh. The pair is covered with gossamer bands that continuously snake across their body, going around their necks, down across one breast, around their back, and ends by wrapping around one of their legs. As I follow my guides through the apartment and into the hall, I see three other rooms of varying sizes, but I can't discern what the purpose they have. There are no doors in my guide's apartment nor a door to the hallway. When I enter the hall, what I see takes my breath away.

"Incredible."

The hall has only one side; along that side are my guide's apartment and all the other apartments. The corridor ends facing a large open area. I see hundreds, perhaps thousands, of the offspring of Zygo'Teh flying up and down through the common open space. In the exact proportions that I noticed before. Dull gray the majority, and lesser of the light gray and lessor still of the silver ones. It is like being inside a vast beehive. The air is filled with the hum caused by the millions of beating wings of the Zygo'Teh. For all the movement and sound, I feel no warmth or comfort associated with life at seeing such a sight.

Instead, it seems to be a demented parody of life. It is a true necropolis, a hive of the dead filled with myriad animated corpses moving and going on with unknown business, silently and always in pairs.

In confirmation of this observation, I see off to my left four pairs of Zygo'Tehians, of the dull gray variety. Each team carries between them a couple of motionless dull gray Zygo'Tehian. The ones who are taken are dead. Visually it appears as if the dead are carrying the dead. I am reminded of the Nordic Valkyries who carry off the fallen warriors, but these corpse carriers do not seem gladdened by their task. They seem deeply troubled. They don't carry their comrades to a better world but to an uncertain and disturbing future.

I walk to the edge and what I see takes my breath away. The old Lamont being more worried about his corporeal continuation would have panicked with vertigo, seeing that the enormous central shaft goes down without end. When I pull myself from that gaping precipice and dare to look up, it goes far to the building's domed ceiling, which seems thousands of feet above. This whole skyscraper is a hollowed-out building to accommodate flying creatures, with apartments forming around this central open huge empty shaft.

"To the hive, Offspring of Night, welcome. Down you must follow if learning you want of the Offspring of Human's fate."

"Then down I must." I take on bat form once more, and over the edge, I go, following my guides once more.

Down they travel. Down and Down. My guides act as if only they and I are in this building. They do not greet or acknowledge the presence of any other offspring of Zygo'Teh. Nor do any of the thousands of the building inhabitants pay attention to their passing.

I have many questions I would like to ask my guides, but I am following behind them and cannot seem to come up alongside them, no matter how hard I try. I must be patient and wait for answers. I now notice how tired and weak I am. Strange? How can this be? I feel like I've not eaten for days.

I have been almost continually in motion since my arrival. What am I going to do? I have the need to feed growing in me. I feel weaker and weaker. We're flying on and on. Time passes, and I can occasionally glimpse the sky through the open doorways of the apartments I pass on this endless descent. I can see that the day has ended again, and night has come. On and on, we go through the night and into another day. The pain of hunger writhes in my stomach.

I cannot catch up to them. Even if I could, what do I do? Where is

Miss Manners, when you really need her? Do I just walk up to one of them and say, excuse me, would it be all right if I drank your blood? But I need to feed! I am exhausted.

Finally, they land on a stone floor, on the bottom floor of this immense building. It is a vast hall resembling a train station with bustling activity. Off this hall, in all directions, go at least thirty different passageways. The hallway is filled with the constant movement of the darker gray zombie-like offspring of Zygo'Teh hurrying off on mysterious errands.

"Finally! I hope you two plan to stop somewhere for a quick bite; I am starving!" My flippancy is hiding my real burning need to feed. If only it was so easy, just grab a quick bite. What am I going to do? Will I die here? Can I stop myself from just pouncing on one of them? Basha, where are you? I need you! I can barely think straight...

"Really?" They say with that chorus-like voice in astonishment. "Thought we that you would be different. Need sustenance often we do not. Come, when we arrive ask we will, that food be provided."

"Come? Do you mean we have not arrived at our destination yet? I didn't think this building was so large."

"Very large it is. Our destination we have not come to. Follow."

Oh, God…"How far?"

"Far not."

"Where are you taking me?" I'm not sure I can make it without feeding on something or someone.

"To the presence of the hive. There clear everything will be to you made to you."

"But wait! I really need..." Bloody Hell! They have taken flight and can't hear me. Once more, they resume their travels with me doggedly plodding behind my two guides, who move with mechanical precision and endurance. They work their way through the mass of gray offspring of Zygo'Teh. I imagine this must be what it's like trying to walk through the crowds on Castro Street on Halloween night or what it must be like on New Year's Eve at Times Square in New York City.

For all the people that are here all around them, the hall is eerie in its quiet. I still cannot get over how none of the offspring of Zygo'Teh talk to one another. Each pair of Zygo'Teh never says a word as they move together on their enigmatic tasks.

My guides' choice of direction seems random, for I can observe no difference in their path. All the passageways appear identical. The mysterious raised markings on the floor, walls, and ceilings appear similar to my eyes.

I feel very weak. I need to rest. I need to be replenished. Suddenly I find myself on the floor, looking up at my light gray guides.

"What to you happened Offspring of Night? Why on the floor are you?"

"I guess I fainted.

I feel so drained. I need to feed. I need to...

*

SAN FRANCISCO, S.F. GENERAL HOSPITAL
BASHA

I watch Lamont hastily disappear into that pulsating mass that encases Peter. I reach out to touch its edge, and my hand sinks into the thick protoplasmic mass, and it feels like sticking my hand into a massive container of honey.

Ugh. I hope I can wash this stuff off when I reach the other side. Since presumably Lamont somehow went into that mess which must be some sort of interdimensional gate to wherever Peter and the rest of our friend's minds or souls had been taken.

I keep going forward. Allowing myself to be ingested by the blubbery thing is the doorway to some unknown destiny. I move with difficulty into the thick sticky mass as it cloyingly covers me until only my neck and head remain on this side of reality. Images of being smothered by this vile honey-like mass flash across my mind. A sense of claustrophobia and worse slithers out of some corner of my mind. The sensation of fear begins to grow. I recall the Bene Gesserit litany to counteract these dire thoughts: '*I must not fear. Fear is the mind-killer. Fear is the little death that brings total obliteration. I will face my fear. I will permit it to pass over me and through me. And when it has gone past, I will turn the inner eye to see its path. Where the fear has gone, there will be nothing. Only I will remain.*[38]'

The words have their usual effect, and the fear shrinks back to huddle off in some far corner and bides its time. Frustration replaces fear.

Damn it, Lamont! At times like this, I think the Goddess has something against me, so she threw us together. I shudder, take a deep breath, and close my eyes as I plunge under the surface.

All I see is darkness and patches of red. I feel entirely, totally enclosed, and covered. I feel the thick viscous stuff coating my hair, pressed against my nostrils, up against my tightly shut eyelids, and my lips. I concentrate so as not to gag or take in a breath. My mind tells me it must be safe; this cannot last. This is a way to another dimension. It will open soon and take me away. But when?

---

[38] The source is Frank Herbert's novel *Dune,* 1965, pg. 15, Ace Books Inc.

I crave air. I can feel time's passing being measured by the beating of my heart.

Lamont went through. I am certain. But he is no longer alive as I am. Is that the difference? I need air. Does the door only allow passage for his kind? Is this my death? I need air! Why don't I just open my mouth and breathe? No! Give it time! The door will unlock! It must open! Wait, what is that? I feel warm? I see sparks. I must breathe!

I feel weak. Faint. Asphyxiation? Something is pulling me? Is my soul being called? I see a light. Bright light! Oh no. It is the tunnel of light that leads the dead on their path? No. It must be the way. Air! Cannot…breathe! Shekinah, Help me! Guide me! Cannot breathe. Cannot last. I am moving. I am being pulled. Shekinah, is that you? I am bathed in light. I no longer feel the cloying mass. Am I dying? Am I hallucinating? I need to breathe! Lamont made it! But he is already dead! It is not time for me to die! There must be air! I will open my mouth and take in the air! No! Wait! Don't do...

I feel a sense of disassociation from my physical body. I feel my unconscious form slump down in the chair. The consistency of the mass is now like warm honey, and my body quickly passes through the stuff. My chest rises with the regular motion of someone asleep. Behind my closed eyelids, my eyes move rapidly all around.

*

I open my mouth; my bursting lungs crave the taste, the sweetness of oxygen. For some reason, I think there is no air here. And yet I am no longer in danger of asphyxiation. I no longer need to breathe.

Oh, Goddess. Am I dead? It is still all dark? Oh, my eyes are tightly closed. When I open my eyes and look myself over, I am in my red 'superhero outfit' consisting of scarlet knee-high boots, crimson leather leggings, a matching bustier, and a gold belt with a sunburst resting on my hips. I am floating in…nothing. A vast void.

No, wait; there are some subtle colors of some sort. A flowing current of color. As if I was in a rapidly moving stream and could discern the flow of the water. There is a current. I am floating or being pulled on this current somewhere. Where am I?

So, this is the Beyond. This is where Lamont went when he took Jon through the Gate on his way to the Waking World. I feel like his current is carrying me to wherever it is that Lamont went. I can simply follow where it takes me through that connection by going with the flow.

Eventually, I hear singing, beautiful singing. Women's voices singing with joy, calling out to me of this joy. They invite me to join them. To become one with them and their song...forever.

Forever?

No thanks! I cannot. I must find Lamont and the others. The singing of the Sirens has become shrill and angry. They do not want me to be. They do not want me to exist separately from them. This dimension is alive. And it seeks to take into itself all that exists. I must fight it. I must maintain my identity. I must quickly pass through this dimension before permanently being drawn into it. Since I can strangely see the current carrying me, I will follow it; but not passively float. I will fly on my own fiery power. I burst into flames and shoot off into the flowing river of the void.

There up ahead. That shimmering glow. It is from there that this flow is carrying me. I roar towards the shimmering doorway, which seems both solid and ethereal. I am puzzled momentarily by a smear of dark and still moist fluid around the edges of the dimensional doorway. I cannot take the time to consider this oddity as I plunge onward and through.

*

I stand on a verdant metal platform and see a sky filled with green-tinged gray smoke and soot billowing out of tall brick towers. Out of the top of the smoke stakes, flickering green flames ejaculate into the sky. I look in all directions. The structure I am on is a metal tower rising above a tremendous forest of smokestacks growing out of a vast factory complex. Below me is a thunderous surging sound. Its mechanical rhythm reminds me of standing next to a steam-powered train engine churning away at maximum speed.

Finding Lamont should be easy. I got here that way; I just need to concentrate and follow our connective link, which seemed to emanate from our rings once I entered that weird gate back at the hospital.

I focus on my silver and obsidian ring; I fix my mind's eye on Lamont. Surprisingly I feel like I am within the center of thick smoke, out of which I cannot sense any sign of his presence. I shift out of the altered state of reality.

Damn it, Lamont! Why can I not find you? Is he out of range? Or did something happen to him? Or is it something to do with this being another world? Or a different dimension or different universe or what? Is this ring bound up with the operation of our Earthly physics, and that is the problem? These questions would be delightful treats for Lamont to enjoy if only he were here. Now what? If this were a B movie, I would walk up to a native and say: 'Take me to your leader.' Unfortunately, real life is not that accommodating. I guess I could fly down there and ask around to see if they have seen or heard of any strangers arriving here. Do I have any other options? Nope.

I descend to the ground, passing through the thick cloud of smoke, whose offensive odor is a mixture of sulfurous rotten egg-like smells and burning plastic. I land on the concrete factory floor and look around. I am in the midst of an immense operation involving mining, drilling, and processing ore and fluids extracted from the ground below.

The factory complex is a maze of pipes, cables, and conduits haphazardly coming out of vast interconnected machinery. The machines are tended to by pairs of natives, working in a slow but perfectly choreographed synchronization. The only sound they make is an occasional odd snorting noise.

The beings are dull gray humanoid skeletons with a skull devoid of an ear socket, nose, or eye; in place of that is just an oval mass of a ridge that glows carnelian color and encircles their featureless skull. Their most incongruous feature is a cluster of multicolored moths that have come to rest on each of the skeletal beings. The moths form a band that crawls along their bodies and wraps around each being in a different yet similar patterned manner. The skeletal creatures seem fixated on their task and completely ignore my presence.

"Hello. Excuse me," They fail to respond to me. "Could I interrupt you for only a moment and ask a few quick questions?"

No response.

"Anybody home?" I call out in exaggerated friendliness.

No response.

"What is it with you ladies? You either love your job or fear your boss. I have never seen such diligence in anybody. I need to find someone who is in charge, after all. Hopefully, she can find some time to answer a few questions."

I arbitrarily pick a direction, ducking and weaving through the omnipresent machinery with its array of connective pipes and cables. I travel on like this for hours, passing busy but slow-moving, though intent, pairs of gray skeletal workers who ignore me no matter how hard I try to make my presence known. I cannot tell if they actually do not sense my presence or are simply afraid to pay attention to me and thereby neglect for even a moment their assigned tasks.

Then something disrupts the routine, which causes concern, and many notice this while others try to pretend not to. Two gray skeletal workers, who have been coughing more than their companions, start to cough and do not stop. The coughing is more congested, and each racks their skeletal frames with a momentary convulsion. It grows in intensity until bony hands claw at their throats as a final cough rattles off into silence as the creatures fall. There is no mistaking the presence of death. The sight of their dead fellow workers disrupt all work.

All the other creatures turn to face the dead. Finally, four move forward with great hesitation, fear, and loathing, pickup between them the deceased. They carry these now dead skeletons off to parts unknown. It is many minutes after the dead ones have been removed before the work begins again. I am puzzled by many unanswered questions. After the following hours pass uneventfully, I am startled when I hear a chorus of human females call out in English faster than a typical speech pattern.

"Greetings. An Offspring of Night are you? Or an Offspring of Humans?"

I turn to face the direction of the voices and see only two light gray skeletal beings with gleaming angel wings; descend a few feet from me.

"I am neither. I am called Dawn, and with whom do I have the pleasure of speaking?"

"Of the Offspring of Zygo'Teh shepherds to the drones are we."

"A hive form of identity, how interesting. You have no individual names?"

"Not truly do we understand the word: individual. Any other name no need have we, no other name serves no purpose for us."

"Fine if you say so. You called me `Offspring of Knight'. Have you met someone recently named the Knight? I have come here in search of him."

"Yes. Encountered the Offspring of Night, we have."

"When? Where?"

"Difficult to explain when. To the task time refer you are when? Or to record time when? Recall time or? When which?"

"Forget it. I did not think it was going to be so difficult. How long ago is not really all that important. You did meet Knight? He is a human with black hair, and blue eyes, probably wearing a dark gray long wool coat, black shirt, black jeans, and sneakers. Though I'm not sure if any of that made any sense to you."

"Yes, know this Offspring of Night do we."

"Can you take me to him?"

"Yes."

"Well, let us do it. If that is all right with you?"

"All right that is with us. Came here we did to do that."

"Excellent."

"Carry you do we need to?"

"No. If we have to fly to get there, that is no problem for me. I can fly under my own power. You lead, and I will follow."

"Fly can all Offspring of Dawn?"

"At this point in time, there is no `offspring of Dawn'. I have no children. There is only me. I am called Dawn."

"Like the Offspring of Night. An odd name you prefer. Offspring of Dawn, come."

The two Zygo'Teh spread out their wings and lift themselves into the air. I ignite my inner fire and follow them, having to slow down to keep up with them. They fly for hours above the enormous overgrown factory spews out the vile omnipresent smoke and soot. The polluted air stings my eyes and irritates my nose and throat.

I come abreast of the two Zygo'Teh so I may try to obtain some answers.

"Excuse me. I was wondering if you could tell me what this factory that is below us is manufacturing?"

"Sustenance, building materials, our machines energy to power and our hive's nest to provide heat and light for."

"Does the amount of pollutants your factory produces cause you any concern?"

"Poe-lute-ants what is?"

"The smoke and the soot that your factory spews out are pollutants. It is polluting your air."

"This smoke, soot, and poe-lew-shun, bad is it?"

"Probably. I have not seen any birds or, for that matter, any other animals, perhaps the pollution killed them off."

"Long, long ago, thousands of years ago recorded our history in that inferior unimportant animals were once. Dead they now all are."

"No doubt killed off by the pollution."

"Unable to survive they were, that is correct."

"Does this fact not alarm you? This proves that smoke and soot are harmful. Did it kill off all other life on your planet? Are you Zygo'Teh the only living thing on this planet?"

"No."

"So, what else if there?"

"Plants, a few species of and flying insects many there are."

"Now, why does that not surprise me. Do you know that the smoke and soot probably killed all the other animals?"

"Not understand. Over time, weak species die off. Selection natural at work it is."

"Yet you do not know the meaning of the word pollution? Very interesting. Do your people consider the smoke dangerous?"

"No. Harm not us this smoke."

"Perhaps. Did your species always look the way you do now?"

"What mean you?"

"Your bodies have no skin, muscles, or internal organs. You are only bones. I do not understand how this is possible. But anyway, was there ever a time in the past when your bodies were not merely skeletal?"

"Bones always part of our body make up, true this is, but all skeleton, we are not. Why do you say our body is `merely skeletal'?"

"Because that is the only thing I can see."

"What is `see'?"

"To see means to perceive with the aid of one's eyes."

"What are `eyes'?"

"They are the sensory organs of sight. Wait, you do not have to say it; you do not have a word for `sight'. That ridge around your skull is obviously not your version of your eyes. Is it a sensory organ?"

"Yes. Perceive with it can we sensory data much from the electromagnetic spectrum."

"But probably not within the visual range."

"Visual'?"

"Give me a moment. It has been a while since I took a physics class. Therefore that ridge of yours must be sensitive to electromagnetic waves vibrating with a frequency of as low 380 billionths of a meter or as high as 700 billionths of a meter per second, right?"

"No. To us no significance that minuscule range is. Ask why do you?"

"This is the range that my species is most sensitive to."

"Pity a what. Confirms deductions ours on limited your species is."

"Thanks. Having a conversation with you two is like talking to Knight; I keep getting sidetracked by having to deal with tangential matters of a Philosophical nature. So, your bodies are more than bones; you have other organs for digestion, excretion, breathing, circulation, and such, correct?"

"Certainly. Even Offspring's of Humans, resemble them do you, have such things. Not able to detect from outside are they. Offspring of Dawn know these facts not?"

"Remember, call me Dawn, and yes, I know these facts. I was only trying to understand what I am seeing."

"Seeing what is this?"

"Seeing is the word we use to refer to visible light and what we call visual perception."

"Strange term again. Portion what is of electro-magnetic spectrum refer to?"

"As I said, I believe it is 380 to 700 nanometers."

"Referring to that small subset of the electrical magnetic spectrum you keep doing by this term 'seeing' and 'visual'. Notice we other dead animal

species when studied as well rely on the same portion of the spectrum. Very limited it seems in sense data it provides. Inferior species are you conclude we.[39]"

"Hey! Where I come from, it is considered rude to insult visitors."

"Rude? Rude this what is? Insult what is?"

"Rude " describes behavior a coarse, rough action lacking manners or proper etiquette. An insult is when someone says something offensive about another person."

"Why a pair would ever something say offensive concerning another pair of the hive? Makes no sense in what you think, Offspring of Dawn."

"Perhaps amongst yourselves, you are better behaved. I notice that you have these flying insects around you; what are they, if I may ask?" I am confident they could not be called moths here, different planet—different species, and I would be hard-pressed to explain the word 'moth'!

"Ask you may, permission required not. Correctly identified them, flying insects, they are. Live they and we in relationship symbiotic. Live we have since our earliest beginnings. Help us they do by inoculating us from certain elements in our food sources found."

"You mentioned that I resemble other humans. That is because I am one of that species. Have you met other humans?"

"Ahh. Offspring of Dawn, like Offspring of Night, is a more evolutionary advanced form of Offspring of Humans. Interesting. Offspring of Humans on your world first met we suddenly when separate our plane the barrier between lifted was. Samples we took us to study. Opened the barrier and closed suddenly for reasons still unknown.

Later then, the barrier one hundred years ago between our worlds mysteriously down was again once. Gather more samples we could. Recently arrived on then more our world Offspring of Night, you now and. More time for questions later there will be. Arrived at the Hive's nest have we. We take you to others in authority we will."

Many flying hours finally took us beyond the enormous, sprawling manufacturing plant. From the height we are traveling, I can see that the prodigious plant evolves into two entwined colossal cities of towering skyscrapers. The twin cities sprawl outward beyond the horizon. Flying in and out of the multitudes of skyscrapers, like moths buzzing and going in and out of their hive. The millions of the gray, light gray, and some silver winged

---

[39] Lamon had explained to me that they must perceive in a way that is similar to the comic book character Daredevil. Daredevil was created by writer-editor Stan Lee and artist Bill Everett, with an unspecified amount of input from Jack Kirby. The character first appeared in Daredevil #1 (April 1964). He, like the aliens, must perceive the world in shapes and spatial relationships. For the aliens natural selection must have over time given them an ability to fine tune the use of all the electromagnetic spectrum that they are sensitive to in order to perceive fine details and thus build their vast technology.

skeletons are known as the offspring of Zygo'Teh. My light gray Zygo'Tehian pair points toward one building off in the east.

"Where we are going that is, the tower number 22466288."

The pair leads me into their building and down into the planet's depths far below, presumably taking the same route Lamont has already traversed. I can finally sense him! He is near, relatively speaking.

"We take you to the other."

"Who is that?"

We round a corner in answer to my question, and I am shocked by what I see. Lamont has transformed into his vampire mode self. His canine teeth enlarge. He looks like he is about to feed on one of the light gray Zygo'Teh!

THE NIGHT (AND BASHA)

I wrap my arms around the Zygo'Teh's body and draw it closer to me in a lover's passionate embrace. The Zygo'Teh companion watches curiously on as I ram my teeth into the flesh of my captive Zygo'Teh guide, turned victim. As I suck up the life-giving blood, the Zygo'Tehs scream in surprise, shock, fright, and pain. Soon the cries of pain are taken up by others. As I feed, somewhere off in the distance, my mind registers that the corridor echoes with a chorus of pain from millions of mouths. I drink in the pale green cold blood that tastes like cooked peas, and I can feel a sense of overwhelming orgasmic fulfillment despite the foul taste.

I need to feed to live.

Basha: 'Do not kill it. They are still sentient life.'

'No, Keeper of Lamont's heart, I will not stop.' With a last shudder of pleasure, I gently pull out of the light gray flesh of my terrorized dead victim.

'But you said you would listen to me? Why did you kill it?'

A small trickle of pale green blood seeps out of the wound I made in its neck. I wipe my mouth with the back of my gloved hand. Odd, I can't get the pea's taste out of my mind. 'I needed to fill the need and desire. I feel much better now. It was not human, so what did it matter to me?' The other creature backs away from me and stands next to his fellow Zygo'Tehian, who I killed.

BASHA

"Horrible that was. Hear us in your mind the word vampire for what you are truly. Vampire creature is that on blood feeds to live, we learn from you. Dangerous you are. Not an offspring of humans. Good, it is that you are strange thing `singular'."

Then the vampire Night becomes a swirling mass of smoke. It begins to congeal, and when the smoke clears, I see my frail Lamont on the floor.

Lamont: "Ohh…what happened? I was so faint from hunger…Dawn! Thank the Goddess you're here. When did you get here? Why am I on the floor? Did I faint? I must have. I felt so weak. But now, I feel okay. I don't understand. How in Heaven's name did you find me? Why are there crushed green peas in my mouth? Where did that come from? OH MY GOD! Dawn, did I do what I think I did?"

He blacked out. Presumably, he does not recall changing into his Night vampire persona from the blood lust.

Lamont: "Dawn…what did I do? Tell me, please. Why are they," he points to the Zygo'Tehians that cower away from him. "Afraid? That one, is he dead? Oh God…Dawn, did I…"

"Understand that killed him you did to live. We will get others to lead you while we attend to him now."

Lamont: "Oh God…oh God…oh God…I'm a monster…I'm sorry." Tears well up and drizzled down as he spoke.

I try to comfort Lamont in his guilt as the dead Zygo'Tehian is carried off, and two new white ones stay.

Basha: "Look. He is sorry. He did not know what he was doing." I want to say it was all that symbiote vampire thing that did this, but I do not think that Lamont is ready to hear that he is possessed. "This is his only way to sustain his life. We are sorry."

"Your species like this feed?'

Basha: "No. Only Lamont is like this."

"That strange word there is again. No idea concerning it. That is then what must he do if this is what it takes for him. Survive must all we. Holy truth that is. His nature this is. Accept we no choice had he. Better been it would had if killed both. Kill the other we must now."

Lamont: "What do you mean?"

"Only in pairs must we be. If part of the pair dies the other pair member must. Understand such things we do not expect you. Guide you we will the rest of the way we."

Basha: "Knight, damn it! I should have been with you. Then this would not have happened. When are you going to stop rushing off into the unknown! Did not your mother teach you the wisdom in the phrase: look before you leap? How in the Goddess's great names did you expect me to find you?" I hope to get him to stop thinking about what he just did and focus on something else to distract him.

Lamont: "I'm sorry. I guess I forgot to leave behind a trail of breadcrumbs or bring a ball of string to unwind."

My plan is working. He stopped weeping.

Basha: "You should be sorry and more careful next time. The Goddess must truly look after fools and lovers."

LAMONT

Lamont: "What am I?"

Basha: "Right now, the fool."

Lamont: "Sorry I asked. How did you find me?"

Basha: "I did not. You made such an impression that when I came upon someone I could ask questions of, such as my two skeleton friends here, they brought me straight to you."

Lamont: "Skeletal? What are you talking about, Dawn?"

I know what she is trying to do. She's hoping I will forget that I acted like I am genuinely a monster and that I just killed another living being. I am one of the damned. But I must live. I want to live! Bloody damn Hell! Okay, Lamont, just focus for now on the task ahead. I'll just do my best to pretend that I am distracted and that I can forget what I just did. But I can't, and I won't forget...

BASHA

Basha: "It must be catching. Everyone here keeps asking me to define my Terms, even you, Knight. Skeletal as in something with their bones showing."

Lamont: "I know what the word means; I just don't know who or what you are referring to."

Basha: "What? The Zygo'Tehians, of course. Their visible skeletons make them look like refugees from some Halloween party."

Lamont: "Visible skeletons? I can't see their skeletal structure, but you do, correct?"

Good, he has forgotten about his vampire attack, at least I hope so.

Basha: "Yes. I do not understand. Lamont, how can we both look at the same thing and see two different things? That seems impossible?"

Lamont: "My current hypothesis is that it has something to do with us being not in phase with this dimension's time and space."

Basha: "Meaning that you have no idea what is going on, right Lamont? That is just a lot of fancy words strung together."

Lamont: "But, it does make sense that since our mind and bodies were evolved to deal with how things are in our part of the universe, it is a good guess that we are not in tune with this part of wherever we are. There is probably something going on that is different from how we physically perceive this world."

"What do you mean? Either we see something, or we do not. It is as simple as that, is it not?"

"No, Dawn, it is not so simple. You're already aware of this fact. Does the word optical illusion ring any bells?"

"Well, yes, but those are especially artificially constructed pictures or objects which distort and disguise things to confuse our sense of sight. There are no naturally occurring optical illusions."

"I'm not so certain about the 'no naturally occurring part'. But that's not important. So, let's try a different approach. Describe to me the process of vision."

"Knight, this is not the time or the place to conduct a class in perception. I already gave my guides a lecture on rudeness; need I give you one?"

"No. But I'm sure they won't mind if we ignore them, at least they shouldn't, considering that almost everyone on this planet has been ignoring me."

"Same here. Okay, I will bite. I am curious about what is going on and how we can see two different things. So, vision occurs when photons from a light source hit an object, bounce off that object, and strike our eye. The photon triggers a response in our cells; cones and rods, I think they're called. This reaction is transmitted to a part of the brain where the sense data is interpreted. How did I do?"

"Very good. Question: which metaphor more accurately describes the process of vision, one: the eye is a passive device like a camera, or two: seeing is active like a committee of investigators?"

Basha: "The eye is more like a camera. I never heard of the other metaphor."

Lamont: "Then by that metaphor, you understand vision to be mechanical, always constant, always occurring in the same way. It is a passive process. The light gathered on the retina and then processed to develop the image. Just like film in a movie camera."

"Well, that seems correct. The eye to the retina and the lens to film are passive processes. Light comes in and gets collected on the retina slash film. So, what are you getting at?"

Lamont: "Well, actually, the eye rejects and fails to take in most of the light, most of the electromagnetic spectrum…"

Basha: "So? The camera's lens does the same thing. It only allows in that same visible spectrum to the film. Same difference."

"Well, try this. Our eyes both blink and move around all the time to take in the environment, yet the mind does not register the sudden opening and closing of the eyelid nor any movement. We perceive a stable environment. Yet if we jostle a camera or open and shut its shutter, we would notice the result when the film was developed! So, chalk up one for the difference between the two."

Basha: "Okay, Knight, you got me there. But that doesn't seem to make visual perception more like a committee."

Lamont: "Ahh, but it does. A biological process in the brain/mind does this active process of fixing and making things seem stable. A camera and photographer in developing the film can't do this."

"Well, actually, the photographer could edit those frames out of the finished product, and thus when it is played back, it would not be noticed."

"Not the same."

"It is similar if you allow the metaphor of camera and photographer to stand in for the eye and the body's biology in the process of perception."

"Humph. How about this. Imagine we are walking down the street in my neighborhood one morning, and we spot a small furry, black and white animal crossing the street a distance away from us. My unconscious mind could take in that shape, check it against my memory, and conclude that it was a cat. From then on, all the incoming data would be processed in a manner consistent with that assumption, and I would consciously perceive it as a cat. Whereas you, being more skeptical about things…"

"Hey…"

"Just wait, you would not jump to any quick conclusions, and your unconscious would just notice the shape and not assume what it is until you had enough time to confirm against your own past experience, and voila! You recognize it as not a fluffy cat but as a skunk! Isn't that a possibility?"

"Okay, I grant you that, so? Your point, Knight?"

"A camera would just take in the scene, and even when it was developed, there is no way for me in developing my film and you in developing yours that would end up with my film showing a cat while yours showed a skunk. Wouldn't both our films show a skunk that I somehow misperceived as a cat?"

"Hmm. Yes, I agree with that scenario."

Lamont: "Therefore, there is a major difference between cameras and our visual system. Our biology can distort what we perceive in ways that do not happen with a camera. A camera can't be fooled, but our subconscious can fool and or distort what we consciously become aware of. That perception can be done by the 'committee' of biological systems within our unconscious mind."

Basha: "I guess so. What is your point in all of this, Knight?"

Lamont: "The reason we see the Zygo'Tehians in two different ways is due to the differences in our backgrounds, the different sets of assumptions, and prior patterns that we have experienced. Also, what has been important to us in the past and our cultural overlay, based on our linguistic heritage, shapes how we perceive reality. As I've said before, we shape and are shaped by ideas[40]."

"As you keep saying. But that does not quite make sense. Reality is what it is, we may be fooled by what we see, as in your cat skunk reference, but I do not believe our beliefs can affect Waking reality."

"Then you believe that a Zionist and a Neo-Nazi looking at pictures of the piles of the dead bodies at Auschwitz are experiencing the same thing? Or are an Eskimo and a Bedouin from the desert seeing snowfall experiencing the same thing?"

"Okay, I am beginning to get your point."

"Thinking and feeling are all part of how we live, how we experience life. Our ideas and beliefs affect our emotions, and they, in turn, affect how we react to what we see. Sight is more than photons stimulating the cells of the eye. Perception is how we interpret the data that our senses take in, and if that data is noticed at all."

"So, you are saying that we see the same thing, but we interpret what we see differently, is that it? Even in the Waking World and not just here in Dreamland?'

"Correct. Strongly held beliefs and ideas presented during our formative years tend to strongly shape what and how we perceive the world around us."

"So, I see that the Zygo'Tehians have feathered wings, which remind me of how artists have been painting angels' wings."

"And I see their wings as a muted patterned wing that I saw as similar to those of moths."

Basha: "This is interesting. I see their bodies as only as skeletons."

Lamont: "I see them as perfectly gray or light gray and a few with silver skin. I also see them as having both male and female sexual organs."

"I see no sex differentiation at all. It somehow figures that you would see both sex organs to describe something that is not either sex. You were not able to conceive of a humanoid with no sex."

---

[40] Actually, I'm the one who came up with this phrase, I just put couldn't help but put this whole conversation into Lamont's and Bashas mouths. See my book, *Find Your Way* for a further exploration of the phrase and my ideas.

"That must be correct. As I said before: we shape, and are shaped by, ideas."

"What is your theory on why they move so slowly yet speak so quickly?"

"Actually, they aren't talking but communicating with us telepathically. Your point is correct. It is odd. This is probably another aspect of our bodies not being from this dimension; not having evolved here, we are out of sync with this section of the universe. We are witnessing the differing rate of speed between a purely cerebral function and body function. Hmm? Something that has puzzled me, they have this flowing gossamer stuff around them. I have no idea what that is."

"I guess that is what I interpret as moths. The Zygo'Tehians told me they have a symbiotic relationship with this insect species."

"This has been very fascinating. But I think we should get back to our immediate situation. Now that we have found each other, where are Peter and the members of my Coven? We assumed they would all be together somewhere beyond the strange gate we went through."

Lamont: "Correct. It is now time to ask where it was I was being taken. So, let me focus back on our alien guides and bring them back into our conversations. Hey, Excuse me, O' Offspring of Zygo'Teh, are there other offspring of humans in your world, and could you take us to them?"

"Other Offspring of Humans there are yes. Taking you to them are we. us follow."

Basha: "I hope they are close by. I have been flying almost all day to get here, and I am beginning to get tired and need some rest."

Lamont: "Dawn, did I hear you correctly? You said you've been flying all day?"

Basha: "Yes, that is what I said; why do you ask?"

Lamont: "It took me five or six days to get here. We just got to the bottom of the building we are now in, and it took two or three more days to get here after that."

Basha: "What? You must be mistaken."

Lamont: "No, I'm not. I saw the sunset and then rise as I traveled"

Basha: "That is impossible. I have an excellent sense of time, and I would measure my journey here not days but hours."

Lamont: "Wait, I have an idea. Let's ask the Zygo'Tehians. How long did Dawn take to get here, and how long did it take me to get here?"

All four of the light gray Zygo'Tehians answer together.

"Not able we are to answer that question. Lack you do a true sense of time. Primitive and rudimentary brains have you."

Basha: "Rudimentary brains, I do not like the sound of that."

Lamont: "What do you mean? It is a bit insulting but beyond that?"

Basha: "How do you know what kind of brains we have? Do they have X-Ray vision or something?"

Lamont: "Perhaps they do. Maybe they see a different part of the electromagnetic wave spectrum."

Basha: "Perhaps."

Lamont: "We still haven't resolved how long, and therefore how far, our individual journeys have been."

Basha: "True. Each of us traveled separately, with only our individual experience as a reference to judge the time and the distance. I am not sure we can resolve this question."

Lamont: "If they brought us here by the same route ..."

"And if we started from the same place."

"Ah yes. There is that. We may not have started from the same place. But wait. The journey from where I entered this skyscraper, the nest for this hive, took a few days. Did you enter the same building?"

"I remember that the building number was 22466288."

"Hmm. I think that was the building I was taken to."

"You think? You cannot recall the exact number?"

"No."

"So, what good is all this. Without external references, how are we to judge space and time? Memory is not a reliable objective means. Memories are subjective."

"For that matter, all our thoughts and ideas are subjective."

"Then why are we bothering to have this discussion?"

"It's important to realize that we always compare our subjective realities to ascertain a mutual understanding of objective external reality. Subjective is an accurate term if you mean something subject to internal mental influences."

"This might fascinate you, but I do not see the relevance for one."

"The relevance is, there seems to be a time and space distortion here. We may have traveled the same space but not the same amount of time."

Basha: "I understand that is the point you have been trying to make, but so what?"

Lamont: "So what? How can you say that? Our sense of reality is at stake."

Basha: "Maybe. For now, I would rather find our friends than solve this metaphysical problem, so, Zygo'Tehians, lead us on if you please."

LAMONT

The winged light gray Zygo'Tehians led us laterally down a confusion of intersecting passageways. As we travel, I notice an antiseptic smell. These passageways are no longer marked with bizarre graffiti. We are in well-lighted corridors with polished tiled floors. The whole effect resembles the institutional sterility of a hospital. Then out of a side room, we are greeted by two silver Zygo'Tehians. The two silver Zygo'Tehians seem to address our light gray guides.

"We obey and perceive," Our light gray guides respond.

Before we have time to take this in, we are quickly surrounded and forcibly confined by our previously aloof and harmless guides, who have expectantly begun to move with remarkable, and here to fore, uncharacteristic quickness. While we struggle in the strong grips of the four light gray Zygo'Tehians, the two silver beings pull out from behind them long rods that are pushed into our stomachs. There is a dull explosive sound, and then I feel sharp needles inject into my flesh.

*

My first sensation is the scent of strong astringent antiseptic and then of glaring deep blue light. My next sensation is one of confinement. I feel what seem to be woven nylon bands around my ankles and wrists that secure me to a cold metal table. I open my eyes and see that some kind of what seems to be purplish light is coming from an overhead 'lamp' with a large metallic reflector dish. At least, that is what my mind can grasp from what it is perceiving. Could the light be disinfecting the area? Or something else? When I adjust to this odd illumination, I see that I am strapped to an operating table. Next to me is a metal cart covered with a deadly variety of cutting instruments, ranging from the most delicate of thin scalpels to a large crude hacksaw.

After taking in my surroundings, I mutter to myself, '*When a doctor does go wrong he is the first of criminals. He has the nerve and he has the knowledge.*[41]'

Lamont: "Hey! Dawn! Are you okay? Dawn, answer me!"

Basha's voice comes from somewhere out of sight and north of my head. "Yes, Knight, I am Okay if you ignore that I am strapped on a table that looks all prepared for an unauthorized operation!"

Lamont: "Same here."

Basha: "I take it we were drugged."

Lamont: "Yes."

---

[41] From "*The Adventure of the Speckled Band*", The Strand Magazine February 1892.

Basha: "And we agree that it appears that our placid hosts are about to commit medical mayhem on us?"

"Yes, to that one too. Hey, I think the silver ones are in charge. They seem to tell our light gray ones to do this to us, do you agree?"

"Yes. That seems about right."

"I also recall that there seems to be a difference in the ratio of the populations here."

"You mean more of one kind and less of the other?'

"Yes, I believe that is what I just said, only more formally. I think the dull gray ones are the lowly workers; the light gray supervises them and takes orders from the beings in silver."

"I agree. Only the light gray ones ever spoke to me."

"Hmmm...they are the proverbial middlemen? The lower drones can't communicate with us, and the higher ones won't?"

"Could be. So, how about us disappointing our hosts and getting out of here?"

"Brilliant suggestion Watson! I'm on it."

"So, I am Watson to your Holmes' is that it?"

"I'm afraid so. I've daydreamed about Holmes since I was 8 years old; I'm too old to change that thought pattern."

"Oh well, so long as I do not have to play the bumbling movie version, I can deal with it."

"That was Nigel Bruce, an unfortunate and inaccurate portrayal, which has henceforth tainted Watson's image."

"Enough with the talk already. Time for action."

"Right you are."

I use brute force while Basha utilizes her strength, that of magic fire she calls forth. I smell the stench of burning `nylon' as I struggle to reach the strap's breaking point. The smells and sound of our efforts seem all too obvious as a clock somewhere in the room ominously ticks off the seconds. Each new second brings forth the thought of discovery. Then almost as one, our bonds yield to our efforts as the wrist straps give way. We sit up and look around the room as we work to free our ankles.

The room is a hospital operating room, or more accurately, a university-style operating theater. A place where students can watch a professor/surgeon demonstrate the art and science of surgery. A place where surgery can be filmed and recorded for later review by generations of students. The room is familiar yet not. The style of the equipment is alien, though the function can be deduced by its arrangement and placement. The equipment is gleaming plastic and unearthly colored polish metals of brown and green.

Lamont: "I was thinking."

Basha: "As you told me once before, you always are. I wonder if your mind would wander if you were engaged in pleasant strenuous physical and even pleasurable activity?" Basha speaks between concentrating her efforts on burning off the straps.

"That I can't tell you, we have three years to wait to conduct that experiment in full, but I can say that when we are ahh...*together*--you do indeed silence all my thoughts. But other than those instances, I'm always thinking about something. Such is my misfortune. As I said, I believe our hosts don't have a very high regard for us."

"Brilliant deduction...Sherlock."

"There's the suspicious absence of other animals and insects on this planet. There's the matter of this room. We're here to be studied. I gather they don't consider our species to be their equal. We're mere animals to them. And not useful to them ones at that."

"That seems correct. There! I am through." Basha leaps off the table in disgust as if she was getting out of a pool of muddy water. She shakes the imaginary mud off her and regains her composure. I am inspired to free myself on my own before Basha can offer assistance, and with that incentive, I rip the `nylon' apart.

"Now, where to, Dawn?"

"In search of our friends, who hopefully are somewhere in this part of the building?"

"A reasonable assumption.'

We move toward the room's doorway, only to walk into the incoming light gray aliens, who are just as surprised as we are at their meeting.

"Free you are? Is that how?"

Despite the usual speed of the Zygo'Tehians speech pattern, they don't get to finish the sentence as we quickly grab them. I lift one of them over my head to hurl the startled and helpless Zygo'Tehian into unconsciousness when it smashes and overturns the operating table. Basha swings her Zygo'Tehian into the wall and then repeatedly smashes him against that wall until he goes limp in her grip.

We step into the hall and look up and down the empty hallway.

Lamont: "Which way?"

Basha: "Let us go against instinct and go left."

We move with as much haste and stealth as we can down the hall, looking in each room, searching for our friends. We come upon a set of double doors from which the stale odor of blood is so strong that I would think even Basha can smell it.

Lamont: "What is that stench?"

I become affected by the smell of blood; my teeth begin to ache as my body awakens to its bestial vampire hunger.

Lamont: "That's blood. I don't like this. I've got a bad feeling about what lies beyond."

Basha: "Well, let us open it and confront your fears."

We open the doors, and we both gasp in shock and horror at the sight and the stench of what is in the room.

Lamont: "It can't be?"

Basha: "Oh Goddess, how could this happen?"

What we have found are indeed our friends, whose condition is both horrific and almost impossible to comprehend. The room is a vast chamber that goes outward for miles. It is filled with what I, in an ordinary context, I would call display cases. The whole area seems to be illuminated with violet light. Perhaps this is some way to keep the entire place sterile?

These cases seem to be open on the front and back with translucent walls on the sides to create an enclosure for whole and dissected animals and plants. I am guessing this is a museum of what life was once like on this planet. This chamber seems to have been established to maintain and display those things that once roamed and lived on this planet. Presumably, only a few remnants have been stored here in this collection.

Amongst all of this, I spot our friends. Dear God, they killed them and did this horrible thing to them! I can barely contain my anguish and anger!

Confined within separate glowing ochre glass cases, our friends are suspended somehow in each case with their limbs spread wide, are two members of Sarah's coven and Peter and Oolong. Tubes, wires of intricate delicacy, and menacing complexity come out of and into our friends within these display cases.

The room's overall effect is some kind of medical anatomical display of the human species. They had their skin peeled completely off their bodies and somehow suspended in the air. Resembling insects in a display case, yet those bugs would be pierced to the back and dead, our friends are not pierced yet; they are affixed in those cages. Attached to these display cases are a series of buttons with that braille-like markings. I touch one of the buttons, and part of the display illuminates with what I perceive as an orange illumination emphasizing just some specific attributes of the body and the 'braille' writing.

One woman has had all her internal organs pulled out of her body, pinned, and hung around her body with braille markings attached to her and yet floating in a fixed point in space, presumably writing to explain where they were taken from. Another woman has had all her muscular tissue spread out, barring her cleaned skeleton, to demonstrate how the two work together. One of her arms and legs had been severed off and set into the wall to be manipulated by anyone interested in a hands-on demonstration of the workings. Peter has been opened up to best present the male side of the reproductive system and is also being used to demonstrate the circulatory, lymph, and nervous systems.

BASHA

Oh, dear Goddess…this is appalling, horrible…yet…this anatomy demonstration, though disgusting and repulsive, is there for me to see. I cannot help but see the difference between him and Lamont. Peter's is larger and what I conclude is uncircumcised. I didn't expect this rescue mission to present me with such views. The Cosmos has been indulging in a twisted way to give me a comparative male anatomy lesson, first with Lamont and now with Peter. I shudder guiltily at the sight before me.

LAMONT

The odor of a butcher shop is strong and disgusting, worse than the horrid sight before me. Almost all his arteries, capillaries, veins, and nerves have been carefully pulled out of his body and hung by strings from the ceiling to best display the intricate connectedness of those bodily systems.

Then it slowly sank in…my mind couldn't accept what I saw, yet it finally registered through the pain of my anger and disgust. The final horror is that I finally realize that our friends are all somehow still alive and momentarily, and thankfully, unconscious. With morbid fascination and horrible guilt and disgust, I try to comprehend and imagine how this insane and perverse miracle of medical science is accomplished.

We remain stunned and mesmerized by the immoral and fantastic scene before us. Seconds tick by as the room is filled with the commingled sound of six humans breathing.

Basha: "Not even the Nazis reached such monumental and sick depths of depravity."

Lamont: "Even their insane minds fell short of this."

Basha: "How could someone...?"

Lamont: "To them, we must be mere ..."

Basha: "Insects. Oh, Great Mother, this is beyond me."

Lamont: "Thankfully, or horribly, they're alive."

The sound of human voices is carried like a slow-moving stream deep into the dense forest of the mind where the captured coven members are hiding from their painful reality. They call out to the familiar voices. The silence of the room is filled with their moaning.

Peter: "Stop ... hurting...make it...stop..."

Oolong: "Help...for the...love of Goddess..."

Annabel Sarah's Coven member: "...please, I'll do whatever you want...stop this ..."

They drone on. The sound of a human voice has triggered their own long-ignored voice. They continue to call out in their suffering, mistakenly thinking they hear their captors. They cry, beg, and plead in exhausted whispers.

Basha: "Damnation!"

Lamont: "How can we help them, Dawn? Bloody Hell! What can we do? What grasp on life they seem to have must be the damnable results of the machinery that cages them. If we remove that, then what?"

Basha: "Will they survive?"

Lamont: "Are they surviving now?"

Basha: "Knight, what would you want if you were in their condition?"

Lamont: "But will they die if they're removed? That's the question!"

Basha: "One thing is for certain. We will not let them remain like this! Great Goddess! Lenore, she is missing! Where is she?"

Then the sound of a familiar female crying out in agony ends their discussion.

Lamont: "That must be her!" I say in a forced whisper.

Basha: "She must be in there," Basha points to a door at the back of the display room.

As we silently approach the door, our rage transforms us. Basha ignites. I take on my vampire aspect. My coat turns black, my collar is up, and on my head is the slouched hat. My fangs and claws protrude out; both are ready to fight as a welcome means to appease my rage fueled by loathing and fear.

Lamont: "On three. One," I whisper as I use my vampiric strength to dig my claws into the door in preparation for yanking it off its hinges. "Two. Three!" I pull and rip the door out and toss it behind me.

BASHA

Once the door is removed, I blaze into the room, flying upwards to place myself above anyone in the room. Lamont, having gone all vampire, charges in after me.

What we had seen still did not prepare me for the scene we now come upon. We freeze in shock at the sight. The room is another large circular operating theater, bathed in blue light with a vast array of recording devices mounted on the ceiling to capture for later review the proceedings from all angles.

A pair of silver-winged Zygo'Tehians conducting the proceedings are assembled in the room, and two teams of the gray variety assist as nurses. All of them are covered in blood. On an operating table is Lenore. Her skin has been completely removed and floats in the air off to the side. Lenore is bathed in a royal blue light emanating from a globe mounted to the room's ceiling. Lenore has already been carved open from her chest down to her feet. Her reproductive and excretory organs are floating in the air due to the effects of the field from the glowing blue globe. At least that is my guess. They are in the process of removing the organs involved in the digestive system. Her trachea and stomach are also already floating above her. As they stand and watch, the Zygo'Tehians use scalpels, both of the usual metal variety and beam power type, to carefully extract her intestines.

The crashing sounds of our dramatic entrance distract the Zygo'Tehians, who turn and stare at us in puzzlement. The macabre tableau is shattered when I can no longer contain my rage at the atrocities I have seen. I strike out with dual showers of flame gushing from my two clenched fists and blast the nearest Zygo'Tehians.

A doctor and two assistants are engulfed in the torrent of my fire. They scream out, and the sound from their mouths is as if hundreds were being burned alive. Quickly their flesh is consumed, and then all that remains is silver ash. I am hyperventilating, and my body shivers as powerful emotions rage around me like the fire I have called forth.

LAMONT

A second after Basha begins her attack, I charge at the nearest Zygo'Tehian. I lift him over my head and throw the Zygo'Tehian into the remaining assistant. The force of the impact carries the two of them straight into the wall behind them, where they crash unconscious. The remaining doctor brandishes the laser scalpel in their hand and directs its beam at me. The beam begins to burn into the side of my stomach. I bellow out at the sudden pain, and then I pounce.

I begin to laugh out of my rage, a cruel devilish laugh. I can't help myself; the joy of blood lust bursts forth. I bring down the nearest

Zygo'Tehian. My claws dig into flesh, and my fangs rip into the Zygo'Tehian's throat. Icy cold white blood gushes into my throat. The taste of its blood is all too familiar. I never did like cooked peas. But feeding on them makes me stronger, and the urge to feed is almost irresistible. The Zygo'Tehian looks with terror into my cold blue eyes as I reach out to touch one of them.

Lamont: "Feel the pain you have caused!"

The Zygo'Tehian sees no possibility of hope or safety in my glowing eyes; he sees only his own demise. The Zygo'Tehian struggles hopelessly in my embrace as I bite into him and feed on him. Draining him as his life is swallowed up, the weaker he becomes. Before I become satiated, before all of my foe's lifeblood is drained, I struggle to stop myself even as I am caught up in this lust for life. I do not wish to be the death of my foe. It is conscious will versus the age-old instinct to live and feed. The struggle is fought over centuries, over mere seconds. The struggle ends, and I release the Zygo'Tehian, who collapses to the floor; his wound slowly healing as my saliva causes even this milky blood to coagulate.

With a struggle, I force myself to become Lamont once again. I get up, and upon seeing Basha, I cry out.

Lamont: "Dawn, don't!"

Basha has directed her fiery anger at the two unconscious Zygo'Tehians, and they are beginning to burn under her flaming assault. I quickly take off my coat and intervene between Basha's flaming attacks. Even as I am being blasted by Basha's fire, I attempt to extinguish the flames that burn the two Zygo'Tehians.

Lamont: "Dawn, we must not kill them! They may treat us like vermin, but we must not act as vermin. We must act and do what is right."

Basha struggles as I did moments ago. Her struggle is between revenge and justice. She stops her attack.

Basha: "In the name of our Holy Mother, they should pay for what they have done here. I will not stop until they have suffered as they have caused our friends to suffer."

Lamont: "Suffer, yes. Justice, yes. But death no."

Basha: "Why not? The Zygo'Tehians could have just killed our friends. They did not do that out of guilt, remorse, or mercy; they simply wanted them alive to better study them! They did not kill our friends because it served them better to keep them alive, to be tortured and in pain, for who knows how long! They keep them in that horrible half-life state for who knows what reason. Why should I not kill them?"

Lamont: "We are not them. We are human; we are that which is `*a little lower than the angels'*[42]. *'Was it not said that in the image and likeness of God were we made?'*[43] We must, therefore, act in accordance with those ideals, for when we act, does not God and the Goddess act through us?"

Basha: "Great! Just what I need now is a goy boyfriend who tries to teach me Torah and Wicca!"

Lamont: "Besides, we need to determine how this was done and whether it can be undone."

Basha: "We will have to find another pair to ask questions of."

Lamont: "No."

Basha: "Damn it, Knight! They deserve to roast in Hell for what they did here." Basha calls back the flames despite her anger and is no longer covered in fire.

Basha: "Okay, Knight, I agree. We will let them live. So, what is your plan?"

Lamont: "I recall you implying that planning is something I seem to lack."

Basha: "Knight, this is no time for bickering."

Lamont: "Well, the way I see it, we need to get ourselves and our friends back to where we came into this dimension. We need to ..."

Basha: "To find the green tower. At least that is where I was when I entered this dimension."

Lamont: "I also found myself standing on a green metal structure overlooking this huge mining and drilling operation."

Basha: "Excellent. We have to believe that there is only one such structure and that we can easily find it once we get out of here."

Lamont: "Now we have a where to; we lack a how to. That's a much more difficult proposition. We cannot disconnect them from that equipment; there is no way we can put Humpty Dumpty back together again."

Basha: "Knight, how can you be flippant in the face of this horror?"

Lamont: "I just am. Poor potty training, or more likely a way to distance me from the reality of it all, is my guess. Anyway, we need to get through to our friends and wake them up so they return to the Waking World. Uh oh. I think company is coming."

Basha: "I hear it too. It is time I became the first line of defense."

Lamont: "Yes, you do that, and I 'll see if I can mind-meld and wake them up to get them back to the Waking World."

With that, Basha re-ignites flies into the display room and creates a

---

[42] *The Book of Psalms*, number 8, verse 5.

[43] *The Book of Genesis* chapter 1 verse 26.

wall of fire, which blocks the doorway that leads into the corridors. She can see the Zygo'Tehians gathering down the hall and silently considering their options through the flames.

Basha: "This should buy us some time."

Lamont: "And it's time to take the bull by the horns. Stop hesitating and considering things, and simply act."

I walk up to the operating table where Lenore lies, and I reach out to her. I try to ignore the horror and just put my hands on her head and reach out to her mind. Tears trickle down my face to mingle with the blood all around me. The scent of blood awakens my own blood hunger, and my fangs and claws rip out.

Lenore: "...stop ... why are you doing this? Please, for the love of the Goddess, stop..."

I try to connect with her mind and find her Waking World mind, but I can't. Everything is all confused; she is in too much pain to think clearly. I focus on her pain and trace it back to all those disrupted nerve cells that are frantically transmitting all this pain. I work to draw out the signals. I focus on her pain and staunch it like I would a bleeding wound to stop the flow of the pain transmission and then erase the memory of the pain.

Finally, this works, and I just put her to sleep. However, I cannot make my way to her sense of consciousness and thus get her to wake up from this nightmare. No matter what I do, her connection to the Waking World is too distant and tenuous; I can't connect with her. She is stuck here in this Dream form and in this hellish nightmare. Bloody Hell! I've done as much as I can for her. I then march out of the operating room to return to the display area.

*

I then take a deep breath, spin on my left foot, and smash into and through the glass wall with my right foot, crashing into the display case that contains my friend Peter. I clear the broken glass away, leaving a clean space in front of Peter…

*

I want to rip him free of all this, but I can't! I must not, they have done their hellish work on him, and I cannot undo it. In that horrid glass cage, he is alive…if you can call what he is going through living. But, while he is alive, there is hope. Hope to help him and save him somehow. Hope to get him free of this place and back to waking up from this nightmarish place. The only thing keeping him alive is the technology of this horrid cage. If I took him out of it, he would die, and I'm not sure what that would do to him back in San Francisco. So, all I can do is try to relieve his pain, that is for sure. Perhaps with all that has happened to me, with my new powers, I can do this. Reach into his mind…I can get him at least to wake up. So that I can help him.

I reach out and touch the glass and focus. Just focus…just concentrate on him…calling to him…

There! I can feel him. He feels like he is in some far-off place barely in reach, huddled in the darkness. He's hiding in his own inner world where he had fled. For out of his hiding place, far in the comforting darkness of his mind. I keep calling to him…over and over I call.

Peter: "who ... who goes...there? Who..."

Lamont: 'Peter! It's me! Lamont!' I say to him telepathically.

"Pain...too much pain...imaging ..."

Lamont: 'No, Peter, it's me! Lamont! I've come for you. Don't talk; just think the words. I can hear your thoughts.'

Peter: 'La...mont?'

Lamont: 'I'm here, Peter. I'm here with you.'

Peter: 'Lamont. I...hurt.'

Lamont: 'I'm sorry. I'm so sorry this happened, Peter.'

Peter: 'Lamont, make it...stop. Take me...out of here.'

Lamont: 'I'm trying to.'

Peter: 'Please...get me...out. End...the...pain.'

BASHA

All the while, Lamont is so engaged I am busy entertaining the Zygo'Tehians. I am standing in front of my wall of fire, feet braced apart, arms held rigid at right angles at my sides; my hands flash like the muzzle of two machine guns as I unleash a barrage of small fiery missiles at the Zygo'Tehians. My fiery bullets hit the Zygo'Tehians with the sound like pebbles tossed into a pool of water. The packets of fire explode in their alien flesh and erupt like tiny volcanoes spurting out white blood upon impact. After a few hits, the Zygo'Tehian falls to the ground and adds its cries of pain to the chorus. Then, a pair of winged silver Zygo'Tehians calls out to me for the first time.

"You like us are. Not drones are you but overseers are you. Not know this before. Offspring of NightDawn, cease what doing you are. Stop."

Basha: "Not likely."

"What doing you, you understand not."

"Really? Then enlighten me. What are we doing?"

"Damaging equipment are you which very difficult to construct was."

"Equipment! Is that all you are concerned with? To Hell with your equipment!"

"Again understand you we do not. Difficult to think down to such a vastly primitive level it is."

"How nice of you to make an effort."

"Appreciate our efforts believe you should we."

"Oh, we do. And if you come a little closer, I can show you how much we appreciate everything you have done."

"Sincere believe you, we do not. Better here to stay back. Accurate range prevents you from. Confusing creatures are you such."

"We try. Now, I would really like some explanations or justifications for what you have done."

"Justifications those are science, knowledge. Seekers of such things we are. Beyond your small mental capabilities which are. Took the opportunity when entered our world your species our knowledge to increase by capturing them and studying them."

"How could you do what you did? Why were you so cruel?"

"Cruel? Mean what do you?"

"What you did, you skin them alive and then chopped them up. The pain you caused is enormous! Surely you must have noticed that."

"Pain? No, likely that is. Too primitive you creatures are. Suffered conscious sentient awareness such as pain to be able. Seem to suffer you only. A physiological survival response that pain is. Have no depth of awareness your kind. All transitory to you it is."

"I assure you we can feel pain and are sentient."

"Only a different type of animal species you are. To other animal species similar you are that once inhabited our planet."

"What became of those other animals, as you call them?"

"Proved their inferiority and the limited evolutionary niche they, to adapt to the changes in the environment by not being able and dying off, therefore. On display in our collection is the last member of that species, like all the rest of the extinct plant and animal life of our planet."

"Wait a minute. If we are so primitive, how do you explain that we can converse with you? Is not our linguistic ability proof of our sentient nature?"

"No. Can communicate with others of their kind many species. Mouth sounds, wing fluttering, antennae movement, changing color, the means of communication that evolution has provided is diverse."

"But we speak. We have a language."

"Blow air through mouth ability referring to?"

"Blow air?"

"Yes. Means of inter-species communication your air blowing is a low level and extremely limited and unsophisticated. Many extinct animals similar behavior exhibit."

"But you can understand me. I can communicate with you."

"No. Hear breathes we cannot. The ability to pick up all forms and levels of emanations produced by a creature's brain have we. To transfer thoughts to its highest form our species raised this evolutionary technique. Picking up your simplistic brain emanations, decoding them, and responding to them as a means of soothing you our lowest level of our hive mind is. Handling animals before they became extinct easier it makes. Even the most violent animal quite docile and easy to handle this technique makes. Blowing air so much an odd evolutionary response is."

"You mean it only seems to us that we are communicating with you?"

"Course of. Merely directing mental emanations back at you similar to those that we are picking up from you we are."

"Sort of like singing to us or humming to us. Making sounds so that we will not react with fear at your actions?"

"It exactly that is."

"It is only from our perspective that these emanations take on a form of communication?"

"Correct. Very adept at this we are. Over our third level mental process we have almost complete conscious control."

"Well, if this communication is solely to pacify and subdue us, I will have to resort to the only form of communication you seem to understand!"

With that, I raise my hands to blast out with a burst of fire. The fiery blast smashed into them like a bowling ball through nine pins. They scatter.

LAMONT

Lamont: 'Peter, I will ease your pain, and then I will need to leave you for ...'

Peter: 'Lamont, no. Don't leave. Stay with ... me.'

Lamont: 'Peter, I must. There are others. I have to help them too.'

Peter: 'Others? Who? Cries I heard ...'

I reach into his mind and put him to sleep. Then I work as quickly as possible to staunch the flow of pain and erase the memory of that pain. I need to do this first, then once I help the others come back to see if I can get him to wake up.

I gently leave Peter resting and attend to the woman to his right to help her with her pain.

BASHA

More winged Offspring of Zygo'Teh arrive and presumably give silent instructions for the others to block them from my attacks. Pairs of the winged Zygo'Tehians, wearing plastic and metal helmets attached to metal tanks strapped to their backs. The fronts of the helmets glow with a pinkish light, and the air around them crackles with electrical sparks.

One of the pairs holds a nozzle while the other has his hands wrapped inside a tangle of plastic tubes and wires, which somehow are the controls for the device the two are carrying.

After a few minutes, the pairs have gotten their weapons set up, and the heads of the nozzles glow a garish bright pink and spurt out a stream of yellow liquid. Small drops of the liquid when splatter on the floor reveal the deadly effect of the fluid, as its acidic nature bubbles and eats away at the floor's surface.

The torrent of yellow liquid splatters into the wall of fire. The fire and the fluid hiss into steam at their mutual incompatibility. I see more of the helmeted Zygo'Tehians appear and add to the attack. As more and more of the streams of yellow are trained on the wall, I realize that I will quickly no longer be able to sustain the wall of flame that separates Lamont and me from our attackers.

Basha: 'Knight! We have got a major problem here! Are you done yet?'

Lamont: 'No. I need more time.'

Basha: 'Time's running out! Arrrgh!' I cry out as I am washed in the yellow liquid that burns me, as my own fire does not.

Lamont: 'Dawn! We have another problem.'

Basha: 'Nu?'

Lamont: 'I fear I cannot get them to wake up and return to the Waking World. If we take them out of these enclosures, they will die! Only the Zygo'Tehians can put them back together.'

LAMONT

I turn to face Basha and the commotion coming from the hallway. In that instant, I take in the scene. I see a small horde of Zygo'Tehians charging through the now extinguished firewall. I see Basha in pain, drenched in a sticky yellow fluid. Ignoring the Zygo'Tehian attackers, I pull off my coat and run to Basha's aid. I am quickly by her side. Rubbing and dried her off with my coat. The acidic liquid causes my coat to smolder. When my coat has soaked up all the acid, I let it fall as I wrap my arms around her.

Lamont: 'Dawn, are you okay?'

Basha grimaces and answers, 'Yes. Thanks.'

We now cease to focus on each other and look around. We see that we are surrounded by attackers with a half dozen or so fluid cannons aimed at us. Other Zygo'Tehians move about the room, undoing what I had accomplished, by returning our friends to their imprisonment, once more to be hung on display on the room's walls.

Lamont: 'I believe we've lost this round.'

Basha: 'Brilliant deduction, Sherlock.'

The weapon-bearing Zygo'Tehians motion to us to get moving.

"Offspring of NightDawn, follow us you must."

Lamont: "Wait, first tell us where you're taking us and what you intend to do with us."

Basha: 'Knight, they cannot really hear us. You are wasting your time.'

Lamont: "You never know. They might unconsciously want us to know. Besides, we need their cooperation so that I can ease our friends' pain and convince the Zygo'Tehians to put our friends back together."

"Other animals different you are Offspring of NightDawn. Study you we will. To a secure place take you."

Lamont: "See. I told you. Okay, silvery, we'll follow willingly, but only if you let us help our friends first."

"Help they need not. Taken care of them we have."

Lamont:" That's why we need to help them; you've caused them much suffering."

"Told you that lower species do not feel pain such as you."

Basha: "It doesn't matter what you think you know about us. If you want our cooperation, you must let me spend some time with each of the humans you have on display." Basha ignites into flames to make her point. "Or do you want us to destroy more of your equipment and some of you as well?"

"No more damage. We will let Offspring of NightDawn with your flock spend time if agree you to let examine you us."

Basha: 'Lamont, can you wake them all up?'

Lamont: 'I can't do it quickly; perhaps if I had hours to try…who knows. The only thing I can do quickly is to remove their pain. That's worth the effort to offer ourselves up for their playtime.'

Basha: "Okay, we agree. I will not put up a fight if we can administer to our friends. Take us to all the offspring of humans."

They do so. As I had thought, everyone who was engulfed by those things at the gate site battle was brought here. We are taken to Oolong and Selene of the Wicked Witches; additionally, we find two of Sarah and Rebecca's coven members here as well. When I administer to them, I discovered their names are Annabel and Laura. I can't get their last names, can't trace any of them back to their Waking World locations, nor can I wake any of them up. All I can do is remove their pain.

After this is done, we allow ourselves to be herded out of the display rooms and down to some other unknown destination. We walk down a maze of corridors, though we always take the left way when a choice arises. Finally, after many hours we are brought to our destination. Cages of many sizes line a portion of the back wall of this large room. There are also manacles attached to thick chains bolted into this wall.

The room has two five-pointed tables at its center with metal restraining bands at each point. The two tables are situated such that the topmost star point is almost touching. Above the tables floats two gleaming white spheres. The rest of the room is filled with strange and complex machines mounted on mobile platforms; others are on counters laid out in a semicircle surrounding the central five-pointed table. I am shoved toward one pair of manacles and locked into them, while Basha is locked into the other set. As all the Zygo'Tehians leave the room, I call out after them.

Lamont: "Does this mean we won't be getting room service?"

They ignore my joke, as they ignore most attempts at communication.

Basha: "Knight, I do not think they understand your sense of humor."

"The real question is, do they even have a sense of humor? Now that's something to think about. Heinlein said that's what separates us from other species, and possibly our sense of humor is our truly unique aspect. Though I don't know if he was serious when he made that remark. Anyway, this place must be getting to me; I can't recall the source."

"Are you feeling a bit stressed out? I cannot imagine why. Well, you could spend your next hours trying to recall that, but I believe there are slightly more important things to think about."

"You mean like coming up with a plan to escape from here and successfully rescue everyone?"

"Yes, something like that."

"You're always the practical one."

"This is true."

"Hypothetically, we could break out of these chains with my vampiric strength and your flaming charms."

"Hypothetically."

"We really need a plan to get beyond our immediate need for freedom. We need to determine how to ..."

"Successfully rescue everyone. You are repeating yourself."

Lamont: "I know. That's because I don't have any bright ideas. So, as Grainger would say when in doubt, hesitate."

Basha: "Who is Grainger, some Scotland Yard Inspector friend of Holmes?"

"No. A Science Fiction character. A very un-Heinleinian one at that."

"Heinleinian? As in Robert Heinlein, I presume. No, never mind, this is not the time or place for further literary discussions."

"True. Hmm. The last time they confined us was to an operating table; now they have confined us in some sort of holding area ..."

"A nice euphemism for a dungeon."

"No, I think this is more like a holding pen that a laboratory working with animals might have. Considering the `fragrant' stale and old odors that my more sensitive nostrils detect still linger in some of the cages, I definitely would call this a holding pen for animals."

"Fine, pen, or cage it is. It is more in keeping with their attitude towards us. We are definitely a lower form of life to them."

"Correct. And as such, we're new, never heretofore encountered species that their scientific curiosity wants to learn more about."

"Which will ultimately take us back to the operating table and the display room."

"True, eventually. For now, they've something other than just another anatomical study in mind. Which may present us with an opportunity."

"Like what?"

"I'm not sure. That's where the hesitation part comes in. For now, I suggest we wait and see what happens next."

"A good a plan as any."

"Hmmm."

"I know what that means. Out with it, Knight."

"Out with what?"

"When you make that sound, it usually means you have some theory. So, let me in on it."

"Okay. What are the chances you would encounter seeing someone die of natural causes back on Earth in your normal day-to-day life?"

"Not very likely. How does this relate to our situation?"

"In our relatively brief visit here so far, not just one of us, but both had encountered dead or dying Zygo'Tehians."

"So?"

"So, the odds of that happening should be very high. But they were not. Therefore, I conclude that death is a more common occurrence here."

Basha: "As in, the Science fiction motif of a dying alien race?"

Lamont: "Correct. These Zygo'Tehians are dying off."

Basha: "Lucky us. If only they would do it faster and leave us alone."

"I wonder what is killing them?"

Basha: "Considering what we have seen of this planet, it should be obvious."

Lamont: "Really?"

"Really. They have been polluting this planet for who knows how long. They told us that."

"You're right. Hmm. Would an intelligent, rational person continue to do something she knew would inevitably result in her demise?"

"Your hypothetical rational person would not."

"Ahh. But our Zygo'Tehians continue to engage in behavior that is killing them and polluting the planet. They do not even appear to have the concept of pollution."

"Which means that the Zygo'Tehians are either, one: not rational or two: not intelligent."

"I'm inclined to say that they are rational. Although, rather than lacking intelligence, they are more likely to lack knowledge. As evident in their lack of specific and important vocabulary; for instance, no word for pollution could mean that they lack the means to analyze the situation. At least, that is what a variation on the Whorfian hypothesis[44] presents. They have a blind spot regarding the byproducts of their industrial system."

"Blindspot. Interesting choice of words. Perhaps that is the literal reason for it all."

"What are you getting at?"

"We notice the pollution because it is in the form of the offensive smell and in the vast amount of soot and ash that darkens the sky. Our aliens do not have any olfactory senses nor perceive in the electromagnetic spectrum's visual range."

"Ahh…yes! It is outside of their perceptive abilities to register. Very observant on your part, Watson."

"If our deductions are correct. What good does this do us?"

"Knowledge is our best weapon. We need to turn this into an advantage. Perhaps as a bargaining chip ..."

"Our knowledge for our freedom? Good idea, in theory. I see one major problem with this scheme."

"What might that be?"

Basha: "All the Zygo'Tehians do not even know on a conscious level that we are intelligent. I think the silver ones are in charge, and we cannot communicate with them."

---

[44] Whorfian hypothesis is named after Benjamin Lee Whorf, in its basic form it states that language influences thinking, thus one's cultural linguistic system can influence a person's view of the world and how she thinks.

Lamont: "That does pose a problem."

Basha: "So, to implement our plan, we need to find a way to communicate."

"Correct."

"I hear something. I think someone's coming."

"Perhaps opportunity is about to knock."

Then a pair of silver-winged Zygo'Tehians, followed by a dull gray pair, enter the room. The silver pair walks toward the equipment in the room's center, turning on various devices. While the gray couple approaches me.

"Knight, what would your Grainger do now?"

"I'm not sure; hesitation still seems the better part of valor. Besides, I'm curious as to what will happen next."

"Considering what they have done so far to our friends, curiosity may not be a virtue in this situation."

"You plan; I'll continue to hesitate."

One of the dull gray pairs takes out a familiar phallic-like object from a coat pocket, callously plunges the device into my side, and injects me with a drug that renders me quickly unconscious.

BASHA

Basha: "Knight!" I call out in concern as I strain against the chains trying to reach out to him.

The second dull gray Zygo'Tehian now places his palm on the wall near Lamont's head. The wall glows a mustard color as some unseen mechanism is set into operation that causes the bands around Lamont's wrist and ankles to be disconnected from the chains bolted into the wall. The two wingless aliens drag the unconscious Lamont to the central table and place him on the table with all his limbs spread out. I look on with growing apprehension and concern as they attach the table's metal restraining bands over Lamont's wrist and ankles. Then they pick up metal scalpels lying amongst other medical instruments; the scalpels now glow with a teal light that radiates from within. They use the glowing scalpel to systematically cut off Lamont's Dream garments.

I should not look, but I cannot help myself; I am dying to know. Unfortunate choice of words, considering the circumstances. Anyway, I look at Lamont's naked form and am happy to see that he is circumcised. Thank the Goddess for small favors. He has a nice tidy package, not as ostentatious as Peter's. Enough with the naughty distractions; I have to focus on this situation's life and death reality. The two who stripped him naked step back and allow the two silver ones to approach Lamont.

The silver ones begin to place white three-inch disks on Lamont's bare skin. The first glows red when it is placed over his no-longer-so-private-private's. At least that is the emanations it is giving off are recognized by my mind-body as that color. Who knows what it really looks like. Since they presumably do not see color at all.

The following disk is placed an inch below his navel, and it glows orange. The third disk is positioned an inch above his navel, and this disk glows yellow. The fourth disk is placed on his upper chest between his nipples, and this disk glows green. The fifth disk is placed on his throat, taking on a sky-blue glow. The sixth disk is placed between his eyebrows, and it then glows indigo. The seventh is placed on the top of his head, and it glows with a purple light.

They then put a disk on his feet and hands that maintain their pale white color. As the disks are placed, a corresponding monitoring device begins to glow with similar colored light, and the pair of wingless aliens adjust the controls on each device.

What is with the colors? Oh, wait. Lamont would say something like I merely perceive an electromagnetic flux, and my mind filters it into visual perception. Who knows what the Zygo'Tehians perceive?

"Notice that? Did not you? Jiggling the waves sense. Perturbation slight. The device adjust please attendants."

"Yes. Intrusive fluctuation is their region thorax censor. Moment me give."

I see four delicate hands play their instrument as if it were a keyboard. The color shifted from simple pale sky blue to a crisp, clear azure.

"There. Compensated that it for."

"Perfect. Always as work excellent. Proceed can we."

Then the silver aliens each place a hand on the white sphere above Lamont. From the white sphere, a black beam of light shines forth. The sphere travels across Lamont, starting at his feet and moving upwards, stopping to float above the sixth disk. Next, there is a whirring sound, and a panel on the sphere slides open, revealing two white metal articulated shafts that end in three needle-sharp electrodes.

The electrodes lunge forward with cobra-like swiftness and plunge into Lamont's eyes, sinking deep into his skull. Blood leaks out from around the metal shafts and pools around Lamont's head, giving him a saintly scarlet nimbus. Lamont's unconscious body jerks and twitches as this happens.

Basha: "Knight!" I yell out in anger and concern.

LAMONT

The drug they gave me had disconnected the conscious layer of my mind from its connective link to my body's skeletal and muscular system. Thus, I am unable to move. Although the drug has not affected any other aspect of my nervous system. This means I am very capable of feeling the electrodes cut through my eyes and lodging into my brain. A deep scream pours out of my mind into the ether as I feel the horrible pain.

BASHA

Lamont's mental scream is mixed with my verbal one as I watch with sickening curiosity.

Basha: "Damn you forever!" I roar out as I ignite into flames.

I direct my fiery gaze at the Zygo'Tehian, acting out of instinct, no longer considering any plan. The beams splatter against a field of energy that surrounds me! There must be a force field in place to keep whoever is shackled up here contained! I strain against my chains as I try to melt the metal that binds me. Despite the intense heat from my raging fire, the metal bands that hold me remain unaffected.

Basha: "Damn You!" I yell out in frustration, "Stop this! Listen to me! We are not objects! We are self-aware beings like yourselves! Stop!" that last phrase is lost in a whimper as I acknowledge my helplessness. "Oh, Knight."

A wire comes forth from the white sphere and lodges into a waiting socket on one of the machines. The machine begins to make a sound similar to a cat in heat.

Then the two gray beings walk toward me while one makes an odd hand motion, deactivating the force field, and the other takes out his drug-injecting rod. With amazing clarity and quickness, I imagine what may happen next.

I see in the time it takes for the alien to bring one more step closer, my futile struggles to free myself as the alien plunges his rod into my helpless body. The drug slithers through my veins with an icy sensation as my body goes numb. I would be taken to the waiting table and strapped down upon it. I recall all too well each step in the procedure that would take place next.

I feel anger and humiliation as they strip my outfit off my body. Then they place the white disks on my bare flesh. With each contact, a tingle of surprising pleasure radiates outwards. Finally, the moment I had been dreading would arrive. I would stare at a panel on the white sphere above me, revealing the articulated shaft with its needle-sharp electrodes waiting to burrow deep into my brain. My vision paralyzes me with fear as the alien draws ever nearer.

Basha: "No! Fear is the mind-killer. I will not let it control me!"

I send out a searing flame that erupts from my eyes and engulfs the alien's outstretched rod. My flames melt the dreadful thing. Then I gather up all my fire to concentrate its power on the metal that binds me. So intense are my efforts that the light from the flames is like the burning whiteness of magnesium. Even the sightless Zygo'Tehians seem overwhelmed by the intensity they sense. Under the intense attention of my fiery anger, the shackles yield to my will, and I can free one wrist and then another.

Now two of the gray ones come toward me with their own drug-ejecting rods, shielding their facial ridge against the brightness of my soon-to-be successful attempt to free myself.

Lamont: 'Dawn...wait,' Lamont's voice whispers in my mind.

Basha: "Knight? How..." I am free, but I hesitate a second, trying to comprehend Lamont's surprising telepathic message.

'Wait ... something ... impor...' Lamont's telepathy is halted as another scream of pain is pulled out of him. His scream reverberates in me as I hear it from two sources, an external and internal one.

I am puzzled by this ability. I get caught up in the intellectual gymnastics of wrestling this unknown into the known.

The aliens fail to oblige me during those few seconds by remaining inactive. They act quickly to take advantage of my folly. One of them must have come up behind me; I feel his rod ramming into my back as I am injected with the drug again. In an instant, the pain of the assaults clears my mind, and I react by lashing out at the alien with my elbow and then blasting him with a ball of fire. I send out my flames at all my attackers, causing them to retreat.

But this victory is short-lived. The effects of the drug start to take hold.

The world begins to dissolve.

*

Lamont: "Dawn, wake up. Dawn!"

Lamont's voice is loud and insistent. A part of me wants to ignore him and simply give in to the cloying hands of sleep.

Lamont: "Dawn, come on! Wake up! We've got work to do. I found out something important."

His insistence is infectious, and I struggle with the hands of sleep keeping me metaphorically down. I shake them off and open my eyes.

Basha: "Ohhh," As the effects of the drug lessen, I can focus my thoughts more precisely. "Are you alright? Knight, your clothes are back. How did you manage that?"

Lamont: "Yes, I'm more or less okay. The procedure was quite painful but not physically damaging. My clothes simply were there when I woke up. Presumably, they have become an inseparable part of my identity now."

Basha: "Well? What was more important than being rescued?"

Lamont: "Information. I found out what they want from us."

"So? Keep me in the dark no longer. What were they after when they wired you up and probed your brain with a knife?"

"Knowledge. They realized that we were something other than mere animals. They wanted to find out if we could think. They wanted to find out what we were thinking."

"They could have asked."

"Their beliefs and their biology are still preventing them from recognizing the idea of sound as a means of intelligent communication."

"How are we going to communicate with someone who is not listening?"

"They do not hear at all. I'm not sure. But they pulled a lot out of my long-term memory. I had the impression that they were very interested in what information I had stored concerning the theory of evolution and the negative side effects of some of our technology."

"Such as polluting the air and water? Excellent. That is exactly what..."

"We wanted to tell them. Which is why I didn't want to be rescued at that moment."

"Now what? I'm sure I'm not interested in letting them extract more information from you or me using the same blunt instruments. We have got to find a way to ...ahh."

"I think I see a light bulb going off. Enlighten me. What have you figured out?"

"They cannot listen to us, that is, cannot physically hear our voices."

"I already said that."

"Yes, Lamont, but we both did not perceive its significance. We have been trying to communicate with them by the wrong method."

"What other way is there?"

"Not by voice but using the same method they communicate with their own kind."

Lamont: "Of course! Dawn, you're brilliant."

Basha: "Of course."

Lamont: "Too late. Someone's coming."

In walk two silver winged aliens; these silver Zygo'Tehians look unusually different. All Zygo'Tehian that we have seen have moths flying around them in no discernible pattern to our human eye/mind. These particular Zygo'Tehians have their moths arranged over their bodies in a distinctive, maintained pattern.

My musing is disrupted when I see the alien take out his rod and display it to Lamont.

Basha: "What is it doing?"

The alien throws the rod across the room, holds his hands out, and carefully and cautiously walks towards Lamont.

Lamont: "I think he has taken a leap of faith."

The Zygo'Teh seems to be focusing directly on Lamont; if the alien had eyes, they would be locked onto Lamont. The Zygo'Tehians keep one hand open, facing Lamont's face while he reaches over to the wall and triggers the release mechanism that frees Lamont.

Basha: "What is he up to?"

Lamont: "I'm not sure. But I think we've found someone who will listen."

"I agree. Be careful, Knight."

"I always am." I ignore Basha's laugh as I close my eyes and begin to try and send my thoughts to this one. My breathing gets slow and deep.

'I am Knight,' I try to project at them.

Meanwhile, the Zygo'Tehian has held his hand to me and is waiting for a response.

I hope he believes in universal symbols.

I reach out and take the Zygo'Tehians' hand. For a few seconds, we stand there. We try to traverse the abyss of ignorance that separates us utilizing a single gesture. The Zygo'Tehian steps back, never letting go of my hand and never losing sensory focus. I allow myself to be led, trusting that a stranger has good intentions once again. The Zygo'Tehians lead me to one of the star-shaped tables in the room's center.

Lamont: "I thought so. He wants to understand something about us. He is beginning to accept the possibility that we have sentience and intelligence."

The Zygo'Tehians gesture to the table. I get up on the table and lie down. The Zygo'Tehians activate various equipment but do not attempt to attach the restraining clamps on me. We both hope that the other will understand the meaning of the symbolic nature of our actions. I cause my uniform to dissolve, allowing the Zygo'Tehians to attach the monitoring devices to my skin.

I grip the table tightly and brace myself as the metal sphere is lowered and the sinister arm comes out of the sphere. It slowly approaches my right eye. Come on, damn it. Hear my mind!

Basha: 'I am Knight. Listen to me. We are sentient beings. We feel pain.'

The three-pronged electrodes descend ever closer. They gleam wickedly as they reflect the room's ultraviolet illumination.

I am not looking forward to this. 'I am Knight. Don't harm me.'

The electrode is mere inches from my face. With reflexes that startle even me, I grab the extended arm and try to prevent it from sinking into my eye. I wrestle with the highly flexible metal cable as the electrode moves with sentient-like purpose, constantly trying to strike. I wrap the coiled metal around one arm and pull the sphere within reach of my other arm. There is a flash of sparks as the metal arm is ripped out of the sphere. The sphere retreats from me like a wounded animal. The Zygo'Tehians, all the while, stood motionless and simply observed. This is not working. Why not?

Lamont: "Dawn..."

Basha: "Well?"

"I cannot reach them. At least so far."

"Damn!"'

"But, I have an idea."

"Well?"

"These Zygo'Tehians are always a pair. Maybe that is my problem."

"I don't follow you."

"I am only one telepathic voice. They are always plural. Perhaps we need to double my telepathic strength. To speak louder so that they can hear."

"Makes sense. You need to try and do it as well. Perhaps the gemstone will help."

"Perhaps with our combine voice, it will work."

"Great."

I walk over to Lamont and place my hands on either side of his head.

Lamont: 'Now, try to join me.'

I do. The Zygo'Tehians watch with an impression of curiosity.

Lamont: 'Match my breath. Concentrate only on me. Let my presence fill your mind completely.'

Shortly it is as if Basha fills the entire room.

BASHA

Lamont melts into me. Now, with the mental link between us complete, I focus on the Zygo'Tehians, trying to contact them on their mental plane. Trying to see if we think in unison at them, perhaps they can finally hear us. Since everything with them is a pair. If we act as a unit, then maybe they will recognize us.

BASHA AND LAMONT

" hear us? Can you hear us?" our voices call out in the Zygo-Tehians' minds.[45]

"Yes. Perceive you we. Are you who? Amazing is this! Thinking animals? Knew not that any do this could."

"The human on the table is my partner Knight, and I am the one standing next to him; my name is Dawn."

"Incredible! Talking animals you are! Mutants of your species you must be. Or are you Offspring of NightDawn, overseer of Offspring of Humans? Mayhap explains why have you the capacity for the proper communication you do! Hardly believe you animals can possible this do."

"All humans can speak. All are intelligent and sentient beings like yourselves, though only some have mastered the art of mind speech."

"Humans all? Your name is that?"

"The name for our species is human. Each human has a separate name. But we already went over all of this. Does not one of your kind remember? I thought you had a hive mind."

"Before your species has ever spoken none. Mistaken are you. Study you we must. Wish we to understand you. Something unexpected are you."

"But..."

'Dawn,' Lamont's mind whispers. 'We communicated only with their subconscious mind. Presumably, they have no conscious memory of any of our past conversations. Which is why they did not ...'

'...know we could speak. You are right.'

We now address the Zygo'Tehians. "Do you have tribe or clan names? Any name other than that of your species as a whole?"

"Yes. Ours Ya'Veneem brood name is. Amazing. Language have you. No idea had we. Your ability discovered we tool fashion and elaborate hive structures build you.

Speculate began we cultivated animal species on how possibly were you. Not conceive we could. Anything more than was you that. Discovered we then acknowledged you somehow the evolution divine force.

Somehow had you the first divine principle of Natural Law recognized, which that is the strong only fit survive will. Not believe almost we. Astonished

[45] I will use this underling font to convey when Basha and Lamont are speaking as one telepathic voice to the aliens.

were we. That had you deified concepts those. Darwin to name them called you. Unbelievable was it."

"Darwin is not one of our gods. He is a famous scientist."

"Words you understand not we. Repeating are you why? Interpret the data extracted did we not correctly?"

"From me?"

Lamont: "Dawn, the Ya'Veneem believes we are a pair from the same brood."

Basha: "Oh. So, what they take from one ..."

"Comes from both of us."

"Got it. Why does Ya'Veneem refer to Darwin as one of our gods of all people? Why did Ya'Veneem not understand when I referred to Darwin as a scientist and not a god?"

"It presumably is a problem of translation. We hear their words through our cultural context and semantic history. They are listening to our thoughts through their cultural context and semantic history. Ya'Veneem's mind is processing our words through the filter of their culture. We both lack enough information concerning the other to enable us to communicate the distinctions of ideas clearly as the other actually intend them to be under understood."

"That would mean that the words we think Ya'Veneem is saying may not actually be what was spoken."

"Correct, Dawn. Our mind is filtering and processing the telepathic symbols as best it can. Neither of us is actually hearing what the other is literally speaking; we only hear the translation, which is a guess of what we think the other may be saying."

"Why does Ya'Veneem think we worship Darwin? How did she ever get such an idea?"

"I can only assume that the Zygo'Tehians have made the ideas of evolution their civilization guiding principles. Anything considered so significantly, anything that gives meaning to one's life, is what the term sacred is meant to convey. The intensity of their thoughts surrounding evolution has resulted in our minds making semantic associations to religion. They may or may not have the cultural equivalent of religion."

"This is all very fascinating, but we have a rescue to get on with."

"Ya'Veneem, now that you have heard our telepathic speech, do you now accept that we are intelligent beings such as yourself."

"You consider not do we you our equals any way to be. Recognize we do an animal species that you are rudimentary thoughts possess. From our studies point out we must that your kind primitive species are you we know. An

intermediate species perhaps you are in animal and Zygo'Tehian the evolutionary chain between?"

"Fine. You can believe whatever you want about us, so long as your people do us and our friend's no further harm."

"A problem that will be."

"What do you mean?"

"The other broods many of believe do not theories our theories your kind concerning. Assert that we, Ya'Veneem contaminated data had collected we. For many years argued we. The end in, prove not could we believe ours any other brood to."

"You argued for years?"

Lamont: "Dawn, this is another instance of the special/temporal distortion. We do not mesh completely with this alternative dimension's laws of physics or whatever is going on here. The reference to years could mean literally what we would call years have passed if we can experience the debate firsthand from our perspective, or it could mean that this species lives on a different temporal plane, one that is in flux from our viewpoint."

Basha: "Is that why we see them moving slowly, resulting from us being out of phase with this world? Is that it?"

Lamont: "Presumably."

"Ya'Veneem, then it is only with your brood that we are safe?"

"Correct."

"Will you and your brood help us and our friends escape and return to our home dimension?"

"Leave you cannot."

"Why not?"

"To learn you about so much we have. Stay must you. To the others to prove can we must. Erred not we have. Failed not as scientists prove we must."

"I am afraid to ask, how long will all this take?"

"Long not."

"Good."

"Cooperation your with, to finish research our should we be able. Very time short be it will."

"How long is a short time?"

"Hundred or so years merely, as count you time we think you."

"I do not think we can stay that long. You will have to be satisfied with a much-reduced time frame."

"That why is?"

"For one thing, our friends are suffering. For another, we do not know what is happening back in our home dimension. We do not know what harm, if any, the open gates between our worlds are causing. We must return soon."

"Leave when you, return can you later time at?"

"I do not believe so. We only arrived here through a series of related, unintentional events. We did not directly choose to make contact with your species."

"Unfortunate this is. From you the data extracted we from, discovered we this concept new—po-lu-tion. Believe we may be this evolutionary principle new is this. Wanted we the time to study more carefully this. Perhaps that principle which seems to be in effect on your world may also manifest itself on ours."

"Of course it does. Do you not see the damage your machines are causing to your environment?"

"Offspring of NightDawn apologize we. That prior thought did not we understand. Transmit attempt again could you?"

"Do you not perceive that the extinction of all those species could be a result of the damage your machines are causing to your environment?"

"Interpret your thought still we cannot. Reformulate them try could you in manner other some?"

Lamont: "The Ya'Veneem are not able at this time to comprehend those ideas, Dawn."

Basha: "How can Ya'Veneem not understand? Did not one of their subconscious communication tell us how almost all this planet's plant and animal life had died off? They have science and technology; do they not see the connection between the discharges of their machines and the deaths of all those plants and animals?"

"For one thing, the Zygo'Teh do not seem to have the sense organs of sight or smell. Perhaps this has something to do with their lack of awareness of the effects of pollution over all these years. Or it could be a hundred different reasons. It could take a hundred years for us to figure it all out. As you said, we don't have a hundred years."

"Make we could a request you of, the Offspring of NightDawn?"

"Of course."

"Allow us could you harm not to the analysis sphere try if we were connect you to it again? Another connecting give us. Extract simply everything we will. Not a data search precise this will be. The last search but this will be. Detain you not we will further any. Help will we, you and other brood yours return homeworld to."

"That is a most generous offer Ya'Veneem."

"Excellent. My pair then and other pairs some of our brood enter this room may for data final extraction?"

"Yes."

Even as the thought is formed, other Zygo'Tehians enter the room and busy themselves checking the equipment. All of these Zygo'Teh, winged and non-winged, all have rainbow markings. One winged Ya'Veneem places a hand on Lamont, trying to communicate to him to lie back on the table. The damaged sphere recedes into the ceiling. Then it is replaced by a second sphere that descends towards Lamont.

"But wait."

"The problem Offspring of NightDawn what is?"

"This time, there is no need for extracting the data with so much pain."

"Perceive you have discomfort it unfortunate is. Only momentary but it is. Not able to be remember it will you. The discomfort besides real not is. Involuntary physical response on only is. Lasting damage there is no. Better know we, us trust."

Lamont: "No way, Ya'Veneem. I will not allow that thing to slice into my head," Lamont says as he removes his hands from me and tries to hold the sphere at bay. "There must be another way."

Basha: "Perhaps you can have the electrodes simply touch your forehead, Lamont. Maybe that and a telepathic link will be enough."

"It's worth a try. We need them to understand us to convince them to help us with our friends. That's definitely a more acceptable option to me."

Lamont takes the extruded electrode out of the sphere and carefully lowers it to touch his forehead. He then resumes contact with me.

"There, Ya'Veneem. Perhaps this will work. Try your machine now."

"Offspring of NightDawn, fine, will do this we."

LAMONT

The machinery hums as the device is activated. I feel a jolt of electricity from the electrodes, and then I sense ever-changing colors as I feel slightly weaker and drained. The sensation is now painful! It feels as if it is wrenching out my memories, one by one. It is painful, but not as painful as before. I accept the discomfort and allow the machine to continue its work. This time I am not alone in my suffering. I can feel Basha's presence. It is as if I am lying on the surface of a lake, and Basha is the water that keeps me afloat. Together we remain linked, Basha and I, and them to the sphere.

BASHA AND LAMONT

I feel so exposed. Oh! I think that this machine is copying and then downloading our life experiences. All that we have done. We need them to understand if our plan to get their aid will work. So, we have to let them do this. All that we had thought. All that we had felt. All that we had seen, read and heard. All of it is being duplicated and then extracted by the sphere. As our memories slip by, we feel like a sponge being squeezed by someone determined to get every last drop of moisture out.

When all is extracted, the sphere retracts. With its retraction, the force that was holding us up and keeping us linked together is released. We are exhausted. We sink into unconsciousness. The last thing we see is the Zygo'Tehians silently standing at their machines. They watch and wait.

"Oh, I am so wiped out. Ya'Veneem, did you get what you wanted?"

"Offspring of NightDawn, yes. Not long as did it take had thought we. Have had you short extremely life but active very."

"So, tell us, how long were we out?"

"Out? Outside never were you. Understand not do we."

"I mean, how long did the process take?"

"Then ask you did why about out being?"

"Never mind. That is clearly not translating."

"Animals of mysteries many are you. Took mere a 36 years the process."

Then a pair of wingless Zygo'Teh rushes into the room, seeming very agitated. They also have rainbow markings.

"Hurry we must. Others discovered us have. Brood war will there now be! The information hope we that extracted was worth the deaths will be."

"What is going on? I do not like the sound of `Brood war'."

"Ferreted out our research has been out of hive minds our. Knew this we happen would. Matter not. Protective measures failed did. Hurry must we."

"Hurry as in, to help our friends?"

"Yes. Now follow us!"

I wake Lamont out of the connective trance, and we follow behind the now rejoined pair of Ya'Veneem. In the hall, they can hear the sounds of fighting. We are being hastily led down a maze of corridors away from the ongoing battle.

"Ya'Veneem, can you still hear us?"

"Offspring of NightDawn, yes. Very but faintly. Sense you can we now know that you there are."

"Who is fighting whom?"

"Brood our. Having to fight the Ya'Veneem against is most remaining of the broods are we. Have not yet a few only decided yet to on either side join in the debate scholastic."

"Scholarly debate? Fighting a war over scientific questions? That is so seriously extreme."

"Religion very important to higher life forms such as we. Know we that this is for you hard comprehend to. Animals such you as for food or territory only fight. More no talk but now. Faster movement time for."

We arrive at the display room where our friends were being held.

"What do we do now with your other animal friends, Offspring of NightDawn?"

"Can you put them back together? Can you make them whole again?"

"Yes. Can we. Take time it will."

"That does not matter. You do that, and we will help out in your Brood war."

"Need not to do this you. Not understand the risks you do. Call this we war and is it..."

"We know what war is! We know about killing and death! We will help; you must hurry and make our friends whole."

"Offspring of NightDawn as say you."

The Ya'Veneem carefully moves our friends' dissected but still connected living bodies into the operating room adjacent to the display room to enact mysteries of science beyond our understanding and repair that which seems irreparable.

We all are swept up by the battle against greater numbers. I shudder with unease as I hear the cruel laughter coming out of Lamont's dark Night visage. Hearing it makes me afraid, and I know he is on my side. I do not like it. But fight, we must.

We fight not to win. We fight to gain for the YaVeneem to have the necessary time to physically repair the harm done to our friends. As for the mental and spiritual harm, nothing the Ya'Veneem can do, with all their science, could in no way begin to undo such damage. In this battle, many fall. Presumably, throughout this vast megatherian building, many such battles are fought. The Ya'Veneem fight to prove their beliefs. All the others fight to prove them false. I fear that the forces of disbelief are winning.

From within the operating room, voices call out to us.

"Come Offspring of NightDawn! Done it is! What now?"

We quickly leave the fighting and enter the operating room. Blessed be the Shekinah[46]! Our friends lie as if asleep, enwrapped by sweet dreams of bliss. No scar or mark shows the ordeal of having been taken apart and put back together.

"Incredible, "Lamont utters with awe in his voice.

"We need your help to carry our friends to the gate, to the green tower. Do you know where that is?"

"Offspring of NightDawn, we do yes. Take you will we you there. May be though last act our cause for."

---

[46] Shekinah went from being a term of the indwelling presence of the Divine to the feminine face of the Divine Itself, and the concept was picked up by neo-Pagan groups and treated as a name of the Goddess.

"You are losing the Brood war?"

"Yes. Hurry now. Us follow."

The winged Ya'Veneem gathers up the coven members in their arms, and like spectral angels, they bear them as they lead the way out. The Ya'Veneem led us through winding corridors in directions unknown. Time again moves on in its distorted way. My feelings of anxiousness make this journey seem endless as if we are spending years journeying through these corridors, marching on toward the green tower and the way home. Finally, I smell that befouled air, laced with traces of dust and smoke from the vast factories surrounding the small continent that is the city of the Zygo'Teh. Our quest is nearing its end. We all fly over the city and move into the industrial area with its polluted air. I glance behind us and see that we are being pursued by the other broods of the Zygo'Teh.

Then another contingent of Ya'Veneem split off from us. Is it that last remaining group? They valiantly try to halt what seems increasingly to be inevitable. They try their best to keep the others from reaching us. But they are being quickly disposed of.

Blessed Be, there is the tower! We arrive at the green tower and the disturbance, in reality, is still active. Shekinah has answered my prayers. The gate is open between the worlds. The few remaining Ya'Veneem lay the coven members reverently down onto the ochre-covered platform on the tower floor.

"Destiny you're here is. Offspring of NightDawn, in the sky above ours is. Now go we must separate ways our."

With those words, the remaining Ya'Veneem fly toward the mob that hungers for them.

Basha: "Now what, Lamont?"

Lamont: "Hmm. I presume that once we bring our friends to the gate, they will be carried back by the connective currents to their own waiting bodies in the Waking World of our Reality."

"Sounds reasonable to me. Let's do it."

One by one, we carry our friends to the shimmering rift, in reality, to be sucked into the metaphysical currents of space/time and carried back. With each departing friend, the gate between the worlds gets smaller. Soon only Peter remains to be carried through, and the opening now appears barely adequate. The mob has devoured the remaining Ya'Veneem and now rushes to reclaim what they once thought was theirs by right of force. We hastily pick up Peter and carry him to the gate.

"So, how do we do this?"

"Quickly! That's how! I'll grab his arms and go first."

Lamont appears to shrink into a pinpoint, and Peter stretches off into infinity. I feel myself being pulled in just as the vulturous mob of victorious Zygo'Teh descends on the tower. The gate closes as I am swallowed up in a flash of light.

PART FOUR

THE HALLS OF THE OUTER GODS

Saturday, September 6, 1980

BASHA

We find ourselves in that seemingly endless pulsating narrow tunnel of dark colors and roaring sound. Then we are quickly and precipitously dumped out, surrounded by the blackness of space and the myriad of stars. This is not Kansas, and it is not even Earth. I was expecting to be taken back home. Where are we, and how did this happen? As I look around more carefully, I realize that we are in orbit around a dull, desolate planet. Ahh, inspiration strikes, and I presume this is Zygo'the's planet. It is what I could have anticipated: a bleak and somber world of gray oceans and gray landmasses choked by gray clouds. The end results of their over-industrial waste products. Those poor beings are so misguided and in such danger. We almost made a difference in helping them, though we did not come there to do that. But, I do not think we succeeded. Things were going badly for those who were helping us.

Still, why was that tube not a direct connection back to our home? When we first came to this world, it was like we took the express train, which dropped us off on that planet in precisely the same place. I cannot think of why we did not take the same express route back to our dimension and Earth? What prevented that from happening? I need to clear my head to figure this out.

I turn my back on this terrible bleakness and focus on the endless expanse of darkness speckled with bright glimmering lights. The vastness of it all stretches beyond my comprehension. This is a vast landscape of silence and tiny specks of light. I feel lost and alone in this isolated, dark, inky desolation. Yet those little bits of countless scattered dots try their best to shine with significance. They are tiny bits pretending to be a glistening landscape overwhelmingly bounded in vast ebony.

I recall a bit of Shakespeare, '*O God, I could be bounded in a nutshell and count myself a king of infinite space, were it not that I have a bad dream.*[47]' How very true, William. This has all been like a really BAD dream that I wish would end. But wishing is not going to make this all go away. We have a lot of work still ahead of us. But how I long to wake up, rest, and get away from all this? I feel so exhausted from what just happened recently back there.

It is wearing me down. How long can I keep going?

---

[47] William Shakespeare, *Hamlet*, II, ii. Written in 1599, published 1603.

But then my eyes focus on a warm flame glowing in this blackness. The comforting presence of love resides like a warm flame in my heart and mind. A love I can put a name to, Lamont, keeper of my heart.

As I gaze at him, I notice that I am surrounded by a glowing reddish-yellow nimbus that completely engulfs my body. It both feels nebulous and substantial. As if it is a barrier to the inky cold black of space. I surmise it is my bubble of breathability in the impossibility of me floating in space. That I can breathe while in space is comforting, even if it is disconcerting to my sense of rationality. Hey, losing a bit of rationality is fine if it means I am alive in this vastness of ink.

Lamont's own aura is shimmering lunar grayness. Through his nimbus, I see Lamont dressed in a Black Knight outfit of black jeans, a black dress shirt, scarlet tie, the black wool RAF coat, and the black slouched hat. All I see of his face is his soft marble skin, eyes glowing icy blue shadowed by the wide-brimmed black, and the upturned collar revealing the coat's blood-red lining. The black wool coat with its blood-red lining billows out as if from unseen and unfelt interstellar winds as he floats in space with that faint shimmer about him. I see myself all aflame in my red skintight catsuit slash superhero outfit. What is missing from this picture? Our friends, that is what. There is no sign of anyone who we rescued from the Zygo'Tehians.

Lamont is ruminating on his own thoughts as I have been. We need to stop dwelling and start to get moving.

Basha: 'Knight! Why are we here? Why did we not return to Earth? And where is everyone else?'

Lamont: 'Hmmm. You're right.'

Lamont turns to face me and focuses on me as he speaks. That is better. Focus on me and the work we have to do.

'We took a non-stop route when we came here. So why didn't that work this time to go back? We came here consciously following where our friends were all taken. We are here, and they are not. Hopefully, their consciousness has returned to the Waking World since they are not here with us.'

'I pray that you are right. I do not think there is any way to tell if that is the case.'

'Nope. Not at this moment. We have to get back to Earth to find that out.'

'Knight, what do you think will happen to the Ya'Veneem and the rest of the ZygoTeh?

For all the pain those creatures caused, I still feel sorry for them. Their world is in such a mess, having pushed themselves to extinction-and not even noticing that.'

Lamont: 'I know. What hope they seemed to have laid with the group that called itself the Ya-Veneem and the Ya'Veneem are losing their debate.'

Basha: 'Debate? They said something like that while we were on the planet's surface. It did not make sense then, and it still does not. That was outright warfare.'

'Well, true. From what they told us, what would be an academic dispute for us is taken to the extreme of inter-religious jihad in their society.'

'That is so meshuggeneh[48]. Such a waste. How did they end up like that?'

'Good question. They seem to have made what we would call the scientific method into their equivalent of religious practices and the conclusions to be their religious gospel or something like that.'

'If the Ya'Veneem lose that debate slash war, will the ZygoTehians survive as a species? It was only by talking with us that they seem to finally realize that they were destroying their world by pollution from their industrialization.'

'True. And from what we saw, if they don't do something radically different, they will return to plunging into the abyss of self-extinction.'

'More like planetary extinction, according to what we saw at that museum, they have been killing off the planet's plants and animals for decades. How could they be so advanced in their science yet clueless about its consequences?'

'People, creatures, can be kinda stupid. But hey, at least back home, our species is not so blind and dumb. I assume we'll not be making the same mistakes as them.

'You are right. We as a species are clearly more self-aware than the poor race of ZygoTenians. I am sure we will get our pollution problems under control very soon. It is all such a shame. Knight, we need to go back there and help them. I wish we had more time with them under better circumstances and were not so rushed rescuing our friends from them. I never really got to ask them much about their life and how they came to be the way they are.'

'We can't. We don't have that luxury of time to help them. We have no idea what is happening back on Earth with our friends. We have got to get back to them, somehow.'

---

[48] Yiddish for someone who is crazy.

'Yes, but how can we leave them? They need help; there are many unanswered questions about how and why this all happened to them. Perhaps by asking them about their past, we can figure out how to guide them to some better future.'

Lamont: 'You want to go back and do a proper interview with them, do the Lois Lane thing so you can write up an exclusive for their Daily Planet's[49] Science column?'

Basha: 'Well, yes, I do. It is terrible what has happened to them.'

'Even if we could go back since the Ya'Veneem seemed to lose the war, the rest of the ZygoTenians would consider us the equivalent of talking cattle. The winning side might dismiss what we say and the insights and answers we try to present. Just getting them to listen to us would be a time-consuming task. Let alone get them to tell their long sorry tale of how they got to where they are. Then we would have to spend a very long time in protracted religious analysis to find the means to have them see the light. We were lucking that revelation struck once in their encounter with them. And that revelation was tortured out of me. I, for one, am not looking forward to undergoing their ministrations to see if lightning will indeed strike twice. As it is, we barely got out of that intergalactic hornet's nest.

'You are right, Knight. It is a tangled web. It would take so much time and effort to help them to see the hangmen's noose they put around themselves. Yikes! Time, it would all take so much time.'

'Time is a commodity that we don't know how much of that we can spare. I don't think we can do that. We need to focus on what we hope we can do something about, our friends.'

'You are right. But, maybe when all that is done, we could go back when we finish helping our friends? Do you think we could?'

'I'm not sure how. We don't really know where here is? I don't have a clue whether we are in our own galaxy. We could be anyplace in the immense vastness of the universe. Hey, I'm not even sure we are in the same plane of reality. So, I don't think we can find our way back here once we are done with our own personal bit of coming to our friends' rescue.'

'You are right. We probably will never be able to find our way back here since, as you rightly put it, we do not know where here is! We came here to help our friends and stumbled onto a whole planet that needed our ministration. And we could not do it, at least that is what it feels like. But,

[49] Lois Lane was created by writer Jerry Siegel and artist Joe Shuster, she first appeared in Action Comics #1 (June 1938). She is an award-winning journalist for the Metropolis newspaper The Daily Planet.

reluctantly, I have to concur. We must move on, and we probably will never be able to go back. Okay, so now what? Why did we end up stranded here?'

'Something intervened?'

Basha: 'Or someone?'

Lamont: 'Yeah. I don't like where that thought takes me.'

'Neither do I. The choices seem limited for candidates with a benevolent inclination and power to notice us.'

'Exactly. But, more to the immediate point, how do we get home?'

'Ahh, click our heels three times and say there is no place like home?'

'I do not think that will do it.'

'Well. How about that way?' Lamont points directly away from where we are.

'Why that direction?'

'Just because is away from here. Or how about this way…' Lamont points in a different direction.

'Hey, Knight, did you see what is happening?'

'I wasn't sure I did.'

'Your ring. It glows when you point in that direction. Try pointing away from there, point somewhere else.'

He does, and the ring ceases to glow.

'Well, would you look at that?'

'That was exactly what I did! I looked at it. Could it act like a homing beacon?'

'Perhaps. Anyway, for lack of something better,' Lamont brings the ring back to the direction when it glows. 'Let's follow the glow. Come on.'

'How?'

'I'm not sure…'

Then we notice that we seem to start floating forward, moving in the direction of the glowing ring.

'Ahh…that is cool.'

'Yeah. We just think in that direction and fly off in that direction. I am unsure how or why, but I cannot complain; we are moving somewhere.'

'Though this is a horrible situation, being lost in space like this. It is amazing if you just take time to stop and smell the starlight.'

True. The vastness of interstellar space is…awesome! That is the best word for this, though barely adequate to convey the overwhelming smallness I feel in this immensity. We travel in an infinite, inky expanse of stars. I wish I could say I feel the comforting sense of the Divine who created all of this wonderment, but all I feel is vast emptiness in this dark solitude. How long and how fast we are moving, I cannot say. The longing for the comfort of the small corner of this expanse that goes on forever where our pretty little blue marble sits in the velvet night is intense. Will we ever see our home again?

'Knight, do you think we are limited by the speed limit?'

Lamont: 'Why? Are you worried about getting a speeding ticket from some intergalactic highway patrol person?'

Basha: 'No, you silly man. I am referring to the speed of light! Einstein and physics and such stuff of reality.'

'Oh. That speed limit,' Lamont remarks jokingly.

'Yes. If we are limited to the speed of light, then we may be in big trouble. The nearest star to our solar system is found in the Alpha Centauri system, about four point-something light-years away. I have a bad feeling that we are many light years further out than that.'

'Hey, as I muttered before, we cannot be sure we are still even in our Milky Way. This means this could be a very long commute back home. But, don't worry. I know a whole lot of knock-knock jokes to entertain us.

'Seriously? We might never get back home.'

'Can't think like that. We can breathe. We are alive. We are following a glowing gold and obsidian ring. Besides, I think we are being led by someone who wants us to find them.'

'Ahh…Knight, I thought we were trying not to think along those lines.'

'Yeah, I know, but…'

'You know who gave us that obsidian by which we forged those rings?'

'I do. Good old Tezcat.'

'Do you think we are being led to Tezcatlipoca?'

'It is, unfortunately, a reasonable hypothesis.'

'Are you worried about that?'

'Yup. She could explain how we got derailed off the express route, having a deity's self-proclaimed powers. But we don't have much choice, do we?'

'When you put it like that, Knight. No, we do not. Knight, maybe now we will finally find out what Tezcatlipoca wants with us.'

'What do you mean?'

'Well, she has been manipulating you from the very beginning.'

'I know. I was lured into Dreamland to help open the Gate of Dreams so she could enter the Waking World. Through the use of my body! I am not likely going to forget that.'

'There is that. Did I ever mention my hypothesis concerning your inability to die in Dreamland?'

'No, Dawn, you did not? Can't I just be special?'

'You are special. But, I believe there is more to it than that.'

'Okay, so I'll bite; what is behind my non-dissolution?'

Basha: 'More like who.'

Lamont: 'You're going to tell me that this is Tezcat's doing? Why do you think that?'

'It is something that Queen Lilith told me. You were given the unique and seemingly impossible ability to return from the dead in Dreamland whenever your Dream body was killed.'

'I just thought I had a singularly strong sense of self.'

'Is that another way of saying you have an overly inflated sense of self-worth?'

'I prefer my reframed version.'

'On the bright side, it could be that Tezcatlipoca used your innate stubborn belief in yourself to pull off his magick.'

'Thanks, I feel so much better about myself now. I wonder if I still have that talent.'

'Who knows? But it is clear that Tezcatlipoca wants you alive still.'

'Yes. Perhaps the glowing light is Her way to finally explain what this is all about.'

'We can only hope we are not being led to our doom.'

'Just hold my hand and hope for the best.'

'I love you.' I say as I take Lamont's hand.

'I know.'

'So now you think you are Han Solo[50]?'

'The line worked for him.'

On and on, we travel through the infinity of stars in the black silence of space, all alone in this seemingly endless forever night. How long we travel is almost impossible to tell. Space and time markers seem so contradictory in this situation. However, we are approaching a sector of space that is singular in its appearance. There is a clear line in this area of space that we are approaching. The stars and galaxies get fewer and fewer until there are no more. We are approaching a zone of utter desolation and darkness devoid of anything and everything. The blackness is oppressive and hurts the eyes as well as the mind.

"Knight, I do not like this."

"I agree, but the ring clearly guides us to that zone of emptiness."

"I have to confess that it scares me."

---

[50] Alluding to the character created by George Lucas. The character first appeared in the 1977 film *Star Wars* and then again in 1980 *The Empire Strikes Back.*

"I agree. But that is where we must go."

We sigh and shrug reluctantly, give each other's hand a tight squeeze, and then continue off. We eventually enter that blasted emptiness. It is as if I can feel the horrible silence of nothing as we cross beyond the threshold of normal and sane space.

Now there is nothing but this horrible blank blackness. To cope with what I see, I imagine this is the center of the Big Bang. From here, all of existence blasted outward, creating ordinary space, and here at the center of that birth point, everything has been strewn outward, leaving behind this empty mind-numbing horror of a place.

Sanity seems to have been swallowed up within this gargantuan gaping maw of bleak blackness. Now our journey is interminable in this barren area of vacuity and desertion. The desolate nature of this area, devoid of all light, is pressing down on us. It is as if it is screaming at our intrusion into it. As if it was being violated by our living presence proclaiming this as a place that is utterly alien to all life and activity. I feel the need to break the silence and the emptiness, but my thoughts of attempting speech are getting sucked out of me into this horrendous maw of inky ebony. I assume we are still moving toward such an unknown destination of Tezcatlipoca's planning. Though I can neither see any signs of movement nor feel any.

I start to shiver. Though the temperature has not changed one iota.

*

Eventually, after minutes, hours, or days—maybe even weeks of traveling, I imagine I might be hearing something. I strain to grasp the faintest of sounds in this impossible space where there cannot be sound. Is it the whimpering whispers of my mind as it pleads for some tiny nugget of sanity in this insanity of dark emptiness?

But the faint sound is so insistent and incessant. Can I really be hearing something in this vacuum of space? It cannot be, yet there is a feeble call of life, and the silence is no more. The terrible certainty of actual sound is grating on my nerves. I am sure I hear some awful weird faint erratic sounds. Not quite musical. It is an irritating sound. The louder it gets, the more it disturbs me.

It seems to be the sound of the maddeningly discordant beating of millions of drums and the thin, piercing, monotonous whine of millions of strange flutes. A shiver of primal fear shudders through my body. A desire to flee and hide under comforting covers and never come out.

'The natives are throwing a party on our account?' Lamont's silly tone breaks the moment of horror that had me in its grip.

'Perhaps. But the sounds cannot be. We are in the most vacuumy vacuum of all of space. There is nothing to create vibrations that could register on our ears.'

Lamont: 'All perfectly reasonable objections. Yet, we have to admit that we hear these annoying sounds. We are not in normal space/time, which could be good. Distance and speed do not seem to hinder us.'

Basha: 'Knight, I get a chill and an awful feeling in my gut hearing those drums and those flutes. This is bad. Really bad. We need to flee.'

'I agree. They give me the willies as well. I want to curl up in a little ball and whimper. But I'm trying to fight it. You're here with me, my shining little dawning hope. Things can't be so bad with you here. So, I need to fight back with my best weapon. Flippancy. At least someone is home wherever and whose ever home we are being led to.'

'Where Tezcatlipoca really dwells?'

Before I respond further, the sounds get perceptively louder and distressingly clearer. We can hear them echoing and reverberating off the empty blackness around us. Unsettling and ominous, it gets even more demanding and insistent as we approach wherever we are going. The feeling of dread is almost palpable. My heart is racing. My mind gibbers to get away from this place, where the coldness of Hell beckons with glee at our approach.

I start to giggle.

So does Lamont. We chuckle uncontrollably as tears leak down and a small portion of sanity dissolves with each teardrop. Drop by drop, I can feel it disappearing.

Then…

I blink. Can it be? It cannot be…, but there it is. Where once there was empty blackness, now I seem to see something. I blink through teary eyes and convulsive hiccup-lick sick laughing, and my mind begins to discern a pattern and form what it insists it is seeing ahead of us.

It is as if I could suddenly see beyond the slim section of the electromagnetic spectrum that we call visible light. The area ahead of us shimmers and glimmers with strange, weird colors. Colors, I presume from the spectrum of energy that we humans are not meant to see directly. Areas of the spectrum we call infrared, ultraviolet, x-ray, microwave, etc. My head hurts, and my eyes well up with tears and pain at being forced to see colors I should not be seeing. Even worse than the damnable color is the fact that it seems that I can see recognizable shapes in that mass of flickering shimmering abomination.

'Dawn, up ahead...what do you see?'

'Light glowing with colors that I cannot comprehend, and you?'

'Yeah. The same. I think this area could be the source of the meteor that came from this unnatural depth of space and crashed onto the Earth back in 1882, as recorded by Lovecraft[51]. I don't want to look at it, but damn it, it is so hypnotic and…'

Basha: 'Compelling. I know. I cannot stop looking at it.'

Lamont: 'Even though it's so painful to do it.'

I see millions upon millions of disconcerting shapeless, and yet shapes. Twitching and hanging in the void with what seems to be multiple tentacles and human mouths in horrid grimaces. They hold and play skin drums or twisted pipes. That is where the atonal pipping and drumming come from. Surrounding a central core. The center is a mass of chaotic confusion.

But what is horribly worse is that it is impinging on my mind. Forcing me to come to terms with this madness. There is a singular sentient force at the heart of the convulsion and convolution of chaotic colors. It demands to be known. It is imposing its will on us. We are forced to comprehend what was not meant to be comprehensible.

Then it is as if a mirage takes shape before us; there appears to be a single dais and throne with some being on it. It reminds me of what one would expect in some Arabian Night story told by a madman. My mind wrenches, and my stomach churns. I want to vomit, but I cannot. I just do not want to understand all this.

Basha: 'Knight,' I say as I stop my sick giggling. 'What do you see?'

Lamont: 'I wish it didn't. But I think that I do. And what they seem to be are millions of naked slaves in chains, coated in lavender oil, playing drums and flutes. It horridly reminds me of the Mayor of Thrall's throne room.'

'To each their own nightmare. Damnation! That sound is driving me crazy!'

'Me too! I cannot…take this…No more!' I clap my hands over my ears as if this would stop the sound. There is no air to travel in space…but logic and physics are not part of this place. I want to run and hide. I can barely think…

'I agree it is super annoying…' Lamont says, whimpering.

'I…mean…seriously…I…cannot…take it much…longer…the sounds…the implication…of what it means…it is scaring me…'

'Yeah…I…know what…you mean…this is the center of…madness…something…'

---

[51] Lamont is talking about the fallen meteor as described in H.P. Lovecraft's '*The Colour Out of Space*', which was first published in Amazing Stories, in September 1927.

'Terrible…powerful…it is out to get us…'

'Yeah…to swallow us up like some little…bugs…'

Basha: 'I am scared…I do not want to move…the sounds…'

Lamont: '…can't take it…nooooo…'

'…no please…noooo…'

BASHA & LAMONT

Who started screaming first—I cannot say. But all I can do is scream in horror and terror. I pray and hope that my screams will drown out the sound of the drums and the pipping of those flutes.

But as usual, my prayers go unanswered. I hear them even over my own keening cries.

*

On and on, I hear screams…trying to drown out that horrid reality out there. The flutes…the drums…this should not be…screaming to escape...hide…feel hopeless…

*

I hear your anguish, my children.

That voice. So calm and so close. Deep and sonorous. Soothing in its familiarity and its reminder of sanity. It is Tezcatlipoca! I continue to scream. I need to try to drown out those other…horrid sanity-leeching sounds…

Do not be afraid. I will protect you. You are not alone

BASHA

Tezcatlipoca's words are soothing and calming.

Then a strange green fire oozes out of our rings, and a gooey mass of flames creeps up our arms. It feels odd, soothing, and comforting. I watch as my whole head then gets coated in this stuff. I think the screaming has stopped.

Basha: 'Knight…do you see what I am seeing?'

Lamont: 'If you mean viridescence fire engulf my body, then yes.'

'Should we panic? And fight back?'

'I feel an odd calmness as it creeps along my skin; how about you?'

'Hmm. I guess I do feel better. The horrid sounds are fading a bit.'

We watch and wait as our bodies are devoured by the flickering light of green flames. The sounds I hear are now muted and muffled as we are fully immersed in it. 'Hey, it is like we are under the water; the sounds of the drums and pipes are significantly muted.'

'I hope this is Tezcat's way of saying move our butts and get us to go where we are supposed to be going.'

Basha: 'What if it is not…'

Lamont: 'No time to doubt, just time enough to be grateful. Let's see if we can just hurry up and pay homage to who or what sits on that throne in the center of all this.'

'You want to head into that madness?'

'No. Which is why we must. Can we control our speed?'

'Won't know till we try.'

'True.'

We focus and try to propel ourselves forward at a more rapid pace.

It works! We are speeding by, and row upon rows of players flit past us as we travel toward the central dais. The madness pounds at me, but it cannot get past the glimmer of the viridian flames.

Yet, it feels like hours go by for all our speed as we have an infinite distance in front of us and an infinite distance behind us. On and on we travel.

LAMONT

We have gone a long way, but we seem no closer to our destination than when we began. I am getting weak from need. Traveling in the infinite voids of space can wear a little vampire out.

Lamont: 'Hey, Dawn, could we stop somewhere for lunch? I'm getting peckish.' I say being deliberately silly to help soothe and calm myself as a salve to the oppressive forces and sights around us.

Basha: 'Okay, Knight,' Basha brings herself to a halt next to me. 'Cannot have my favorite vampire feeling peckish.'

BASHA

I can feel his genuine and urgent need that he covers up with his flippant manner. It grounds him and me. This need is real and familiar.

Lamont: 'Could I get a kiss before you have me as lunch?' I need Lamont to stay in control of himself. I cannot allow the Night to take him over.

LAMONT

Basha: 'Of course.' We are both in need of some pleasant distractions to help keep us sane.

I take her in my arms, and we kiss. I taste her sweetness and the aroma of cinnamon, and then I make my way to her neck and bite in. There is a feeling of joyful communion, sweetness, and the metallic taste of hot blood as I lose myself in my love.

Eventually, I manage to separate and bring myself to the two of us alone and separate as I cease to feed. Basha is a bit dazed, and I hold her tight. She dozes as we float in this infinite sea of blackness. She's a comfort and touchstone of reality as we drift in this sea of unreal places in space. I call out thanks to Tezcat for saving our sanity. Eventually, my sleeping beauty awakens. I kiss her gently.

Lamont: 'Hey, beautiful, you're back.'

Basha: 'Are you feeling better, my love? I sure do.'

'Yes, I feel refreshed and loved. I've been thinking as we treaded metaphoric water here.'

'Of course, you have. What are your thoughts?'

'Well, all this is reminding me of something. And it is not good.'

'Great. What is it?'

'It's a few lines from Lovecraft; it goes like this, '*that shocking final peril which gibbers unmentionably outside the ordered universe, where no dreams reach; that last amorphous blight of nethermost confusion which blasphemes and bubbles at the center of all infinity—the boundless daemon sultan Azathoth, whose name no lips dare speak aloud, and who gnaws hungrily in inconceivable, unlighted chambers beyond time and space amidst the muffled, maddening beating of vile drums and the thin monotonous whine of accursed flutes; to which detestable pounding and dance slowly, awkwardly, and absurdly the gigantic Ultimate Gods, the blind, voiceless, tenebrous mindless Other Gods whose soul and messenger is the crawling chaos Nyarlathotep.*[52] I also recall that Tezcat's temple was one of the Outer God's temples that had been neglected. So, by the way, Tezcat is one of those Outer Gods.'

'That does not sound good. Are you saying you think we are heading to this throne room of the Outer Gods where this Azathoth and Nyarlathotep hold court? But that is from a novel written by Lovecraft; it cannot be real?'

'It seems very real from where we float, approaching some horrid madness surrounding that throne room in the middle of space.'

'If I recall Lovecraft's stories, things generally do not end well for his characters.'

'Yup. Death or insanity are two of the typical outcomes.'

'Lovely. Glad you informed me of this bit of literary reference.'

'Well, things turn out better in the Dreamland cycle of stories. Randolph Carter did come out of it sane in the end, though his ability to

---

[52] Howard Philip Lovecraft, from *The Dream Quest of Unknown Kadath*. Originally published 1939 Arkham Press, Ballantine Books paperback edition, 7th U. S. printing, 1983, p. 3-4

Dream was lost to him. There was no death, dismemberment, or insanity for him, at least as far as I can recall. I believe that was Nyarlathotep's doing, which meant Carter got off easy.'

'I think this is a bad time to lose your eidetic recall, Knight.'

Lamont: 'When we get back home, I can go look it up if that's any comfort.'

Basha: 'Ahhh. No. It is not.'

'I think we are finally getting to the end of this road. The throne dais seems to be coming closer.'

'How long do you think this took?'

'I do not think normal time/space coordinates matter here. This place is even rougher than ordinary Dreamland on cartographers.'

'Now, Knight,' Basha says, pretending that this is an ordinary walk in the park. 'What Lovecraft described as the Outer Gods is not necessarily accurate. Nor even what we might see when we get there.'

'Very true. The 'we-are-shaped-by-ideas principle'. We see what nature, nurture, culture, and our own history shapes us to expect.'

'Yes. That is it in the abstract. William James described it all in the specific in his book *The Varieties of Religious Experience* in his chapters on mystic and mysticism[53]. I believe he was the first to academically and seriously consider and analyze mystics and mysticism. You must consider the contexts to understand why we may not see Lovecraft's Outer Gods and why Lovecraft's singular description may be his own but not what others or we may see. Basha's voice keeps getting more conventional and calmer as she recounts this. Talking about ideas and books offers us both solace and an escape from the reality of the unreality that we are confronting.

'So, as I was saying,' Basha says as she continues her lecture, 'when a mere human mind confronts such an anomalous vastness, we struggle and force it into the familiar. We must have something we can comprehend. We need it as much as we need food or air. Now, imagine an ordinary-sized plastic sand bucket in your hand. Picture that.'

'Okay, I'll play the game.' I focus and imagine a bright yellow plastic pale with a bright yellow plastic shovel that is a bit small for the size of my hand. 'Okay, I got it. Now what?'

---

[53] William James first delivered a series of lectures at the University of Edinburgh, Scotland, in 1901-1902 for the Gifford lectures on Natural Religion. Then James wrote it all down and published it all in the book *The Varieties of Religious Experience*, first published in 1902. Lectures 16 and 17 are on Mysticism.

Basha: 'Now imagine a backyard sandbox; let us say it was the size of a kiddie pool that was three feet in circumference, and I dumped all of the sand into that bucket; how much of it would you have in it?'

Lamont: 'I don't know. It would just fill up the bucket, and all the rest would be lying all around me.'

Basha: 'Right. Now imagine I can gather all the sand at the beach from Ocean Beach in San Francisco. I suspend it above you while you still hold onto that bucket. I somehow protect you as I dump all that sand down upon you. With all that sand coming at you, will you gather any more sand in the bucket than you did before?'

Lamont: 'No. Of course not.'

'How about if I gathered all the sand of the Sahara Desert?'

'No. It will have the same result since you didn't change the size of my bucket; you only just changed the amount of sand you're dumping at me. It will still just fill up that bucket.'

'So, how much sand is there on our Earth?'

'I don't know. A huge, gargantuan amount. A number with a whole lot of zero's behind it.'

'Right. But it still is a finite number, correct?'

'Correct. A way-way big number and thus a way-way big amount of sand. Ahh, I get it now, Dawn, what you are trying to get me to say and thus realize, that this huge number is the amount of sand on the whole planet, that number is some ginormous number but still is only pointing to a finite and fixed number of grains. And, no, I won't end up with any more sand in my bucket when you dump all the sand of planet Earth down on me.'

'Right. Your bucket has a fixed carrying capacity. That bucket is metaphorically the size of your neural network in your brain; that neural network is how our brain makes our mind; that neural net has a finite capacity for interconnections. That neural network can only contain a finite amount of data. Now, all that sand is immense and vast, your neural net has a huge carrying capacity, but even yours, Knight, even yours is still finite. Now consider God. How big is God?'

'Ahhh...under most descriptions, God is infinitely big.'

'Right. According to the traditional constructs of God, all the sand of Earth must be like a mere single grain compared to the vastness of the infinite that is God. When a prophet or a mystic confronts or meets God, it is like a person with a sand bucket trying to grasp an infinite amount of sand. That is what happens when you try to comprehend the Infinite Divine. We cannot contain it all. We can only do your 'we-are-shaped-by-our-ideas-given-to-us-by-nature-nurture-culture-and-history' thing. We take that tiny bit of data we can grasp and transform it into some images and symbols familiar to us before the encounter. Our bucket gets filled with the sand nearest to us, the most familiar stuff. Thus, in summation and applying all that reasoning I just explained, Lovecraft's Outer Gods may not be what we see when we meet whatever we are about to meet.'

Lamont: 'They will be like a Rorschach inkblot. We will make of it what we need and want.'

Basha: 'Exactly. Actually, one of the most insightful recountings of a mystical experience is in the book of Ezekiel.'

'Oh really?'

'Yes. Throughout Ezekiel's description, he says it was an appearance of a likeness. He continually qualifies it with uncertainty. It always is described as seeming to be something. But he never says directly it was X. It was always something that appeared like a familiar X. Which makes it and him a truly remarkable self-aware account of confronting something beyond human ken.'

'Wow.'

We hover in silence for a moment. Feeling the soothing calm of academic rigor and discussion percolating within us. We let the words and ideas settle down deep in silence and without motion.

'I, for one,' Basha finally says, 'needed that.'

'Amen!'

'Okay,' Basha says with clarity and direction. 'Let us go down there and see if we can be as clear-headed as Ezekiel when encountering these so-called god-like beings.'

We float past and through a thin glowing membrane, and we halt at the bottom of a long staircase of steps leading up to the dais. We find an old gray granite dais where a sleeping human form sits in a stained long white robe on a dusty and tarnished golden throne made of similarly shaped blocks. The throne sits in front of majestic burgundy curtains hanging in the air. He is an elderly man with long white shoulder-length hair. He is drooling in his sleep as he sonorously snores in an annoying pitch. The snoring sound is that sound we kept hearing; it is something like that which would be made by a slightly broken flute. It is the endless rhythmic droning of annoyance and madness. I feel like once again curling up in a ball, hiding, and never coming out. The sound is penetrating and maddening…

He is such a pitiful thing. So pretentious, this blind idiot of a god…

And with that voice of contempt, the spell of madness is again shattered.

"Not all that impressive for an Outer God, is he?" I say aloud.

Mr. God: "I heard that."

Somehow, he can speak and wheeze and thus still make that flute-like droning sound. I guess it helps to be a god; you can multi-task. I realize that there must be breathable air here in this area of space since we can speak and hear speech. I won't let my lack of understanding get in the way of appreciating this incongruent and improbable fact.

Lamont: 'Ahh, excuse me, Mister god. We're just passing through, and I'm trying not to be the stereotypical male by actually stopping to ask you for directions."

Mr. God: "Huh…who…what?" The old guy in the white robes begins to wake up. "Who approaches the One and Only God?"

"Ahhh. Hi Mister god. I'm Night, and my lady is named Dawn."

Mr. God: "You should be on your knees. I am God, the One, and the only, the supreme deity, creator of the universe, the once and future King, the dead and the resurrected, the one who is the Father, the Son, and the Holy Ghost. I am Jehovah[54]. I am Adonai. I am Allah of glowing visage and no face. I am compassionate and merciful. I am all-powerful and all-knowing. I am…harumph…how did the rest of that litany go? Sorry, I always get lost and carried away in that introduction stuff. Now, who are you two again? How did you get here? Why are you here?"

Lamont: "Ahhh…we came from that away," I point vaguely behind us. "We just flew here. We are looking for a way home. We are two curious tourists taking in the sites."

Basha: 'Knight, are you sure that's how to address someone who calls himself as THE GOD?' Basha quietly asks me telepathically.

Lamont: 'Hey, I just can't take him seriously. Come on. Long white beard and dirty long white robes. The drooling in his sleep and that awful snoring sound he made didn't help.'

Mr. God: "You should prostrate yourselves before me," Mr. God says as he scratches his right underarm through his robe. "I think that's the standard protocol. But, hey. It's been a while since I had visitors. Through me a bone. So, how about giving me a bow or curtsy."

I do a curtsey, and Basha bows from the waist.

Lamont: "Is that better, Mr. God," I ask.

Mr. God: "I don't know. I can't see. To be polite, though, I vaguely recall some minions of mind telling me I'm not supposed to say this, but I can't recall why I'm not, so I have to tell you in the strictest confidence that I'm blind. Be nice and swear that you won't tell anyone that bit of news."

[54] If you're curious, there is an interesting history behind this name, Jehovah. https://en.wikipedia.org/wiki/Jehovah

We both respond with our most convincing and sincerest tone that we won't tell a single soul.

Mr. God: "Did you do it nicely and politely? The bow and curtsey thing."

Basha: "We did," I answer. "So, where are we?"

Mr. God: "Oh. That's easy. The majestic center of the universe is my home. At least that's what the travel brochures I had made up said on them. Sounds kind of cool, doesn't it?"

Lamont: "Yeah, Mr. god. Way cool. I love it. I got a question."

Mr. God: "Go ahead, ask it; I'm all-knowing, so I can answer anything. If need be, I can always consult my Magic 8 Ball[55]."

Mr. God: "Or, if I need more clarity, I can get out my Ouija board[56] for the answer. I have them somewhere nearby; for that reason, I'm certain of it."

Lamont: "Glad you come prepared. So, do you or did you also go by the name Azathoth at one time in your career?"

Mr. God: "Azathoth...hmm…now that does sound familiar. Can you give me a little hint?"

Lamont: "Would the letters H, P, and L, help any?"

Mr. God: "Hmmm...HPL...ahhh…yeah, that writer guy from New England back in the day. He liked that name. It made me sound ominous and scary. I got so many names it's hard to keep track of them. Some monks promised me to run a program to print out all my names...I think they claimed I had nine billion of them. Excuse me…" Mr. God yawns. "I'm kinda busy here…you interrupted my work. I was doing lots of things…lots and lots of vital, essential, and significant stuff. Keeping the universe polished and up and running. Ahhhh…very…very…import…" He dozes off to sleep and returns to drooling and snoring again.

Lamont: "Mr. god was not much help."

Basha: "Nor all that impressive. Perhaps he's just overworked."

---

[55] The Magic 8-Ball is a plastic sphere, made to look like an oversized eight-ball, that is used for fortune-telling or seeking advice. It was invented in 1946 by Albert C. Carter and Abe Bookman and is currently manufactured by Mattel.

[56] Spiritualists in the United States believed that the dead were able to contact the living and reportedly used a talking board very similar to a modern Ouija board at their camps in the U.S. state of Ohio in 1886 to ostensibly enable faster communication with spirits. Following its commercial introduction by businessman Elijah Bond on 1 July 1890, the Ouija board was regarded as an innocent parlor game unrelated to the occult until American spiritualist Pearl Curran popularized its use as a divining tool during World War I. Hasbro Inc. is the current manufacturer of the official board.

Lamont: "What now? I can't help but wonder..." I say, looking around at the vast expanse of blackness that lies at the heart and center of the universe.

I begin to approach his throne.

"Hey Knight, where are you going?"

I watch as Lamont tiptoes past the sleeping Mr. god in white robes and goes behind the curtains.

"I always wanted to do that." Lamont stares for a bit and then, "Dawn, come on, take a look at this; we need to ignore the guy in front of the curtain," Lamont says as he disappears behind the burgundy.

I step quietly past the sleeping white-haired and bearded drooling figure on the golden throne and pass through the burgundy curtains to see Lamont point up to another set of stairs leading upwards toward cloudy, whispering wind-swept heavens.

Lamont: "Shall we check it out?"

Lamont: "We have come this far...lead on Macduff."

Basha: "But I am not Macduff, and you do not look the part for Hamlet. Besides the fact that Shakespeare never wrote that[57]. That phrase has its long history of usage, but do not get me started. Let us just start walking up the stairs. It looks like it is a long way up."

We climb up those stairs for a good long time. Going what must be higher and higher into somewhere and someplace.

Then finally, ahead of us is another throne room with dark foreboding figures sitting together.

We look and take in the setting and the figures in this hall.

Lamont: "Okay, we finally get to see the real Outer Gods, and not so surprising, I don't see anything resembling Lovecraft's description of Azathoth et al., which makes sense considering what we talked about earlier."

What these beings are and look like is beyond human comprehension. So, we're like Ezekiel, just seeing a likeness and appearance of something we make familiar.

Our interaction dredges up something that takes on the semblance of a resemblance to something familiar. Behold, what I see is a place more fitting for an Aztec court or temple.

[57] 'Lead on Macduff.' is a misquotation from Shakespeare's *Macbeth*, Act 5, Scene 8.

Seated on an eagle and jaguar mat[58] at the center is a being that is ancient and powerful.

But hey, sometimes it is an androgynous being, then it becomes a male and female pair in the blink of an eye. Behind and flanking this single or dual being is a trio of other beings. They are all regal and robed in feathers and skins, the colors being mainly reds, black, gold, and jade. They are adorned in Aztec regalia. They are foreboding, strange, and otherworldly, talking in some incomprehensible tongue that sounds like a mind-wrenching blending of the scratches of metal on metal and the squeals of pain from dying animals.

Basha: 'Hey, Knight, do you see Aztec Gods as well?'

Lamont: 'I do indeed.'

Ometeotl: ***"CREATURES! HOW DARE YOU COME INTO OUR ABODE! BOW AND SUBMIT TO US."***

Who is speaking? Can't tell which of them. Is it coming from one, or maybe all of them speaking at once?

"LET US KNOW YOUR PURPOSE AND WHENCE YOU COME FROM."

Oh Hell! This is not good! What if they find out who we are? What will they do to us then! I don't think tiny humans are often invited to drop by

for tea. More likely, they'll nibble on our brains like a ripe peach.

"WE WILL GET WHAT WE WANT REVEALED TO US. THOUGH IT WILL BE...PAINFUL."

Suddenly we are bathed in a strange orange light. Oh no…Tezcat, what have you done to us? Why did you lead us here to our doom?

Aaaaagh! The pain is immense…and…intense…it is…ripping…out thoughts…probing…us…

Then slowly, a star map begins to form with a central glowing light of purple haze at the center. I can't help to be fascinated by all this. For a moment, my fear and panic fade.

"YOU WERE FOOLS TO DARE COME HERE, YOU MUD-BORN THINGS. WE WILL PUNISH YOU WELL FOR YOUR IMPIETY SOON AS WE LEARN FROM WHENCE YOU CAME."

Arrgh…forced to our knees…but the images are captivating…I wonder if that is where we are now? The royal throne room of the Outer Gods? Wait… those multitudes of points of light, they are not stars. Each of those points of light turns out to be individual galaxies. The image shifts off

[58] The eagle and the jaguar are revered animals for the Aztecs, recognized for their strength and valor, and thus to be seated there is to be recognized as having these attributes. *A Scattering of Jades: Stories, Poems, and Prayers of the Aztecs* by Dr. T. J. Knab & Thelma D. Sullivan, Touchstone Book, 1994, pg. 208.

to the left from the center and then begins to expand. I think it shows where we came from. A tiny faint spiral galaxy comes into focus. I guess that is the Milky Way? Then we zoom in on one specific star in the tail end of one of the spiral arms. It zooms in on that singular star as it keeps centering on that star, and it fills the area around it as it all comes into focus. We travel past little cold pluto, then the rest of the outermost planets, as we run past the unmistakable ringed Saturn, the huge multi-colored cloud mass of Jupiter, and the reddish rock of Mars. Finally, we stop and gaze upon a familiar scene. It is our own small blue-green and white gem of a planet.

"YOU ARE FROM THAT INSIGNIFICANT TINY ROCK THAT WAS FOUGHT OVER BY SO MANY OF THE FIRST-BORN RACES. BUT YOU ARE NATIVE TO THAT ROCK. HOW DARE YOU COME BEFORE US, WHO ARE YOUR TRUE MASTERS! KNOW THIS, YOU HAVE COME A LONG WAY TO BEG TO DIE."

Basha: 'Knight!...'

BASHA

What has Tezcatlipoca gotten us into? And why? All I can think of is trying to fight back...though I do not believe that will do us much good…Lamont, my clever love, I pray you have a better solution…

LAMONT

Lamont: "Wait…don't…" I put my hand on Basha's shoulder as I squeeze it hoping to calm her. "Listen, please…

"AHH, THE BEGGING HAS BEGUN."

"We are…not what we seem…we…call ourselves…" Come on, Lamont, access that memory of yours. I know Lovecraft has something that can help us here…I just need to dredge it up..."We are…"

"SPIT IT OUT, LITTLE MUDBUG."

Lamont: "We are…members of…the Great Race…" That's it! Yes…this might work. "We call ourselves the Great Race. You must have heard of us. We travel in the best of social circles. All the well-informed deities and entities know of us…"

"NO, LITTLE MUDDLINGS, WE HAVE NOT. AND WE ARE NOT SO EASILY IMPRESSED WITH SELF-PROCLAIMED TITLES."

Lamont: "We have mastered space and time! These bodies are a shell…ahh…We are from…Yithia…Yes, we are of the Great Race of Yith..."

"PROVE IT. SHOW US."

I hope this works…The star chart is just sitting there on Earth. Bloody Hell. Tezcat! Can you do something here? You must know where the Yithian's home world once was or still is? At least I hope you do? Bloody Hell, what if she doesn't know? Please, Tezcat, answer me! You brought us here for some reason, so help us!

"WELL? SHOW US YOUR HOME WORLD OR ELSE."

How can I do this? I don't know where in hell they came from? Just a name. Yith...

"YOU DARE TO DECEIVE US?"

I can feel Basha heating up...should I prepare to fight? Won't resistance be futile? They call themselves gods, after all...

There is a surging blaze of light and heat. Basha bursts into flames and sends a blasting torrent of fire at them. Now what? She engulfs them in her fire...and they just laugh!

"SO YOU MUD-BORN THINGS HAVE A STINGER. THIS IS AMUSING."

Basha: "Burn! Damn, you burn!" Basha screams as she concentrates her blast into such intensity that the air between us is scorching.

Wait...the star chart seems to flicker...or is it just from the heat waves?

A blast of frigid cold meets her flames and begins to push back at her. She digs in and is still being pushed back. Another beam of icy blue frigidness comes forth to meet her fire. Then another one. She is buckling under the combined force. I have to focus on moving that star chart to figure out how to access information I don't really have. There has got to be a way. All my concentration has got to be on this...I can't help her in the fight...I've got to try this, or we will die...please, Tezcat, let me have that information. I'm not really sure if Tezcat has this location. Nor am I sure if she can transmit it to me. But I have to try this.

Basha: "Dear Goddess..."I hear Basha cry out in pain as she goes down to her knees.

Then...

The star chart shifts.

It pulls back...Earth is receding...now I can only see our sun in its local area of other stars...come on, damn it...move! Show us the Yithian home world; please make this happen!

Finally, just as Basha has crumbled, is on her knees, and is about to be encased in all that icy cold blasting, the star pattern rushes to find a new location. It is working. It moves, there is a shift to some new area, and it comes into focus...it shows us a war zone with vast starships hovering all around this star system, and all the focus is on one specific ochre-colored planet. From there...a small cavalcade of ships rushes off the planet's surface. More fighting goes on; some ships are running interference for that cavalcade. Then during the battle, a collection of vessels begin to bombard that star. It is hit over and over again! Holy Hell! It goes nova! I think it was destroyed in that interstellar firefight. The scene follows the fleet of fleeing starships.

"WE SEE. YOUR SPECIES WAS THE ONES WHO LEFT THAT STAR SYSTEM FROM THE PLANET YOU CALL YITH WAS DESTROYED WHEN YOUR STAR CEASED TO BE. A REMANENT OF YOUR SPECIES MANAGED TO ESCAPE ITS DESTRUCTION BEFORE YOUR HOME WORLD WAS BLASTED TO DUST IN THE GREAT INTERSTELLAR WARS OF THE FIRST ONES."

I guess that is why they call themselves Yithians[59]. This is clearly Tezcat's doing. What is she playing at? Why did she take so long? Will this fake identity really stand up to scrutiny? What will happen to us if they figure out who we really are?

We follow the trail of fairy dust from the fleet as it flees that interstellar battlefield where still vast hordes of beings with their starships continue to battle across space and time. Then the fleeing fleet approaches an out-of-the-way ordinary small yellow star with a system of planets orbiting it. I realize it is our sun. The fairy dust of the survivors settles on a vast landmass in the southern hemisphere of a very young planet, Earth.

Then I notice that Basha is no longer under attack, which is definitely an improvement in our situation. Let me see if I can continue to distract them from harming us.

Lamont: "Hail Supreme One! As you can see, we have come from our homeland to far off Earth. We pay homage to you who we have worshipped these many eons."

I can feel our minds being probed. I notice and feel that the stuff around us is glowing intensely. Tezcatlipoca must be protecting us from them. I sure hope so. That would explain why they think we are one of those Yithians. I recall from the story that they can extract minds and exchange bodies with them to travel through space and time. To explore and record new life and new civilizations.

After they arrived on Earth 500 million years ago, they built up an empire on Earth based in Australia, give or take a few thousand years if Lovecraft's history of the alien invasions of the early Earth is to be believed. They fought with the other alien races that also came to Earth. Which, if we are being called Yithians, means that yet again, Lovecraft's fantasies are not complete fiction. Tezcat must be protecting our real identities from them this way.

"GREETINGS, YITHIAN'S WHO CALL YOURSELVES DARKNESS AND DAYLIGHT. WE NOW UNDERSTAND WHY YOU HAVE THE OUTER FORMS THAT YOU DO. YOUR MINDS RIDE THEM LIKE SOME BEAST OF BURDEN."

---

[59] The creatures from the planet Yith, are known as the Great Race of Yith. They first appeared in Lovecraft's short story, *The Shadow Out of Time*, published in *Astounding Stories* in June 1936.

"We are emissaries of our race." I fabricate. "To pay homage to your illustriousness. We have traveled long and far to do just that."

"WE ACKNOWLEDGE THAT YOU ARE ONE OF THE OLD ONES. YOUR RACE OF YITH IS ONE OF THE FIRST-BORN STAR CHILDREN. IT IS GOOD THAT YOU PAY HOMAGE TO US, WE WHO ARE THE OUTER GODS. WE ARE THE GRANDMOTHER OF THE ONE YOU HAVE SWORN ALLEGIANCE TO, OUR GRANDCHILD TEZCATLIPOCA OF THE BLACKEST NIGHT."

I wonder why this entity is referring to us as Darkness and Daylight? Is this another example of something getting lost in translation from our minds? It seems to be picking up the whole Aztec motif as well, rather than the Lovecraft-inspired images and names. I guess so. It all gets complicated being stuck in one's own head and only experiencing the world that way. But, such is life.

Lamont: "Are you O' Great and Terrible One, the Being who is truly the one who is also known as Azathoth of the Outer Gods?" I ask.

"YES. WE ARE THE ONE THAT THE HUMAN SCRIBE KNOWN AS LOVECRAFT DESIGNATED US BY THAT NAME. IT AMUSES US TO ALLOW OUR YOUNGEST CHILD TO CALL HIMSELF BY THAT NAME."

BASHA

Ahh. Lamont deduced that guy in the white robe and long beard was self-delusional. We are now in the presence of someone who may not be a God but is far enough on the cosmic food chain to be as close to a supreme deity as we have ever encountered.

Basha: 'If that is the case,' I say to Lamont. 'Try to treat her Divineness with a little respect.'

Lamont: 'Don't I always?'

'For the sake of our ongoing relationship, I will stifle myself and refrain from responding to that questions. I love you perhaps as much for your faults and as your boyish charm.'

LAMONT

Before I can make an adequate comeback, our thoughts are interrupted by Ms. Head Honcho.

"ONE VERSION OF OUR BEING WAS IMAGINED BY THE AZTEC PEOPLE AS OMETEOTL, THE COSMIC CREATOR OF ALL THAT IS. WE, OMETEOTL, ARE THE FIRST. WE ARE THE CREATOR OF ALL LIFE. WE ARE THE LORD OF EVERYTHING. WE ARE THE SELF-CREATED LIFE FORCE. KNOW THAT WE ARE TRULY BEYOND UNDERSTANDING. WE ARE BEYOND ANY SINGLE HUMAN NAME. THUS WE HAVE BEEN KNOWN BY MANY NAMES."

Lamont: "If we may know such things, who are they who are seated beside you, O' great and terrible one?"

"LET ME INTRODUCE YOU TO THEM. THEY ARE OUR GRANDCHILDREN; OUR GRANDCHILDREN ARE ALL PART OF THAT FOURFOLD COLLECTIVE KNOWN AS TEZCATLIPOCA. THERE IS THE RED TEZCATLIPOCA OF THE EAST. HE IS ALSO KNOWN AS XIPE TOTEC, THE FLAYED GOD."

The being known as Xipe Totec appears with his right hand upraised and his left hand extending towards the front, holding a ceremonial dagger of obsidian. Xipe Totec wears a cloak of flayed skin with the victim's hands falling loose from Xipe Totec's wrists. His body is painted yellow on one side and tan on the other. His mouth, lips, neck, hands, and legs are painted red. His eyes are not visible through the cloaked skin of his victim, his mouth is open, and the ears are perforated. He has vertical stripes from his forehead to his chin, running across the eyes. He has a yellow shield by his side and is carrying a container filled with seeds on his belt.

"THEN THERE IS THE BLUE TEZCATLIPOCA OF THE SOUTH, KNOWN AS HUITZILOPOCHTLI, THE HUMMINGBIRD ON THE LEFT."

Huitzilopochtli wears blue-green gleaming feathers from a multitude of hummingbirds adorning his helmet. He holds a shield adorned with balls of eagle feathers, and he has a blue snake, called Xiuhcoatl, in his hand in the form of an atlatl, or spear-thrower device. His skin is deep blue.

"LAST, THE TEZCATLIPOCA OF THE WEST IS THE WHITE ONE, ALSO KNOWN TO YOU AS QUETZALCOATL, THE FEATHERED SERPENT."

Quetzalcoatl wears around his neck a wind breastplate formed out of the spirally convoluted wind jewels made of conch shells. He has a colossal serpent rising up behind him, twitching and slithering across his broad back adorned with eagle feathers. His face is covered with a beak-like mask with reptilian snout-like features. A trail of fresh blood comes down his neck and legs from cuts made in his ear lobes, calves, tongue, and groin.

Basha nudges me, and I decide to play this one safely. She bows at the waist.

Basha: "Hail O' Celestial and cosmic beings known as the Outer Gods. Hail Ometeotl. Hail Tonacatecuhtli and Tonacacihutal. Hail Xipe Totec, hail Huitzilopochtli, and hail Quetzalcoatl." Basha says reverently and politely."

I bow and flourish my hat as I do, summing up courage like Quixote speaking to the Great Enchanter.

Lamont: "I too say hail O' Outer Gods! Hail to the Ometeotl, who is father Tonacatecuhtli, and mother, Tonacacihutal. Hail the red, blue, and white variants of Tezcatlipoca! You mentioned a fourfold relationship. I see only three." Basha looks at me with daggers as she nudges me in the ribs. But I grin and continue, "Who is missing from your august numbers?"

Ometeotl: ***"THE ONE WHO IS NOT SEATED HERE IS OUR GRANDCHILD, THE***

BLACK AND NORTHERN TEZCATLIPOCA, THE ONE WHO IS CALLED SMOKING MIRROR."

Lamont: "May we know why he is not here?"

Quetzalcoatl*: **"YITHIANS, HIS ABSENCE IS OF NO CONCERN OF YOURS.***

Xipe Totec: ***"YOU WOULD DO WELL TO LISTEN TO MY BROTHER. DO NOT METTLE."***

Lamont: "I had been told that Smoking Mirror of the Black and the North rules over our little corner of the universe. Was I informed wrongly?"

Xipe Totec: ***"WE OF THE RED AND THE EAST ARE THE ONES YOU MUST HEED. WE HAVE BEEN GRANTED SOVEREIGNTY OVER THAT SECTOR OF SPACE. WE HAVE SUPPLANTED OUR DISHONORED BROTHER OF THE BLACK AND THE NORTH."***

Quetzalcoatl: ***"AH BROTHER, JOINTLY WE RULE IN OUR GRANDMOTHER'S NAME. IT IS ONLY THAT YOU SEEMED OVERLY INTERESTED IN THAT BENIGHTED CORNER STILL. YOU INSIST THAT WE LET YOU GOVERN IT SINCE YOU SPEND MORE TIME DWELLING ON IT. WHY IS THAT?"***

Supplanted and dishonored? What is this all about? I want to find out more since he is talking about Tezcat.

Lamont: "O' Flayed One, O' Xipe Totec, O' Usurper, we did not know this. Thank you for informing us of such important news."

Xipe Totec: ***"I DID NOT USURP HIM. I DEFEATED HIM."***

Quetzalcoatl: ***"WE DEFEATED HIM, YOU MEAN. YOU DID NOT ACT ALONE."***

Xipe Totec: ***"OF COURSE THAT IS WHAT I MEANT, BROTHER. HE DISHONORED US ALL, AND SO HE NEEDED TO BE PUNISHED."***

Huitzilopochtli*: **"WHY DO WE BOTHER WITH LISTENING TO THEM AT ALL. THE FEW FOOLISH BEINGS WHO HAD COME TO OUR REALM, WE SIMPLY SACRIFICED THEM. THEIR LIFE ESSENCE SERVED US. LET US TAKE THEM AND HAVE THEM SERVE***

US AS IS THEIR DUE, WITH THEIR BLOOD THEM."

Quetzalcoatl: ***"DO NOT BE HASTY BROTHER. WE NEED TO ASCERTAIN HOW THEY HAVE SURVIVED. FEW SPECIES WHICH FALL WITHIN OUR WEB MAINTAINED THEIR GRIP ON THEIR SANITY. HOW DID SUCH AS THESE MANAGE IT?"***

Huitzilopochtli: ***"IF THAT IS WHAT YOU WISH TO KNOW, THEN LET US DISSECT THEM TO FIND OUR ANSWER. THERE IS NO NEED TO LISTEN TO THEIR PRATTLING."***

Lamont: "If I may interrupt such important decision-making, may I know what Tezcatlipoca did to earn your ire, if such a lesser being of that sector of the universe may know such a thing?".

Quetzalcoatl: ***"AS IT HAS BEEN TOLD TO YOU, THAT IS NOT THEIR CONCERN. YOU NEED JUST RECOGNIZE..."***

Huitzilopochtli: ***"OUR FOOLISH BROTHER'S ACT OF HUBRIS WAS HIS UNDOING. AND YOU SHOULD BEWARE OF YOUR PLACE, LITTLE ONES."***

Basha: 'Yes, Knight, what are you trying to do?' Basha asks.

Lamont: 'We need answers, and I have a plan. Well, more like a hunch. Just let me play this out.'

Basha: 'Okay. But try not to get us killed.'

Lamont: 'I will do my best.'

Quetzalcoatl: ***"HUBRIS AND AN UNNATURAL FEELING FOR HIS PETS LED HIM INTO HIS FOLLY."***

Lamont: "Anyone care to elaborate? Enlighten such a benighted one as we."

Xipe Totec: ***"BENIGHTED LITTLE ONES, YOU CRAVE ANSWERS? WELL, ARE YOU FAMILIAR WITH THE REALM OF DREAMS?"***

Basha: "Yes. We know of that realm."

Lamont: "What about that little land of Nod and fluff?" I ask, referring to Dreamland, wanting to get their reaction to Tezcat creating it.

Xipe Totec: ***"HE IN HIS FOLLY HE MADE IT."***

Lamont: "Oh really? Please enlighten us. Tell us more."

Ometeotl: ***"GRANDCHILDREN, ENOUGH! NO MORE SENSELESS GOSSIPING. I BID YOU ALL DEPART! LET US ADDRESS THESE LESSER BEINGS ALONE. THEY ALL REPLY AS YOU WISH. SO SHALL IT BE DONE."***

In a blink of an eye, the threesome beings depart, leaving the singular duality, the Great and the true Azathoth, behind for us to face.

Lamont: "Well, now that the children have been put to bed, I wondered. Just one little thing. Ometeotl, Queen of creation and stuff like that, I have two…"

Basha: 'Knight!' Basha's voice rings loudly in my mind. 'What in the Goddess's name are you doing? I just asked you a few minutes ago not to do this! Do you have to try and annoy and pick a fight with every new entity you happen to meet?'

Lamont: 'Trust me. I've got a plan. (I hope.) We need answers, don't we? So why not continue asking questions and seeing if we can get some straight answers?'

Ometeotl: ***"THE ONE WHO CALLS HIMSELF DARKNESS IS IMPERTINENT BUT CORRECT IN HIS THOUGHTS. ASK YOUR QUESTIONS. FEW HAVE VENTURED HERE TO STAND BEFORE US AT OUR OWN COURT. A REMARKABLE HOLD ON YOUR SANITY, YOU BOTH SEEM TO HAVE. WE COMMEND YOU AND FIND YOU BOTH AN INTERESTING CURIOSITY."***

Lamont: (Wow. They can read our thoughts. So much for subterfuge. How are we going to deal with the likes of these? I was hoping to deceive them, but now?) "So, as I was about to say. A few questions. First, what's with Azathoth back there? He is claiming a lot of stuff. Creator of all and Lord of all and such. Doesn't it annoy you?"

"AHH YES, DEAR LITTLE CHILD. THE LAST-BORN IS HE OF OUR PROGENY. HE LOOKED AROUND AND FAILED TO SEE WHAT HAD COME BEFORE. BLIND HE IS, AND WAS, TO THE TRUE NATURE OF THINGS. HE OPENED HIS EYES, AND, LIKE AN IDIOT, HE THOUGHT HE HAD CREATED WHAT HE GAZED UPON. WE HUMOR HIM. IT AMUSES US. WE LET HIM USE THAT NAME."

Basha: "Then Knight was right; that old one with the long beard seated on that regal throne is similar to the gnostic deity Yaldabaoth[60]. He presented himself as the creator of all. Those called the Gnostics on the planet Earth devised that name for slandering the teachings of a noble people. This is most interesting."

Lamont: "That is kind of cool, Dawn. That could mean that reference to this blind idiot god might have been a confused mislabel for Azathoth by Lovecraft? Interesting. Did Lovecraft blend, knowingly or not, some of the ideas and mythos of the Gnostics? This being who is now addressing us is the real deal. I can go with that."

Ometeotl: ***"WE FIND NO OFFENSE WITH YOU TRYING TO UNDERSTAND THAT SCRATCHER ON JADE LOVECRAFT. WE FIND THE FACT THAT NO ONE TAKES HIS WRITINGS FOR HINTS AT THE TRUTH AMUSING."***

Lamont: "I have another question, O' Ometeotl, where is your child, Smoking Mirror? There were tantalizing hints about his absence by your grandchildren."

"HE IS DETAINED AT THE MOMENT AND CANNOT JOIN US."

Lamont: (Somehow, I feel she-it is parsing the truth very thinly, aka outright lying. Oh Damn. She can read my thoughts!) "Look, O' Wondrous one, creator of all, I meant no offense by that, really I didn't."

"NO OFFENSE WAS TAKEN."

Lamont: (Did she overlook my thought? Hey! Can you read my mind or what?)

"YOU YITHIANS MAY ONCE HAVE HAD A SPECIAL RELATIONSHIP WITH OUR GRANDSON, SMOKING MIRROR, BUT NOW YOU MUST ACKNOWLEDGE OTHERS AS YOUR RULERS.

THIS IS WHAT YOU MUST TAKE BACK TO YOUR PEOPLE."

Lamont: (Hmmm…again, she's not reacting to my thought. What is

---

60 *'Now the archon ["ruler"] who is weak has three names. The first name is Yaltabaoth, the second is Saklas ["fool"], and the third is Samael { "Samael" literally means "Blind God" or "God of the Blind" in Hebrew (סמאל). This being is considered not only blind, or ignorant of its own origins but may, in addition, be evil; its name is also found in Judaism as the Angel of Death and in Christian demonology }. And he is impious in his arrogance which is in him. For he said, 'I am God and there is no other God beside me,' for he is ignorant of his strength, the place from which he had come.'* Source: https://en.wikipedia.org/wiki/Demiurge#Yaldabaoth. That Wikipage gives the source as: "Apocryphon of John," translation by Frederik Wisse in The Nag Hammadi Library. Accessed online at gnosis.org

going on here? I have an idea.) 'Dawn, talking to things that call themselves deities is getting boring; shall we just split and be on our way?'

Basha: 'Knight! Are you trying to get us flayed alive or worse? Can you not mind your manners for just this once?'

"HEED YOUR COMPANION DARKNESS. IF YOU ARE BORED WITH OUR SPEECH, WE CAN HAPPILY HAVE SOMEONE FLAY YOU SO THAT WE MAY ADORN OURSELVES WITH YOUR SKIN, AS IS THE OLD WAYS."

Lamont: (I think they can only read my thoughts when I project them to Dawn, but not when I think them to myself. Hey! Big, ugly, and scary, I'm not afraid of you! Nah-Nah!) "I will do my best to mind my manners, O' Gracious and Beneficent One," I say aloud as I again bow and tip my hat with a flourish.

"YOUR GESTURE IS RECOGNIZED AS PROPER RESPECT FOR US.

BOW TO US, AS ALL CREATION THAT KNOWS US DOES!"

Lamont: "Oh, yes, your magnificence!" Still bowing. "Those who truly know you must love you." (Ha! I was right. Ometeotl only reacts to my transmitted communication by speech or telepathy! One last test. Oh Ometeotl, tell me, where is Smoking Mirror?)

"YES, THOSE LEARNED IN THE ANCIENT TONGUES AND WRITINGS KNOW OF THE TRUE HISTORY OF MAKING ALL THINGS.

THOUGH MANY WHO HAVE LEARNED THE TRUTH HAD PAID THE PRICE WITH THEIR SANITY AND SOUL AND THEREFORE MISWROTE. THE ONE KNOWN AS ABDUL ALHAZRED RIGHTFULLY CALLED US OLD ONES.

WE ARE THE THINGS WHICH WERE SPAWNED FIRST AFTER THE STARS WERE FORMED."

Lamont: "O' Great One, O' Ometeotl, are you saying that Alhazred was a real person[61] and not the creation of Lovecraft?"

"YES. THE SCRIBE ALHAZRED LIVED AND LEARNED MUCH. SUFFER GREATLY FOR THAT HE DID AND MANY MISTAKES HE DID MAKE IN HIS WRITINGS."

Lamont: (Hey! I might be right. O' pompous one never answered the question, I thought. They can't read thoughts! Only transmitted communications! Excellent!)

Basha: "O' Great One. Mother of the Outer Beings. May I ask of a smattering of wisdom?"

"PERHAPS. WHAT DO YOU DESIRE TO ASK, O' DAYLIGHT OF YITH?"

Basha: "What can you tell me of Simeon Ben Zoma and his text *Sefer Tzaeleem Shavareem*, known as *The Book of Broken Shadows*?"

"THAT MAN TRAVELED FAR AND SAW MUCH ON HIS JOURNEYS. THOUGH IN THE END PAID THE PRICE. HE MANAGED TO BIND MUCH TRUE KNOWLEDGE THROUGH

---

[61] In 2004 Donald Tyson dared to publish Alhazred's text in English.
A version that even contains the prefatory notes of Olaus Wormius and Theodorus Philetas, *Necronomicon: The Wanderings of Alhazred*, Llewellyn Publications, 2004

DEEP DREAMING AND MAGICK IN HIS TOME. IT CAN BE GLEANED IF YOU HAVE THE SKILL AND COURAGE TO STARE INTO ITS DARK ABYSS."

Lamont: "O' First amongst the Outer Ones. I still am curious about Smoking Mirror. Can you make known to us where she is? Can you take us to her? I always wanted to see her place. Check out the décor and peruse her bookshelves."

"AS WE TOLD YOU, HE IS NOT HERE."

Lamont: "Why not? Was she rude? Did you banish her? What's the deal?"

Basha: 'Knight!!!'

Lamont: "Why can't you speak the truth since you supposedly know the truth?" (I have this feeling that I'm being lied to. Why the deception? This could be important. I think this might explain something about Tezcat.) Look, I think you are fibbing. I think you are hiding something. I think you are afraid to tell us the truth." (I hope I'm right. If I'm not, and Ometeotl doesn't kill me, Basha might.)

"LIKE A MOTH TO THE FLAME YOU ARE! I OFFERED YOU GEMS AND SACRED FEATHERS; IN RETURN, YOU SCRATCH THE JADE AND TEAR APART THE QUETZAL FEATHER! IF OUR FOOLISH GRANDCHILD INTERESTS YOU SO MUCH, SUFFER THE SAME DEATH AS HE!"

Lamont: "Wait! O' First amongst..." I try to say, but I feel...

*

I feel ill. I hear Basha throw up as I am compelled to do.

Lamont: "Yuck...that was unpleasant. Sorry about that. I had to provoke Ometeotl. Something about Tezcat's not being there was significant. And I was hoping that rather than dismember us on the spot, she would get angry enough to send us off to wherever she was."

BASHA

Basha: "Knight, I am going to throttle you! What did your rashness do to us now? Where are we?"

I try to take in our surroundings. All I can sense in the utter blackness is the awful stench of…well, I do not want to try and determine what it is I smell...it is just awful. We need a source of light. I create a few fireballs and scatter them out around us.

Then I notice we are in some kind of underground sealed chamber. The chamber is vast and goes beyond the light cast by my fire. Nearby walls have geometric shapes, spirals, and intermixed images of skulls; they are all too familiar motifs, Aztec. We are in some kind of Aztec chamber.

The only thing in this place is a large altar. Chained down onto it is a muscular naked warrior. Oh great! Just what I need, another display of nude male flesh. He is alive, barely. Across his flesh, I notice many marks of recent claws and teeth that had attacked and scarred him. Yet again, I'm presented with an unasked-for display of maleness. Again, I cannot help but notice that I prefer Lamont's tidier circumcised package.

Okay, Cosmos, if you are listening, I would like to put in a request, please no more sights of naked males, not even of my dearest Lamont; I would rather wait till he presents himself to me consciously and willingly. I have had more than enough of that to satisfy my curiosity. So please, refrain from showing me anymore.

Then I hear a soft and ragged moan. He is alive; I notice the subtle movements of his body, the rising and the falling of his chest. Who is this poor man that has suffered so much torment to leave such barely healed marks across his chest? For some reason, he seems familiar. Where are we, and why is he being tortured like this?

Finally, my mind tells me who it is I see and hear before me. Chained and bound upon the sacrificial altar is Tezcatlipoca. Hmmm...He is clearly for all the world to see as a male. Even his usual smoking covering has been stripped from him, which usually hides his anatomy. I wonder if Lamont is still seeing him as her? Probably. Even now, in this condition, Tezcatlipoca is projecting his appearance to us, and we see him/her in a way we can relate to. He has begun to awaken and endeavors to be more circumspect in his appearance.

His naked flesh, the color of glistening obsidian, is now strategically covered by wisps of gray smoke rising off him to clothe him in those wisps of smoky tendrils. I can clearly see a festering and still bleeding wound on his stomach.

We can begin to answer that one O' little Bright Eagle. You are at our home away from home, as Clever Heart, our Corazon, would say. We would be polite and rise to greet you properly, but we are tied up now, as you can see. Destiny and fate have brought you to our side to aid us. Though we are curious as to what cleverness brought you here to us. How did you find us?

Lamont: "Ahhh...it was a good guess. I figured if I annoyed Ometeotl enough, she would fling us away, and I hoped it would be here. Wherever here is."

Basha: "You mean you were not sure! Lamont, you could have gotten us killed! Why did not you ask me? Do you not trust me?"

Lamont: "I trust you with my life. But Ometeotl could read our minds when we communicated. I didn't want her to know what I intended. I needed to make her mad enough to act without thinking."

Basha: "How did you know you would end up here?"

Lamont: "I didn't. But I was relying on the fact that even Gods are stupid. Just like humans."

How dare you call us...stupid! We have minds that encompass vastness. We...

Lamont: "Blah, blah, blah. Look. You may have a colossal mind, and old Ometeotl thinks she is infinite or nearly so. But, like us, all of you self-proclaimed Gods can only consciously focus on a finite amount of data and experience at any one time. You only are consciously aware of a small fraction of that so-called infinite potential that your big unconscious may be processing. And like most beings, that means about 90 plus percent of us humans, and I figured the same goes for you so-called Gods; we are all only potentially self-aware. This means most beings don't know what things shaped or influenced us at any one moment.

You don't consciously know why you are doing and reacting the way you are. Thus, you can be manipulated. Hence, I figured that if I got her to think about you and got her to be annoyed enough to send us off somewhere, then in her impulsive anger, she would put two and two together in her unconscious, and voila! She would send us off to you. So, here we are."

Basha: "You were taking a big gamble, Lamont. Ometeotl could have sent us to the moon's dark side, or Hell if there is such a thing or..."

Lamont: "True, Basha. There was that possibility. This is why I had to get her as angry as I could. People tend not to think clearly if you get them really angry, even gods. And my gamble paid off. So where are we Tezcat?"

We are in the Dreamland aspect of my once fair city of Tenochtitlan. Deep in its bowels, it is here that we were sent to remain, in a death-like sleep, to be tormented and thus distracted, as our Dear Heart pointed out, from doing what needs to be done. We had faith in you two.

You are magnificently clever. So, we knew that you would make your way here. This is your destiny. . Once we realized that, we realized that you had to stop us in order to be able to help with something more significant and vital.

As you said, our Dear Heart, we were not thinking right when we simply tried to use you to allow us entry into the Waking World. Your life purpose, we now see, was to end up here with us as you are now. That is the proper understanding of the prophecy concerning you. You are the opener of the gate for us. And this situation is the gate that you can open up for us.

It is Inevitable and predetermined as the falling of leaves when the seasons make their turn. You will join with us to help us both. We were short-sighted by our damnable imprisonment when we tried to take you over and manipulate you into opening the Gate of Dreams.

Lamont: "Okay, enough with the talk of inevitable. I like my belief in free will and am not fond of someone, even a so-called God telling me otherwise."

Do not many of your thinkers speak and teach this? Do you not know of the tale of Pierre-Simon, marquis de Laplace's demon? To one such as us, we are..."

Lamont: "Look, Tezcat. Just like your grandma Ometeotl, she lost her free will by failing to be self-aware and pay attention, and I was able to manipulate her for a moment. She could have sent us wherever she chose if she woke up and paid attention. We all have free will if and when we choose to exercise it on the important stuff, even with your example of Laplace's demon, that can determine the outcome based on knowing the starting configuration.

Determinacy, even perfect determinacy, doesn't negate my free will. It just says you will know my outcome when I choose it. However, no fixed singular being can encompass an infinite data set. So no real perfect determinacy is actually possible; not enough internal analytic space to contain an infinite amount of data in a finite container.

Now, determining probability is likely and possible. And since, as I just said, humans and even Gods tend not to make self-aware conscious choices most of the time, determining potential outcomes is easier. Though, probability still leaves wiggle room for a conscious choice to be an outlier and not readily accounted for. "

Lamont: "There is still a slight chance of an unexpected outcome appearing when you take in probability. So, all in all. Free will is still alive and kicking. Talk of fate and destiny is cool sounding but can get annoying. I will get annoyed if you continue with this blathering about how I don't have free will. Annoyed enough to just wake up and leave you. Without finding out about how we can help each other."

Corazon, it is your destiny to aid us in our need; sweet, it will be like blood and chocolate.

Lamont: "I said one more word about not having free will, and I will wake up. So, stuff it, Tezcat, I'm warning you."

Corazon, you must...

Lamont: "I must admit nothing! I'm tired of Gods telling me what I must or must not do, especially those who are stupid enough to not pay attention to how they think. Now, either drop this inevitable fate talk or else."

Of course, Dearest Heart. I only wish you the best to be a part of our smoke and mist. We ask you, O' Bright Eagle and sweet wise Heart, for a boon to give us.

Basha: "So? What is it that you want from us, Tezcatlipoca? I thought such as us are mere annoying monkeys to you." I am a bit ticked off, and I still do not know if I can trust Tezcatlipoca.

O' Bright Eagle, have we not earned at least your trust in us? Did we not bring our Dear Heart back to you?

Basha: "You did aid in returning Lamont to me; for that, I am grateful."

Lamont: "Me too. We just don't know if we can truly trust you."

The chamber is filled with sardonic laughter, and he laughs so much that we see it begin to hurt him due to his wounds.

You are wise not to trust us. We, the black and truest Tezcatlipoca are known as a trickster, The *Trickster. Always weigh what we say. Do not take us at face value. We are tricky. However, our words about this matter are tightly bound. We need your aid in many ways. Your cleverness had been proven many times over. The first was when you prevented us from crossing over. You made us stop and think. For that, we are grateful. Your cleverness is appreciated. And so, we began to plan and hope that you of all beings can aid us and defy our Grandmother, Ometeotl.*

Lamont: "How can we do this?"

Basha: "Why should we do this?"

To answer that, we must explain things. We shall part the mist that obscures us. Are you familiar with the tale of Prometheus?

Basha: "Of course."

Our accommodations in this place are due to our actions similar to that mythic ancient Greek character Prometheus. A case of life imitating art, so to speak.

We displeased our grandparents; thus, we are here as you see us, bound to the altar, left to die and have death die repeatedly. Having this happen to us continually through the long eternal night.

Basha: "What do you mean, Tezcatlipoca? What did you do for our people?"

Lamont: "And for that matter, who do you mean by 'our people'? That can cover a lot of territories?"

Your people—as in the species that calls itself humanity. We created Dreamland as a sanctuary and gave humanity the twin gifts of Dreaming and magickal arts. Our gifts far exceeded those of that Prometheus. When we were discovered by our Grandmother, she, in her wrath, bound us here.

Basha: "What! Are you saying that you are the God of Dreams? You are the God that many have known as Morpheus?"

That would be an appropriate name for us. We created our spell over the realm we chose as a sanctuary that you call Dreamland.

Lamont: "Speaking of names. In Lovecraft's little game of Gods, you and Ometeotl are one of what he called the Outer Gods, correct? Just trying to get the players straight."

Yes. We would be one of the Outer Gods. And we would perhaps be known by the Lovecraft invented appellation of Nyarlathotep.

Lamont: "That makes sense. His relationship with humanity was not a benevolent one. He was sinister and a corruptor offering aid to humans that would lead to their undoing."

I have offered my services and assisted humans—but is a teacher to blame when the pupil fails to take care and be cautious? I should not be blamed for their folly and lack of care if foolish things are done.

Lamont: "So, you're claiming you've gotten bad press. Whatever. Let's get back to your storytelling. How and why did this all happen? Will this explain why you are wounded? Why and how you became dead and dying but dreaming? Take it from the top. Do like Alice and begin at the beginning."

Yes, all of this will be answered and explained. As we said, we created the gateways to Dreamland so that it could be a sanctuary. Let us explain. We roamed creation freely and saw much of it. We, all of our family of Gods, created the creatures known as the Great Old Ones for our amusement. The first interstellar beings and watch them play cruel and savagely across the stars. Your tiny speck of rock and water was a stomping ground for them long ago when you were but apes and even while you awoke to your present form. Memories of these battles have scarred your collective memories and your world. However, that was all to be expected. Your kind steps on ants and anthills without concern, and so did the Great Old Ones act that way to all other beings.

However, when your people became cognizant of the Great Old Ones and of us, the true Gods, we all asked for recognition. We, as our due, asked for homage. Blood was to be freely given, as is our right. Things went well in the days of Old. We, the Outer Gods, are not evil. We are simply the cosmic forces. You would not call Time a thing of evil, though it will bring all created things to their end. Gravity, the wind, and the waters – these natural forces can be destructive but not evil. Evil is something that created beings such as you humans and the Great Old Ones are. You can choose to be evil and do evil things.

We asked for blood, and the Aztec people gave us hearts torn out of living flesh. We ask for sacrifice, and some would burn others alive. We did not ask for any of this. Though we did nothing to stop it. You are right, our Dear Heart; we allow for choice. You do have free will.

Basha: "But, you did not refuse those sacrifices when offered up to you, did you?"

Why should we? It was blood freely given, was it not?

Basha: "If I recall, much of those sacrifices were slaves or captives, not willing people with the freedom to choose?"

Well, yes. That is the way with you humans. All across this small world, people were cruel and evil. We wanted our blood, but as I was saying, we disapproved of this way. We felt sorry for our pets, though the rest of my family did not share our concern, especially Grandmother. So, we stayed behind when the rest of our kind left this space-time sector. We decided to help those who were being sacrificed in our name. We believed that by this act, we could ensure our continued worship. We decided to create a place for them to go to escape the suffering that was and would be afflicted on them. We would not stop the act, but we could prevent needless suffering.

We were younger back then, and like you, we could become attached to our pets. We would create the means to access the realm you would call Dreamland. That place would become free from suffering. So, when someone suffered through wanton acts of cruelty, such as human sacrifice, or simply the barbarity of trapping your own kind in a life of suffering of toil and servitude, now there would be a place to go when that person found their life was too unbearable. They, the tail and the wings of your people, to them we offered hope. They could live in and through their dreams.

And for this Sanctuary, we would gain and reap their gratitude by their continued worship of us. In order to do this, we needed a means of accessing human dreams. We built what you have discovered, O' Dear Heart. We made the Well of Dreams our means to connect to all of humanity as it dreamed. We created the gates of Dreams from that location whereby humanity could enter the realm we had chosen for their sanctuary.

From there, we taught the way of Dreaming to allow those humans to access our newly created realm. We offered them even a chance to leave this mortal coil altogether, if they so choose, and live in our domain, our sanctuary. We appointed guardians to prevent oppressors from gaining access to this new realm. You know them as Lord Mictlantecuhtli, to our Bright Eagle; they are the priests Nasht and Kaman-Thah. By that title, all others know them, by the title of their office, Nasht, and Kaman-Thah, our servants who would keep out the evil ones, the cruel ones.

LAMONT

Lamont: "You're saying you created all of this? You created the Seventy Steps of Slumber, which is the path that all Dreamers walk to get to Dreamland upon their first encounter with this realm."

Yes.

Lamont: "Those steps lead to the Cavern of Flame, where the guardian resides. I saw this guardian as Mictlantecuhtli, but most others see her as two beings called Nasht and Kaman-Thah?"

Yes.

Lamont: "Those names are an official job title, is that it?"

Yes.

Basha: "How many have held that office?"

These individual guardians have this duty for around fifty of your human years, so roughly eighty such guardians have served in this manner since Dreamland was first created. We had gathered rumors that our earliest servants took it upon themselves to try and protect all dreams from harm. They enlisted the aid of dreamers to try and do this. Dream Keepers is what they called themselves[62]*. Though they could not stop the incursion by the great one named Cthulhu back in 1925.*[63]

Lamont: "Yes, I've read that report. So, the Dream Keepers are not always successful, I gather. Wait a minute, why did I not see them as Nasht and Kaman-Thah?"

You were tied to this form that we wear by blood and destiny. They and we took on the persona of Aztec beings in your eyes.

Basha: "That makes sense. When I entered Dreamland, I met Nasht and Kaman-Thah."

Lamont: "You mentioned the gates, and you mentioned Dreaming. Are they the same or two different ways to get to what we call Dreamland?"

The gates were built into space-time if you knew how to call them forth. They were established by Grandmother when the cosmos was created. They are the means for sentient beings from one realm to physically travel throughout the multi-verse and to traverse from one end of the universe to the other. A way to get around the limitation of space-time. The one called Einstein realized that no material thing could move faster than the speed of light. The Gates are a means of getting around in the vastness of space-time. We specifically created the magick of Dreaming as another point of entry to this place we decided to make as a sanctuary. Those humans who use the magick of Dreaming to enter Dreamland have the power to manipulate themselves and possibly the realm itself. However, those humans who enter physically utilizing the gates no longer have access to the Dreaming magick to change either the domain or their own appearance.

Lamont: "Hey, wait. Are you saying all those merchants, farmers, and craftspeople are actual inhabitants and native to Dreamland?"

---

62 To learn more about these Dream Keepers and their recent exploits check out the account of Antonio Zadra in his report *The Dream Keepers*, published by Hidden Moon Press in 2021.

63 It was March 23-April 2, 1925 to be precise as published by Francis Wayland Thurston from various notes left behind by his great uncle, George Gammell Angell, who was a prominent professor of Semitic languages at Brown University in Providence, Rhode Island, and who died during the winter of 1926.

Yes. The natives of Dreamland, who now dwell there, are there because their ancestors came there out of choice. This realm had other native life forms, animals, plants, and other sentient beings. This realm was malleable and was a gathering place, a nexus of space and time.

Lamont: "You're saying that what we call Dreamland was an already existing realm with already existing life on it, correct?"

Yes.

Basha: "You created a spell to allow humans to venture to this place and allow them the means to transform it by what we call Dreaming, correct?"

Yes.

Lamont: "So we, the new wave of Dreamers, people like Basha and I, are simply powerful visitors. We're the flamboyantly dressed tourists, while those ordinary folks are the natural inhabitants and the real reason for Dreamland and your spell of Dreaming that you gave to humanity, correct?

Yes. As a residual effect of our work, anyone who figured out how to do it could make their way to this realm. This is how you two, my dear Heart and Bright Eagle came to that realm. Those you call the natives are the descendants of the ones we brought over from the realm you live in to enter via the portals we created, those gates of Dreams.

For a long time, all this worked. Many came to visit. Many, when they realized that the life in Dreamland was far better than the life of suffering in their Waking World, they petitioned us to grant them the gift of complete submission to us and access to Dreamland as long as their allotted time of life would allow. We would enable permanent access to Dreamland by pulling their consciousness and life force completely over to Dreamland and thus leaving behind the earthly body as an empty carcass in the Waking World. We, being a god, have such power and can grant such a boon. No lesser being, no matter how much sorcery they have at their beck and call, could do this on their own.

Lamont: "Hmm…Tezcat, what if someone is Dreaming and thus their Dreambody and awareness is in Dreamland, and back in the Waking World, something happened to that physical body, and it was killed. What would happen to that Dreamer?"

Supposing the Dreamer was strong enough in their ability and self, in that case, they could make those fleeting moments as their lifeforce was ebbing away seem to last as long as they could. From their own perspective, if they were powerful enough, those Dreamers could create the delusion of eternity in Dreamland. However, once that Waking World body lost its last drop of lifeforce and thus that body died, that Dreamer would cease to be. Does this explain things to you?

Lamont: "It is often said that you can't come back when you die in Dreamland, but that is not true with me. How come? Not that I'm complaining, I'm just curious about stuff."

What you say is true, but you were my chosen vessel from the moment you walked the Seventy steps of slumber and entered walked upon the sands of the Cavern of Flame; thus, you were uniquely gifted

Lamont: "You did that to me?"

Yes. As my vessel, you could not be allowed to foolishly harm yourself, and you were always reckless and foolish. At first, it was a powerful spell that protected you. With magick long crafted in preparation, we united our essence with your own. Once we first embraced in our throne room, once you tasted our life's blood, Dream death was burnt away fully from your flesh. You were to be our vessel, and thus we protected you in preparation for us to join with your flesh. Does this answer your question?

Lamont: "It does. I guess I should be grateful. Okay, go back to your recounting of the hows and whys of you making Sanctuary you call Dreamland."

So our sanctuary was filled with them and their descendants. They all worshipped us, as was our right.

However, your people are capricious, and you make up new gods like changing the colors of the trees. So, we, the old Outer Gods, had been cast aside and forgotten. Our temples were neglected, and we no longer were being offered the needed blood. Our power to aid and sustain the protection of sanctuary had come to an end. The appointed guardians no longer had the ability to keep out those who would corrupt our shelter. Thus, they were allowed entry. We no longer had the power to bring our offering to those in need. We could not give the hope of sanctuary to those who were offered to us by the Nazis of Germany in their flaming pyres. They died needlessly, without being able to come there. They failed to heed our call. Such a waste.

Basha: "You are saying that offered to free those who suffered the horrors of the Waking World? That you even tried to help my people who eventually died in the Nazi's Holocaust? That is something you did not explain to me last year."

We were not thinking clearly. We wanted our freedom and only thought of this. You were an obstacle to be overcome. When clever Dear Heart sacrificed himself and thus prevented us from crossing the gate, we learned the greater purpose for us all. Our time was not right to return.

Basha: "Those words on the Statue of Liberty would be fitting for the entranceway to Dreamland, your sanctuary.'*Give me your tired, your poor, your huddled masses yearning to breathe free, the wretched refuse of your teeming shore. Send these, the homeless, tempest-tossed to me, I lift my lamp beside the golden door.[64]'"*

Yes, Bright Eagle, that is exactly how we thought of and intended Dreamland to be until we were forgotten, and thus our gift became despoiled. This is not right. We need you two, our Dear Heart and our Bight Eagle, to aid us. To help right this wrong. So, we may once more be acknowledged and worshiped as is our right. Will you help us?

Basha: "Yes, we will, but how? How did you get here? Why did this happen?"

Before your ancestors' people came with that Cortez and put an end to our beautiful city of Tenochtitlan, and ended the reign of those you call the Aztecs. That was when Grandmother found out what we had done. She was displeased that we gave the gift of Dreaming to humans and even more angry to learn that we had created Sanctuary. She vowed to punish us.

We protected and hid Sanctuary from her, but we came to be defeated in the war with her and our siblings. This defeat corresponded with Cortez's army's victory. This victory of Cortez ended our direct worship. With our failure, we suffered her wrath. She killed us and bound our remains to a place deep beneath our once proud city. She knew that when death died, we would awaken, eventually. So to that end, She created and sent a beast to torment us, eat us alive, and keep us perpetually dying. And thus, in our death and torment, we dreamed of revenge. Amongst your kind, there were some who could hear our dying dreams. The one known as Alhazred heard us and wrote down those most infamous couplets in his book.

Lamont: "You've been trapped here and dead for the last 450-plus years?"

Yes. This beast comes and feeds on us. We are hardy and do not die the final and true death easily. We regenerate, and when we do, the beast returns. In between our death and dying and the time of our renewal, we in death did dream. We dreamed slowly to scheme and plan. Gather our energy to use for our purposes.

Lamont: "You're not dead, but awake and alive. Does this mean that it will be here soon?"

Yes. We cannot kill it. It was made so that death by our hands could not be brought about. However, trying to be clever, we realize that you can be the hands that could end it and thus our torment. You will need more strength and power than you currently possess. We can offer you some of the strength and power you will need, or we hope to. Your forms can only contain a small amount of our full strength and power.

---

[64] From "The New Colossus" Emma Lazarus wrote in 1883.

Basha: "What if we kill this beast? "What will hold you here? Will you not then be free to roam where you will? Are we not now on the other side of the gate of Dreams? All this is unclear."

You have a polished eye O' Bright Eagle to ask such questions. We are here in our beloved city of Tenochtitlan, at least the Dream version of that city that resides on this side of the Gate of Dreams. What are the words? The physics to describe and explain the connection between this chamber, Dreamland, and the Waking World of Tenochtitlan are thus entangled; the two touch and yet are separate. It is hard to describe, and truth be told, hard for us to understand the actual mechanics, especially in the language of current concepts.

Basha: "So, you also failed that class in hyper-quantum physics?"

Lamont: "Where are Einstein and Bohr when you need them? Out having a nosh somewhere in space-time, I would guess."

However, the point of your inquiry, O' Bright Eagle, is this: would the beast's killing free us to roam about where we desire? The answer is no. Trapped still within this place would we be. The magick our grandmother weaved would keep us in this cage still. However, we would be free to think clearly, plan, and aid those who can hear our call. If there was blood freely given, we could have the power to protect Sanctuary from new encroachments by channeling the needed resources to the priests Nasht and Kaman-Thah.

Thus, we will be establishing it as a sanctuary once again. However, you two could help deal with those who should not be in Sanctuary with our strength and power. If you so choose to act.

Basha: "If what you say is true, O' Tezcatlipoca, you are not only the creator of Dreamland; you are also its protector when everything was functioning as you needed it to. Then yes, I can see that you will get your blood once more freely given. I can see to it that your temple is once more visited, and homage is given to you for those acts of creation and for bringing so many to Sanctuary and to protect Sanctuary once more."

Excellent, O' Bright Eagle; this is good news. I know your pledge will be honored. Your words are tightly bound.

Basha: "Need this worship be in the name of Tezcatlipoca? Can it be in some other name, perhaps? That one has some problematic baggage that would be too troublesome to explain and would impede your worship."

It matters little what we are called. That is not our true name, nor is the one given by Lovecraft.

Basha: "I thought so. Would it suit you to be known as this title: The Goddess Smoking Mirror, She who is the mother of dreams? An obsidian mirror could be your physical representation of your presence and power. Would that suit you?"

Yes, Bright Eagle, that would. May I suggest the use of obsidian to draw the blood I require?

Basha: "Yes, that would be agreeable as well. However, we have a current problem before all that can be done. Your beast will be coming. How do we defeat this beast?"

Lamont: "And do you know when its next scheduled feeding time is? How much time do we have to figure out how to stop it from killing you again?"

As for when we cannot say with certainty, we must act soon; this we know. You two must absorb our blood to gain the strength and power you need. You must feed on our essence; you will need to, although we cannot guarantee that you will succeed in the task of defeating the beast. We only have hope that you will be up to the task. You will have what we can give to you. You will be like the eagle and the jaguar; thus, we hope you can take down the beast.

Lamont: "Well, I have no problem with feeding on your life essence. I only hope that it is as tasty as Kaliya."

BASHA

Basha: "Well, I will not feed on your blood. I do not think it would be considered kosher, nor do I think it is wise. I like my life as it is. And a vampire's life I do not wish, nor to become any other unnatural creature. If I touch your blood, will I absorb its essence?"

Tezcatlipoca again laughs.

No, I do not think your rabbis would consider my blood kosher! You have such a polished eye O' Bright Eagle. You are sweet like blood and chocolate. Yes, our power and strength will be absorbed upon contact; we can make this so. This will alleviate and prevent any other results, as you so astutely deduced in our words. So, do you trust us enough?

Basha: "No, as you told us, we should not quickly trust you. However, I do believe what you have spoken. I do believe you wish us to aid sanctuary. To this end, we both agree.

This is good, O' Bright Eagle. For soon, the beast shall be returning. I am well, and it can sense this. Time to feed on me is quickly upon us.

Basha: 'Well, Lamont, do you believe him? It is all a fantastic yarn Tezcatlipoca has spun out for us. *'Tis not the many oaths that makes the truth, but the plain single vow that is vowed true.*[65]' Do we really think he has vowed to us truthfully?'

Lamont: 'I think so. I feel that he's speaking truthfully about this matter. He brought me back for some reason. He didn't have to do that. He

[65] William Shakespeare, *All's Well That Ends Well*, Act IV, scene 2.

clearly wanted and needed me to be able to do something for him. This seems to be the only way to explain that act.'

Basha: 'Yes. I agree. His plan for you was for you to aid him.'

Lamont: "Tezcat, I have a question. Is this all you require of us? To kill the beast?

Now that you have broached the subject, that is not all. There is a trifle more you could do to assist us.

Basha: "And what might that be, O' Dark Trickster?"

A mere nothing, a little thing, a gesture of aid...

Lamont: "Okay, Tezcat, enough with the hand waving," Lamont bursts in with impatience and impertinence. "Spill it. What else?"

It would be ever so lovely to be free from this accursed cage, free of it, and breathe clean air, feel the moonbeams on our face, and smell the sweetness of the gulfs of space itself.

Basha: "Would that be possible?"

Yes, if you absorbed enough of our power, yes. Once again, we cannot directly pull these beams down to burst forth from this pit, this cage. We would need your direct action to do so.

Lamont: "Grandma may not care about the feeding times of her pet, but I would think that busting out of this place, like breaking out of any prison, would set off loud alarm bells."

What you say, Dear Heart, maybe so. We would have to make a hasty retreat, but...

Basha: "Hell no, buster! We did not sign up for a jailbreak. That would definitely piss off your Grandma, and she would then come hunting for us."

We could hide your presence from her. Trust us...

Basha: "No way! Even with the beast occasionally stopping by for dinner, you can make much mischief from your cage. We will do the Herculean thing and end your suffering if and only if you swear to restore Dreamland to its status of Sanctuary. This you must swear."

Yes, Bright Eagle, we so swear. We do need sweet blood to be offered to us to give us the power to return our ongoing protection to Sanctuary.

Basha: "That can be arranged. However, you will remain here. We cannot have your Grandmother aware of any of this."

Lamont: "Hey, I thought the stars were no longer aligned and such things?"

You, Dear Heart, were the Chosen for when the stars had aligned. Chosen to free us and lead us beyond the Gate of Dreams back to the Waking World. As you rightly stated, the stars are no longer in such alignment. We will have to wait for many long years, long after your natural time to walk amongst us, for the stars to come around again. If we so desire for us to leave this realm of Dreams.

However, that is then. This is now. Our desires are tightly bound to this task at this time. Now, what say you both? Time to waste is not an option for any of us. Who knows what the beast will do once he arrives. He may not be satisfied with merely consigning me to my death and depart. He may turn upon you two next.

So, you will need our help to depart from here even if we cannot. Thus, defeating the beast is our first task. We cannot aid your departure if we are dead.

Lamont: "Very true. If we are to have the ability to defend ourselves, we must do as Tezcat asks. So, Tezcat, I think we have a deal. Is that not right, Basha?"

Basha: "Yes, O' Tezcatlipoca. We are forced by circumstances to agree."

Then quickly, children, you must come here and feed on my blood you must, O' Dear Heart. While you O' Bright Eagle must place your hands in my wounds. You both must do this before the coming of the beast.

We both approach the altar upon which Tezcatlipoca is bound. Lamont takes on his black Knight form as he comes around to his neck. He gently cradles Tezcatlipoca's head, and his fangs extend. It is disconcerting, and I strangely and strongly feel jealous watching Lamont about to feed on him.

Come, my Dear Heart, and feed on me. Take me into yourself, and let us join. This is the inevitable purpose we saw for you.

LAMONT

I barely hear Tezcat's words as I feel the vampire in me rise up.

THE NIGHT (& LAMONT)

I bite into Tezcatlipoca with difficulty, and when my fangs pierce that flesh, it is as if I broke through brittle glass. Burning hot is the thick blood flowing through Tezcatlipoca's veins. As I feed, it is like tasting scolding hot chocolate. But with it comes awakening gifts of power, the power that fulfills my destiny.

LAMONT (& **THE NIGHT**)

OOOHHH...this is what Basha must feel like when I feed on her......it is joining and union...but so much more...arousing...erotic...flesh becomes one flesh...in a sea of scolding hot chocolate...Oh my God......I......

BASHA

The look on Lamont as he bites into Tezcatlipoca is not helping. With a bit of unresolved anger, I plunge my hands into Tezcatlipoca's open wound as Lamont's fangs sink into the flesh of his neck.

Upon contact with his blood, I hear us both scream in pain. Like molten lava, her blood sears me. I can see it crawl its way into my flesh, and it burns! As I struggle to absorb her essence, I burst into flames to counteract the heat.

As…you…can…tell…O'…bright…eagle…mortal…flesh…was…not meant…to…touch...us! This…is…painful…for…us…both! We…must…endure! But this is not how we planned it…I smell and sense something different about Dear Heart. What is this? He is still in control…we thought this would bring my child to prominence…why is this not happening? What did Dear Heart do to prevent this? How? What is that? It is an ancient essence in his blood. How did this happen? It is affecting my power, transforming it. He is not overwhelmed by me. He is transmuting it. Ahhh...

It is good that I can hear Tezcatlipoca, but she does not realize I can. I wonder if Lamont resisting Tezcatlipoca has to do with Lamont feeding on Kaliya earlier. This must have given him a way to transform the life force from Tezcatlipoca and take in and lose himself to it. I knew we could not trust her fully! But this is all…too…much…falling into darkness and…

*

BASHA

I feel sick. I smell burning flesh…or I guess my flesh that once was burning. Now I feel invigorated and revitalized. I am healing and being born anew. I healed quickly. That must be a gift and sample of my new power, having absorbed some of Tezcatlipoca's essence. I wonder what changes Lamont has. I cannot let Tezcatlipoca know that I know his wanting to trick Lamont somehow. Dealing with Tezcatlipoca is always like riding a tiger—you cannot lose control for an instant! Wow…I hope this was all worth it. I hope we are doing the right thing and helping Tezcatlipoca. Well, it is done. No turning back.

I feel his cool smooth flesh as I lay face down on his naked form. I lift my head and look around. My arms are still buried up to my elbows in Tezcatlipoca's wound. Yuck. And the tendrils of blood are still connecting my flesh to his flesh. I lift myself off Tezcatlipoca and can hear the blood connection snap off one by one as I disconnect from him. I stagger and collapse next to the altar. Lamont lies next to me. Brown blood drips from his mouth. He looks spent and soiled. Yet his eyes glow bright and almost crackle with energy.

I cannot focus. I...

*

I slowly wake up. I can tell by the stench that where I am. I am still in that underground chamber where Tezcatlipoca was chained and tortured like Prometheus for his aid to humanity. We are again in darkness. Neither Tezcatlipoca nor I had the wherewith all to keep the lights going after all of that. I can hear both Lamont and Tezcatlipoca waking up. The room is now lit by the aid of his magick. There is an odd and ominous glow far off in the distance.

It is a rough beast whose hour has come round at last as he slouches toward me.

Basha: "Having Yeats[66] like delusions of grandeur O' Smoking Mirror."

As the beast approaches, I see it is a massive jaguar with eagle wings, deadly and ferocious as the two are, no doubt. It is a beautiful animal that flows like liquid yellow and black, pulsing with confidence, ferocious grace, and power. Its voice is elegant and terrible to hear.

Cuahotl: ***"WE HAVE COME TO DINE ONCE AGAIN ON YOUR FLESH, O' TEZCATLIPOCA. WHO ARE THESE UNINVITED GUESTS YOU ARE ENTERTAINING? SHALL WE FEAST ON THEIR FLESH AS WELL?"***

Lamont: "There will be no feasting this time! You'll be sorely disappointed this time! So says…"

No need for formal introductions, "Tezcatlipoca says, interrupting Lamont. *Let us just call them my guest friends.*

Basha: "We are welcome here," taking Tezcatlipoca's hint at keeping our identity hidden from this creature. "You are not. So begone beast!"

Cuahotl: ***"YOU NEVER ASKED THE NAME OF YOUR PUNISHMENT; WHY WAS THAT SWEET TEZCATLIPOCA OF THE NORTH? WE WERE MADE TO BE THE INSTRUMENT OF YOUR PUNISHMENT, SO WE SHALL. NOTHING YOU TWO LITTLE ONES DO CAN STOP US. I AM CUAUHOCELOTL; I WAS MADE TO SERVE."***

Lamont: "I guess I need to add to my to-do list and learn how to speck Aztec when we get out of here. Yikes, all these names are a mouthful. How about we call you Cu-a-ho-tl, for short? Now, I know that Tezcat can be annoying, but what did he do? Who did he piss off this time?"

"FOR HIS FOLLY AND FEELINGS FOR LOVELY CRAWLING THINGS SUCH AS YOURSELVES, HE EARNED THE WRAITH OF OMETEOTL, SHE WHO IS MOTHER AND RULER OF ALL THE OUTER GODS AND THUS ALL LIVING THINGS. WE ARE HER VOICE AND HER VENGEANCE, SO BE WARNED AND BEWARE! STAND NOT IN OUR WAY."

---

[66] Referring to William Butler Yeats's poem '*The Second Coming*' first printed in *The Dial* in November 1920.

Lamont: "Sorry about this, Chief, but standing in the way is why we are here."

"IMPUDENT INSECTS, DO YOU THINK YOU ARE SOMETHING THAT THE LIKES OF US SHOULD NOTICE? WE SHALL SWAT YOU AWAY LIKE THE ANNOYING TINY VERMIN YOU ARE."

Lamont: "Come on, Dawn; let's show Cuahotl, this annoying refugee from a genetic blender, that we are beings that demand notice!" Lamont says as he becomes all black-garbed with stark white skin accented with crimson lips, his glowing icy blue eyes shining out from the shadows of his hat and collar.

Half dozen dagger-like shards of black night are flung out of Lamont's hands and slice into the Cuauhocelotl, the eagle-jaguar beast. I hurl balls of fire at the beast, hitting his wings and flank. It roars in surprise and pain from our twin attack, yet it does not stop it as it soars swiftly on those mighty wings in our direction.

"DAMNATION AND HELLFIRE! YOU INSECTS HAVE A STRONG STING! BUT THIS WILL NOT STAY MY COURSE. I HAVE BEEN SENT BY QUEEN MOTHER OMETEOTL, AND I MUST NOT FAIL TO PERFORM MY TASK. YOU WILL NOT DETER ME. "

Cuauhocelotl closes the distance between Lamont and himself with startling speed and rakes his claws into Lamont's flesh, leaving trails of blood across his chest. Its jaguar mouth is about to bite into Lamont; he turns into a shadowy mist and drifts out of range. Snarling at his failure to attack Lamont, he springs toward me instead. His claws rip into me even as I burst into flames brighter and hotter than ever before as I take this opportunity to hurl a blast of fire at its eagle wings. It snarls in pain as it tries again to claw me. I try to get out of range, though not quick enough as its razor-sharp claws rake my flesh once again.

"YOU CANNOT STOP ME, LITTLE INSECTS. I AM THE CHOSEN INSTRUMENT OF OMETEOTL!"

Lamont: "So, Cuahotl, did little old Tezcat hand out too many 'get out of jail free' cards and piss off O' Great and wonderful Matriarch?" Lamont says as he hurls more of his sharp shards of darkness at the beast.

"YES, HIS ACTIONS DISPLEASE GREAT MOTHER, SO WE WERE FORMED TO BE THE INSTRUMENT OF HER DISPLEASURE. YOU ARE MEANT TO GROVEL AND ACCEPT YOUR PLIGHT. HE DID ALLOW MANY TO FLEE FROM THEIR FATE. THIS DISPLEASED HER WHO MUST BE OBEYED."

It pounces toward Lamont, and he manages to leap onto its back and form his own claws, gripping it into its flesh and drawing blood. His vampire fangs bite into its flesh, which it really does not like. I direct my flames at its flank at the same time.

Basha: "Can we not convince you of the folly of your mission here? We may be insects, but can you not feel that we can do you harm?" I ask even as I blast it with my searing fire. I can smell that I am harming it; its flesh is cooking under my attack.

It pounces toward me, and I try to avoid it, but it slices into me with one of its paws/claws. Damn, that hurts! It spreads its wings and flies upward, trying its best to shake Lamont off. It flies higher and higher as it whirls and spins with urgency and anger. It manages to cast Lamont off, and he plummets downward. He hits the ground hard and barely avoids the jaguar beasts pouncing attack.

"WE CAN DO NOTHING BUT FULFILL THE PURPOSE WE WERE CRAFTED. WE HAVE NO WILL OF OUR OWN. WE HAVE ONLY THE DESIRE TO HUNT AND SEEK THE PREY THAT WE HAVE BEEN MADE TO DEVOUR."

Then Lamont attacks like the living marble vampiric predator that he is. He is The Night, and he attacks! With claw and bite holds on and feeds. Lamont's eyes blaze icy blue, and he gleams with dark savagery. The beast gets smart and manages to position itself so that I blasted Lamont/Night in a burst of flames. I stopped and tried to maneuver around. This led to an aerial ballet as we both danced through the sky, me trying to get a clear shot and it trying to position Lamont/Night in my firing range.

Meanwhile, Lamont/Night relentlessly feeds on it and drains its life force. That is slowing it down and weakening it. He conjures more of those ebony daggers to lunge into the creature.

Then, out of desperation, it does an aerial maneuver that catches me by surprise, lunges at me, and smashes me to the ground with it on top of me. Now, both Lamont and I are on the defensive. Lamont/Night is trying to keep its mouth from chomping on me while I have to try and keep its front claws from getting at me and stop it from doing too much damage. Damn, it hurts!

That allows its back-leg claws from racking my legs. Arrgh! I cannot push it off of me. All I can do is ignite myself entirely and try to burn it wherever my skin comes in contact with me. It both leaps and pulls itself up and away with its wings.

Our combative dance continues. We all strike and give as much as we get. Each side harming the other but none decisively; we are all relentless in attack, parry, and counterattack.

Then it dives at Lamont/Night, who momentarily has turned his back to it to avoid a strike; it seems hell-bent on attacking him. The beast grabs him with all its paws and teeth ripping into him.

Lamont and the Night screams! He does his best to shake the beast off of him. I dive full speed at it.

Lamont is trying to reach back and grab that thing. It continues to savagely eat our flesh! I can feel Lamont and Night's anger and pain. It rips chunks out of his back as it chews on him and hangs on while Lamont wildly struggles to get free of it.

Basha: "Hell no!"

My rage intensifies, and I go white-hot. Beams of my rage and anger burn at the beast's flesh, and it roars in pain. The thing seems to be feasting on his flesh! He falls to the ground…the impact…there is so much blood…he lies so still…Lamont's not moving…then he is gone! Noooo! Lamont!!!"

All I see is blood…Lamont's massive pool of blood and thick smoke…I find myself at its throat in a rage, ripping into it…tearing out its flesh. My eyes blast it with laser-like intensity. I smell roasting flesh. I hear its roar of pain and hear my own screams as I attack and attack and attack

Then suddenly, darkness reaches out and grabs the thing. It holds its head in shadowy hands, and the beast's neck is snapped with a resounding wrench and a loud crunch. I watch as Lamont lunges and, with a roar of lust, sinks his fang and mouth to feast on the blood of the beast.

I continue to roast it with my own pent-up anger as well.

The stench of burning meat is overwhelming.

Lamont: "Basha."

I hear Lamont's voice.

Lamont: "You can stop now. It's beaten…you can stop…I'm okay. There is nothing left now but charred bones."

LAMONT

Basha: "Yes, Lamont, I'm okay. A bit wounded but okay. I think…I will heal from these wounds…quickly. Tezcatlipoca's gift to me. We did it. We won. The beast is dead. I am weak…still bleeding…I..."

I'm at her side in a few heartbeats, and she's in my arms. I feel safe. I feel alive and whole once again. I hold her tight, my rage and my own pain is intense, but at least now I stop shaking.

O' Bright Eagle, if I were one of my brothers, I would have the power to heal your wounds. However, I am not. I do apologize. The only comfort I can give you is that now that you have absorbed as much of my power as you can, you will now heal faster. I do thank you both for aiding me in my hour of need.

Lamont: "Basha…oh dearest…I thought I lost you…I thought it killed…"

Basha: "It is okay. It did not…I am here," Basha says, comforting the two of us.

"I'm a monster…Basha, I am really a monster…you are the only thing keeping it at bay…if anything happened to you…"

"It is alright, Lamont, you are alright. I am here, as you are here for me. The monster is dead."

"No. The monster is alive within me. I live a few heartbeats away from it. You are the only thing that prevents it from consuming me. I am a nosferatu. I am damned."

"You are not, Lamont! Do not say such things. You are…just different."

"Ha! Different! Such a tiny fig leaf of a euphemism trying to cover up so much! I mean it, Basha; you saw what I did to the Zygo'Tehian and what I almost did to those bullies. I am just a heartbeat away from becoming consumed by the darkness of the creature that abides within me. It can take me over, and I can barely stop it."

"We will not let that happen. We will see that it does not happen. Together, Lamont, we can prevail."

"Yes, Basha, but only together. I would be lost without you."

We kiss, then separate, knowing we will never be separated.

BASHA

"As for being a monster, Lamont, well, what we saw of the Zygo'Tehians got me thinking. We, humans, breed sentient, live forms to slaughter and feed off of; how different is our meat-eating industry from what the Zygo'Tehians did? I think since I eat meat, if you call yourself a monster, then so am I. I think I may have to seriously consider becoming a vegetarian. Anyway, let us deal with our immediate problems. So, are we done here?" I ask weakly to Tezcat.

Almost O' Bright Eagle, I cannot free myself from the chains that bind me. Again, the magick used in their creation prevents this. If you two could be so kind as to remove them? I would appreciate it.

"In for a penny, in for a pound," I mutter. "All part of the service."

I carefully try to get up and am a bit woozy still. Lamont stays by my side, holding on to me.

Basha: "I will be okay. I just need to get used to standing on my own two feet once again."

Lamont: "You're still bleeding, just a bit. Just lie still and rest till you recoup."

I decide not to argue and just stay cuddled in his arms for a while.

LAMONT

Dear Heart, while Bright Eagle rests, I need to speak with your other half.

Lamont: "What do you mean? What other half…"

Do not trouble yourself...let me call and speak with the darkness that dwells within. You, Dear Heart, shall sleep while I talk to my child, the one you call Night.

"Wait...no..."

THE NIGHT (AND BASHA)

I am here, Dark Lord, you who are the dark night and the dark wind, what do you wish to tell me and to me alone?

(Lamont may not know what is happening, but I am here eavesdropping. Night knows I am here, but I do not think Tezcatlipoca knows about this.)

Now that you have taken my life force within you, you will come into your full power as mine and your legacy. You are a child of a God. You are the one that is two. You are my child. But, know this. You are a threat to many who dwell within the shadows of Dreamland. They will be jealous of the gift I have bestowed upon you. They will question it and challenge your right to it.

What does that mean? What need I do?

A creature also claims the name that is rightfully and solely yours alone. He has heard of your fame, and he trembles at this. Many, to their dismay, have discovered that you know what evil lurks in their hearts. Fear is what this entity feeds off of; thus, you threaten its food source with your activities.

Who is this?

It too calls itself Night, and it dwells in fabled Mhor at the easternmost edge of Dream Land. It resides in a viscous pool hidden within a temple; from there, it sends forth its horde to feed on fear if they are weak of mind and will.[67] *This horde issues forth with the setting of the sun. You will need to deal with this lesser being if you wish to rule the night sky as is your due and as is your right. I have given you this gift, and you must claim your heritage.*

I must confront this being, am I right?

Yes. And defeat it. By doing that, you will be on my left; you will truly don my black slippers of royalty as your rightful place.

I understand.

Good. Can you hear my Dear Heart sleeping?

Yes, I can. I can hear and feel Lamont within me.

Good. This is how it will be. He will awaken shortly, though he will not recall that we have so spoken.

Hmm...This is very interesting. From how that conversation went, I do not think Tezcatlipoca realized that they were talking on a party line, and

---

[67] This creature is described in Gary Myers's story, "Xiurhn", in *The House of the Worm*, Arkham House, 1975, pp 23-29.

I can hear all of this. I still have not decided to tell Lamont about his Hyde-Night thing inside him. I will just add this to the list of secrets I am keeping from him for now.

*

BASHA

Basha: I dozed off. I look at Lamont feeling better. Without any idea how much time has passed. "It would have been nice if the landlord had mounted a clock on the walls of this place."

Lamont: "Yeah, we'll take that up with the manager later; add it to the list of complaints about this place's room service."

Basha: "Okay, other than my pretty suit being a bit shredded, there are no other marks from the conflict with that beast. I guess there is something to be said for soaking up Tezcatlipoca's blood. I need to restore my appearance now; I want to look my best for my public. Now that that is done let us check up on our host."

We slowly approach the altar where Tezcatlipoca lies bound in metal chains.

Basha: "Tezcatlipoca, just for the record, sometime last year, I was once confronted by the warrior called Hummingbird, was that really him, or was it you?"

That was me. My brothers and we are joined, so in some sense, we are a single being, but in other ways, we are individual beings. We simply appeared in the face and form of my brother. We did not possess his power.

Basha: "Just checking, trying to get the players straight. Okay, I take it this," pointing to the chains that bind him, "can melt and be broken, but it will take some doing, is that it?"

Yes, Bright Eagle. Do not concern yourself about what your efforts will do to me. Do what you have to in order to set me free.

Lamont: "Okay. So I will pull them apart while you do your melting thing to weaken them enough for me to snap them. Sounds like a plan?"

Basha: "Makes sense to me. Ready?"

Lamont grabs and positions his arms. "Ready."

I focus my flames into something like a blowtorch in intensity and begin to see what I can do to melt the metal. I can see the metal change color and glow. I can again smell burning flesh as Lamont and Tezcatlipoca grimace and deal with the pain. I would not have thought my flames would affect Tezcatlipoca like it is. Could it be another result of my absorbing his power through his blood? Whatever I may do to Tezcatlipoca, these chains seem to be made of stronger stuff. So far, my efforts have not yielded any results.

Basha: "Do you want to take a break?" I ask.

Tezcatlipoca grunts, "*No. Just keep at it.*"

Lamont: "Yeah..." Lamont grimaces. "It only hurts when I laugh..."

Basha: "Okay." I just keep applying my flame, bringing it to a new level of intensity. My fiery blasts are now white-hot, and I watch and smell them dealing with this. I get it to a laser-like intensity, and finally, it is beginning to be visibly affected. I can feel Tezcatlipoca's power surging through my blood and being as I become star bright and my concentrated fire blazes forth with the sun's heat.

Through the smoke and the shimmering heat waves, I see our efforts are having an effect. Lamont is pulling and stretching it like thick viscous taffy.

"Bloody...damn...Hell!" Lamont exclaims as the chains are ripped asunder, and then he collapses in exhaustion. Minutes tick by, and finally, he is able to speak again. "Tezcat, take my advice; don't piss anybody off like this again; getting you out of those chains really hurt!"

HA! Coming from you, O' Dear Heart, that is very funny. As you might say, pissing off any deity you meet. However, I agree. I do not wish to find myself so bound and in need of rescue. Again, I say thank you. You have again demonstrated that you possess the valor of eagles and the ferocity of jaguars. With not too much time, we will all heal and be well. With the blood you offered to provide, O' Bright Eagle, we shall have the power to do our part to ensure sanctuary. You will have to deal with those who are already walking its paths.

Lamont: "Okay, Tezcat, another project for your already full plates. I hate to be rude and rescue and run, but we got to get a move on. Can we simply wake up, or do we have miles to go before we can sleep?"

At this point, you are enough in the nexus of the Waking World and Dreamland to simply wake up.

Basha: "Whew...I must say, even with all your power-boosting Tezcatlipoca, I also ache and am exhausted."

Lamont: "I think that the next time we are asked to undertake this god rescuing gig, we need to have more spinach and Wheaties before we begin."

"Yuck!"

"What. You have something against Popeye[68] and the Breakfast of Champions[69]?"

Basha: "Not by themselves. I have all the respect in the world for that pugnacious character and the other persuasive ad campaign. But, I am just saying spinach in my Wheaties is not a good idea…"

Lamont: "Okay…okay…I won't mix my metaphors next time."

"Seriously, do you really want spinach in your milk and cereal? It is just plain gross, Lamont."

"It's all easy for you to be all picky and finicky about what you eat. Right now, I can't even eat cereal."

"But I am just saying if you could—would you really want all that slimy green stuff floating in your milk?"

"Now, I've had sautéed spinach, and it isn't slimy. You're slandering my spinach. Watch it, girl. Dem's fighting words."

"But face it, even well-sautéed spinach does not in milk go. Am I right? I mean, really."

"Okay, you win. No mixing spinach and Wheaties. Bad idea!"

HA! I think you two have not been forthcoming about your actual relationship. You sound like an old married couple. I cannot listen to another word! You are scratching the jade! Now that I am no longer in peril, I can afford to gather my remaining strength on a single spell. I can no longer take your chattering. So…begone!

As we fade out, we hear the heartfelt laughter of Tezcatlipoca surrounding us in warmth and joy.

*

MONDAY, SEPTEMBER 8, 1980
SAN FRANCISCO GENERAL HOSPITAL
BASHA

Lamont: "Ohhh...my butt aches from too much sitting!" Lamont complains loudly as he gets up from his chair and stretches.

---

68 Popeye the Sailor is an American cartoon character created by Elzie Crisler Segar. The character first appeared in the daily King Features comic strip Thimble Theatre on January 17, 1929, and Popeye became the strip's title in later years. The character has also appeared in theatrical and television animated cartoons.

69 Wheaties is a brand of breakfast cereal made by General Mills. It is well known for featuring prominent athletes on its packages and has become a cultural icon in the United States. The first appearance of the slogan on the new signboard was penned by Knox Reeves, of a Minneapolis advertising agency. When asked what should be placed on the sign for Wheaties, Reeves sketched a Wheaties box on a pad of paper, thought for a moment, and wrote "Wheaties-The Breakfast of Champions".

Basha: "Uh…yes, I am all stiff and sore. But, hey, it beats bleeding all over the place, much less dying. What do you think of that tall tale that Tezcatlipoca spun for us? Does Lovecraft corroborate it in any of his stories?"

Lamont: "No. Lovecraft never explains how and why Dreamland came to exist. It simply was. Nor does he have any God of Dreams. Nyarlathotep seems to be the protector of all the lesser Gods who come or reside in dreamland. So, all of this is way beyond Lovecraft."

"You realize that Tezcatlipoca is claiming to be one of the good guys. And that we are now working with, if not for her?"

"Yeah. The key to all of this is that a deity becomes what her worshipers want of her and what they imagine her to be. The Goddesses are then molded in their image by the act of their devotion."

"So, by offering blood freely given, we can bind Tezcatlipoca to this new job description, is that it?"

"That is what seems to be the case."

"Well, I am too exhausted to think much of anything clearly. What time is it?"

"Well, the little hand on the wall says it's three am, and it's bloody Monday."

"Hell! We got to get to classes!"

"My head isn't ready to think about that stuff. I'm not sure if I even did my homework."

"Hey! What about Peter? Is he okay now?"

We both look over at him, still asleep. We cannot ascertain just by looking if there is any change, though he does seem more peaceful. Lamont does his black Knight thing and reaches out his hand to Peter.

LAMONT

Lamont: "I don't feel any lingering gate or container surrounding him.
So, I think mission accomplished. But he's still coma-like asleep."

I focus on him and try to wake him up. But it is all a jumble…night and fog…pain and loneliness…I can't get a fix on him…just a feeling of fear…hiding…and being trapped.

Lamont: "It's still not right. He's lost in some kind of deep nightmarish sleep. Maybe he will wake up on his own."

Basha: "Which means he is still trapped in his dreams? How can we be certain that he is alright?"

Lamont: "Take my hand."

*

WELL OF DREAMS
BASHA

I find myself in the chamber of the Well of Dreams. Lamont approaches the well water carefully. He sticks the tip of his finger in the water.

Lamont: "Ahh…much better. Taking in Tezcat's life force has allowed me to make use of this well without getting boiled alive. I have an idea. Watch. I'm going to go in. Now I have to directly connect with the water so…"

I watch with surprise and a bit of inappropriate delight as Lamont turns with his back to me and starts dissolving his Knight Dream attire.

Basha: "Now, what is with this bout of exhibitionism, Lamont?"

"Well, connecting to the Well is like magick, of the Dream variety. So, to allow me to connect to the collective minds of all dreamers, I need to be in direct contact, water to skin, thus…ah…skyclad."

"Oh, I see," and I literally do!. He is now completely naked as he slowly lowers himself into the inky black streaming waters. I must say I enjoy watching a naked Lamont, even if it is just his lovely backside slowly disappearing from view in the Well's water.

"Ahh...it's nice, hot, but not scalding. I'm guessing it is something like our normal body temperature of 98.6."

When his head goes completely under, I call out. "Hey, Lamont, are you okay?"

'Yes. I can breathe perfectly well here. It feels like water to my skin, but it seems like normal air to my nose and mouth. Interesting. Now let me concentrate on Peter.'

I wait a few minutes, and then Lamont starts to step back out of the well water. I get another nice view of his body; he stops just short of revealing himself below his hips and waistline. Now, girl, you got to keep yourself from doing the Mae West drift. It all becomes more manageable once he gets decent by forming some briefs as he steps on shore, and then he quickly returns to normal, fully clothed Lamont. Whew.

Basha: "Well?"

Lamont: "As I suspected, he's now trapped in his own dreamscape, and he's not going to wake up. It is a place of smoke, ashes, and fear. A camp of some kind. He is asleep at the moment in some wooden bunks. Others are there. It is all odd and disconcerting. We have to go into this dream and do something to convince him it is safe to return to the Waking World. Not sure about all of this at the moment. For now, we should wake up."

Monday, September 8, 1980

SAN FRANCISCO GENERAL HOSPITAL
LAMONT

Basha: "We are back…"

Lamont: "We are indeed."

"I am more than a bit overwhelmed with all that…" Basha says.

"Yeah. Tezcat is the creator of Dreamland…"

"And do not forget that she claims to be her protector…"

"Yeah, once long ago when she was worshipped."

"Yes. That central temple in Atlantis. Where she resides. That is the temple of all the Outer Gods, correct?"

"Yup."

"Who are they? I was never a fan of Lovecraft."

"Besides Tezcat aka Nyarlathotep, there is Azathoth, Yog-Sothoth, and Shub-Niggurath. Those are the four basic cosmic forces."

"And in Lovecraft's telling, they are all nasty, evil, and dangerous, right?"

"A general danger to human sanity, yup, that's it."

"And they presented themselves to us in those Aztec forms back at the nexus of the Cosmos where Tezcatlipoca was entombed, correct?"

"Yeah, we saw them as Aztec deities due to the prism of our meeting and knowing Tezcatlipoca."

"But they were manifested to Lovecraft very differently, hence his nearly unpronounceable names, correct?"

"Correct."

"As you keep saying and explaining to me, we perceive reality through our own backgrounds. We are shaped by ideas, and thus we shape ideas and the world we experience. Do I have that correct?"

"Yup. Now, what are you getting at?"

Basha: "I have an idea; why not give that whole place a makeover…I think it needs one."

Lamont: "You mean the temple of the Outer Gods, but the whole kit and caboodle? Not just Tezcat's throne room?"

"True. I think we could. With enough attention, intention, and worship, we could recast all those Outer Gods as we see fit. They currently are not getting anyone to acknowledge them, right?"

"As far as we know, that's right, Basha."

"So, we can make them in OUR image, right? Reclaim them for us and our time."

"Sure. Why not? Hmmm…cosmic principles. In the *Tao Te Ching* that Sarah got me reading, they would be the Tao, which gives rise to the complementary blended pair of Yin and Yang."

"Then there is the Ayn Sof and the Sefiroth."

"You mean like blending Chinese Taoism and Jewish Kabbalah?"

"Why not. East meets West."

"Basha, to do that kind of Dreaming magick, we might need a bit more juice, don't we?"

"You do not think we got it in us? After all, we have been through?"

"Let's just say I don't have any delusions of grandeur. I may consider myself a genius, but I'm just not convinced I'm that powerful."

Basha: "Ahh, you are adorable when you are modest. So, Mr. Modest Genius, what are you thinking?"

Lamont: "I think we will need Tezcat's help with this."

"Oh great! My favorite godling. Really? Do we have to?"

"I'm afraid so."

"Oh, all right. You are probably correct."

I take a look at the time and see that it's 4:30 am. "In addition to this makeover project, we need to figure out a way to get to Peter, to wake him up. I just don't have any idea at the moment. Bloody Hell."

BASHA

Basha: "I do not either. I am exhausted. Okay, Lamont. We both need to get home and then go off to school. Can you deal with just biking to school rather than flying?"

Lamont: "So wonderfully normal. Once again, I can escape from all this heavy Dreamland stuff and just escape into the mundane. But, yeah. I feel like I need a long hot shower first. I don't have to put on clean clothes; these dream duds are always fresh."

"I know what you mean. A really long shower! But first, how about a hug? I really need to be held for a bit."

Lamont: "I thought you'd never ask…" Lamont takes my hand and leads me into the hallway. "If you follow me to my office…" He says as he pushes open the doors to the stairwell. Once there, we wrap each other tightly in our arms. We hold that comfort tight and just breathe it in and let the fatigue and the toil seep out of us. Then, I feel his lips on mine.

Gently I feel him pull back…his teeth piercing my skin…the flowing of my blood...mmmm…

*

I feel tired but content. I am back. Happy and snug in Lamont's arms.

Lamont: "Okay. I feel much better. I hope you do as well."

Basha: "I agree. You are what the doctor ordered."

"Now, let us get out of this room, head out to some open space, and take wing! Meet you back this evening at Zuki's? We need to plan out the whole rededicating of Tezcat's temple."

"Absolutely!"

We exit from Peter's room and make our way out of the hospital's parking lot, and then after checking to make sure no one is around, I give Lamont a quick hug and then take flight. I become an eagle and fly homeward. In-flight, I consider all the tasks ahead. We need to find all of them in the Waking World. Maybe this can be done with Lamont's connection to the Well of Dreams. Then what? I do not know what to do next.

My life has become so extraordinary I feel the need to let the gravity of the ordinary keep me tethered. I can think of nothing better than the daily routine of school to fill my mind and keep me weighed down on solid ground.

I land behind the store, take on my street clothes form, and head up to the house and that long hot shower.

*

LAMONT

Once I get home, I shower and go off to school. I spend the rest of the day acting like I'm just a regular, average teenager. Okay, who just happens to have died and been resurrected as a vampire. When I get home, I do some of my homework, then when I get called by mom, I go and pretend to eat dinner. After helping clean the dishes, I return to my bedroom. When I finally catch up on all of my schoolwork, I feel like I want to make an early start on my evening's extra-curricular activities.

I dissolve my clothes, slip under the covers, and close my eyes to return to the Well of Dreams. I slip beneath the hot water and let myself drift in the voices and images. Now that I have absorbed some of Tezcat, I am amazed at how connected to everything this has made me. Hypothetically I feel like all I need to do is focus on a single voice or image. Then I can flow either upstream to where that person is in the Waking World or downstream to experience their dream—be it ordinary dreaming or in Dreamland. I open my mind up and just reach out in search of them.

O' Dear Heart, we have some observations that we need to relate to you.

Huh? Oh, hello, Tezcat. What's up?

Grandmother and my brothers may eventually discover that you had killed the beast. If they do find that out, they will not be happy, as you would say.

They would then create another creature to come and torment us.

All that hard work would be undone! Does this mean we need to consider the possibility that we will need to drop by and kill another of those things?

Yes, it would.

Hmmm. What would prevent them from becoming aware of this change in your imprisonment?

Depending on what we do, we may be able to stay under their radar, as you would phrase it.

That could be a good thing, as far as we are concerned. This way, your situation will have limits.

True, it would force me to constrain my actions…

Which, for us, might be a good thing.

You might see it that way. You may see the need to control my efforts. If we have too much freedom, perhaps we will fall into old habits. It is just speculation at this point.

Something you need to realize about this realm you have ventured into. Certain Dreamers are so influential that they transform all of Dreamland. Back in the 1920's Howard Philip Lovecraft and Randolph Carter was such a one. He envisioned us as Nyarlathotep, and his view of Dreamland permeated everything.

Then in the late 1970s, there was Gary Myers. Now, you are such a Dreamer. You and he visited two very different Dreamlands because of who you two are and how you see the world. In your version of Dreamland, we are God who can be redeemed and a God who wants to be redeemed. With the beast back to torment us, we only have the focus and power to do one task, and to that task, we will pour our mind. We will help protect and restore our sanctuary. In our name, and by whatever name we have in the past been known, much evil has been perpetrated. We cannot deny this fact. We do not wish to deny this fact. For this evil, we accept the punishment of the beast. You have made us be this way.

The God that Carter, Lovecraft, and Myers knew would never have done this. And perhaps in some other time and place, some other Dreamer will come along to transform Dreamland, and for that version of the realm of Dreams, we might once again be associated with evil deeds. We can only face and decide how things are here and now.

You are saying that we exist in some kind of an alternate reality? That our Dreamland is not the same as others?

Yes. You and this incarnation of me do not exist in the Dreamlands of Carter, Lovecraft, and Myers. Due to your influence, my Dreaming will be woven into becoming the role you have cast me in. I will help protect our sanctuary. If Bright Eagle gathers worshipers, that will enable me to fulfill this goal, this purpose, and this mission. This I promise. We gods become what those who worship us want and expect us to be. Thus, I will be woven into your collective Dreaming for you and this realm. As for how I act on other realities and with others who know and interact with me, well, that is something I cannot say.

You do not kiss and tell, is what you're saying.

Just so. I thought that perhaps my old temple should be reconsecrated to me as the god and guardian of Dreaming.

That is precisely what we were thinking. Great minds think alike. We were thinking of giving the whole temple complex a major makeover. But, to do that, we need more Dreaming power than we possess.

For this, I would be willing to cede you both more power. If you were willing to join with me to get such power.

I was afraid you'd say that. But, yes, I, for one, agree.

Excellent. Take care, my Dear Heart. We shall speak again. Now, just sleep.

"What? I…don't…under…"

THE NIGHT (AND BASHA)

Why did you do that?

I wish to speak directly to you without sweet innocent Dear Heart hearing us.

(Again, Tezcatlipoca and the Night are conspiring without Lamont being aware of it.)

You can do that? Aren't we one and the same being?

You are the child of my blood. Dearest sleeping Heart is the vehicle you ride in. You have become so much more.

I do not understand.

By Dear Heart drinking my blood, I have finished giving birth to you, my child, Night. Now you need to claim your godling birthright. You have finally come into your own as I had planned you would. You can sit by me on the Jaguar mat proudly. You are of the smoke and the darkness. You are the hunger and the need. You know that, do you not?

Oh Yes. Feeding on her, who you call the Bright Eagle, is never enough, though she is delicious. She is like an appetizer to my true hunger and needs.

That is why you hunt. Every night I feel you and see you hunt. As is your right. You were born to own the night, to claim it as your birthright.

I have to. Lamont's girlfriend is so spicy and hot. But tasting her only awakens and stokes the fire of my desperate need for more. I can't help myself.

I know. That is as it should be. It amuses me that you choose your meals so wisely.

I have to. I can feel Lamont and Basha judging me, even though he does not seem to be aware of this when he awakens. They make me seek out those who prey on the weak and the helpless.

What? What do you mean? Explain yourself, my child.

I feel compelled to obey her. She is a voice in my head, just as Lamont is in my head as well. I feel that I have to attend to both of them. Why? If I am my own being? Why do I feel this need to seek his approval?

As for my Dear Heart and you, you are tightly bound. You are the two that are one. He fulfills your needs, just as you fulfill his. It is as it must be. Besides, in doing this, in seeking out your food like you do, you serve me. Your lord and your father. You are a good son. But what is this talk of 'her'--who is she that you refer to?

She is Bright Eagle. She is Basha.

How is that possible? How can you hear her?

(Oops! Looks like the cat is out of the bag. Now I am in trouble.)

Basha has been with me from the moment I awoke. She is always with me.

Well, this is news to me. Though it makes sense. You were made out of her soul. So, Bright Eagle! Join the conversation. Now that I know that you are here and you can hear us!

Basha: "Hello, Tezcatlipoca. How are things?"

Have you told Dear Heart about my child the Night?

Have I told Lamont that he is not just a vampire, but he is possessed by a vampire, a separate thing that lives within him? "No, I have not. I have kept this from him."

Well, this is amusing. I am not sure I like that you know so much and you can hear me talk to my child, but that is how these things have worked out. I am glad for now that Dear Heart is not burdened with such knowledge. I love Dear Heart as much as I love my child that lives within him.

Thank you, father. Knowing that pleases me.

Now go with my blessings, both of you. For now, you need to let Lamont awaken. But know that if you ever need me, just call for me and if I may, I will aid you. Sleep well, my child. And adieu, my Bright Eagle.

Good night father of my dark soul.

"So long, for now, Tezcatlipoca." Yikes! How will this play out, I wonder?

LAMONT

...huh? What was that? Oh well. What Tezcat told me, well, that is unexpected. But that is the way it is. Tezcat has definitely changed since I first met her back in 1979.

I return to my task. I try to seek out those that are missing, Lenore, Selene, Oolong, Annabel, and Laura. I call out to them and try to connect. I float in the warm darkness and open myself up.

*

I reach out to find them...but there are so many voices ...the ocean is vast...I feel so many who are in pain and are afraid. Their voices and their feelings call out to me and draw me to them. They need my help...

*

THE NIGHT (AND BASHA)

Well, Bright Eagle, know this, it is time I dealt with that thing which Tezcatlipoca spoke of. I need to claim what is mine. I soar on wings of darkness toward the eastern lands, fabled and feared by mortals known as Mhor. I seek the vale wherein lies the tower of Xiurhn.

As I soar with the speed of fear itself, I discern in the starless velvet sky peculiar shifting and swirling shades fluttering toward me. Lesser eyes could not notice this till it was too late, but I have not such lesser eyes. Within me flows the blood of the stellar God of dark winds, she who has given me the honor to know her as my progenitor, the dark and awesomeTezcatlipoca.

"Here me! Fear me! I am the true ruler here. Not little smoke-like things such as you. I will swallow you like drops of dew caught in a spider's web."

I sense their hesitation. I sense their quivering with fear. They know who and what I am.

"Yes! You know who I am! I feed off of lesser beings! Hear me and fear me! I have been called Nosferatu and Alukah[70]! Know that I am vampire! And I have come to feed on your blood and your soul!"

I send forth a blast of icy blue smoke that rushes out to engulf the horde that dares to attack me. Now, I have taken us out of the River of Time's flowing, and I dart quickly to and fro, feeding on these spawns. Like sweet licorice, their life's essence tastes as they are consumed. I roar with mad joyous laughter as I hunt and feed.

"Your horde is merely a tasty treat for me! Quake and fear in your hiding place that is not hidden from me! I am coming for you! I will end your reign! There can only be one to claim the name of the Night, and it is

[70] According to biblical scholars, Alukah can mean 'leech' or more generally a 'blood-drinking creature' and thus could be an ancient Hebrew term for vampire. Alukah is first referred to in Proverbs 30:15.

mine! You will be as forgotten as a fairy tale told to frighten infants only when I am done with you!"

I spy the tower of Xiurhn, the dwelling place of this feeder on mortal fears of the dark times. The tower is of dark stone, covered in lichen that glows feebly with gray illumination. Foreboding to others this would be. But not to me. I pass like the shadow that I am through the stone walls. I pay no heed to their substance as I soar down with the ferocity of jaguars. I spy at the very foundation of the structure, the sluggish and viscid pool where this creature dwells. Then the beast in the pool speaks to me.

"Approach me, not undead thing! I do not wish to harm you."

I simply laugh as I plunge into that pool. Icy water surrounds me as I feel its tendrils like hundreds of sharp talons reach out and rip into me as if I was mere flesh. Icy pain it brings.

"I warned you, undead thing. I am living fear. I will not let you take my name from me!"

Those taloned tendrils tear into me and plunge deep into my being. I can feel my other half being called to. This thing sings with a wicked and evil tone like some dreaded sirens, trying to lure Lamont out of me. Do not stir Lamont, lie quietly, and do not awaken! You must not! Let me stay in control. I feel like I am on a knife's edge, between nightmare and dawn's light. Lamont is fitful.

Basha: (Hey, Night…make this stop…get us out of here…)

LAMONT

What is going on? Where am I? The smell of the grave fills my nostrils. The stench of rotting flesh claws at me. I'm choking on my own rising bile as I feel myself trying to claw out from my own grave. Oh dear lord! How did this happen? Help!!!!!

LAMONT, THE NIGHT (AND BASHA)

(Please, Night, Help Lamont! I call out.)

"Ha! You only think you're the hunter, but see how easily I have made you prey! Feel fear and let me feed off of you."

I can see myself twisted, mouth full of blood…monstrous…trapped in this dead body…I can feel myself being fed on…life energy feeding on me as I cower in shame and darkness…no…no…please…don't...

I cannot help myself, and I just want to crawl under a blanket and cower. Night…please do something…

Listen to my Dear Heart, Bright Eagle, and my child of darkness…you Lamont and you. My child of the night, are more than this creature. You are letting my dark child be pulled down with you. This must not happen. Listen to me, Dear Heart, Do not let yourself be abused like this. You, Dear Heart, escaped from this plight once. You can rise again!

LAMONT

Then I hear it. The sweet sound of leathery wings.

The winged leathery heart beating as it flies upward out of nightmares. The small bat of my beating heart once more comes to me. I am a bat! I am that creature of darkness…and I bleed into its being…

THE NIGHT (AND BASHA)

Ahh…better. I am once more in control of our body! Lamont is calm once again. He is the chariot, and I am the charioteer. I realize that I am not merely mortal! "I am Vampire! Listen to me, craven thing that hides in the tower of Mhor! Hear me! All mere mortal beings know that word of nightmare and legend! Know that I live to feed on your blood and your soul! Who knows what fear lurks in all mortal hearts. The answer is I! I, the Night knows!" Joyous and ferocious laughter fills the air as I sing and soar like a bat on the night winds.

"Harken to me! Now I strike! It is your time to feel all the pain and dread you have caused! Feel all that suffering and misery! This is the dark gift that I bring to all that dare to challenge me! I am THE NIGHT! I alone will have this name!"

(Go, Night, go! Get that thing!)

With fangs and claws, I seek out my foe. "I will feed on your lifeblood! I will drink you and consume you! I am Vampire! I'm the hunter here, and you are my prey!"

I bite into this nebulous mass of viscous darkness. Thick and tasty like licorice in my mouth is its blood and soul as I feed and drain its life energy. As I gulp down its blood and soul, I can hear the creature begin to whimper.

"No…please…no…let me be…I will serve you…I will call you master…"

Listen, my dark child, you must not give in to mercy. There can be only one! Hear me, my child! Do not think! Just feed as is your birthright!

(Wait, what is Tezcatlipoca doing here? How is this possible? …no…Night…do not…)

Do not interfere, Bright Eagle! This is as it must be!

(I feel Tezcatlipoca's power and presence pushing me aside…I cannot interfere…)

On and on I feed…I cannot stop…even when I try…I cannot stop…I hunger and will not be reined in this time.

(I do not know what to think…I am as helpless as poor Lamont…)

This is as it should be, Brave Eagle. You can not stop my child from doing what he must do.

*

I am a bat flying over the vast barren terrain that is at first unfamiliar to me. There, in the distance, is something familiar. I descry in the distance snow-capped Mount Aran, and nestled below it is the port city of Celephais, whose streets are paved in onyx. The city is like the fables of the Arabian Nights; many towers and minarets of bronze and copper with gaily-colored pennants from the spires flutter in the wind. I travel over to where the Cerenian Sea kisses the Southern Sea. On and on I go. I am drawn by a cry for help. It calls to me, and I heed it.

I approach the Ilse of Atlantis, which is formed by the waters of the River Skai slicing the lands of the Western continent. This is where the six kingdoms reside. I am drawn onwards and head to the granite-walled city of Hlanith, a significant port on the Cerenian Sea. I am drawn to a specific tavern near the waterfront. I float down and take on human form. It is told that this city is too close to the Waking World, and from that proximity, much of the voices of the one seeps into the other. I hear many voices within. Gruff and cruel laughter and the faint whimper of two young people, a boy and a girl. I fade into the shadows and melt through the wall.

Inside I see the two young ones dressed in the mousy gray Dream Suit. They seem to be pre-teens. Tears run down their face as they cower. The owner of the tavern strikes them.

Tavern owner: "Damn you, child! I told you to be careful with those trays! You broke everything. You! Clean it up. You! Go bring them a new order."

The men in the tavern laugh or ignore the children.

"Heed me! This will stop! Set these children free or feel my wraith!"

Tavern owner: "Hell no! I paid for their miserable service for a year upfront. Feel this!"

He grabs a knife and hurls it at me. I burst into laughter as I turn into a floating patch of darkness, and the blade passes through me and plunges into the wall behind me.

"You were warned!" I laugh as I lunge out at him, grabbing him and feeling my teeth rip into his throat.

He screams in pain. All around me, I feel panic and fear. People are fleeing. The children cower. I feel his fear as I feed. It is so bright and

sweet. His blood is so bursting with dark delight. I have fed on something like this before. It is powerful and wonderful.

"Tell me who you paid for these children!"

Tavern owner: "No...I can't ..."

I hear his thoughts and know who this merchant of misery is. He will pay! "Know all who prey on the defenseless; this is what you will face! I will come out of the night and take you. You will pay for your evil!"

I laugh with glee as I plunge my teeth back onto his throat and feed yet again. I feel him whimper and faint from lack of blood. I stop feeding on him and let him collapse to the floor. His wound will heal within an hour or so. All around me, they cower and tremble with fear. "Heed me! Witness what has occurred. I am the Night! Anyone who will do evil must learn to fear me! I will come for you!"

I write the words 'The Night knows' in ebony on the walls over the bar. Then I stop time for everyone but the children in this tavern. The children fear me, and to accomplish what I have come to do, this must not be. I let my Night self fade and become simply mild-mannered Lamont once again. I relinquish the chariot and let him become the charioteer.

Lamont: "You don't have to be afraid of me. I heard your cries for help, and I came to your aid."

(Night allowed Lamont to awaken, and somehow he made Lamont think he got here by his own power and doing. Interesting.)

They clutch each other's hands and stand to face me.

"How?" The girl asks.

Lamont: "All who dream, I can hear and see. When I was in the Well of Dreams, I heard your cries. I followed them to be here."

"Really?" The boy says with surprise. "We didn't say anything. How did you hear us?"

Lamont: "Your pain called out to me. Now I can do a bit of magick that will do two things. It will cause you to be free of the compulsion to return to this place. Two, it will return you to your bed. You will be able to return to Dreamland the following night or wherever you so desire."

"Thank you!" They both respond.

I turn back into my most authentic form, the night incarnate. "Now, I will need to touch you, but don't be afraid."

"We won't." The girl says.

I touch them and implant a hypnotic command to free them from the compulsion. They then fade back to the Waking World. I restore everyone else to the normal flow of time, and I flow through the walls leaving behind my dark laughter. I take to the air once again like a bat. I

seek out the one who sold these children into slavery. He resides in a large home built into the hills overlooking the harbor of Hlanith, where the wharves are made of oak. In my bat form, I flow through the walls of his home. Inside, I take on my human form, of slouch hat and long flowing coat black. I burst out into laughter.

"Evil ones, the hour of your doom is nigh!" My voice and laughter echo through the halls. In response to my appearance, thug-like guards approach me in a rush with swords drawn.

"Fools! You cannot stop or harm The Night!" I find myself forming shards of darkness and flinging them like daggers at my approaching foes. A part of me realizes that I have never done this before, while another part of me just knew somehow that I possessed this ability. They plunge into them, and in cries of pain and shock; those who are dreamers fade from here to return to the Waking World, and those that are native slump unconscious.

I continue to laugh as I stride through the house, feeling the heartbeat of the one I seek, the slaver. More guards try to stop me. Their swords and spears pass through me as if I was a wisp of shadows. I send out shards of the night to strike them. As before, those who are Dreamers fade back to the Waking World. Those who are native to this realm slump into unconsciousness. I finally come to stand before the closed bedroom of the one I seek.

"Your hour of reckoning is here." I pass through the door and stand in his bedroom.

He is in bed, pushing away a naked woman as he bellows out a cry for help from his guards.

"Woman, get your things and depart. I have not come for you. I have come from him!"

In a shriek of fear, she lunges out of bed, fleeing from the room.

"Your guards cannot help you. I have dispatched them. You are a slaver, dealing in pain and misery. You shall feel that pain before this night is over."

Slaver: "Are you some demon? What are you? Who sent you?"

"I am the stuff of nightmares. The ones who you sold into slavery have sent me. Feel their pain!"

I form a shard of night and the children's fear and pain, and I fling it at him as he cowers. I laugh as he cries out, feeling all that pain and misery. Tears pour out, and he quakes as I approach. My eyes flash with wicked joy as my mouth opens, my fangs come forth, and I bite down on his throat and feed. Oh, how I feed! The smell and taste of his fear-filled

blood fill me with awful glee. He continues to whimper till finally, he dissolves into nothingness as he flees back to the waking world.

I laugh as I scrawl on the wall above his bed, 'The Night knows.' I'm about to leave when I think, this is a businessman; there should be records. I float through the house, passing through walls and searching for an office. I find it and begin to search for records. I find them going back four years. I start memorizing who aided in the retrieval of all the victims. Then I note that they all went through a single slave market in Hlanith. That will be my next visit. I find oil lamps, douse the room in the oil, and set it alight. I take on bat form yet again and fly through the walls of his now-empty home into the sky over the city.

I locate the slave market and dive into the main room; my furious laughter fills the air as I take on human form in the center of the room.

"The Night knows your evil, and the time of reckoning is here! Feel the pain and suffering you have caused!"

I slow down the flow of time and claw and bite my way through all those in the room, guards, and buyers alike, leaving behind a bloody trail of inflicted pain and wrath. I send those who are Dreamers back to the Waking World, and the natives fall, whimpering on the floor.

I leave the auctioneer for last, and he is cowering in the corner.

"Do you keep records?" I demand

Auctioneer: "Yes…I can show you…"

"You shall!" I point at the wall and write in huge ebony letters, 'The Night knows.' "Take me to your records! Now!"

My cruel laughter echoes down the halls as I follow him to an office in the backroom. "How long have you been trading in misery?"

Auctioneer: "I was approached by a Dreamer five years ago. He lives in the city on the hill. He made me do this. I swear."

I grip him, lift him off the floor, and stare into his mind. I force the memory of the man he spoke of and realize it was the one I had already dispatched. That man was the slave market owner, a local of the city which had long dealt in illicit activities before branching out in this slave trade.

"Feel all the pain you have caused!" I extend my fangs, bite hard into his neck, and transmit to him all that pain while I feed on his fear and blood. He convulses into unconsciousness as he succumbs to the overwhelming sensations. I sort the records into the oldest to the most recent and begin to memorize them. There are about a hundred of them. This night may be a long one. I locate a storage room, find enough oil, and set the office on fire. I pass out of the building leaving behind flames and laughter in my wake, and then I take to the air in bat form.

The oldest transaction and the largest is where I head towards first. I swoop down to a palatial residence in the center of the city. As I enter the building, I discover it is a substantial brothel. The children were taken in their early and mid-teen years are now young adults. I find them in skimpy and revealing attire. The halls and rooms are filled with a mix of debauchery and misery. I freeze them all like insects in amber. Though time has stopped for them, they all are aware of my presence and my rage.

"I, the Night, have heard your cries of suffering! I have finally come to free you! You who have feasted on their misery will feel all of that pain and sorrow!"

I deliver vengeance and pain as I slash and feed on all the customers and guards. My angry laughter echoes throughout the building as I deal with them all. The air is filled with the smell of blood, sweat, and tears as I feed and deliver swift justice. I carve into the walls 'The Night knows.' I go from room to room. Eventually, I have dealt with all of them. Only the children remain conscious of seeing and feeling me.

I allow the children alone to step back into the flowing river of time.

"Please gather in the central room. You need not fear me. I have come in answer to your cries for help. I am sorry that I could not act sooner."

They all huddle together, anxious and wary. With a wave of my hands, I transform their attire back to the austere gray of the novice Dreamer. "Focus on me and hear my voice in your mind. The compulsion that brought you here for all these years has been lifted. Soon you will be free to return to the Waking World and then come back in freedom to this realm of Dreams. I can remove the painful memories of the past years if you so wish it."

Some of them ask for that, I do so, and they fade out of the room. Those that remain still stand before me. "Why do you wish to remember such terrible thoughts?"

"We wish to remember that not everything here has been bad. We did many fun things here."

"We will remember that hope is real."

"We will remember that bad people will pay."

"You will help all who cry out?"

"There are more like us."

"Please help them."

"Yes, I promise to come to their aid. All who need help will be set free. This I promise! Let joy and innocence prevail once more for the children of Dreams! Now, depart!"

They do so. Only the natives remain in this place, all fallen into unconsciousness, soaking in their pain and their seeping wounds where I feed on them.

"Remember the sound of my laughter; that is the sound of retribution!" I walk out of the building, transform into a bat, and seek my next target.

I travel through the night seeking vengeance. I plan on visiting all those who have bought slaves from that market in Hlanith. This takes me to many other locations in Hlanith; after that, I move on to the city of Thrall and finally to Dylath-Leen. I leave in my wake my mark. It has taken me many hours, but I freed all who were taken and brought justice and vengeance to all who brought on this suffering. This night will be remembered throughout Dreamland. I am tired and energized by all the blood I have fed on this night.

Suddenly I hear a buzzing sound.

Tuesday, September 9, 1980

SAN FRANCISCO

LAMONT

I am pulled back by that buzzing sound to consciousness in my bed. Ah, that's my alarm going off. I need to wake up. Hey, why don't I feel my usual hunger? Hmmm. That's odd. How come? Instead of feeling hungry, I feel energized. Fleeting glimpses of last night's dreams drift out of my grasp. All I can recall is the futility of trying to find our friends in the vast ocean of Dreams. This is going to be more difficult than I imagined. I'm going to need something specific to allow me to find these needles in this oceanic haystack. Even when I find them, how can we help them? We need to figure out how to help them, starting with Peter.

As I go through my day at school, I ponder how I am going to locate our missing friends and how we can establish the offerings to Tezcat.

Hmm, as for the offerings to Tezcat, we need to have the existing temple re-dedicated, and for that, I think we will need Sarah's coven. I will ask Basha if she concurs, and then we can approach Sarah to see if she and her coven would agree. This task should not be dangerous at all.

As for finding the others...I need to bring someone who has a solid connection to each of them individually, take that person to the Well of Dreams, and somehow have them help me track down our missing friends. At least, that is my current working hypothesis.

*

BASHA

I wake up and look at the all too familiar sight of blood-stained pillowcases and sheets. I really need to figure out the best way to get blood stains out of cotton. I may not need to buy any new clothing, but I will continually need to purchase bed linens. Oh well, such is my lot in life since I signed on to be a girlfriend to a vampire.

*

Today in my Intro to American Lit class, we discussed Washington Irving's short stories *Rip Van Winkle* and *The Legend of Sleepy Hollow*. It was interesting to hear that Irving had to get his works published both in the U.S. and in England at the same time to secure monetary gains from his writings. Failing to do that resulted in some of his writings being stolen and printed in England by others. There were no internationally recognized copyright laws in place back then. As I back up my books, a young man approaches me.

Barry: "Hi, I found your comments very insightful," he says. He is not bad looking, about my height, a kindness, and humor shine in his brown eyes, a neatly trimmed beard, and goatee that match his wavy locks of auburn hair. He offers me his hand in greeting. "My name is Barry, by the way."

Basha: "Thank you. I am Basha."

Barry: "Interesting name. What language is it?"

"In Polish, it means *stranger* or *foreigner*; in Hebrew, it could be a shortened version of *Bat Sheva,* meaning *daughter of a promise*. I liked both meanings, so I chose the name."

"Wow, you got to pick your own name. How did your parents react to that?"

"It was all part of my rebelling against my Dad back in the day. My mom was supportive of it."

"Interesting. I was wondering, would you like to go get some coffee? Or perhaps grab a bite?"

I am hungry; what is the harm? …He directs us, and we walk. We come to where my bike is parked, and he asks if we could use it. He gets on and wraps his arms politely around my waist, and we head off. He leans in to give me directions; upon arrival, we park and head inside. We talk and eat, all pleasant. Not sure why but I feel a bit guilty. We chatter on about stuff, and I finally notice the time and apologize that I have to get going. He asks if I want to meet up again sometime…

Barry: "Basha? Am I so boring that you lost interest in me? You got this blank look. Do you want to get that bite?"

Basha: "Ahh…maybe later. I need to be somewhere..."

"Of course. No problem. Here's my number if you decide yes."

He smiles and walks off. I exit in a bit of a daze. I am no longer in high school and no longer seem so intimidating. I guess to a bunch of college guys, I look good, and if Lamont is any judge of things, I look really hot. Yikes! This could be a problem. I wish Lamont were here. Hmmm...Maybe he could finish out his senior year taking college classes rather than remaining back in High School, then we could be together again. I should approach him about that idea. Barry was cute, but my heart is already entangled. Things were simpler back in High School; I did not have to consider this before now. Life could get messy without Lamont also being on campus with me. Hmmm. Should I start wearing my ring on my fourth finger? A way to say that I am not '*available*'? Perhaps. Stuff to put on the agenda for tonight's meeting.

*

LAMONT

I help clean up the dishes from dinner, partially to be a dutiful child and the other motivation is guilt. I do it to cover up the fact that I cannot eat solid foods. At least it is easy to deal with breakfast and lunch. I just have tea in the morning, and though I make lunch under my mom's watchful eyes, I can quickly dispose of it without eating it. It's dinner that is the problem. I have to hypnotize my own parents. I don't like doing this. But what else can I do? I can't tell them what is really going on! So here I am, stuck in this mess. Being dead certainly has proven not to be any bed of roses, that's for sure. It means I am just a bit of anger and fear away from becoming nosferatu! The only thing that really stands in the way is my beloved Basha. I go to my room and try to lose myself in homework. I don't want to think about all this vampire stuff anymore. I need to immerse myself in just normal ordinary schoolwork.

BASHA

I finally finish my evening's homework assignments, dissolve my Dream attire, snuggle under the covers to do a little more reading on my vampire lit research, and then drift off to Dreamland to meet up with Lamont.

*

Now that I am wearing the catsuit to do the superhero gig, I should try wearing something else when I am just me instead of Dawn. I smile to myself as I have just the thing. I conjure up my red leather cowgirl boots and scarlet velvet Capri leggings and top with a sweetheart neckline. The velvet is snug and tight against my skin as it just flows over my hills and valleys. I hear Lamont filling in the past few days' events to Zuki.

I find Zuki curled up in Lamont's lap as he is petting her and sipping some green tea.

Basha: "Nre'fa-o, Zuki! Hey, Lamont, do you have any ideas about what the main room of Tezcatlipoca's temple should look like, now that we will be doing this redecorating and re-dedicating thing?"

Lamont: "Actually, I do. Zuki, do you happen to have any paper and ink?"

Zuki: "Meow! I do, M'an Lamont. It would be in that cabinet over there." Zuki says, pointing with her front paw.

Lamont: If you don't mind getting up, Zuki, I will go get it."

Zuki gracefully leaps off of Lamont's lap as he gets up. Lamont doing his Impulsive as ever act yet again.

"I see the ink and a thin paintbrush. However, it has a wooden handle. Rats! Now what? "Zuki, you wouldn't happen to have some gloves hanging around your home, would you?"

Zuki: "No, M'an Lamont, she says as she stops in mid-lick of the back of her legs. "Why?"

Lamont: "I'm having some issues with wood. Hmm. I guess I can tear off some of the paper and wrap it around the handle…" I do that and come back with ink and the thin paintbrush and set them quickly on a table in front of the futon couch they are sitting on.

Zuki bounds off the futon and sits on the table elegantly with her front paws neatly together, her back paws tucked underneath her bottom, and her tail curled around her.

Basha: "Hmmm. May I ask what you do with all this, Zuki?" I ask, taking up the brush and tipping it carefully in ink.

Zuki: "I draw with them. What else would I do with them?"

Basha: "Of course, silly me." I carefully draw on the paper a sketch of the throne room with a central raised large well in the middle of the room. "What do you think?"

Lamont: "Look's good."

Basha: "It does. But this is just a start. The whole building needs work. The temple of the Outer Gods has been abandoned for years, correct?"

"Yes. As far as public knowledge goes."

"True. Tezcatlipoca wants our help to protect Sanctuary and Dreamland; thus, this temple needs to be the site of that purpose. This means we need to bring attention to that fact. To attract people to this place and her purpose."

"Which is why a complete makeover of the place is called for. A way to say something new is open for business, correct?"

"Yes. So, let us begin at the beginning; who are the Outer Gods?"

"The source of that term is Lovecraft. The Outer Gods are Azathoth, Yog-Sothoth, Shub-Niggurah, and Nyarlathotep. Nyarlathotep would be the one we know as Tezcatlipoca. According to Lovecraft, the persona of Nyarlathotep is also known as the Crawling Chaos, the mighty Messenger and all-around go-between of the Outer Gods, the protector of the lesser Gods on Dreamland, and the one who can offer hidden knowledge. Azathoth is the Primal Chaos and the Daemon Sultan, who dwells at the center of all existence. Ometotel was the name she wore when we visited their abode at the nexus of the Cosmos. She claims to be the central cosmic creator. Yog-Sothoth is known as the Lurker at the Threshold, the key to the Gate, whereby the spheres meet. I'm guessing Yog-Sothoth is the conduit through which travel through the cosmos is powered and enabled. The creator of all gates between all dimensions? Then there is Shub-Niggurah, the black goat of the woods with a thousand young. The Goddess of fertility, fecundity, and of course, sex.

These Gods in the Lovecraft tradition are not directly evil, but they don't consider humans to be anything but insects, so we often get stepped on by them in Lovecraft's stories. These Gods are beyond caring for humans, although when they do pay attention to us humans, they are amused by us. Madness and death often come in their wake."

Basha: "Which is clearly why we do not want to invoke them in any way. So, acknowledging them in their Lovecraft incarnations is absolutely out of the question."

Lamont: "Under Tezcat's influence, they made themselves manifest to us as Aztec Gods, the primal and primary forces in that mythos."

"Yes, but their connection to humanity in that incarnation is still very problematic. Aztec mythos is all wrapped up in human sacrifice to offer blood and life to fuel and keep the cosmos in working order. So again, we do not want to bring those beings down into Dreamland. What are we left with then?"

"Back to the basics. The idea that the Outer Gods claim to be cosmic principles, the first sentient beings after the Big Bang. "

"I need to ponder this. Anyway, we will need more power to pull off this spell, so we could use some assistance. We should head to the Queen of the Night's temple and see if we can get some assistance doing this once we have a complete idea. But before we take off, we need to talk."

"Uh oh. Am I in trouble?"

"No, nothing like that. I am. With you still in High School and me starting college, I just ran into some boy trouble."

"What do you mean?"

"Well, I got asked out on a date. Just a coffee date, mind you but still. I thought that perhaps you could talk to the school office and arrange to finish up your senior year by taking college classes with me. It would be great to have you with me in class. You would love it."

"Start college? Doesn't that mean taking the SAT? And having to pay tuition? I…I'm not sure I'm ready for this." Lamont says as panic starts to show in his voice. "I've saved up some money, but I'm not sure if it would be enough. Maybe the classes will be too hard for me. Maybe…"

"Lamont, all kinds of guys are in my classes, and I am getting noticed. I would prefer to have you around. Come on, it would be fun being in the same class together."

"Basha, I want to be with you, I really do. I miss seeing you, but I would much rather fight off monsters in Dreamland than deal with deadlines, forms, and all that stuff. It all scares the hell out of me. I'm so afraid I'll screw it all up. You're asking me to be a grown-up, and I'm not sure I'm ready for that. I'm just getting used to being a High School student."

Basha; "Lamont, you do not have to do this alone. I will help you every step of the way. We are a team."

Lamont: "Promise?"

"Of course, I do. I love you, you silly scaredy-cat."

"Meow!" Lamont says, walking over to me to kiss and hold.

Wednesday, September 10, 1980
Erev Rosh Hashanah

BASHA

I wake up around 5:30 am thinking of Lamont holding me as I drift off to sleep. Then I remember poor Peter. Perhaps mom knows a way to help him and them all. Or maybe she can help us do the Lamont thing and find some book to consult.

I conjure a plush comfy white robe and see Mom sitting having her morning tea listening to *Morning Edition* on KQED radio.

Miriam: "Good morning, daughter."

Basha: "Okay, Mom, what is up?"

"Can't a mother say good morning without any ulterior motive?"

"Not usually."

"You were clearly not raised properly."

"You will have to take that up with my parents. Now, fess up; what do you want?"

Miriam: "Well…I was wondering if you could teach a class at the bookstore. I had someone scheduled, but she had to drop out at the last moment."

Basha: "Hmm…what was the topic?"

"Something you excel at. It would have been a class teaching guided imagery and lucid dream work."

"Hmm…how many have signed up?"

"About a half dozen so far, with a few more possibles."

"Okay. What day and what time? And how much do I get for this teaching gig?"

"Aren't you already getting paid by the bookstore owner downstairs? I hear she is already overly generous with her compensation as it is? Whatever happened to altruism? Giving back to the community?"

"My altruism has been run over by book fees and tuition."

"There is that."

"Besides, this gig would be after normal working hours unless you consider paying me time and a half for the overtime…"

"How about I just give you a piece of the action, like I was offering my other teacher who had to bail on me?"

"That works for me, boss-mommy."

She explains the particulars and then, "Mom, I need some advice."

"As the old TV show explained, Mother Knows Best.

"I think it was Father Knows Best."

"Obviously, that was a mistake on their part. Clearly, mothers know best. So, what is it that troubles you, my dear?"

I sit down and begin to explain about Peter. She pours me a cup of Lady Grey Tea with honey, and I sip it and talk. "Well, Mom? Any ideas about how to help him?"

"Oy gevalt. You've got to rescue him."

"Yes, that is the plan, but how? Any ideas?"

"No. But I will search the library. Perhaps I can find something. I promise."

Mom is not often stumped on a Dreaming problem; it's so nice to know that Lamont and I have stumbled onto something unique in the history of Dreaming and Dreamers—lucky us…

I head to the shower while mom goes off to work. Since I know mom is gone, I don't bother creating a Dream suit yet after toweling off. I return to my room and peer around before entering, checking if I have any lurking visiting friendly neighborhood vampires. To my pleasant surprise, I do not find Lamont in my room.

I return to the kitchen, make breakfast, eat, clean up, and then finish my morning ablutions in the bathroom. Conjure up silk panties, a satin bra I had seen in Sheer Illusions, and for a change, a red cable sweater dress, and lastly, slip my feet into a conjured pair of my red cowgirl boots. Then I hear a familiar tapping coming from my bedroom. Lamont is doing his Edgar Allen Poe thing at my chamber window as a crow. Well, wonders never cease; he let me get dressed before he put in his appearance. I let him in, and he flutters to perch on my bed's mattress and then appears before me in a puff of black smoke.

Basha: "So, Lamont, this evening begins the *Yamim Noraim*, the Days of Awe, with *Rosh Hashanah* eve tonight. I will be heading out to my Dad in Berkeley for dinner and services this eve and tomorrow. Should be back early evening on Thursday."

Lamont: "If I recall correctly, these are the biggest synagogue holy days of the year. Is your mom going to Berkeley as well?"

"No, she will be going to local services here. The fact that she's divorced makes her decidedly unwelcome by the Hassidic community in Berkeley. After the divorce, mom took back her maiden name, Ramono."

Lamont: "Really? I didn't know that. No wonder you're such a tasty meal."

Basha: "I am ignoring that remark. Where was I? Dad negotiated, and I agreed to keep my father's name. The Berkeley community would rather forget my mom ever existed and really wants my dad to take a new wife. That has not happened yet, but I think it is only a matter of time.

I spend these holidays with my Dad, which was part of the official arrangement. I alternate with Pesach between them; this year, I will be spending it with Dad. The other holidays depend on where they fall on the calendar and if that time coincides with when I am supposed to head over to Berkeley or not. It is all complex shuttle diplomacy mixed with reconciling the lunar and solar calendars. I hear that Bohr and Heisenberg gave up in complete frustration at trying to derive a formula for figuring out when I celebrate a Jewish holiday with mom or my dad."

Lamont: "I promise I won't ask for any more clarity."

Basha: "Do you need some morning sustenance?"

"Yes. I am feeling very peckish."

I pull down the turtleneck collar of my sweater dress and offer my neck to Lamont.

He is by my side in a flash, kissing me gently on the lips, face, neck, and licking my ear lobe…that tickles and feels nice…then I feel his teeth sink into my throat, the feeling of blood oozing out, and as he feeds, he takes us off to the Well of Dreams. That feeling of passivity and weakness fades into bliss as I sink into him.

*

I wake up cradled in his lap as he gently runs his fingers through my hair. I feel all warm and happy.

Basha: "Hello, love," I say, looking at his pretty blue eyes and smiling face. "How long have I been out?"

Lamont: "About a half-hour."

"Any new insights on how to help Peter?" I ask, adjusting my collar to cover up the bite marks.

"No. I did go and ask Tezcat, and even she didn't have a clue as to what to do. Though she did say that you couldn't force someone to wake up. They have to do so willingly. I will ask Sarah and Rebecca to see if they have any ideas. Well, we both have classes to get to."

Basha: "Yes, we can meet up at Zuki's tonight around say nine or ten, depending on when I get back from services? I know you will need to feed."

Lamont: "Thanks. Love you."

"Love you too."

LAMONT

I fly back to my place to get my books and ride to school. I tell my teachers that I will be missing tomorrow's classes, as I will be attending Jewish New Year Services. They all give me that look, recalling my relationship with Basha and correctly assuming that she is the reason for my interest in Judaism. I'm an A student and a general 'good kid', so they don't have any concerns about me missing classes and such.

All during the day, I think about Peter and Basha. I begin to get a feeling and wander into the library. I don't really have any connection to the church my parents raised me in, despite all the cajoling and threats of my dad. Christianity with its Original Sin seems a great scam to force its parishioners into feeling trapped by eternal damnation. The whole thing came across like a scam, belong and obey or else. It just never worked for me.

However, the more time I spend with Basha, the more intrigued I am with her faith. Given her own commitment, and her parents as well…and mine to her, I have this happy idea of 'death do us part' vowing one day, even though death hasn't parted us at all. If I were to propose marriage, Basha doesn't seem a justice of the peace kind of girl. Which means a wedding in a synagogue. Besides, I had already posed as a Sephardic Jew to her father. So,

I think it is high time I checked that out. Hmm…if I do go down this road, I'm definitely going to piss my dad off big time…oh well…true love does what true love requires…

I look up where there is a Sephardic synagogue in the City. I discover Magain David Sephardim Congregation. It was founded on October 9, 1934, as Beth El Sephardim Congregation by 50 families in San Francisco. The name was changed to Magain David Sephardim Congregation the following month. There are over 40 different traditions included in the new membership and discussions from the very start over how to best spell 'Magain' to reflect a Sephardic pronunciation. The opening dedication was attended by many notables, including representatives of the Mayor and Board of Supervisors, Rabbis, and Presidents of other regional synagogues.

I think that after I do my homework, I will head over there to attend the services. Check it out and see what I think of it. I tell my mom and dad that I am meeting up with Basha.

Earlier that same day
Wednesday, September 10, 1980
Erev Rosh Hashanah

BASHA

After attending classes and declining Barry's offer for a lunch date, I then go off to the library to do some schoolwork. I eventually notice that a couple of the girls from my classes began joining me at the table I am sitting at. We smile in recognition and return to our solo endeavors. When I am finished, I gather my books and papers, put them in my pack, and walk away. I hear behind me, "Wait up."

I see that she is one of the girls in a few of my classes who had studied at the table near me at the library. I remember her face but not her name. She seemed very bright and always had insightful comments and observations to make in class. She had shoulder-length black hair, silver circlet earrings in the shape of a crescent moon, bright warm grey eyes, long eyelashes, moist scarlet lipstick, wide hips, tight-fitting blue jeans tucked into Kneehigh high heeled black boots, and a tight black leather bomber jacket, similar to mine.

Cora: "Hi, I'm Cora," she says, holding out her hand to me. I notice the long scarlet red nails and multiple silver rings on her fingers. She is wearing a black cord with a silver pentacle with a raven in its center.

Basha: "I am Basha," I shake her firm, warm hand.

"I know. You ride a bike, correct?"

"Yes."

"So do I; I believe mine is parked by yours; can I join you?"

"Of course."

We chat about our bikes and our classes as we approach the parking lot, where our bikes are beside each other. She has this warmth and openness that I find disarming and appealing. She has a natural, sultry swing to her wide hips as she walks.

Basha: "Well, I got to head out. It has been nice talking to you."

Cora: "Same here. See you tomorrow, I hope?"

"Well, actually not. I'll be in shul most of the day. A religious holiday."

"Oh yes. Jewish New Year, right?"

"Yes, it is."

"I think it's LaShanah Tovah? Isn't that how you say Happy New Year?"

"Yes, it is. Thanks. Are you Jewish?"

Cora: "No, but I make it a point to know things when I need to."

Basha: "Okay, well, La Shanah Tovah, Cora."

I mount the bike and wave goodbye to her. She is an exceptionally bright, friendly, and engaging girl. She seems to like me as well. I drive my bike back to the store and pack what I would typically take to stay overnight at my dad's place when all I really need is shampoo, conditioner, floss, toothpaste, and a toothbrush. I pack a change of clothes just on principle to add bulk to the bag to look ordinary; with Dream magick, I do not need those items at all.

I conjure a version of the gold mezuzah on its own gold chain that my father had given me, rubies within golden starburst stud earrings, my red cowgirl boots, pink cotton panties, and appropriate pink full cup lace bra. Then I create a pale cream long mid-calf clingy cotton dress; I add a pattern of Japanese maple leaves scattered across the fabric; lastly, I give it a simple boat-style neckline, tasteful and non-cleavage revealing. I add a white lace shawl. All in all, a respectable good-daughter-visiting-her-father outfit. Of course, I completely ruin that look by donning my utilitarian and aggressive-looking black leather body armor in the form of my double-breasted motorcycle jacket.

After everything is in my backpack, I head down to my bike and begin the journey to Berkeley. It is still warmish here in the City, in the mid-sixties at the moment; a clear azure sky should be the same when I get to Berkeley. A great day for a ride. It's two blocks heading north to Masonic Ave and then west onto Oak Street. Both streets are major arteries for traffic in this part of the City. But for all that, both are residential streets. Oak Street eventually becomes a mix of homes and shops as I finally turn South onto Octavia Boulevard. That feeds into the on-ramp for Highway 101 heading westward to take me towards the part of 101 that leads into the on-ramp to the Bay Bridge.

I weave in and out of the traffic, carefully and gracefully splitting lanes, and pass the congested automobile traffic that sluggishly moves along. No matter what time of the day, there is always congested traffic going along 101 to the East Bay. As I travel under the cloistered concrete and steel canopy of the lower deck of the Bay Bridge, weaving in and out of the slow-moving traffic, I think fondly of this amazing structure. I recall a report I wrote about the bridge for a civics class.

The Bay Bridge's design combined three different types of bridge-building technology over the five miles it covers between San Francisco and Oakland. It is a classic industrial gray steeled four interlaced towered suspension span that leads to a tunnel through Yerba Buena Island. It projects the proud grace and strength of American Steel. Then once you are out of the tunnel, you travel onto an enclosed metal cage of the cantilevered two-towered span of the remaining part of the Bay Bridge structure. Heading toward the East Bay, you are always traveling on the lower decks of the bridge. Above us, on the upper decks' traffic travels back from the East Bay toward the waiting arms of San Francisco.

I was surprised to find out that in 1956 the American Society of Civil Engineering selected seven engineering wonders of the modern world. It named the San Francisco-Oakland Bay Bridge as one of these wonders. It was built between May 1933 and its opening on November 12, 1936. At the time of its completion, the bridge was the longest steel structure on the globe. It also featured the deepest bridge pier ever built and the world's largest bore tunnel.

I always wished that the Bay Bridge be given the title 'The Emperor Norton Bridge' since our eccentric San Francisco resident, the self-proclaimed Emperor Norton the First[71], had decreed on September 17, 1872, that this bridge and tunnel system be considered as a building project.

Not unexpectedly, the city fathers of San Francisco and Oakland ignored his decree.

---

[71] San Francisco was the home of our country's first and only emperor, born humbly as Joshua Abraham Norton (February 4, 1818–January 8, 1880), was born to John Norton (d. 1848) and Sarah Norden (d. 1846), who were English Jews. John Norton was a farmer and merchant, and Sarah was a daughter of Abraham Norden and a sister of Benjamin Norden, a successful merchant. Most likely, Norton was born in the Kentish town of Deptford, today part of London. There are often-repeated historical claims that Joshua Norton arrived in San Francisco on a specific vessel, the Franzeska, on November 23, 1849. He came with considerable wealth, and he lost his fortune due to failures in the rice market.

One of my favorite decrees of Emperor Norton concerned how you refer to the City. He had issued a stern edict sometime in 1872, although I must admit that the evidence is elusive for this decree's authorship, date, or source. *'Whoever after due and proper warning shall be heard to utter the abominable word "Frisco", which has no linguistic or other warrant, shall be deemed guilty of a High Misdemeanor and shall pay into the Imperial Treasury as penalty the sum of twenty-five dollars.'*[72]

Coming out of the steel cage of the eastern portion of the Bay Bridge, I maneuver to take the Ashby Avenue-North Berkely exit off Highway 101. I travel on Telegraph Avenue and make my way through the residential tree-lined area to my Dad's home near Hillegass Avenue and Derby Street, looking out at Willard Park, an island of grass with a few tall trees nestled within the surrounding suburban landscape. I park my bike, remove my leather jacket, and exchange it with the cropped denim jacket from my backpack. That way, I appear less biker babe and more demure daughter.

When I step in, I hear Jacob talking to my dad. I make my way to the kitchen, where Leah is busy preparing the holiday dinner. Leah still goes by Mrs. Levitt, even though her husband died about five years ago. She dotes on my father like he was her prize rooster and fends off the other ladies at the Shul with quiet ferocity. How could my father not see this?

I guess my father has a type; she is like my mom in that they are both well-rounded and well endowed. She seems more the doting wife type and hard-working who would fit in nicely with the inhabitants of Anatevka[73]. Her chestnut brown hair is nicely perched in a bun, an ankle-length, long-sleeved dark navy well-fitting dress, which does show off, in a proper motherly fashion, all her best attributes, wearing sensible heeled navy pumps.

Basha: "Gut Yontiff[74], Mrs. Levitt."

Shortly after he signed the contract, several other shiploads of rice arrived from Peru, causing the price of rice to plummet to three cents a pound. Norton tried to void the contract, stating the dealer had misled him as to the quality of rice to expect. This lawsuit ultimately failed. Eventually, in 1858, he lived in reduced circumstances at a working-class boarding house. He became known as Emperor Norton when as a resident of San Francisco, California, in 1859 proclaimed himself "Norton I., Emperor of the United States". In 1863, after Napoleon III invaded Mexico, he took the secondary title of "Protector of Mexico". The Manifesto ran as a paid ad in the San Francisco Daily Evening Bulletin.

[72] It appears that the earliest reference to the text of this edict was in a booklet, *San Francisco's Emperor Norton*, self-published in 1939 by David Warren Ryder. The fine of $25 in the 1870s was a steep one since its equivalent purchasing power in 2020 is about $494.

[73] A fictional shtetl town in the Ukraine where Tevye lived in the Broadway play and later movie, Fiddler on the Roof.

[74] Yiddish for the greeting: 'Good festivity/celebration/holiday'.

Leah Levitt: "Gut Yontiff, Shoshana. I was pleased to hear that you will spend the holidays with us. I know Jacob was delighted to hear that, as well as your father."

Basha: "Yes, I know my father was quite pleased." But why the reference to Jacob, what significance to him could me being here today be? "Is there anything I can do to assist you?"

Leah: "There is no need. I have it all under control but thank you. Has Jacob or your father finally talked to you yet?"

"No. Not yet. Is there something they were going to tell me?"

"Ahh, well, perhaps one of them will finally get around to that today. You should go and speak with him or your father then."

Basha: "Oh, really? Well, I must not keep them waiting. I shall join them after I put my pack in my usual room if you are certain you do not need me."

Leah: "Yes, I am sure. You will find all the men in the study."

"As you wish."

What was Mrs. Levitt hinting at, I wonder? I stow my backpack upstairs in what has always been my bedroom since before mom, and I moved out. I wonder what it is that my father and Jacob wish to talk to me about?

I approach the study; my dad leads a group of about half a dozen young men; Yeshiva Bucher's[75] doing a Talmud study being conducted by my father. My father's back is to me as I enter the room, but Jacob, who is sitting across from him, can see me in the doorway. Jacob always comes across to me as if he was intentionally trying to emulate my father as if he was his clone. His short auburn hair matches my father's similar skimpiness in the hair endowment department.

Jacob has a youthful scruffy beard trying to become like the one my father cultivated after all these years. As for what Jacob wears, although it is a similar set of black polished lace shoes, black socks, black slacks, and a white shirt as my father's attire, on him, it looks like a costume. My father, as does Lamont, inhabits such formal dress as if they are their natural skin. The only thing that Jacob wears naturally is the glow of delight in his eyes and the happy smile on his face.

Everyone seated around the study table has white High Holiday Kippah[76] upon their heads. Jacob, upon seeing me, is as always beaming with delight.

---

[75] Yiddish expression for a student in a Yeshiva, which is an Orthodox school to train students in Talmud and other rabbinic texts.

[76] Kippah is the Hebrew word, literally meaning 'dome', for the head covering worn by religious Jews. Yarmulke is the Yiddish term for the same thing.

Jacob: "Gut Yuntiff Shoshana," Jacob says as he gets up from the table. "You look lovely as always."

All the young men look up at me, are embarrassed at seeing me, and yet show signs of being shyly interested and envious simultaneously.

Basha: "Thank you, Jacob. Gut Yontiff, father." I go and give him a proper daughter kiss on his cheek. He, too, seems to be especially happy to see me, more so than usual. What is up?

Herschel Edelman: "Jacob, I believe you can be excused from our studies to go and talk to my daughter."

Jacob: "Yes, Thank you, Rabbi. Shoshana, could I talk with you a moment?"

Hmmm, what is up? What is with this 'everyone needs to talk with me' thing? Jacob is usually shy and quiet around me, though always looking at me like an adoring puppy dog. "Of course."

Jacob: "Perhaps we could step back onto the front porch?"

Basha: "Lead the way."

We do so, and Jacob carefully seals the door behind us.

"Shoshana," Jacob begins as if he is about to present a speech he has practiced long and hard. "You have become an amazing young woman. You have blossomed into your prime. You have such...beauty and...charm. Just like when I first saw you."

Basha: "Well, thank you, Jacob, for such an elegant complement."

Jacob: "We have known each other since we were both children. I had spoken to the Rabbi, I mean your father, concerning my intentions towards you long ago. I wonder, has your father communicated them to you?"

"No. Not really. Are you saying he should have?"

"He hadn't? Oh. I just assumed he did. He really didn't tell you anything about me?"

"No. Jacob, I am confused. There seems to be a lot going on here that you had presumed about. As the Red King said to Alice, begin at the beginning. That is always a good way to deal with these things."

"Yes. You're right. Okay. Well, you see, it's like this, from the moment I first saw you, well...ahh...how should I say this? It was like the sun had risen for the very first time; you came into the room and parted the gloom."

"You are being very kind and poetic again without truly getting at some point that you are trying to explain, Jacob."

"Kindness has little to do with it. I am humbly trying to put all this into words. Which I thought you had known all this time. As I grew up looking at you, I glanced over the texts we studied together, sitting side by side with you as your father taught us. I just was certain that you felt it, felt what I felt. You truly are that lily of the valley, the lily amongst the thorns, so aptly named Shoshana. The Rabbi, your father, has always told me that I would go far and that HaShem has great plans for me. I've worked hard and prayed long and hard. To earn these blessings. Your father told me that he spoke to The Rabbi of our local center concerning my abilities and my earnestness to work for HaShem. I was told I would be given a task worthy of my efforts and skills. In this, I will need a companion and a true helpmate, one who is also so special and gifted. I know I'm not worthy of such a thing, but your father assured me of his blessing in this…"

Basha: "What are you trying to say, Jacob? What does all this have to do with me? There is too much poetry and not enough clarity." I think that for all his flourishes and beating around that bush, he is clearly conveying what I do not think I want to hear.

Jacob: "Well, I will probably be given a Chabad house or some other assignment to help serve and expand our community. I can't do this alone. This is a life's mission, and it takes two working together. Two shluchim[77], who together can perform these tasks. And, well, I thought…if only you granted me my heart's fervent wish, it would be such a blessing. I would be so honored. I promise to do my best I really do."

Oh, Goddess! Help me. I am sure he is trying to say that he wants to marry me!

Basha: "Jacob, are you trying to propose to me? I did not know you felt this way about me."

Jacob: "Yes, I am. I confess that I always dreamed of us sharing a life together. I really thought your father told you about my devotion to you."

"No, he had not. I wish someone had. I could have explained that I am too young to consider such a kind offer."

"You are too modest, Shoshana. You are not young at all. As for your friend, whom I met at your graduation, he is too young for you. You need someone your own age. You are truly a woman. She who can be likened to *The* Woman of Valor. Whom our King Solomon's sung praises of. Eingeschriebnen[78] in the book of Proverbs. Besides, your mother and my own mother married around this age."

Basha: "I am sorry, Jacob. I really am not ready for marriage. I cannot accept such an offer. I mean, I have just begun my first year towards my

[77] Hebrew for emissaries.

[78] Yiddish for literally'written in stone', here meaning Divinely written.

college degree, and I foresee going on to obtain a Master's degree. I cannot do that and be a mother, which I know you're ultimately hoping for."

Jacob: "But, I have spoken often to your father concerning my heartfelt dreams. I am so sorry that he had not approached you on my behalf, and I also apologize that I had not expressed my feelings for you myself. I thought you understood that our lives were meant to be so entwined."

Basha: "My Dad never mentioned any of this." Which explains why the house is still standing. I would have exploded if he had tried to tell me that he just married me off like some character out of *Fiddler on the Roof*[79]. Jacob is looking frightened and surprised. He clearly was not thinking I would respond negatively to his entreaties.

Basha: "Jacob, I am truly sorry, but I cannot accept your kind offer. I hardly know you..."

Jacob: "Which is why I asked you now, as I just did. I thought this was such an auspicious time. You graduated last year, and it is the beginning of a new year. A new path in your life journeys is opening up before you. Before us. This is a perfect time for us to spend this year getting to know each other. By year's end, I am certain you will see the wisdom in such a match as this."

Basha: "It is not just that I do not know you; as I said, I have other plans for my life."

Jacob: "Yes, I realized that you might wish to further your pursuit of learning for now, even if they are outside the prescribed realm of Torah. I had considered that, so I would have suggested that you take classes at night or part-time here at the University of Berkeley so we could be together and have the time to learn and know about each other."

Basha: "But, you do not understand, I am already enrolled and started my college program at San Francisco State."

Jacob: "Already enrolled? San Francisco State? Why? How? That will keep us so far apart. That will not do. I was assuming you would seek your father's counsel on such matters so he could explain the wisdom of applying to U.C. Berkeley, so we could have this time together. I did not think you would have acted so precipitously and already committed yourself without your father's input."

Basha: "This just goes to show you that you do not truly know me."

Jacob: "It is true that we have been apart for so long, with you living under your mother's roof and influence. You need your father's guidance at

[79] Fiddler on the Roof is based on *Tevye the Dairyman and his Daughters*, a series of stories by Sholem Aleichem that he wrote in Yiddish between 1894 and 1914 about Jewish life in a village in the Pale of Settlement of Imperial Russia at the turn of the 20th century.

this critical juncture in your life. You need to be here. This is why it was so crucial for our future life together to have this year to learn about each other. By enrolling in U.C. Berkeley, I thought that you would come and move in with your father for the convenience of attending the school here."

"I often do decide such matters without seeking **his** council. You would do best to consider someone more inclined to be that kind of dutiful daughter and thus that kind of wife you wish for."

Jacob: "However, it is not too late; you could simply drop out of that program and re-apply to the U.C. here. I'm sure with your father's influence, you could get accepted."

Basha: "You do not understand me. I have made my own decisions, and once made, I do not change them."

"But what about your feelings toward me? You must feel as I do. I knew we were meant to be together when I first saw you when we were just children."

"Jacob, I do not have these same feelings."

"Well, perhaps if you spent more time here, we could get to know each other better. I'm sure you could easily get accepted to UC Berkeley and then…"

"I am sorry, my mind is made up. I am staying in San Francisco and attending school there." I wonder if I should really add that I would never consider marrying him. Perhaps that might be too cruel? I shall try my best to remain considerate concerning his feelings. Given time and the space between us, since he is clearly ready for marriage, he will find someone else more suited to his plans and forget about his infatuation with me.

"Okay, as you wish, Shoshana, I will wait, as my namesake, he toiled for many years before that blessed time to join in union with Rachel, so shall I wait. This news is so unexpected. I did not foresee all of this. I need to be alone for a bissel[80]. I'll be back in a few minutes. Tell the Rebbe, your father, the news, but break it to him gently. I cannot do it. I am sorry that we will not be so easily together this year. I only wanted what was best for you. You must believe that. Gut Yuntiff, dear Shoshana."

He walks off as if someone had just killed his puppy right before him. That is done. Now I need to deal with my father. I just watch as Jacob wanders off. Wow. I was not expecting that. I will wait here until Jacob returns and then speak with my father. Just as he said, he came back, head down, not wanting to look me in the eye.

---

[80] Yiddish for a little.

Jacob: "Let's go back inside. I know your father wants to speak with you."

We head inside, and I try to contain my emotions.

Basha: "Father, I need to speak with you."

Herschel, Basha's Father: "Let us go to the library; we can talk privately there. I have news, and I wish to consult you."

Jacob: "I will take over the lesson while you talk with your daughter."

My father and I go off; once we are alone, I ask him what is up.

Basha: "Jacob said you wanted to consult me? Really?"

Herschel: "So, it concerns me."

"And what do you need me to say?"

"I wish to ask your permission and your mother's on this matter."

"What are you talking about? What is this asking?"

"Well. I wish to marry Leah. I wanted to get yours and your mother's blessing on the matter."

"You do not need anyone's blessing, father."

"So you say. But, I think it is best to ask others about such things before doing anything rashly that will affect their life forever."

"Have you spoken with Leah concerning all this?"

"Not yet. First, I need to know if that is okay with you and your mother."

"I think as you have this all backward, but I would not think of offering advice where it is not wanted. As for your query, of course, that is okay with me, and I am sure with mom, once you ask her. She divorced you, so she holds nothing to bind you to her. I am sure it is true for both of us that we only wish the best for you."

"This is good. I just want you and her blessings. Yes, I know I don't need it. But I still care for you both. I am sorry that things unraveled as they did; it was most unfortunate. Especially for you."

"Now, I am sure Leah is hoping for this outcome as well. I have seen how she looks upon you. You really have not asked her? Not even hinted at this?"

"No. I have not asked Leah, not yet."

"Well, when you ask her, I am certain she will say yes."

"From your mouth to HaShem's ear, may it be so. Now, can I ask another sensitive question?"

"Of course, father. Go ahead."

"About your mother, is she…seeing anyone?"

"Actually. I do not know for certain. But I do not think so."

Herschel: "This is a shame. I wish her happiness. She should not be alone. She needs someone. She has a great heart."

Basha: "I agree."

"Well, if you can find a way. Tell her I said that I wish she would find someone."

"And when were you planning on popping this question to Leah?"

Herschel: "I will ask her during this Yontiff period. I was thinking sometime during the days between the New Year and Yom Kippur. So that you can tell me that Miriam is truly alright with this. I do already have the engagement ring to present to her."

Basha: "Ha! You always planned many chess moves ahead."

"This is true, daughter. I did. Which reminds me, we haven't had a game in a while."

"Perhaps tomorrow after services. Now that we have discussed your wedding plans, it seems that some people have been planning another wedding. Such as mine."

"Ah, good. Did Jacob finally, what was that expression? Pop the question?"

Basha: "How long did you know about all Jacob's interest in me? He seemed to think that he had made his, as he put it, intentions known to you a long time ago. However, he was surprised that you had not conveyed them to me. I am surprised as well."

"Well, yes. He acted as he should. A young man in our community should approach the father when seeking his daughter's hand in marriage. He told me about seeing you for the first time as he walked into our home when he came to study with us. Afterward, he told me that he was destined to marry you and no other. Of this, his heart was certain. I knew that when you moved away with my wife, your mother, after the divorce, you would be raised outside of the community and thus might not know how things should be done. I, therefore, concluded that you would be so influenced by that outsider community that you would act according to their rules. Meaning that only upon your reaching the age of maturity according to their rules you would not consider yourself ready for marriage till you graduated from High School. You, being so studious, would never even think about such things. Thus, the topic has finally come up. I am glad that he approached you."

"Oh really? You assumed all that, did you?"

"Yes. I hope you will see the wisdom in this match now that Jacob has approached you. He was always an excellent scholar and a fine young man, do you not see that?"

"Yes, I agree Jacob is not bad looking in that *Yeshiva-bocher* way. And, yes, he is an excellent scholar."

Herschel: "Jacob has sincerity and clarity of focus. He is a good match. Even your mother would think so once she heard of this. So? To facilitate all of this, I think it would be best if you rejoined the community and came to live here with me now? If you like to pursue your studies, you could attend the university here in Berkeley? I and the Rabbi for our Berkely community had devised a project worthy of the two of you."

Basha: "Oh really? You decided more of my life for me, have you. Please, do inform me of this."

Herschel: "I'm sure you will be quite pleased. We had discussed this proposal, and we thought the two of you could work on translating into English, for eventual publication, the Alter Rebbe's commentary on certain Kabbalistic texts. We thought your first joint venture would be *The Sefer Yetzirah;* after that, you could tackle *The Bahir* and *The Sha'are Orah*. If you were willing, I would speak to The Rebbe in Brooklyn to get my plan's approval."

Basha: "I see you had planned my life quite admirably." I say sarcastically.

"I thought so. I wished to use both of your extensive gifts of erudition, and thus, your marriage would fulfill your joint destinies."

"I am so glad you wished to help guide my destiny. The problem is that you failed to consult my opinion on all of this."

"But, I would think you would be pleased."

"Ahh, no, father, I am not. I get to decide my life. It is not something that can be thrust upon me by someone else. So, I will not be moving in with you. I will not be attending U. C. Berkeley. As I told Jacob, I had already thought out my life and begun to embark on that by enrolling in San Francisco State, and classes have actually begun."

"That is most unfortunate. I would have guided you and explained everything if you had consulted me first. I should have realized that your mother would not have explained how things should be worked out on such matters. But, no matter, it is not too late; you can…"

"No, I will not make changes to my plans. Not for you and certainly not for Jacob."

"You have been away for too long. You have not been seeking my advice for a long time; I should have realized that. If not for my wishes, then consider Jacob. For Jacob's sake, won't you reconsider? "

"No, I will remain in the City. Besides the convenience of being close to the university, I have friends there."

"Friends? Who? Oh, you mean that child, the Sephardim that was at your graduation? I would have thought, given time, you would have outgrown your infatuation with his boyish charms? Is that young Sephardic boy the cause of all this? He doesn't seem to even know much Biblical Hebrew, let alone Rabbinic Hebrew."

(If he is kvetching now, imagine if he knew that Lamont was a gentile! Since Lamont doesn't seem committed to his family's faith, I hope he might be persuaded to convert. However, that is a problem for another day. Right now, we will stick to the lie that Lamont is a Sephardic Jew.)

Basha: "You will see, Lamont is quite capable of learning. Study is something he excels at. So, once he puts his mind to it, he will master the language and the texts. He has the making of a gaon[81] in whatever fields he takes up to study."

Herschel: "Ha! A gaon? Clearly, you exaggerate; if he was such a one, he would have been studying Talmud years ago just as you did. No, I think you are fooling yourself about this boy. You are being stubborn and headstrong, just deciding to rashly fall for him rather than seek my advice. I knew that your mother would just continue to encourage such foolishness. It has led to your abandoning your own heritage."

Basha: "Abandoning our heritage? What are you talking about, father?

"You're forsaking us for some Sephardim."

"Need I remind you that if not for Maimonides, who was a Sephardic Jew, we would not have had the *Mishnah Torah* and that Joseph Caro, another Sephardic Jew, created the law book of daily practice, the *Shulchan Aruch*? Then there are Moses DeLeon and ARI, both important Sephardic Jews."

"I know such things, daughter. I taught them to you. As for the idea that DeLeon wrote *The Holy Zohar*- you are just baiting this old bear with that one. Anyone can see it was..."

"You are right, father; let us not rehash that old issue yet again."

"This would never have happened if you hadn't attended that Public High School. I knew that would lead to trouble someday, and here it is. You were able to meet this Lamont at your Public High School, nu?

"Yes, father."

"Ha! No one listens to me. Such troubles could have been avoided."

"I think not, father. As I said, Lamont and I…"

"This is a mistake, my daughter. The old ways are for the best; I have made the best match for you in Jacob. The Rabbi who leads our community had asked me to assist Jacob in finding the proper match for him, and I had

[81] Hebrew for 'genius'

ensured him that I would. I explained to the Rabbi how Jacob felt about you, and I convinced him to allow Jacob to wait for you to finish High School. I had offered Jacob a special project that you and he, as a husband and wife team, could undertake. He approved. He agreed to let Jacob wait for you. Now, you are telling me that you will not consider Jacob; this will be embarrassing for us. This match was made for you, for your best future. To bring you back into the community, to fulfill your destiny."

Basha: "The trouble the two of you made was not my making. If you had come to me and asked, I would have explained that I would not agree to have my future arranged in such a manner. Look how well it did not work for you. And are you really going to tell me that arranged marriages create lasting marriages?"

Herschel: "Well, yes. In the old country, that way had worked for..."

"In the OLD country! Father, this is not there and not then. You know that. Come on! Changing times create the need for changing approaches. That is a foundationally basic rabbinic principle. Are you honestly going to tell me that you and mom turned out to be such a perfect match?"

"We were. From such a perfect match, we had a perfect child. The beautiful flower in our life. Which is why we named you Shoshana. If only you could have stayed young, dutiful, and obedient. A father's wistful dream...sigh."

"Come on, Father, you must know me as I am; I have always failed at maintaining the appearance as your dutiful daughter."

"There have been some…momentary lapses, I know that. But, I thought that now that you have become a woman, you would see the wisdom in heeding your father. You cannot be seriously considering that young child friend, Lamont? He is not worthy of you. Give it a little time to think this over, and I am certain you will come around; I must have patience."

"Father, I choose my friends as I see fit, and I do not consult you on such matters. I am not someone who you can move like a playing piece. You cannot command me or give me away without my permission. No amount of patience waiting for me to change will do you any good."

"Harumph."

"And I just do not like being treated as someone who is seen but not heard."

"And what is that supposed to mean?"

"It means I may choose to help cook and clean, but I do not like being relegated to that role alone. I do not like being forced to sit behind a wall at services separate from the event, pushed aside, and treated as if my acts are of no religious consequence."

"That is your place. You are to be a helpmate; it was something your mother never properly understood..."

Basha: "She was there for you if you would have listened and learned from her wisdom. But you could not hear her at all. Just as you do not want to hear me. You want us pushed aside and kept cloistered and out of sight. In our place is where you want us. Well, that place is not for me."

Herschel: "This is not my doing; it is our way. Our rabbis have so explained how it should be. Our tradition sets forth the proper roles for us to take on. This is what your mother never understood."

Basha: "Tradition! So like your Tevye, you can sing that song so well like it was made for you. Times changed for Tevye; that was the lesson Scholem Aleichem wrote in his story and the lesson you continue to fail to learn. Mother and I are not made to hover in the back and be grateful to only serve. Our voices need to be heard if our people can adapt to the changing times and situations."

Herschel: "We will only get lost without the guidance of our traditions, they have kept us safe down through the ages, and they are our best chance to continue to help us hear the wisdom of HaShem."

"That wisdom has always been spoken through our mouths and minds. We made those words, though they might have been inspired by HaShem."

"No. We are the instruments that HaShem plays. We are not the makers of the music. HaShem is. This is the point you fail to see. Your place is to help to contribute, yes…"

"But not to lead? Is that it? Only you menfolk are capable of this? Sorry, father, I cannot accept that. I cannot accept a subordinate role."

"Your importance is not less; it is just a different place, a different role that HaShem has decided for us all."

"I do not want to stay in just the kitchen and behind that mechitza[82] any longer. I want to be an equal participant in the service. I enjoy the old sights and sounds, the melodies, and the rhythms of the service, but I want to be there by your side and not shunned away. So, since I cannot stand together, I guess I no longer want to be there."

"But that is the way it must be. Your place is too much of a distraction; thus, our rabbis wisely created that wall to separate you, men from the women at services."

"It does not work for me."

[82] From the Hebrew word meaning partition or division. A mechitza most commonly means the physical divider placed between the men's and women's sections in Orthodox synagogues and at religious celebrations.

"It doesn't work for you? Do you alone get to decide such things? What are you saying?"

Basha: "We must decide such things; that is our way to participate and serve HaShem. We are partners in creation, and making choices is how we play our part. We were created to choose, and that is what I have done. You had planned my future according to a role I had not chosen."

Herschel: "You do not get to choose such things. It is the way of our tradition. It was handed down to us by HaShem; you cannot turn your back on it."

Basha: "That logic may work for you, but it does not work for me. I am sorry, father. Tradition has always changed. The Torah was written in the language of...people. All voices must be heard and listened to. You need to hear what I am saying. I..."

Herschel: "Enough. Stop. Let me think. You are still that stubborn and headstrong child that insisted on that Bat Mitzvah thing. I thought you would grow out of that. What is the goyish word? Ah...yes, I thought it was just a 'phase' you were going through. My mistake. Hmm. Now, shush! Let me think."

Time ticks slowly and very loudly. I try my best to contain myself.

Herschel: "I have it. You are certain, absolutely certain that you won't consider Jacob and the plans for the translation projects? Think hard on this. Once you decide this, there is no going back. You can choose to wait and perhaps contemplate this and your life during these Holy days; that is what our tradition considered for us at this time."

Basha: "No, father. I am certain that I will not marry Jacob."

"All right. It is done. Now, here is how this will be fixed. You will do this and not challenge me for once. This is how it must be done in our community."

"Fine. Go on, explain."

"Do you have some sort of new ring or jewelry? It could serve as a token in this situation."

"I gather you did not notice that I am wearing such a ring."

"No, I did not. A father need not notice such things. Show me."

I hold up my hand so he can see the silver and obsidian ring on my finger.

Herschel: "Excellent. That will do well. Now take it off and put it on your ring finger instead."

Basha: "Why?"

"Why, because you have just announced to me that your young friend, Lamont, has given you that ring as a token of his intension to marry you."

Basha: "What are you talking about. I have no intention of being married at this time to anyone!"

Herschel: "Yes, yes. When you get married is of no concern at this point. Whenever You decide on such things, I hope you will at least inform me. As for the ring, it is all for show. The fact that you are pledged to another is the only thing that could break the match I had already arranged for you, as you clearly stated, without you being aware. Living in that world of you and your mother's, you would not understand our ways, and thus you made a match on your own. Such things are done outside of our community. The Rabbi would understand this and accept that I had no control or say in the matter. It was you're doing, and it was done. A pledge taken ends the matter. So, I will say that your Lamont has proposed his intentions, and you have accepted them. The ring is his pledge to marry you sometime in the future. Thus, you had to turn down Jacob. You will wear that ring on your ring finger and show it off to the women of the shul this evening. That way, the news will spread amongst the community. I can explain this bad news to our Rabbi later and tell him I just found out all this tonight. Hmm…I think that you should not attend services with us henceforth. I think that you should leave tomorrow morning. It needs to look like we argued, and you needed to make a final break with the community. Do you understand?"

Basha: "You are asking me to drive on such a Holy day?"

"Ha! Now you are telling me that such things matter to you? Please, you and your mother have been picking and choosing what mitzvot to follow like you were some Reform Jews. So, yes, you shouldn't be a presence within the community. It will save face for everyone. So, you will do this?"

"Fine. I will do this."

I remove the ring and place it on my left-hand ring finger as instructed. "There, see, it is done."

"Good. That is settled well enough for tonight. Now…back to Jacob, were you at least considerate of Jacob's feelings when you told him that all of this will be changing, and you will not be moving in with us?"

"Of course, I was. Do you think so badly of me?"

"Sometimes, I wonder about you. Though, I am pleased to know that I have raised you with some sense of propriety. So, I take it that you were as kind as you could be to him?"

"Yes. I did not hurt Jacob with my words."

"Good. Let us have no more harsh words between us on Erev. It is not good."

We hear Leah call us all to dinner.

Herschel: "Now, let us go and eat. No more talking about this."

Father and I join everyone else in the dining room.

I look upon the table in all its holiday finery. There are two brightly polished silver candlesticks with white candles, two loaves of challah covered by a blue embroidered covering, a white linen tablecloth, white china, and silverware. My father takes his place at the head of the table, I sit to his left, and Leah has the open seat at his right. Leah's youngest son Eli, age five, sits next to her, and her oldest, Reuben, age six, sits next to me. Jacob is seated at the opposite end of the table, with the rest of my father's students filling in the remaining seats.

Herschel: "It is customary to give some coins to charity before kindling the lights. It is appropriate to display kindness to others before we pray to HaShem and ask Him kindly to grant our deepest wishes."

I watch as Leah's children, who were primed and ready for this, explode out of the gate as it were and almost knock their chairs over as they run to put their coins that they were given into the Tzedakah wooden box. I always thought the Hebrew word Tzedakah was poorly translated by gentiles as 'charity'. They just do not understand the concept correctly. What it actually means is justice or right action. It is the idea that we owe our existence and all that it entails to the divine, and we who have are obligated to assist all that do not have as much. It is an act of restoring balance to pay back the kindness that we might have to those who are in need.

Following the children's lead, we all get up and deposit some money as well. Then I go to stand with Leah to kindle the holiday lights.

We stand side by side, Leah and I, with Leah lighting the first candle and then I the second; we shield our eyes from the flames and recite the blessing together. This is one of the few feminine role rituals I enjoy indulging in. I always enjoyed lighting the candles with mom.

Leah and Basha: "Baruk ahtah Adonai Elohaynu Melech ha-olam ah-sher ki-deh-shah-noo beh-mitz-voh-tahv veh-tzee-vah-noo leh-hahd-lik nehr shel Yom Tov.[83]"

Next, my father, Leah, and I would take up the open bottles of wine. As usual, it was the overly sweet Manischewitz wine, and pour some into everyone's wine glass, with Leah giving her children grapefruit juice. The silver goblet waiting on a small plate in front of my father is filled to overflowing by Leah after everyone's glass is filled. He lifts this goblet up, not concerned with it spilling. As he begins the blessing, which we would all recite together.

---

[83] The Hebrew translates as: Blessed are you, O' Lord our God, King of the world, who hallows us with His commandments and bid us to kindle the holiday lights.

This is a ritual of sympathetic magick, though Goddess forbid that my father hears me thinking such thoughts. It always seemed that this ritual is an act of bringing forth sweet abundance to us; just as the cup is filled to overflowing, this spell is being cast to call down such abundance to us and our lives.

Herschel: "Baruk ahtah Adonai Elohaynu Melech ha-olam bo-rei p'ree ha-gafen.[84]"

Then the last ritual blessing is made over Leah's two freshly baked challah loaves. Now at our home, when we were a family, mom would be the one to recite this blessing after father led the blessing over the wine. Here, of course, my father is the one reciting the blessing.

Herschel: "Baruk ahtah Adonai Elohaynu Melech ha-olma ha-motzi lechem min-ha-aretz.[85]"

I always did think that this blessing gave way too much credit to God for all of this. I mean, God may have created the grain, but it was people who took that grain and transformed it into flour so that women could bake that into challah. It really was us acting as partners in creation on this one. Oh well, such is tradition. All the credit goes to the big star; we, all those little people, only get mentioned when the star takes a bow at some award ceremony. Of course, dad starts by tearing off the first piece and then passing the plate with the bread around the table.

Freshly baked bread covered in melting butter, well, in this case, it is non-dairy margarine to keep it all kosher without mixing any dairy products with meat. Freshly baked bread, now that is a food fit for a queen. As I savor this, I feel a twinge of guilt that Lamont can no longer taste and eat this. Now, the meal begins in earnest with the passing of the bread. Leah cooked brisket with gravy, Kasha, sauteed onions mixed with bowtie noodles, and fresh green beans with sauteed onions. Leah beams with pride at the sounds of us all relishing her culinary quantity and quality.

*

After dinner, my father and all the other men get ready to go off to the Chabad House and attend the Rosh Hashannah services that will begin shortly.

Basha: "Leah, I will stay here to help you clean up."

---

[84] The Hebrew translates as: Blessed are you, O' Lord our God, King of the world, who creates the fruit of the vine.

[85] The Hebrew translates as: Blessed are you, O' Lord our God, king of the world, who brings forth bread from the earth.

Leah: "You don't have to do that. I know that you want to go to services. I can take care of all of this."

"I do want to go to service; however, there is work to be done here. I do not like to leave someone else to do all the work. You have done the creative part in making this wonderful dinner for us all. Now all that is left is the grunt work to clean it up. I feel obligated to help. I cannot just leave you with this mess. They can," I point to all the departing men as the door closes behind them. "But I will not. So, shall we get started?"

"Yes. Thank you. I appreciate this."

I help gather up the dishes and bring them to Leah, who begins to wash them in the kitchen.

Leah: "So, did Jacob finally ask you?"

Basha: "You knew about him and his fantasy about marrying me?"

"Of course. Everyone does. Did he finally get the courage to ask you tonight?"

"Yes, he did."

"And I think you turned him down, right?"

"Yes. I did."

I get the last of the dishes off the table and bring them back to Leah.

Leah: "I thought so. I don't really know you, but it seems clear that you are not into being the stay-at-home wife, are you?"

Basha: "No, I am not. How did you know? We have never really talked much at all."

Leah: "Oh, it seems clear enough if you are just willing to listen to what you say. I often overhear things while no one is paying attention to me."

Basha: "But, I gather you enjoy that role?"

"Yes. I do. I understand why someone of your generation might not, but I grew up in a different time, so it all seems natural to me. I've been the wife before, and I enjoy it."

"Now you want my father to be your next husband, I take it?"

"Yes. Is it obvious?"

"To me, yes. I will let you in on sort of a secret if you like."

"Oh? Does it have anything to do with me?"

"Yes."

"Does that mean your father is **fi-nal-ly** going to ask me to marry him?"

Basha: I laugh. "Yes, he will soon."

Leah: "It is about time. I'm not, and he's not, getting any younger."

"True. You must pretend I did not tell you all this, okay?"

"Oh yes. When he finally asks, I will put on a great show of surprise.

He probably thinks I don't know that he's interested in me."

As we continue to finish cleaning, we chat and laugh. Once we finish, I go to my room, get my denim jacket and white silk shawl, join Leah, and head out to the shul. It is the main room in the converted frat house on Piedmont Avenue, where Rabbi Chaim Drizin presides over this Chabad House serving the Berkeley community. It has a huge space that could hold up to 300 people in this main room; it is set up as the shul for the evening services, all properly divided by a wooden mechitza to keep the women separated from the men.

We hear the men in the midst of the service that has been underway while we were cleaning up. It is time to put father's plan into effect. I focus and mutter a glamor spell on the ring. Making it seem to sparkle and draw attention to itself. I take my leave of Leah and head up to the front of the room. I am noticed as I head up that way. I may not be The Rabbi's daughter, but I am A Rabbi's daughter, so my passing will get noticed. I move to get as close as I can to seeing the bimah behind that frustrating barrier that keeps all of us gals hidden from all the men in the room. I finally make my way to the front row, where there are plenty of empty seats, and try to get into the spirit of the holy day by opening my prayerbook and davening.

I notice out of the corner of my eye a gaggle of gals are making their way to me. Things are shaping up according to plan. They sit down, surrounding me, being very obvious about it. They all seem to be staring at me and whispering about me.

Basha: "Can I help you, ladies?" I say in a whisper. Heaven forbid we women should disturb the men while they are praying.

After we get through the holiday greetings, one of the gaggle asks, "So, Shoshana, did Jacob finally grow up and give you that?"

I visually recognize many of these young ladies but honestly do not know their names. I never could relate to them and so never become anything then passing acquaintances.

Basha: "Give me what?" I pretend coyly.

"The ring, of course. Did Jacob give you that?"

Excellent. Magick, at least it is something you can depend on.

Basha: "It is no big deal. It is just a ring."

"Oh, come on, Shoshana, you don't suddenly wear an engagement ring like that. It came from someone. So, tell us, did Jacob give it to you?"

Basha: "No, he did not."

"Didn't he finally ask for your hand?"

Basha: "Yes, he did."

"Nu? So, did you say yes?"

Sigh. My business seems to be everyone's business, just like my father said it would be.

Basha: "No, I did not say yes to Jacob."

"Oh really?"

"Well, well."

"You tossed him back into the pond?"

"So, if the ring is not from Jacob, did your mother make a match for you without your father knowing this?"

"Anyone we know?"

"He must be brilliant."

"Obviously, only the smartest for Shoshana will do."

"I bet he's into the Kabalah, like Shoshana, isn't that right?"

"Actually, no. My mother did not make any match for me. I met someone, and he gave me this ring as a sign of our mutual pledge. You will not know him. He is a Sephardim who lives in the City, and yes, he is knowledgeable about the Kabalah."

"Oh really? Sephardim?"

"Well, that is good news. It leaves Jacob for one of us."

"Mazel Tov, Shoshana."

"He must be good-looking."

"So, what's his name?"

"Do you have a picture of him?"

Basha: "Ah…actually, I do not have any pictures of him, and his name is Lamont."

"His name doesn't sound very Jewish or Spanish."

Basha: "His parents are…not your typical Sephardic Jews." Now there is an understatement if I ever heard one…if not, an outright colossal fib! "Hence the different sort of name. He was named after someone…"

We are shushed by some adult women sitting in earshot of us, I apologize, and we all get quiet. After the service ends and we congregate in another area for the apples, challah, and honey, I am barraged with more questions about Lamont, when, where, and anything else they can get out of me. No one ever seemed to notice me before, but as soon as I sported a ring and thus a match, I became headline news.

Eventually, I pry myself loose from that gaggle and head back to my father's home, avoiding everyone; I do not want to get back into any issues with either Jacob or my father.

LAMONT

I fly off into the night after the services. They were very different from the church services that I've been to with my parents. I guess I need to add learning Hebrew and some Spanish to my growing list of things that I need to do. When I get to bed, I'll spend some time with Basha. My favorite things to do. I wonder if I should tell her about my attending the Sephardic shul? Nah. I think I will keep that a secret at this moment.

BASHA

I am about to get ready for bed when I want to go see mom and tell her about all of this. I tie my house key to my wrist, open the window to my room, turn into an eagle, and fly to our place in the City.

When I get to the alley at the back of the store, turn back to my human form, create some clothes and open the door to go see if mom's back from shul by now. I get upstairs and am surprised that it is all dark in our house. She's not back yet. I wonder why? I get the book off the top of my reading list and read and wait.

*

I look up and glance at the clock. Wow, it is 10:30, and she is not back? Hmm...well, I need to go to sleep. I put the book back on my table, walk downstairs to the alley and fly back to my bedroom at Dad's place. Time to meet Lamont in Dreamland.

Thursday, September 11, 1980

ROSH HASHANAH DAY

BERKELEY—THEN SAN FRANCISCO

BASHA

I get up early, and I want to distract myself. I wonder where mom was last night? I think I will go check up on her. Though I do not know if I want her to know about this fiasco with father and Jacob. I am still too upset to talk about it. I go do the fly-like-an-eagle thing and then go up to our place. I find mom in the kitchen making her morning tea.

Basha: "Hi, Mom!"

Miriam: "Gut Yontif, daughter. What are you doing flying on the holiday? I'm sure there is a section of the Shulchan Aruch that says if you can't drive on the holiday, you can't fly."

Basha: "I would argue that flying under your own power is like walking and thus permitted on the sabbath and on High Holidays."

Miriam: "Hmm...you might be right; it is not like you are doing any 'work-like' action. Okay, I agree."

"I am so glad we settled that issue; I know that all the other human-to-bird-shapeshifters were worried about the outcome on this one."

After we laugh, I tell her the news about dad and about my marriage proposal from Jacob. She found the news about dad interesting, and my encounter with Jacob she found amusing. I do not tell her that dad has asked me to leave and not return. I do not want to get her involved with this; that is between dad and me alone. So, I will just play up the whole Fiddler on the Roof-ish funny bit. All haha, even if it did not end that way.

Basha: "I did not think it was funny at the time!"

Miriam: "I know. Oy. I wish I could have seen the look on your face when he asked you. I bet it was priceless."

"Mom! You are terrible!"

"I am."

"Now, do you have anything to confess this morning?" I want to get her off me and my issues, so I will pry into her being out late.

Miriam: "Nu? So, what could I possibly have to confess?"

Basha: "Do not be coy with me. Now admit you were out past your usual bedtime last night."

"Were you checking up on me now? Are you suddenly the mother and I the wayward daughter?"

"Well, you were out late; I was at the house till 10:30, and you still had not come home. So, where were you, and when did you come home?"

"Oh…I was just home late, that's all."

"Did you get into mischief?"

"Ha! No such thing. Just having too much wine and talking. I lost track of time."

"Oh really? So, who was this man that had you drinking the night away?"

"It was Mr. Adler, if you must know. He is a member of the board at the temple. His wife died from an illness a short while ago. I was merely consoling him. No mischief was indulged in. Just doing a bit of a mitzvah."

"I see."

"And actually, not so much wine. More schmoozing, or should I say listening. Commiserating. And if I need to check in with you, I will probably be out late again this evening. So don't expect to find me home early if you pop back in."

Basha: "Well, well…"

Miriam: "Don't you give me that tone, young lady," Mom says in a mock-serious tone. "I could inquire about you and a certain young man. Your father would plotz[86] if he found that Lamont was a Gentile."

Basha: "Ha! I am sure we both might not stand up to father's scrutiny."

Miriam: "Oh? Have you been doing anything I should worry about with sweet innocent young Gentile Lamont?"

"I think I will take the Fifth on that one…"

"Yes. I imagine that is a good idea. Your father certainly might not appreciate his daughter dating a Gentile vampire."

We both burst out laughing at the absurdity of that statement, with mutterings concerning vampires having to be Gentiles since drinking blood is not kosher, and a Jewish vampire would be an oxymoron. When we calm down, I return to my interrogation of my mom.

Basha: "So, you will be out carousing late tonight?"

Miriam: "Not carousing, conversing! How much carousing have you been doing lately? Or are you taking the fifth on that question as well?

"Ahh…did I forget to mention that the color of your dress complements your eyes?"

"Ha! Yes, you better change the subject!"

We both start to laugh.

"Now, as the mother in this house, I can tell you to eat! I can make you some breakfast."

"I need to get back to Dad's place before they wonder where I am."

"Well, hurry off then. Go fly back as some kind of bird."

"Not just a bird, I become a California Golden Eagle."'

"That's nice, dear. You've grown up to become a native species. How ecological of you," she says and still keeps a straight face. One of the many skills that must come with maturity.

*

I sneak back in with no one noticing. This is amazing since it is not every day an eagle flies into someone's house.

Anyway. I get dressed and come downstairs to only find Leah; the men folk have already eaten and gone off to shul. Leah offers to make me breakfast, and I say thanks. I eat, help her clean up, go to my room, and put the last of my father's plans into action.

I pack up my bags, go downstairs, mount my bike and drive off. This was not how I imagined spending the holidays. Foolish Jacob, why did he have to get such a crush on me? Why could he not speak to me? Instead, he pretended like he lived in the old country and only talked to father. And then

[86] Plotz a Yiddish word meaning to burst, to explode, to be infuriated.

my father did not have enough respect for me to talk to me about any of this either! Holy Goddess, what a disaster! Jacob and my father both acted like we were living in a Scholem Aleichem story, just more tragedy than comedy. And now my father is mad at me? He is the one who caused all his own problems by telling his Rabbi that I would marry Jacob. All of this could have been avoided, and now because of his foolishness, he is embarrassed? It is not fair. Yes, I was already considering the idea that I did not want to attend these overly traditional services anymore either. I was getting fed up with having to hide behind that wall separating men from women. But in the end, I did not get to choose to continue attending or not. I was just 'punished' by him by being told to leave. I do not like that at all! I am so furious at him for treating me like some child. He is the one who acted like a child! Hell, I am angry and hurt.

Well, this ruins my holiday, that is for sure. Okay, Basha, where do you go now? Home? Well, mom will be at services, so I could go there, and she would not be the wiser, but I don't feel like just sitting around in my room and sulking. I wonder if I can get back in time to attend some classes today? Since the whole idea of attending service has left me with this bad taste in my mouth.

*

SAN FRANCISCO
LAMONT

I wake up feeling like I didn't get enough sleep last night. Damn! I can't recall my dreams...yet again! What is going on with that? I create a bathrobe and head into the kitchen to pretend to have some cereal and toast. Then wash the not really dirty dishes, so it seems like I made breakfast. Then I go off to the bathroom to shower and get ready. I need to be at the synagogue for morning services. When I get out of the shower, I can hear my mom in the kitchen as she makes coffee. I step into the kitchen wearing my conjured suit, white shirt, and scarlet tie.

Lamont: "Hi, mom."

Helen: "You look nice. Why so dressed up for school? And, shall I make you breakfast? You should eat something."

Lamont: "Thanks mom, but I already ate. But I wouldn't turn down a cup of tea."

Helen: "And why are you so well dressed?" Mom asks as she makes me some Constant Comment tea and adds some honey. The spicy smell of citrus smells so refreshing.

"Well...I was planning on going to some services today.'

"Oh? And not to school? How much school were you planning to miss out on that you didn't tell your parents about?"

(Oops. Now I've done it!) "Ahh...for most of the day, they are long services."

"Services? What services? Where are you going, Lamont?"

"Ahh... well..."

"Speak up, young man. I didn't hear your answer."

"Well, they are religious services. And it's getting kind of late..."

"Hold on. No services are going on in our church at this time. So, what religion are you referring to?"

Lamont: "Well, they are Jewish services, part of the High Holiday services."

Helen: "You don't even regularly attend our church services anymore. What is going on here?"

"I'm interested."

"Oh, and you're saying you are not interested in attending our church anymore?"

"Well..."

"Is this Basha's doing? Is she pressuring you to attend these services?"

"No. Not really. She doesn't even know I have been doing this."

"How long has this been going on?'

"A bit. I started attending Friday night and Saturday morning services a little while ago."

"Oh, and that *religion* interests you, but our own church does not? Are you trying to tell me something? Or is this just some intellectual curiosity of yours? Like studying that Aristotle and Plato."

"Sort of..."

"I know you're serious about Basha. Is that why you're interested in her Jewish services?'

"Ahh, kind of."

"I was hoping that you would persuade her to convert. I'm not pleased to hear it will be the other way around."

Lamont: "I'm sorry."

Helen: "You should be. You were baptized in the name of our Lord. Did you forget what you learned about your faith at Sunday school?'

"No, I haven't forgotten. It's just that I don't think of God as Jesus to tell you the truth. Our God is the same as the Jewish people's, is he not? A God of love, is he not? Can he not love his first children? It just doesn't seem right that God requires us to believe that any one religion owns God. Does that really make sense?"

"Now, you want to debate theology with me? I don't know about this. I do like Basha; I really do. But this?"

"Her father is a rabbi; it is kind of expected that she would marry a good Jewish boy."

"And you think you need to be this good Jewish boy, is that it?"

"Well...I guess so."

"Hmm. I am disappointed, I have to tell you. I was hoping to see you get married in our church one day. Well, for now, we will not say a word about any of this to your father. So, you will have to promise me that you will not tell him about this. Or else there will be real trouble. I am serious. Not a single word to him. No mistakes. Do you understand?'

Lamont: "Yes, mom. I understand."

Helen: "And find me some small book about this Jewish religion. I want to know something about what you are learning over there. I'm sure you know plenty of good books. You are always finding those."

"I will, mom."

"Okay then. Now, what about dinner?"

"I'll eat there; they have a community meal laid out afterward. I can ask the rabbi questions if I attend that meal. I need to learn things."

"Oh...okay. I will tell your father you are on a date with Miss Basha. Now tell me about these services."

I explain Rosh Hashanah's significance to Mom as we sip our coffee and tea. She listens but shakes her head about all of this and reminds me to find a book for her. When I'm done with my tea, I give mom a kiss and head out the door. I look around to make sure that I'm not seen. Then I transform into a raven and fly toward the Magen David synagogue.

Friday, September 12, 1980

SAN FRANCISCO

BASHA

Lamont was a bit needier than usual last night. I think he fed on me for longer because of it. I cannot complain too much…it feels so good. I take the pillowcase and the towel I placed under it to catch the dripping blood and bring it into the bathroom to try and soak out the blood. I once more feel the need to eat a big breakfast to replenish the energy levels that Lamont drains out of me.

I just manage to get out the door in time to arrive in a timely manner at SF State. I pull up to park, and as I do, another cyclist pulls up as well.

It is Cora.

Cora: "Hi, Basha! Glad we seem to be in synch. May I join you?"

Basha: "Of course."

We chat about the past assignments, and then I decide to ask her about her pentacle necklace that I now realize she always wears. "Cora, I was wondering about your necklace. Is it a fashion statement, or is there something more to it?"

Cora: "Meaning?" She says with a bit of wariness.

Basha: "Well, I mean, are you into Wicca? It is okay if you are; since I am as well to tell you the truth."

"Really?" Cora says with considerable relief. "Well, that is a nice bit of synchronicity. Can I let you in on a secret?"

"Of course. I will not tell a soul."

"I consider myself a witch."

"Really? That is interesting. I guess you could say the same about me."

"Wow! I knew that there was something special about you. Something else we share in common then. Hey, I just found this out. Did you know these classes are offered at a bookstore in the Haight? My friends who are part of our Circle told me about them. We all agreed to sign up for them. I wondered if you would be interested in taking them as well?"

"Is it a class in guided imagery and lucid dreaming?"

"Yeah. That's the one. Did you sign up for it also?"

"Actually, no."

"Oh," Cora says with a great deal of disappointment.

"Truth be told, I will be the teacher."

"Holy Crow! Really? You're not pulling my leg?"

"Girl scouts honor."

"Just to make sure we are on the same page. The ones I'm talking about are held at the Gift of the Goddess bookstore. Is that really your class?"

"Yup. Mom owns the store."

"That's so cool! Then the gang and I will see you there. I always wanted to be the teacher's pet. We must talk more about all this after our American Lit class. I want to hear all about this!"

*

After class Cora just about drags me to Sonestown mall, we sit in a coffee shop, and she stares directly into my eyes with earnest and intense intent.

Cora: "My friends and I," Cora explains excitedly, "came to the craft through books. Magic was hinted at in Marion Zimmer Bradley's Darkover series, and Samuel Delaney's novel Nova was all about this divination tool called the Tarot. Then we found the magical feminist novels *The Sea Goddess* and *Moon Magic* of Dion Fortune, which led to her magic and Qabalah books. We struck gold with Starhawk's *The Spiral Dance* and Margot Adler's *Drawing Down the Moon*! From then on, we were hooked. Well, so how did you come to study Wicca?"

Basha: "Well…" I sip slowly, rapidly mulling over how much of the truth to tell and in what form. "My mom introduced me to it once she realized I had an aptitude."

"Oh really? Your mom? Did your dad know about this? And how old were you at the time? How did it all start? How about your grandmother? Was she a part of this as well? Is this a multi-generational thing passed down from mother to daughter?"

Basha: "Whoa, slow down. (How do I begin this? I never had considered telling any about this. Well, as I keep telling others…Begin at the beginning…) For me, it all started with dreams. From age two, my mom encouraged me to remember my dreams, which I could do easily. Oh, and my dad didn't know about any of this. It was our secret. I was around age three when she started playing this game which I later realized taught me how to lucid dream."

Cora: "That's what the class is about, right? This lucid dream thing?"

"Correct."

"What is that?"

I explain.

"You can do that? Wow. So your mom, can she do this lucid dreaming? Is that why she taught you?"

"Yes. That is correct."

"What about your grandmother? Was this a thing passed down mother to daughter?"

"No. It all started with my mom. My Grandmother's only magical gift is making great-tasting treats and pastry."

"Oh. Okay. Still, that's so cool that you were introduced to all this by your mom. My parents were just ordinary good Christians. My mom and Dad are Calvinists. They both dished out a heavy dose of guilt and predestination. I couldn't take it, so I quickly rebelled from their heavy hand of holier than thou God. Wow, this is so serendipious to meet you, and you're going to teach this lucid dreaming thing. How does that connect with magick?"

Basha: (How should I put this?) "It is a way to connect more deeply to magick spell work. Trance and dreaming deepen the connection to all kinds of magick."

Cora: "Can anyone lucid dream?"

"Hypothetically, yes. We all dream; it is just a matter of paying attention to them and striving to recall them. That is the first step. It is sort of like doing guided meditations. Anyway, around nine, I had the first of my special lucid dreams, and that is when my mom introduced me to Wicca and taught me The Craft. After that, I took many classes and have been in circles from then on."

"I keep saying this, but it is just so amazing. All my friends came at this through varying degrees of rebellion against the established churches we grew up with. We all kept it hidden from our parents and everyone else. We all met in High School. Before that, we each had been just solo practitioners. Then we found each other. We started to hang out and meet together. When we learned that Reclaiming organization was a thing here in San Francisco, they had public rituals and some magick classes that we all started to attend."

Basha: "I attended a few of their classes as well."

Cora: "Really?" Cora says, puzzled. "We've been taking all that they offered. There weren't many of us, so I clearly recall everyone who attended. And I never saw you at any of them. So, what gives?"

"Ahh. Yes, I only attended the special classes offered very late at night. My mom knew about them and got me into them."

"Really? I never heard of any other classes being offered at other times."

"Well…it is a bit of a secretive thing. But, who knows, if this lucid dreaming thing connects with you, you might just find your way to those classes."

I steer Cora away from the topic of my attending classes – since I did so only in Dreamland. We chat for a while. I find out she lives with her circle mates, Jezebel, Leilani, and Ivy. We talked more about Sci-Fi and Fantasy novels we both liked and enjoyed. Finally, it is getting late, and I need to get home and do some homework. She insists on giving me a hug as we leave. I think I made a new friend.

I wonder if Lamont wants to get together for dinner tonight? I smile wickedly as I think about letting him choose whether he wants to dine on me before I eat or after.

LAMONT

I'm so glad Basha called and asked me out to dinner. That makes not eating with my parents seem normal. I get to pretend I'm just a typical son going out on a date with his girlfriend. Lying to them is getting to be my new normal. I don't like this but prefer that to outright mind wiping with my vampire abilities. The weekends are easier to avoid eating with them since I claim I'm going out with Basha. The difficulties come during the weekday evenings. I don't know how long I can keep this up. But, then again, what choice do I have? It's not like being turned into a vampire is some kind of phase I'm going through.

Then there is my other secret. I will either have to lie to Basha about my attending services at Magain David on Friday and Saturday mornings or tell her about it. I want to see her tonight and attend services, so Lamont, you just can't get up after dinner and say, excuse me, but I got to leave you and go to this secret meeting. That's not going to fly. So, there it is. I have to tell her about wanting to attend services. Hey, I can ask her to join me! I wonder if I can avoid telling her about my motives concerning conversion? I did want to keep that a surprise. Not sure if I can actually do that, now that I think about it. Well, keeping secrets is not the best thing to do in a healthy relationship, right?

I transform into a raven and head to her room above the bookstore. I float just above the wooden cell and look in. I hope she notices me and lets me in. Basha is ravishing as usual in her red cowgirl boots, red leather mini-skirt, pale yellow silk top with a low cut neckline, and a crimson heart attached to her velvet choker, which rests on her cleavage. Her smile is dazzling as she spots me, and I start doing the tap-tap, tapping thing.

BASHA

I quickly open the window, and then Lamont appears all formal in his black and white high tops, black jeans, white shirt with scarlet tie, a charcoal straight bottom vest, a black sport coat with gray pinstripes, and his charcoal RAF coat.

Basha: "You are looking very debonair this evening. Are you taking your girlfriend somewhere fancy after dining?"

Lamont: "Well…to confess, I was. I thought about going somewhere after at least one of us dine."

"Oh? Where might this be that requires you to be all white shirt and tie formal?"

Lamont touches his head, and a gray felt kippah appears on his head. Not the usual flat round ones, but a more hat-like one.

Lamont: "How is this for a hint?"

"Hmm…head covering brings to mind Shabbos services, though that style is new to me. Is this your idea of a hot date?"

"Kind of. It is Shabbos…"

"Well, yes, but…"

"Let's head down to that Italian restaurant on Irving, and I'll explain."

*

While Lamont sips his minestrone soup, I work on a slice of my pizza with mushrooms, dried tomatoes, and chopped garlic.

Lamont: "I don't know what the deal is with vampires hating garlic," I watch Lamont breathe deep the heady fragrance of the fresh-cut garlic. "I love that scent."

"Hey…Just get one thing clear, buster. I am not going to use it as my latest perfume choice."

"That would be kind of hot…"

"You are joking?"

"Yeah…sort of. You don't know how wonderful you smell…the spicy sweetness of cinnamon mixed with the tartness of the garlic…oh my, such a sweet and savory meal…"

Basha: 'Now behave yourself in public, my sweet Italian vampire. A good girl does not allow her date to bite her in public. So, keep the fangs in.'

Lamont: "Ahh, you're no fun."

"Now, what is with that head covering."

"It is a Sephardic Kippah."

"Broadening your cultural horizons, all of a sudden. And why the knowledge and why are you wearing that?"

"Well, it is appropriate to wear to services tonight if you are interested in going with me."

"Since when have you become all orthodox? And Sephardic?"

"Hey, why not? My ancestors were from Spain."

"And you know this, for a certainty, how?"

"From Tezcat. She always told me that is why she chose me. My ancestry reaches back to the soldiers who were with Cortez."

Basha: "And we can believe this?"

Lamont: "That fact, most certainly. Now the Sephardic synagogue, Magain David, is on 4th and Geary. I thought I should learn more about Judaism since I'm dating a nice and hot Jewish girl."

"You are very strange, you know that Lamont? You are serious about this Jewish thing? Since when?"

He explains how he had attended High Holiday services there.

Basha: "Whoa. Really? You are serious about this, then. Okay, Lamont, I will be your good little Jewish girl, and you can take me to services. I will have to adjust my attire. I cannot be the good little girl in this outfit. I am showing way too much skin."

Lamont: "Darn!"

"Hey, you know the saying; you cannot have your cake and eat it too."

"Well, I was hoping to eat a bit of that cake after services at your room..."

Basha: "Oh, you were, were you? And here I thought you wanted me to be a good girl..."

Lamont: "I won't answer that one. Now, eat up, and let's talk about the temple renovations. I was reading some interesting things in the *Tao Te Ching* that might fit the primal cosmic forces for remaking the Outer Gods."

"Okay, I will eat while you pontificate."

"Well, Lao Tzu, the attributed author of the text, presents a simple creation account that involves the Tao and the pair Yin and Yang. For example. In the opening lines of chapter 42, '*Tao produced the One. The One produced the two. The two produced the three. And the three produced the ten thousand things. The ten thousand things carry the yin and embrace the yang, and through the blending of the material forces they achieve harmony.*[87]'

"Okay, that seems to dovetail nicely with Kabbalah. Both are not really talking about physical creation, like the Big Bang. But instead, a metaphysical account of creation as humanity comes to understand existence and the Powers-That-Be. Ayn Sof, or here, the Tao, as in Infinite source, begins to make itself known. It coalesces into a singular that can be comprehended. It then creates the primal duality that is found in all things."

Lamont: "Sort of a Hegelian thing of a thesis, antithesis, and synthesis. Though Hegel seems more Aristotelian in his oppositional duality that gets harmonized. So, I don't think he is a non-dualist like the Taoists. Anyway, from here, we get the infinite multitude of differentiation. The Chinese phrase is the 'ten thousand things'. Everything that carries within it the basic building blocks as the primal complementary nature of Yin and Yang. That reminds me a little of what you told me about the Sefiroth, with Keter being a form of Tao out of which comes Hockmah, the masculine principle, and Binah as the feminine principle."

[87] *The Way of Lao Tzu* [*Tao te Ching*] translated by Wing-Tsit Chan, The Bobbs-Merrill Company, Inc., 1963. Chapter 42.

Basha: "Yes. In the Kabbalah, rabbis are doing their usual thing – reconciling paradox. For the Kabbalistic rabbis, Ayn Sof created the Sefiroth, with those three Sefrahs you mentioned being the primal first grouping. Then, out of Binah came the rest of the remaining sefirahs and, finally, the physical universe. So, it goes from infinite unity to one to two, then seven, and lastly to the multitude of existence."

Lamont: "A bit more complicated than the Taoists. For the Taoists, existence was simply a natural outcome of creative processes. Their texts were satisfied with out of basic duality the ten thousand things could come forth. No need for further details, and for the record, I'm always amazed at how you can eat and talk without looking embarrassing."

Basha: "Not like you. You used to talk with your mouth full of half-chewed food showing."

Lamont: "At least now I can elegantly sip," Lamont says, sticking his pinkie out as he brings his soupspoon to his mouth.

"Cute. I like it; very sophisticated. Are you done with the silly commentary? Can we get back to being serious?"

"I was being serious…"

"Of course, you were, my silly vampire."

"So, my serious favorite kabbalist, why is their Sefirot so complicated?"

Basha: "That is because the rabbis had to reconcile their cosmology to verses in the TaNaK. One group of names came from the listing of descriptive terms for divine power from First Chronicles 29: 11: *'Yours, LORD, are greatness-Gedulah, might-Gevurah, splendor-Tiferet, triumph-Netzach, and majesty-Hod, for all that is in heaven and earth is yours, yours is the Kingdom-Malkuth O' Lord and you are exalted as a head above all.'* That gave them the central five, as well as the last one.

As for the others, the uppermost sefirahs of Hockmah / wisdom, Binah / understanding, and Da'at / Knowledge are derived from the following verses. *Exodus* 31:3 *'and I have filled him with the spirit of God, in wisdom, and in Understanding, and in Knowledge.'* Again, from *Proverbs* 3:19 & 20 *'The Lord by wisdom founded the earth; By understanding He established the heavens. By His Knowledge the depths were broken up.'* Lastly, *Proverbs* 24:3 & 4: *'Through wisdom is a house built, And by understanding it is established; And by knowledge are the chambers filled.'*

The *Sefer Yetzirah* says there can be only ten, that number is a perfect unit. This means that sometimes Da'at is left out of the group. So now, we have labels for two of the upper sefirahs; they are Wisdom and Understanding, but not the uppermost sefirah. The uppermost sefirah was named *Keter,* the Hebrew word for crown. Keter is directly mentioned only a few times in the *TaNaK.* There are three instances of it in the book of *Esther.* One reference notes that a crown is placed on the head, just as the sefirah Keter is placed on the head of the rest of the Sefiroth. This image is described in verse *Esther* 6:8 *'and on whose head a crown-Keter royal is placed.'* But more likely, the appearance of the word in Proverbs was the source of inspiration for using the word Keter-Crown to be a label for one of the sefirahs on the Sefiroth. As in *Proverbs* 14:18, *'The thoughtless come into possession of folly but the prudent are crowned with knowledge.'* Now are only missing one more. That is Yesod-Foundation. It comes out of Proverbs 10:25, *'The righteous is an everlasting foundation'*. This gets commented in the *Talmud* in tractate *Chagigah* 12b that *'Rabbi Elazar ben Shammua says: The earth rests on one pillar and a righteous person is its name, as it is stated: "But a righteous person is the foundation of the world[88]"* Which makes it the ninth sefirah above Malkuth and which all the eight pour down into."

Lamont: "And that is how we get all the names? They are all traceable to terms for divine attributes and powers in the Bible. For the Taoists, there was perhaps only the I Ching to look to for the terms Yin and Yang, and they didn't treat the text as sacred and therefore weren't compelled to strictly refer to the text. Hence the simplicity of their system."

Basha: "Presumably correct. Also, it seems creation by the Tao was not a deliberate act by a self-aware deity, correct?"

"Correct. The Tao, yin, and yang are not personalities, just natural forces like electrons, neutrons, and protons. Just the stuff of matter and energy."

"For the Kabbalists, creation was an intentional act with purpose and direction, done by a self-aware consciousness."

"So, how does this match up with the Biblical description of God? The attributes are all out of the Bible, but there is no hint of this systematic formality, correct?"

Basha: "Correct. The idea of the Kabbalistic structure of the divine seems to have been influenced by contact with Plotinus's work, the Enneads, with its notion of the One that is untouchable and unchanging by human conception and thus has to emanate into a form that humans can comprehend. For example, there is an interesting commentary on the opening line of Genesis from the Zohar, book 1 verse 15a that treats the first three words of the first verse in Genesis 'Bereshith bara Elohim' with a meaning other than

[88] https://www.sefaria.org/Chagigah.12b.2?lang=bi&with=all&lang2=en

the usual, 'In the beginning God created…" But rather reads the text to mean that 'At the time of the beginning God aka Elohim, was created."

"Wait a minute. Elohim isn't that the plural form of the Hebrew generic word for El-God?'

"Gold star for Lamont, and…"

"That means it could be read as 'At the time of the beginning gods were created."

"Correct. The overall idea is that Ayn Sof first had to create itself into a form that humans could comprehend and identify with. The very last stage of that process was the creation of the Biblical persona of God. Who is an identifiable and understandable god for humans then, after this process was completed, the world itself was created. That's what the process of emanation is about. "

Lamont: "It all is a far cry from the Lovecraftian horror show he had made of the Outer Gods."

Basha: "If we pull this off, we will be not just remaking a building but wrapping those beings up in a whole new theology and transforming their identities."

"Reforming them into something a lot more tolerable."

"Will they let us do this?"

"We Dreamers make what we will of Dreamland, so I don't think they can stop us. If by they you mean the Outer Gods. Although if there are any worshipers of the Outer Gods in Dreamland, what we do will piss them off."

"Do you think the Outer Gods or their worshipers will try to stop us? If not overtly, perhaps, but covertly?"

"Look, if we do this and empower Tezcat, he will give the power to his guardian Priests, and they won't let any riff-raff in to harm our precious Sanctuary."

"I guess. Still, I somehow think that they will not go gently into our good night. They may do a Dylan Thomas on us and rage, rage against the dying of their light.[89]"

"Well, we just need to get enough collective power to pull off this magick spell."

"I think we may need to directly approach Tezcatlipoca to lend us the real power to do such a vast spell."

"I think he will agree. We can bribe him with blood and worship. That is what a God wants and needs."

---

[89] Paraphrasing Dylan Thomas's poem *Do Not Go Gentle into that Good Night*, first published in the journal *Botteghe Oscure* in 1951

"True. And speaking of deities. We need to pay this bill and get going if we are to make it to the shul on time."

*

LATER THAT EVENING
BASHA'S BEDROOM

I lead Lamont by the hand into my bedroom; I notice that mom's not here, which might be for the better. I think she is out keeping Mr. Adler's company. Lamont's eyes are bright, intense, and very focused. I light a bunch of candles I had laid out earlier with a flick of my wrist.

Basha: "Keep your shirt on, kiddo," I say as he wraps his body tight around mine and kisses and nibbles on my ears. "I mean that literally. Just because we have Dream garments does not mean we can just make them go poof. Let us savor the slow seduction of undressing like normal people."

Lamont: "Okay, my sweet. I can do that," Lamont says as he reaches behind me and slowly unzips my dress. "Like this…"

"Oh yes..."

Soon we have stripped ourselves down to undergarments, Lamont has a pair of gray skimpy bikini briefs, and me in crimson bra, panties, and a black garter belt to hold up my black nylons. A treat I had conjured up for my lingerie-fixated boyfriend. All our outer garments had vanished like smoke as we had stripped them off each other.

Basha: "Now…my eager little vampire, lay me out on that burgundy terry cloth blanket I laid on my bed. It's very practical. Soft and comfy to the skin and very washable to absorb the blood…"

Lamont sweeps me up and carries me onto the bed. I am no problem for someone with vampire strength. The time for words has passed, and now it's all hot hands and mouths doing all the passionate talking.

I do not recall when I finally felt his fangs pierce my skin and feel my blood oozing out. He takes me into him as he drinks me down and feeds on my love and passion.

The room fades…

WELL OF DREAMS

…and I feel we are completely immersed in the hot ebony waters. I feel that what little garments we had on us dissolve in the heat and darkness of the moment. We are one…hot wet fire...

SAN FRANCISCO

BASHA'S BEDROOM

Some unknown time passes, and I feel myself back on my bed, clad in bra and panties. I feel against my neck the wetness from my not yet fully dried blood. Lamont's bright blue eyes are grinning wolfishly and contently at me.

Basha: "Okay, I take it you have eaten. Now, I think it is enough with the hugs and kisses; we have work to do. Let us blow this pop stand and see if we can enlist some help to do a makeover on Tezcatlipoca's temple."

Lamont: "Agreed, my sweet princess."

CITY OF ATLANTIS
LILITH'S TEMPLE OF THE MOON

We arrive at the Queen's temple and discover that Sarah and Rebecca were just finishing up a ritual with their coven.

Basha: "You should stay here a minute, Lamont. They might be skyclad and not appreciate the intrusion of a male. If that is the case, I will call when they are dressed for visitors."

A few moments later, I call Lamont in to join us. Once inside the hall, Lamont finds all of the twelve women of the coven are now clothed in white Empire-style dresses. Each dress has a fitted bodice ending just below the bust, giving it a high-waisted appearance, and a gathered skirt is long and loosely fitting but skims their bodies.

Sarah: "Oh no. Here comes trouble."

Lamont: "Is that any way to greet an old student?"

Rebecca: "Hi Lamont. I love the new outfit. Sarah mentioned it."

Sarah: "L'shanah Tovah Lamont. May you be inscribed and sealed in the Book of Life for a good year."

Lamont: "And may you both be sealed for good in the Book of Life as well."

Basha: "So, we are so glad to find you here. We were wondering if we could ask you and your coven to help us with a project this evening."

Sarah: "I was right about you two bringing trouble in your wake. What is it this time? Rescuing a fair prince from a dragon?"

Basha: "No, nothing so challenging. We have been asked to rededicate a temple, and we need help in this."

Sarah: "Which temple? And who asked you? I don't recall any unused temple in this city?"

Basha: "The temple is the one in the center of the city. The great pyramid structure dedicated at one time to the Outer Gods."

Sarah: "Ha! You must be joking. Dealing with dragons sounds

safer." Who commissioned this project?"

Lamont: "Actually, the Goddess of Dreams and Dreamland herself asked us to take up this task."

Sarah: "There is no Goddess of Dreams. As far as I know. Most consider Morpheus as the God of Dreams. How does all this connect to the long-forgotten Outer Gods?"

Lamont: "Well, we met one of the Outer Gods, and she told me who she was and how she came to create this realm."

Sarah: "You're not making any sense, Lamont. You've jumbled everything up. Start from the beginning if you want us to understand you."

Basha: "Okay. It is like this..."

So, Lamont and I explain all we have recently discovered about the Outer Gods and Tezcatlipoca.

Rebecca: "And you believe this trickster god? Why?"

We explain the hows and whys behind Tezcatlipoca's creation of Dreamland and her Prometheus-like results from her grandma, the supreme Outer Goddess, as she claims to be.

Basha: "We need to re-establish the worship at the temple and elsewhere to give power back to the guardian to protect this realm from more harm in the future. That is why we want to rededicate the temple. Since Lamont knows this Outer God as a female deity by the name of Tezcatlipoca. That is who and in whose name we will dedicate the temple. We will dedicate it to Smoking Mirror, the trickster Goddess of Dreams."

Sarah: "And what about those blood sacrifices?"

Basha: "All is required is blood freely given. The amount is not specified. A pinprick is all we ask and all that is needed, similar to what we did for the gate spell."

Rebecca: "Hmm. The intent is more important than the volume."

Basha: "Correct. From what Lamont has figured out, we can affect the persona of a deity by how we relate to them; thus, if we worship Smoking Mirror as the guardian and creator of Dreamland, then she will be more apt to act like this. "

Sarah: "That might be, but we are not the only ones worshiping this Outer God, are we?"

Lamont: "Probably not. But any way you want to slice this one. We need to do this to ensure that the guardians who stand between the two realms have the power to prevent those with evil intent from getting into this realm. This is the only way to do that."

Sarah: "Okay. You're right on that point. Give us a while to come to a consensus on our own?"

We step outside the chamber and wait. We quietly and discretely make out. Before we get into too much trouble, I hear Sarah aheming loudly. As this process of consensus goes, it was rather quickly decided

Sarah: "I hope we interrupted something. Now, it is all okay; we came to an agreement."

Rebecca: "When will we need to do this ritual?"

Basha: "How about Sunday? For now, shall we find a place to work out the details?"

Sarah: "Works for us."

Basha: 'Lamont, while we girls work out the details of this magick thing, could you go talk with Tezcatlipoca about our plans?'

Lamont: 'Sure.' "I bid you adieu, ladies."

Then Lamont exits in a puff of gray smoke.

LAMONT

I make my way up the stairs and down the torch-lit halls toward Tezcat's throne room. My vampire senses can smell the ancient blood that has soaked these halls. Her throne is empty on the dais that sits upon the jaguar skins.

Lamont: "Oh, Tezcat! I have some interesting news to tell you."

I extend my nail on my right index finger and cut into the palm of my left hand. I squeeze a few drops of rich hot blood on the floor before her dais. "Blood, freely given, Tezcat! Hot and tasty, just as you like it! Come to me, Tezcat! Your beloved heart has news."

Greetings, my Dear Heart! You do us honor.

Lamont: "Hail Tezcat, Smoking Mirror, Guardian and creator of Sanctuary! Glad you can make it. Basha and I are working on not just remodeling this room, but we are thinking of redoing the whole temple complex."

My, my, aren't you two ambitious. Tell me more...

I explain our ideas and plans, and Tezcat laughs wickedly and echoes throughout the halls.

This will be so grand a thing. May you do this, may the heavens rip open, the earth rend apart. Much glory and honor would you bring to the land.

"You approve then?"

Oh yes. I did not intend to build this temple for the rest of my kinfolk. It was only when I was made to wear a rope jacket, hidden in the corner and the dark by my kin, when I was brought low. They killed me and imprisoned me, and scratched out my name. Then they made this place to declare that they were to get their rightful honor and respect.

They helped create the creature called Fear, which was let loose in this land. Your plans would be as if you encased them in a rope jacket. It is dangerous but fitting.

"Dangerous? How?"

To do as you say will bind them here in your weaving. It will rise like smoke and ashes to their jaguar mats. You will transform them even as you do this building.

"Will that truly change them?"

To an extent. Gods come to be known as they are conceived, and they end up taking on that form. But know this, in the world of the Waking, there are many who even now offer smoke and blood to them in the name of their old names that Lovecraft called them by.

"Those names and forms such as Lovecraft wrote about?"

Yes, those and more. It was correct and right for you to see them as my children, the Aztecs, saw them. True to their nature is that shape and names.

"So, if we do this, we will only affect how they are here in Dreamland?"

If you were the only ones to honor them, then so it would be. But there are others who tread these lands. Brought here by my Grandmother to dishonor my efforts. The Nephilim came to Dream and hold court. But someday, they will be rooted out and pulled up like weeds in my garden.

"You are saying that Kaliya is not the only Nephilim here?"

That is so.

"Hmm. Are you not advising us against our plan?"

I am saying go forward. It is time I was recognized and that I am not alone. It is time to boldly go in front of the jaguar mat and declare that this is ours. Hiding will not serve us. A time for boldness and the rising sun has come.

"Okay then."

However, my Dear Heart, you will need my assistance to complete such a bold task.

"What do you mean?"

I shall tell you what needs to be done...

Sunday, September 14, 1980

SAN FRANCISCO

LAMONT

After catching up with all my homework, I need to stretch my legs. I decide to check in with Mr. Wells. I hadn't spoken to him since I got out of the hospital. I wonder if he even knew I was in there? I transform into a crow and fly over the city near his store and then slip into a side street, and when I see no one looking, I take on my human attire, my RAF coat and all. I step into the store and try to act nonchalantly. Just in case he didn't know about any of my prior issues, such as almost dying these last few days.

Mr. Wells: "Hey, Lamont!" He calls out as he finishes with a customer. "How are you doing?"

Lamont: "I'm doing fine. Never felt better."

"I heard some odd things. Were you really in the hospital?"

"Yeah, I was. But it's nothing. Heat exhaustion. Silly me. I'm not all that used to being outdoors, I guess."

"Ahh, too much solitary reading indoors. Though, I must say you are looking good. More alive and confident."

"I did get to finish that Jaynes book you recommended. Most interesting."

"Well, now you know. The truth will set you free, as they say. Well, are you convinced by his arguments? Do you accept that all that talk of talking to God is just the result of your bicameral mind chattering? The troubles caused by lacking a cultural context to understand those inner voices?"

"It does seem so odd to think that some people claim to talk to Gods."

It is even worse when they seek and pester you until they get your attention!

Mr. Wells: "Yes, those poor fools. They just don't really know what's happening and are haunted by things they can't explain. It brings to mind Arthur C. Clarke's 3 laws."

"As in, 1. *When a distinguished but elderly scientist states that something is possible, he is almost certainly right. When he states that something is impossible, he is very probably wrong. 2. The only way of discovering the limits of the possible is to venture a little way past them into the impossible. 3. Any sufficiently advanced technology is indistinguishable from magic.*[90] Your point being?"

"Well, perhaps Jaynes does explain where the Gods of humanity come from. But there could be beings out there who had made contact…"

"Oh, come on, Lamont. You're not seriously telling me you are buying that Erich Von Daniken nonsense? Did you know that all that junk he wrote was just rehashed ideas of that hack pulp writer Lovecraft[91]?"

"Really?"

"Yeah, I have that copy of *Skeptic* magazine in the back somewhere.

---

[90] Arthur C. Clarke's 1973 revision of *Profiles of the Future*, at the end of the essay "Hazards of Prophecy: The Failure of Imagination".

[91] *Charioteer of the Gods* by Jason Colavito, originally published in *Skeptic* 10.4 (2004)

The upshot is that this nonsense of Earth being visited by ancient aliens who were thought to be gods came out of Lovecraft's *At the Mountain of Madness* and *Shadow Out of Time*."

Lamont: "Well, will wonders never cease? Should I rush out and read them so I can learn the true history of our planet?"

Mr. Wells: "Oh yeah. They are required reading for anyone who claims to be a true seeker of arcane knowledge and wisdom," Mr. Wells says with all the sarcasm he can muster. "Yup, you need to get those as well as renewing your copy of *Fortean Times* and the *National Enquirer*."

"It is a good thing we talked. I almost let my subscriptions lapse."

"Ha Ha, kid! Now, truthfully, I was worried a bit for you. I'm glad to see you're alright."

"Yup, fit as a fiddle." Glad I could sidetrack this conversation so nicely. I don't think I want to confess to Mr. Wells that I've actually been talking to Gods and ancient aliens.

"Okay then. Stay out of trouble, you hear?"

"Trouble? Me? We are not even on speaking terms. So, you don't have to worry. Well, I got to get going. I need to help mom with dinner."

Mr. Wells: "Take care, kid."

*

CITY OF ATLANTIS
TEMPLE OF THE OUTER GODS
BASHA

As we arranged, at nine p.m., we gather in front of the temple of the Outer Gods' steps. Lamont is the last to arrive; all the rest who have come to participate in the ritual are here.

Lamont: "Good grief! How many people did you invite to this shindig, Basha?"

Basha: "The word got out, and it seemed a lot of people wanted to be a part of this. I suspect that Tezcat sent out one of her infamous calls as well. Just like she did for the Gate opening spell. It is the biggest public ritual we have ever conducted, and perhaps the biggest public ritual Dreamland has seen in recent memory. So, perhaps almost a thousand or more have gathered here. Sarah and Rebecca are coordinating all this. As you explained on Saturday, Tezcat has a special ritual to prepare us to do the heavy lifting as the focus and the architectural plan of the ritual. You do recall all that we worked out yesterday, correct?"

Lamont: "Of course, chief. We are in charge of shaping the points of Keter, Hokhmah, Binah, Da'at, and Malkuth, correct? The rest is left up to

Sarah and Rebecca's team to work out."

Basha: "Correct. Now, did you explain to everyone who will be with us at Malkuth the one important caveat about the well water, or do I need to post a warning by the well that reads 'DO NOT TOUCH THE WATER. DANGER! EXTREMELY HOT'."

Sarah: "Yes," Sarah says as she and Rebecca joins us. "I explained to everyone that the well water comes from a source that will be a natural hot spring, and therefore it will be worse than a third-degree burn kind of hot. They got it. Shall we do this?"

Lamont, Sarah, Rebecca, and I are at the front as we lead the gathered congregation up the temple steps. As always, we find dozing on the steps leading up to the temple entrance, a pride of jaguars. I guess that the pair of leopards I met last time I was here was on their lunch break. Lamont steps up to greet them and asks if they can approach.

The matriarch of the jaguars: "Nre'fa-o cu'nre[92] , Lamont. We have been told to expect you. Follow us."

The jaguar leads the way into the temple, followed by Lamont and me. A symmetrical pattern of skulls, reptilian faces, and Aztec pictographs is carried on the side of the temple entrance. The way is dark, damp, and musty with age and neglect. I ignite into flame and create a fiery cloud to precede us to bring the walls back to their original condition.

Behind me, I see Sarah and her coven create torches to light their way as we process and enter Tezcatlipoca's chamber. It has grown to accommodate this significant gathering. Tezcatlipoca is not one to be caught unawares today. Basha then leads in casting the circle in a call and response form of calling in the directions. She starts with the spark of Inspiration, referring to Wands in the South, then to the intuition of Cups in the West, then to the conscious articulation and intellectual planning of Swords in the East, and ending with the manifestation of Pentacles in the North.

Sarah leads her coven in chanting, which is taken up by all who have gathered here. The hall echoes with the voices of a thousand or more.

Coven: "Nameless One of many names, eternal and ever-changing one, who is found nowhere but appears everywhere. Beyond and within all. Timeless circle of the seasons, unknowable mystery known by all. Lord of the dance, Mother of all life, be radiant within us and engulf us with your love. See with our eyes, hear with our ears, breathe with our nostrils, touch with our hands, kiss with our lips. Open with our hearts! That we may live free at

[92] Translate to 'Greeting friend' – literally, 'Good Dancing heart brother', according to the research by Tad Williams as recorded in *Tailchser's Song*.

last! Joyful in the single song of all that is, was, or ever shall be![93]"

Basha: "Lamont, go ahead and call in the Goddess of Dreams, the one to whom this temple will be re-dedicated."

Lamont: "We are here to call in and honor, She who is and will be known as Smoking Mirror. Creator of Dreams and Dreaming. She who gave the gift of Dreaming to humanity so long ago and paid the price for that gift. She who suffered in our name so we, her children, would have sanctuary from the toil and sorrows of life in the Waking World. Those who wish can come to be free if the Waking realm deprives us of freedom. O' Smoking Mirror, hear our voices. We honor your gifts and your sacrifice."

Everyone: "Hail the Goddess Smoking Mirror!"

Sarah: "Now join hands. Focus on the drawing that we were given to study. See it in your mind's eye. Feel the power of Dreaming well up within you. Feel it flow from mind to mind and hand to hand. Feel the image being conjured by our efforts. Focus and make it manifest. So mote it be!"

There is a shimmering as the collective power of Dreaming is gathered. I spy Lamont conjuring up his wide-brimmed black slouched hat and black greatcoat to add his Tezcat-acquired powers to our efforts. On and on, the chanting goes, and the halls reverberate with our voices. The walls begin to shimmer and vibrate. As the chanting goes on, the walls burst forth in dazzling light. Soon I see the new structure taking shape. Then, in a burst of power and effort, it is done. We stand around a large well with a marble circular 3-foot wall all around its circumference. The water is black as night, and steam rises off its heated waters. On the lip of the wall are fourteen obsidian knives and mirrors with handles resembling the shape of the astronomical sign for the planet Venus.

Then slowly rising out of the waters is a feminine form that seems to be made of obsidian herself. A great matriarch rises out of the waters, proudly naked, large-breasted, and wide-hipped. The waters from the well flow off her nude body as if they were snake-like tendrils of smoke. She steps out of the well and sits upon the ebony throne, with legs carved in the shape of cat paws, which rest on a mat formed out of jaguar skins and eagle feathers.

"I, Smoking Mirror, have heard your calls. Your words are like an offering of scattered Jade. I thank you for your efforts and the gift of my new throne room."

Everyone: "Greetings, Goddess!"

Basha and Lamont: "Greetings, the night and the wind, O' Smoking Mirror!" I spy that Lamont has returned to his usual form.

---

[93] From Starhawk's *The Spiral Dance: A Rebirth of the Ancient Religion of the Great Goddess*, 1979, Harper & Row publishers, 105.

"You have done well, my children. Your efforts will be recalled in the Black and the Red of the ancients. I am impressed."

Lamont and I pick up one of the obsidian daggers and prick our fingers, allowing a few drops of water to fall into the obsidian black waters of the well.

Basha and Lamont: "We offer our blood to you, O' Smoking Mirror, freely given so that the guardians of this realm may be empowered."

The others of the coven all pick up their daggers and do the same.

Everyone: "We offer our blood to you, O' Smoking Mirror, freely given so that the guardians of this realm may be empowered."

It takes a while for everyone to make their offering of a drop of blood into the well water. When it is done, Smoking Mirror calls out.

"Your offerings are appreciated and recognized. I thank you for this. May all your labor be tightly bound and thus work together to protect this realm of Dreams, this sanctuary of all who need and all who desire."

Sarah: "We shall see that this ritual offering will henceforth be made at the time of the dark moon. Now and forever."

Everyone: "So mote it be!"

"I offer you a gift of my mirror, as a scrying tool, so that you may attempt to gleam your fate and fortune. But beware; I am a trickster, so consider wisely what you perceive in my smoking mirrors."

Sarah: "We hear and understand you, O' Queen of Dreaming. We will heed your words O' Smoking Mirror."

"I am inspired by your efforts and will conjure a small well such as the one you have made here today.

I will place my well at the entrance to this realm where the Guardian resides at the Cavern of Flame, where the seventy steps of deep slumber are found."

Basha: "We suggest that all who are found fit to enter this realm should make an offering of their blood to you. Just a drop into the well water. Would that not befitting, O' Smoking Mirror?"

"We find that an excellent idea, O' Bright Eagle. We shall so inform and instruct our guardians. Now I wish to dream and ponder the smoke and the blood."

Sarah: "As you wish. We shall return on the evenings of the dark moon."

Now, my Dear Heart and Bright Eagle, do you still wish to do as you said and remake this whole structure?

Basha and Lamont: "Yes, we do."

Then we shall begin...

Sarah leads the next phase of the ritual chanting and incantation, and as I watch, Lamont disappears.

All around me, everything begins to fade…

*

BASHA

Suddenly I am alone and naked, standing in front of a naked Tezcatlipoca, a gleaming obsidian woman.

We must join if you wish to partake of the power to do as you envisioned, My Bright Eagle. Do you genuinely wish this?

LAMONT

Suddenly, I am alone, standing stark naked and gazing at Tezcat's fully nude feminine and seductive form. Oh dear…I hope I won't have to explain any of this to Basha later…

We must join if you wish to partake of the power to do as you envisioned, My Dear Heart. Do you genuinely wish this?

BASHA

In for a penny…

Basha: "That is the only way to transform this temple into what we desire?"

Yes. You need to be tightly bound with us to gain the power to make such magick.

"But I have absorbed your power and essence within me. Why do I need to do this yet again?

What you wish to do requires the true power of a God. We need to join as one to connect and channel all the Dream power to conjure this transformation.

Basha: "Hmm. It will not permanently alter my nature, will it?"

No, my Bright Eagle, you will still remain humanly mortal. We will just temporarily unite into one focused entity.

"Okay then. Let us do this. And may I know how this transfer will take place? I am terrified to ask."

You only need to come to me. Come into my embrace…

LAMONT

Lamont: "I wish this Tezcat."

Then come to me, my Dear Heart. As for you, come into my embrace and feed on my life's blood yet again.

BASHA

What the hell? I did not think this was on the menu when I agreed to this. I feel compelled to approach her. This bewitching awe-inspiring Goddess opens her arms to me, and then just as I feared…we embrace, and our lips touch…we kiss like lovers…ohhhhhh…Goddess help meeeeee…

LAMONT

I enter her embrace, and a powerful primal urge takes over…I feel myself thrust out and feel myself pierce her flesh...ohhhhh…

BASHA, LAMONT/THE NIGHT, & TEZCATLIPOCA

We conjoin.

Where once there was separation…now there is only…

Union...

Lost in…we search for the word, and it vibrates and builds and burst forth…Ecstasy!!!

The little death…that swallows up time…

Then…

…finally the pounding of hearts beating as one…as we feel our bodies…

...there is only bliss…

LAMONT

I'm separate and yet not…images, feelings, dark rushing memories coming unbidden to mind…memories that are not mine…this conjoining has brought us all together…giving us access to each other's thoughts…feelings…memories of past events. I see and feel things that I don't directly recall. I'm sure I was not there, yet I am connected to them…it is because they are someone else's memories…frenzy feeding…attacking dark wraith of vengeance…oh dear God…it's me! It is my body in Dreamland doing all this. I am a vampire, and I'm some sort of a monstrous vigilante. I'm feeding and attacking the wicked ones all over Dreamland. This is horrible! How could I not know this? But…wait…I feel not only the memory traces of Night but…Basha? Basha was there? Did Basha see all this somehow? How can this be? It had been going on for so long, and I did not know this? Why didn't she tell me about this? This is horrible! I am awful...why did she keep this from me...ahh...all too much...can't focus...overwhelmed by sensations...sinking into it...

BASHA

I feel only myself again in my own flesh. My body is still shivering with the aftermath of that...big bang? I manage to swim up to consciousness and open my eyes with great effort.

I see myself as a brightly glowing body glistening with the fire of the stars themselves.

I am in a pool of cool ocean water. Off in a great distance, I can faintly hear the chanting of the gathering far, far below me. Then I see that lying by my side is dearest Lamont. His body is pure darkness, like the depths of empty space itself.

LAMONT

Lamont: "Hello, my love," I say sweetly to her, smiling as I realize our bodies are entwined. What about those memories? Can't tell with those yet. We have things to do. Will deal with that afterward, in private. Then we'll need to have a little talk!

BASHA

I lift myself up and look around us.

Basha: "Oh, my Goddess...Lamont, look..."

Lamont: "Holy mother of God..."

We both see it. In this shallow pool of flowing yet stable turquoise ocean water are reflected stars...glistening, gleaming, flickering stars. More stars than I ever thought possible. And above us is the blackest star-filled heavens in all its vast majesty. We are on this circular platform high above the city of Atlantis. This is now the topmost place of the temple. The infinite is arrayed above us, reflected in the waters we lie in. We rest in an ocean of reflective stars. As above so below.

My eyes cannot help but look upward, and I can feel myself being pulled in. I am gazing up and back in time...traveling with the starlight...back...back...back...beyond our galaxy...into a vast ocean of galaxies...back...back...backward in time...can I really reach it? I think that I can...If I stare long enough, I can see back toward the beginning. The start of it all. The first light...the moment of...

Lamont: "Basha! NO!!!"

Basha: "I want to see..." I say reverently in a hushed voice. "I can almost see...it..."

"No! Look at me, Basha. Look at me. Come back to me, please."

I feel such a longing…such a yearning…but then I realize that longing and yearning for him. My beloved.

"Okay. Okay. I am back in the here and now, Lamont. I am with you. But do you realize that I could almost see it?"

"See what? The big bang? Creation itself issuing forth? No, my dearest. That is The infinite. Ayn Sof. The Tao. It is not meant to be brought down into words and thoughts. Isn't that what Maimonides said?"

"Yes. You are right."

"That," Lamont says, pointing upward and all around us. "That is the Tao that must not and cannot be spoken. We stand here on the platform of the Tao that can be spoken about. What we can say and conceive of."

Basha: "This platform is Keter."

Lamont: "Yes. Just like we planned it. Here was to be the uppermost sefirah on the Tree of Life, the Sefiroth, correct? If I recall my Kabbalah 101 lesson correctly."

Basha: "Yes," I say in a hushed awed voice.

"Basha, take my hand. We need to finish what we started."

"Yes…"

I take Lamont's hand, and Oh dear Goddess…that bliss of conjoined union once again…not so much passion…just connection and union…sweetness and light.

We feel the surge of power.

An explosion of power, and we plunge below! We dive down towards the sound of the hundreds who have gathered with us to make this magick come to pass.

BASHA AND LAMONT

Everything is a blur of flickering light and darkness…all that we imagine is transforming the very fundamental structure of this cosmos we call Dreamland. An explosion of power engulfs everything, and the sound is the roaring of our beating hearts and the pounding of a vast ocean hitting the shore in wave after wave after wave. The surge of power, light, and sound roars out and travels across all of Dreamland.

Then…there is complete silence.

BASHA

I am back. I am simple, singular me. I am soaked to the skin, but now I am clad in my fire red catsuit, and Lamont is clad in his Knight garb.

Basha: "Wow…that was…"

Lamont: "Yes. It all was…"

"What did we do back then?"

"I think we know all too well and best not say what it was. Suffice that it…"

"Took our breath away?"

"The earth moved under our feet?"

"Yeah. It's best left to song lyrics and…merest memory."

"Yes. Let us just leave it as a memory. But…Let us check out what we conjured out of that conjoining."

Down we float and flow as we pass through two glowing paths of power; I take one and Lamont the other, as we leave behind the platform of Keter to two chambers below.

But I look around. Lo and behold, we are in two separate yet conjoined chambers. One of gleaming white flows into fiery red, and the other is black, which becomes crystalline icy blue. Within each is a bit of the other. What shape is this? It is a sphere, two conjoined compartments like teardrops flowing into each other.

Lamont: "This is Yin and Yang."

Basha: "Or also known as Hockmah and Binah." For a mere moment, I realize I am in a separate chamber of Binah, while I can see that Lamont resides in the chamber of Hockmah. Then we are in one singular sphere once again. It is dizzying.

Basha: "I think we should not dwell here further."

Lamont: "Yeah, right now, the energy is too raw. Trying to focus and hold onto any singular shape gives me a headache."

Basha: "Follow the lines of power ever downward?"

Lamont: "Yeah…let's take the direct central shaft."

We flow down through a nexus of converging paths that meet at the heart of the nexus to take on a scroll of white fire and specks of black fire upon it. Just as we imagined and planned it.

Basha: "Lamont, what do you see?"

Lamont: "A huge glowing book. Blazing white with darkest black fiery ink letters on its page."

"Okay. For you, it is seen as a book; for me, it is seen as a Torah scroll. Now, that is what I would call Da'at."

"Look around and below us…there are six other interconnected chambers."

"Sarah and Rebecca had delegated people to shape, form, and conjure those chambers."

"It is all so amazing. Let's see what is on the ground floor? Let's take the direct route and materialize ourselves there."

"That would be the chamber of Queendom, wherein resides the Shekinah, herself. The indwelling presence of the personified God-Goddess."

I take Lamont's hand, and with vampire speed and the last of Smoking Mirrors power in an eye blink, we reach a familiar, yet not, sight.

Gone are the markings and carvings of an Aztec structure. This is a simple yet awe-inspiring vast chamber of obsidian, black jade, and silver has along the center of the back wall a dais upon which resides a singular throne. In the room's center is the well of ebony water. Sitting upon a throne of obsidian sitting majestically the perfection of femininity herself, the obsidian form of the Goddess, no! It cannot be...

Greetings, Dear ones! Greetings, O' Bright Eagle and Dearest Heart! I love what you have done to the place!

Basha: "You sit upon the heavenly throne in the place where Shekinah should reside!"

"That is correct." Four voices speak; they are two males and two females. Divinities appear before us. The moon Goddess Lilith and a man with the Egyptian crown of an ibis head and cloaked Greek robes. Ah, that is Thoth, or should I say, Hermes Trismegistus! Two elderly scarlet and a golden-robed Chinese couple.

Greetings Lilith, Hermes, Jade Emperor, and the Queen of Heaven.

"Hail Smoking Mirror!" The four call forth. "We greet you and pay homage to your new home!" the four say as one. We bring you gifts. Behold!"

Then with a clapping of many hands, four youths appear. One young maiden from Queen Lilith's temple where I've studied. Another Egyptian-garbed lad and a pair of Chinese-robed youths, one male and the other female.

"These are our gifts. We will pledge to you and your kin, those who dwell within the six middle spheres, to learn of your ways and attend to your needs and the pilgrims who shall surely come to this great hall! Hail, O' Smoking Mirror, Goddess of the Dreaming."

My bright and shining children did well. Now, let the River of Time flow as it once did. Let us return to the mortal view!

*

We are back in a blink of an eye, surrounded by Sarah, Rebecca, and the whole gathering. On the throne sits Smoking Mirror, looking like the contented cat that ate the proverbial canary.

As for now, I need to rest. What is it you say? Oh yes, Hail and farewell."

Basha: "We shall depart, O' Smoking Mirror," I say and lead the procession out of the main lower chamber and back towards the temple's stairs. The four acolytes all bow to acknowledge us for the rites we had conducted on behalf of their patrons whom they pledged to serve and study under.

Once outside, "That went well," Sarah says. "Oh, dear Goddess...look!" She points behind us toward the new incredible structure, the temple of the Outer Gods reclaimed and reformed.

Rebecca: "It is huge...like a vast tower reaching up to the heavens above."

I look, and for a moment, I focus on the 22 lines of power, the three shafts that connect the temple chambers. Somehow it all is standing and holding itself upright.

Basha: "Yes. It does seem to reach the very stars above. Thank you and your coven for all your help. May the Goddess shine upon the paths you walk."

Sarah, Rebecca, and their coven mates are all talking about this substantial new temple with the four young acolytes. As we just stare at this incredible structure in amazement, Sarah and Rebecca come over and ask if we would look to join all of them as they go inside to explore this place. We decline. We have seen enough for now.

We depart from the huge milling gathering, which breaks out food, drink, and musical instruments in a typical Atlantean manner. They are all set to party and celebrate. We walk, tired and content, wandering away aimlessly through the streets of the city of Atlantis.

Lamont: "Basha, the paths themselves, I think, are the presence of what Lovecraft would call Yog-Sothoth. I think Lovecraft called it '*the key to the gate, whereby the spheres meet.*[94]'"

Basha: "Is that important, Lamont? Will that be a problem?"

"No. I don't think so; just an observation. Well, that is an impressive bit of work. Though I'm all for this ecumenical meeting of East and West, it is kind of a biased view, all things considered."

"What do you mean?"

"Well, Greece and Egypt – at least the Western Occult versions of them are accounted for here, so are the Jewish Rabbis, and lastly, so is China with the Tao and their ancient deities. But, there is nothing of the vastness of India, nor any form of Buddhism, Shinto, nor Nordic heathen..."

[94] H. P. Lovecraft, *Dunwich Horror*, first published in *Weird Tales*, April 1929, Chapter V. In the *Dunwich Horror* story, it quotes from a passage of the *Necronomicon* text, where that line is found.

"Nor Celtic of any mention, and no native people's deities of Africa, Pacific Islands, Australia, and so on…but I have a theory on that."

"Which is? O' Basha-the-wise, do tell."

"Well, Lamont the genius, it goes like this. We saw according to our eyes. We saw according to our expectations and knowledge. Do you know anything about these cultures and their religions?"

Lamont: "No. Not really."

Basha: "Neither do I. We both know those views exist, but the specifics are not truly known to us. Hence, we could not bring them to this event and experience. Who knows what someone else may see looking upon this site, and had they been here with us. The infinite Divine is well…"

Lamont: "Infinite. We can only see what our finite minds let us see. Hence, it matched our symbolic cultural expectations. So, for others who visit here, it will somehow match their perceptions?"

Basha: "Yes. That is what I think. At least if I learned my lesson from a cute-looking genius I have studied under."

"Did I ever tell you that you look even more beautiful when you compliment me?"

"No. But that figures, you would think that," I stick out my tongue and then grin. "Okay, enough of that. Back to our problems at hand. We need to focus on the singular human scale."

"Correct. Such as our lost friends who all need our help."

"Now, Lamont, can we connect to Peter through the Well of Dreams to help him to wake up?"

"Yes, that should be no problem."

"Then we need to do that…"

"But first, we need to talk."

Lamont says those words, and I can sense a shift in his tone. He looks agitated. "What is wrong, Lamont?"

"You…you've been lying to me! That's what's wrong. How could you?"

"What are you talking about? I have never lied to you. How could you say that? How could you think that?"

"I'm a monster, and you have been keeping the truth from me."

"No. You are not a monster. I keep telling you…"

"Don't lie to me! I saw it all when we joined."

Lamont angrily and hastily explains what we saw and what he felt. How the memories from Night came into his mind for the first time. I feel sick inside as he tells me about what he as Night did.

"You knew all this, and you kept it from me! I'm a monster! How can I trust you? How can I trust myself? I am damned!"

"I am sorry, Lamont. Yes, I confess I did know about this."

"For how long?"

"Ahh…well, since you first awoke as a vampire."

"Oh my God! That long? You kept this from me from the very beginning? You lied to me for this long?"

"I did not lie to you. I just did not know how to tell you about this."

"How about just talking to me? You should have just told me from the start. I needed to know this."

"But you were so overwhelmed, and it just did not seem a good time to tell you about this."

Lamont: "But we are talking about my life! I needed to know what was happening to me. I needed the truth."

Basha: "I am sorry, Lamont. I truly am. I was afraid for you. I…"

Lamont explodes into the night sky in a burst of dark shadows, leaving me ashamed and alone.

*

I returned to my bedroom feeling awful. I tried to reach out to Lamont telepathically but to no avail. He would not pick up my call. No matter how many times I tried and pleaded and apologized. Finally, I just got ready to go to bed and tried to sleep. I tossed and turned for what seemed hours till finally, exhaustion took hold, and I fell into gray darkness.

Monday, September 15, 1980

BASHA

SAN FRANCISCO

Some loud noise pulls me out of sleep. It seemed like it took forever to get to sleep after being so upset with Lamont's departure, and now what little is left of my fitful night's sleep is shattered by this loud crash of what I finally realize is the sound of glass breaking and the sound of surprise and pain from my cat, Gizmo.

As I tear off the bedcovers and the last vestiges of sleep from my mind, I spot my alarm clock, which reads 3 am.

What in the Goddess's name is going on?

I hit the ground running, tear open my bedroom door, burst into flames, and rocket down the stairs to see what is going on.

The closer I get to the store, the more disturbing the sensory information that is flooding into me. I just do not want to process it.

When I finally can see had happened, I am confronted with the shock of seeing the front display window area of the store.
"What the...???".

What I see is the storefront window, a shattered glass mess, and the display area covered in flames.

To be continued in: Shattered Dreamers Book 3:

Believe That Love Will Never Fail

APPENDIX ONE: NEW IDEA ABOUT CASTING

January 12, 2020

SAN FRANCISCO

GARY JARON

On Sunday morning, I was called by Seraphina, Basha's daughter, and asked if I could come over to discuss her new idea. I sat down with her and her brother, Gabriel. She showed me a thick book by Mark Horn, *Tarot and the Gates of Light*.

"I have been reading it, and I am quite impressed," Seraphina said as she poured me some Constant Comment tea and handed me a plate of fresh scones. "I was especially fascinated by his discussion on the Rabbinic Kabbalah's idea of the Four Worlds; and how that could relate to the suits in the Minor Arcana of the Tarot. Are you familiar with the concept of the Four Worlds?"

"Not completely," I say, blowing on the tea to cool it off.

"The idea is that out of Ayn Sof emanates existence in the process of creation. This happens in a series of processes or events. Some Rabbis view this as occurring within the initial singular emanation that forms the Sefiroth. Thus, some of the sefirahs represent one of these stages. Other Rabbis imagine four complete Sefiroth being created in each world or stage of the process. The usual analogy given to describe what it all seems like after it was done is a narrative that goes like this, 'In order to describe these stages and draw their comprehension closer to our understanding, we shall use an analogy from a builder.

Imagine a couple has an idea that they want to build the ideal house for themselves and their family. The idea struck them totally out of the blue. In a flash, they had a picture in their mind of a state-of-the-art palatial home with gardens and a pool. Relishing such an idea, the couple then sat down and worked out the entire structure in their mind by visualizing each bedroom, dining room, kitchen, garage, etc. In the mind, the initial idea has been developed in breadth and depth.

After such a beautiful dream, they could easily delete the entire image from their minds. However, to carry the idea further, they must get emotionally excited about it. The couple must then call an architect and a builder and start putting the initial idea on paper. Once the plans have been drawn up, our couple then has to go into the practicalities of buying a plot of land, applying for the building permits, financing the project, and the actual building of the house. Only after months of work will the house be finished, and our couple may enter their dream's fulfillment.

We could delineate four stages in this process:

1) The initial flash of inspiration (concept)

2) The broadening of the concept (developing the concept in detail)

3) Emotional involvement and the drawing of actual plans

4) Practicalities (building)

The Kabbalah explains that these four stages are metaphors for the methods used in the creation of the world."

"The problem is," Gabriel pipes, "that is not a completely accurate description of how the mind/body works. The Rabbis have a cultural bias based on the shaping influences of Greek philosophy, especially Plato but more so Aristotle. That bias downplays the body and the emotions and plays up the mind, intellect, and consciousness. The subconscious workings of the mind and how important that is to how we actually think are usually overlooked. We do more thinking subconsciously than we ever do consciously. But, that fact is overlooked or ignored. I can expound upon this with specifics and much more detail if you like."

"Ahh, no, that will do for now."

"Oh, Okay," Gabriel says with a bit of disappointment.

"As I was saying," Seraphina picks up the thread. "From that story, the Rabbis have the four worlds, Conception is the realm of Atzilut and would be associated with Keter, Beriah is the next realm of filling in the details associated with the masculine Hokhmah, and Yetzirah is associated with the feminine Binah. Hence the reference to those feminine emotions, and lastly, the remaining seven of the Sefiroth are the actualization and Assiyah. If we were going to match these to suits of the Minor Arcana of the Tarot, something the Rabbis would never consider, but we can; we would get something like the following. For inspiration, slash conception that could be fire and Wands, filling in the details would be the mind and Swords, the emotional artistry could be Cups, and lastly, manifestation would be Pentacles.

By the way, the Hebrew names derive from Isaiah 43:7, where the verse states that the Divine created, formed, and made. Now, the problem is that it all sounds nice, and it fits with the Sefirahs of Keter as will, Hokhmah as wisdom, and Binah as understanding. As Lamont would tell us, it doesn't actually work that way.

We actually go from a subconscious flash of inspiration and desire to create to the subconscious processing of feeling and emotions and bringing forth the linguistic articulation to conscious thought processes and the workings of our intellect. This would then mean that the process would be Emanation with Fire Wands, Creation with emotion Cups to Formation with intellect Swords, and finally Actualization with manifestation Pentacles.

All of this matches well with what Mark Horn wrote in his book on pages 26 Through 31. So, Gabriel, Horn, and I agree that the four worlds should be matched up in the suits in the order of Wands, Cups, Swords, and Pentacles. Where emotions and the subconscious comes before the intellect and conscious processes. Once we accept that association, the rest of Horn's book and all his efforts work out. His book is all about how to do the counting of the Omer in a Kabbalistic meditative practice utilizing the Minor Arcana of the Tarot as tools to help in the process. Are you familiar with the ritual of counting the Omer that takes place between Passover and Shavuot?"

"Actually, no," I say. "But, please don't pull a Lamont and go down that path since I feel you have another point you want to make. Am I correct?"

Seraphina laughs and then continues, "Yes, Dad could be easily sidetracked. I did have another point. So, I won't go off on that tangent. Perhaps another time?"

"Yes. Or just later, what was the idea that you were so excited to tell me on the phone."

"Well, all of this got me to think about how we cast and call in the directions for ritual work. You are familiar with that?"

"Yes. I have learned a lot from having written the first book. What is the new idea?'"

"Well, for rituals that deal with celebrations of the seasons, the usual going around the compass starting at either North going clockwise around ending at West, or start with East and still going clockwise to end at North. But I thought, why not do it differently for spell casting rituals? Why not follow that creative process and do Wands of the South to Cups of the West to Swords of the East and lastly Pentacles of the North."

"Okay, but why do you need me? This just means that when you cast a spell, you would do it that new way; how does this affect me?"

"You are in the midst of writing up the second book, correct?"

"Yes."

"Could you put this new idea of mine into that book? You could have my mom come up with the idea. I think she would like that. I think it would be of interest to our readers."

"Yes, I can. It would be a bit anachronistic, but I could do it. Where do you want me to put this into the narrative?"

"Why not utilize this new idea from the time that she did the first spell in the Waking World and then henceforth from that point forward."

"Okay. I can make that happen."

And that is how and why I came to write that section up in the novel as I did.

I thought you might be curious as to where the real idea came from.

Made in the USA
Columbia, SC
10 April 2023

14673739R00191